Catherine Cookson was born in Tyne Dock, the illegitimate daughter of a poverty-stricken woman, Kate, whom she believed to be her older sister. She began work in service but eventually moved south to Hastings, where she met and married Tom Cookson, a local grammar-school master. At the age of forty she began writing about the lives of the working-class people with whom she had grown up, using the place of her birth as the background to many of her novels.

Although originally acclaimed as a regional writer – her novel *The Round Tower* won the Winifred Holtby award for the best regional novel of 1968 – her readership soon began to spread throughout the world. Her novels have been translated into more than a dozen languages and more than 50,000,000 copies of her books have been sold in Corgi alone. Fifteen of her novels have been made into successful television dramas, and more are planned.

Catherine Cookson's many bestselling novels established her as one of the most popular of contemporary novelists. After receiving an OBE in 1985, Catherine was created a Dame of the British Empire in 1993. She was appointed an Honorary Fellow of St Hilda's College, Oxford in 1997. For many years she lived near Newcastle-upon-Tyne. She died shortly before her ninety-second birthday in June 1998.

'Catherine Cookson's novels are about hardship, the intractability of life and individuals, the struggle first to survive and next to make sense of one's survival. Humour, toughness, resolution and generosity are Cookson virtues, in a world which she often depicts as cold and violent. Her novels are weighted and driven by her own early experiences of illegitimacy and poverty. This is what gives them power. In the specialised world of women's popular fiction, Cookson has created her own territory'
Helen Dunmore, *The Times*

BOOKS BY CATHERINE COOKSON

NOVELS

Kate Hannigan
The Fifteen Streets
Colour Blind
Maggie Rowan
Rooney
The Menagerie
Slinky Jane
Fanny McBride
Fenwick Houses
Heritage of Folly
The Garment
The Fen Tiger
The Blind Miller
House of Men
Hannah Massey
The Long Corridor
The Unbaited Trap
Katie Mulholland
The Round Tower
The Nice Bloke
The Glass Virgin
The Invitation
The Dwelling Place
Feathers in the Fire
Pure as the Lily
The Mallen Streak
The Mallen Girl
The Mallen Litter
The Invisible Cord
The Gambling Man
The Tide of Life
The Slow Awakening
The Iron Façade
The Girl
The Cinder Path
Miss Martha Mary Crawford
The Man Who Cried
Tilly Trotter

Tilly Trotter Wed
Tilly Trotter Widowed
The Whip
Hamilton
The Black Velvet Gown
Goodbye Hamilton
A Dinner of Herbs
Harold
The Moth
Bill Bailey
The Parson's Daughter
Bill Bailey's Lot
The Cultured Handmaiden
Bill Bailey's Daughter
The Harrogate Secret
The Black Candle
The Wingless Bird
The Gillyvors
My Beloved Son
The Rag Nymph
The House of Women
The Maltese Angel
The Year of the Virgins
The Golden Straw
Justice is a Woman
The Tinker's Girl
A Ruthless Need
The Obsession
The Upstart
The Branded Man
The Bonny Dawn
The Bondage of Love
The Desert Crop
The Lady on My Left
The Solace of Sin
Riley
The Blind Years
The Thursday Friend

THE MARY ANN STORIES

A Grand Man
The Lord and Mary Ann
The Devil and Mary Ann
Love and Mary Ann

Life and Mary Ann
Marriage and Mary Ann
Mary Ann's Angels
Mary Ann and Bill

FOR CHILDREN

Matty Doolin
Joe and the Gladiator
The Nipper
Rory's Fortune
Our John Willie

Mrs Flannagan's Trumpet
Go Tell It To Mrs Golightly
Lanky Jones
Nancy Nutall and the Mongrel
Bill and the Mary Ann Shaughnessy

AUTOBIOGRAPHY

Our Kate
Catherine Cookson Country

Let Me Make Myself Plain
Plainer Still

ROONEY
&
THE NICE BLOKE

Catherine Cookson

PATHWAY

TRANSWORLD PUBLISHERS
61–63 Uxbridge Road, London W5 5SA
a division of The Random House Group Ltd

RANDOM HOUSE AUSTRALIA (PTY) LTD
20 Alfred Street, Milsons Point, Sydney,
New South Wales 2061, Australia

RANDOM HOUSE NEW ZEALAND LTD
18 Poland Road, Glenfield, Auckland 10, New Zealand

RANDOM HOUSE SOUTH AFRICA (PTY) LTD
Endulini, 5a Jubilee Road, Parktown 2193, South Africa

Published 2001 by Pathway
a division of Transworld Publishers

A catalogue record for this book is available
from the British Library
ISBN 0593 04990X

Printed in Great Britain
by Clays Ltd, Bungay, Suffolk

ROONEY

Catherine Cookson

PATHWAY

Author's Note

All the characters in this story are fictitious and bear no relation to anyone living or dead. Although some actual place-names have been used, Filbert Terrace and the house Honeycroft are entirely imaginary. The story is set in South Shields, but the particulars relating to the Corporation workers are those of another borough.

Contents

I

THE MP

Being Friday night The Anchor was busy, Saloon, Bottle and Jug, and Bar. In the MPs' corner, away from the piano and the dartboard, sat four men. Let us come into the open here; an MP in Shields did not stand for Member of Parliament, but Muck Pusher. In The Anchor, any man who lifted a dustbin or pushed a broom, went under the pseudonym of an MP, and the title often followed him up certain back lanes of the town.

Joseph Rooney Smith had been an MP for the Corporation for fifteen of his thirty-five years, and as time went on he had been more and more thankful that he was employed by such a body. The Corporation was no jumped-up business that could be affected by supply and demand, by slumps or wars; the Corporation went steadily on, and in Rooney's opinion gave a stamp of security to its employees.

But all of Rooney's fellow-workers were certainly not in agreement on this point, and the terms 'daft', 'dim', and 'loopey' had been attached to him when from time to time, in the face of strong opposition and demands of rights, Rooney had put forth temperate arguments, made up of short sentences such as 'Let's be satisfied, man.' 'Just compare us the day with afore the war.' 'If you get it in one way, man, they'll just take it off you in another.' One answer that was nearly always thrown back at him was, 'If you had a wife and bairns you'd be singing a different tune.'

Rooney happened to be the only unmarried member of his particular gang, and although he was not aware of it, the envy of three of them. Fred Hewitt, Bill Stubbly, and Albert Morton were apt to say, 'You don't know you're born, Rooney.' But Danny Macallistair, their ganger, never said this, for Danny was happily married.

At one time Rooney's pals had added, 'Wait till you get hooked, man.' But it was some years now since they had said that, for they were all agreed on one point concerning Rooney, he was too cute to be caught. With skill and surprising determination in so meek a young fellow they had seen him evade four widows and two spinsters during the past ten years.

But being untrammelled with the cares of matrimony did not mean that Rooney was without his troubles. Escaping the blessed state seemed to complicate his life to such an extent that at times like tonight he was weary of it.

Fred, nudging Bill, winked and said, 'She after your blood again, Rooney?'

Rooney pushed his coarse, fair hair back from his forehead and under his cap, and took a drink from his pint mug before answering, 'She's a proper tartar. I can't get in or out for her, man. All I want is peace and quiet and some place to sit of an evening. And can I get it? Why won't they let me have a house on me own?'

'You're hoping some,' put in Bill. 'And eight of us in three rooms! Don't be daft, man.'

'But I've had me name down for years, Bill.'

'Aye, you might have. So've I, an' hundreds of others. Just thank your stars all you've got to worry about is escaping women. The time to worry is when you can't escape . . . Which reminds me, as if I wanted reminding' – Bill finished his beer in one gulp and then his sentence – 'she'll be waitin' . . . in a hell of a sweat. I'd better be making a move.'

'Where you goin' the night?' asked Fred.

'The usual, the Palace . . . her mother's comin' in to see the bairns. So long . . .' Bill rose, buttoned up his coat, adjusted his cap, then patted Rooney's shoulder, saying, 'Cheer up, man. Go and get bottled up and give her a hammering. That'll scare her off.'

Rooney smiled but made no comment. And Fred, rising and going to the counter, said, 'Just one more for me, an' then I'm off an' all. What about you, Albert? Comin' yet?'

'No,' said Albert dully, 'not yet.'

Fred did not return to the corner but, drinking up a quick half-pint, waved his hand towards them and followed Bill.

Rooney and Albert sat on, not speaking. Rooney's eyes moved over the room, past the line of men standing at the counter to the group around the dartboard, along the table under the window, and back to Albert again. Albert was in a mess. He was the youngest member of their gang, being only twenty-nine. He had been married a year and his wife was already playing fast and loose with him. Albert would stay on till closing time; he wouldn't go home because there'd be nobody there. And if you asked him where his missus was the night he'd say, as he invariably did, 'At her mother's.'

15

It was funny, Rooney thought, the things that kept people in the same place. There was Albert sitting here rather than go home and sit alone, whereas all he himself wanted was to go back to his room, have his meal, put his feet up, and have a bit read, all alone.

Whenever possible, Rooney worked his life to a pattern. Each dinner hour he brought his bait to The Anchor, in preference to going to the canteen, and, accompanied by a pint of beer, he ate his dinner. Monday night he called in and had two pints before going to the pictures. During the winter he generally spent the other evenings in his room, with the exception of Saturday night, when after having been to the match in the afternoon he might take a walk up to Horsely Hill and the dogs; afterwards calling in at The Anchor and adding to his usual two pints a double whisky, no more, no less. During the summer he had a leaning towards fishing. This was the pattern of his days when no-one interfered. But when a landlady wanted to . . . get thick, everything went wrong. If only he could bring himself to go into lodgings until he could come by a house of some sort, life, he knew, would become much simpler. But he couldn't . . . because of his bits and pieces.

Rooney's furniture had a meaning for him which he found impossible to translate into thought, much less into words. It was part of his security, as was his job on the Corporation. His furniture was home, some place that belonged to him, no matter what its surrounds might be. The deep meaning that the furniture held for him went back into his past, to his early youth, in fact to the day his mother died. It was from that day of release that furniture began to have a meaning, for when his mother was carried from the house his father began to live again. The perpetual look of worry left his face, his rounded shoulders squared themselves, for no longer would he come home to find his wife sleeping off her drink, or be warned by a sympathetic policeman to collect her from outside some bar or other to save her from being taken into custody yet again.

They had been living in Hebburn at the time, and his father had sold the few remaining pieces of furniture that his mother had been unable to dispose of to supply her drink, and had moved to Shields. And there, in a furnished room, he had started, almost with the eagerness of a lad himself, to gather together a home for them both.

Rooney never looked back to those years spent with his father without pain for the happiness they had held, and in moments of deep loneliness he would ask himself why they had been brought to such an abrupt close. If there had been an illness leading up to it he could, in a way, have accepted it; but there had been nothing. One night, after having been for a walk, his father had sat down in his armchair, put his hand to his waistcoat, gave a little gasp, and died . . . Heart failure, they said it was. And it left Rooney without a relative in the world. He had nothing, only his job and his furniture.

The furniture had been bought piece by piece over the years until two rooms had been completely furnished, and the buying of each piece had been in the nature of an adventure, among second-hand shops tucked away in side streets, in stables, even in front rooms of houses. From among these troves of conglomeration they had acquired a bed, a fine brass one without a dent or mark on it, and an equally fine feather mattress, a Scotch chest of drawers of good quality, an odd tub-shaped dressing-table with swing mirrors, a drop-leaf table, two kitchen chairs and two armchairs, all of different styles, a Welsh dresser, plus various pictures, linoleum, and mats. He was a man of twenty when his father died, yet he grieved for him as a child would have done. He ached inside for the closeness that was no more. All he had missed in his mother's care his father had made up for. They had been like brothers, pals; they had comforted each other in a wordless way for the nightmare of life they had been forced to endure. And once deprived of this comfort the past had leaped back into Rooney's present. It was as if his mother had died but yesterday instead of seven years previously, and he saw all women as prototypes of her.

'Get yersel' married, man,' Danny Macallistair had said; 'there's nowt like it. There's plenty of lasses around, good lasses. You only have to look. Don't take no notice of them what's always on about their women, it's only talk half the time.' Danny was in his forties then and had been married only three years. The three years had since grown to eighteen, and Danny's attitude had not changed in the slightest.

But what, thought Rooney, was Danny's life to go on compared to all the others: Bill, with his six bairns and his periodical rows, Fred with a real sloven of a wife, and Albert, whose wife lived in dance halls. Even without the memory of his mother to deter him,

Rooney's cautious nature would have found sufficient deterrence against marriage in the lives of his work-mates. And it wasn't as though he had never been tried by the arch-temptress herself. He had, twice. First, in his great loneliness, and then again at the age of twenty-five. It was the lass who had backed out of the first effort, but in the second it was himself, for he had discovered in time that although the lass had thought quite a lot of him she had thought very little of his job and was determined to force a change once they were married. Rooney did not like change in any form, and the only thing he would have changed then and now in his life was the place that housed his furniture. His idea of heaven was a house with his own key to the front door. He might be called upon to share the back yard, but to have his own front door was the summit of his ambition. But as Bill had said, what chance had he?

'Rooney!'

Stoddard, the bar manager, was beckoning to him, and he rose and went to the counter.

'Hear you're on the hunt again, Rooney?' The manager spoke under his breath and smiled quizzically.

'Yes. That's about it,' said Rooney.

'Do you know Johnny Casson, him over there, near the dartboard, beside old Foley? He's a newcomer here.'

'No,' said Rooney. 'I've seen him about, that's all.'

'Well, as far as I can gather his mother-in-law's letting rooms. I heard him on about her last night.'

'Oh?'

'Will I call him over?'

'Aye, do.'

19

'Johnny!'

A small, dark man turned and looked towards them. Then handing his dart to the older man he made his way over.

'This is Joe Smith, better known as Rooney,' said the manager.

Rooney and the slight dark man nodded.

'He's lookin' for a room. Can you do anything for him?'

The manager drew a cloth over the counter before moving away to attend to his customers.

'Me name's Casson . . . Johnny Casson,' said the little man. 'And aye, I know of a room. Me mother-in-law's startin' to let. In Filbert Terrace.'

At the mention of the street name Rooney's eyes widened just a fraction. He knew every inch of the layout of the town, and Filbert Terrace, although not up to Westoe or the Harton end by a long chalk, was quite a way above the streets in which he usually sojourned. Yet this Johnny Casson looked a very ordinary type of bloke.

'It's a fair biggish house,' said Johnny. 'Seven rooms and an attic. The old girl's got to let, her youngest's gettin' married next month. And if she wants to keep the house on she's got to do something, you see.'

Rooney asked no further information about the room, but very quietly put forth two tentative questions.

'Will she be livin' alone? Is she a widow?'

Johnny's brows contracted a little. 'Aye. She's a widow, but she's not livin' alone. There's old man Howlett, her father-in-law, and Nellie, her niece.

20

They'll still be there when the young one goes . . . Why? Do you want a widow on her own?'

Rooney, jerking back his hair, exclaimed. 'No fear! No fear!'

'Oh, it's like that, is it?' Johnny's eyes twinkled. 'Well, you need have no fear of owt like that. She's had seven bairns, five lasses and two lads. The lads were killed in the war, and the last of the lasses, as I said, is gettin' married. The old girl's over sixty, although you wouldn't think it; she's still quick on her pins.'

'It's an unfurnished room I'm wanting.'

'Well, you could have that, I think. Doreen, that's the one what's gettin' married, she has her things stored in one and she's taking them next week. She's got part of a house up Westoe end.'

'It sounds all right,' said Rooney. 'But there's one thing. You know I'm on the Corporation . . . collecting?'

'Oh, that. Well, beggars can't be choosers. I work in the docks meself. But between you and me the old girl fancies herself; she would like to be something. And so would the rest of her tribe. My Betty's about the only one who doesn't think she's the cat's pyjamas. And I can tell you she's gone through it because she married me. Old Ma Howlett wanted them all to have white-collar types. I can tell you I was a come-down . . . Have a pint?'

'No. Thanks all the same,' said Rooney. 'I've got a pal over there.' He nodded towards Albert. 'When could I go and see Mrs . . . your mother-in-law?'

'Ma? Well, I suppose I should warn her first. I'm on me way round there now. Friday-night schedule . . . all

21

the gang of them except the eldest one, Queenie, call in on a Friday night.' Johnny paused and rubbed his hand over his mouth as if wiping froth away, then, with the twinkle in his eye deepening, he added, 'Take you round now, if you like.'

Rooney looked down at himself. He wasn't in his working clothes, but he wasn't wearing his good suit, just the odd coat and trousers he wore of an evening. But commenting to himself that if he went to live with these people they'd certainly see him worse than this, he said, 'All right. I'll just tell me pal.'

Going back to Albert, he said, 'I've got the chance of a room, I think, Albert.'

'Where?' asked Albert without much interest.

'Filbert Terrace.'

'Filbert Terrace? Goin' up, aren't you? They won't have your bits and pieces there, man.'

'Well, I can only go and see. So long.'

'So long,' said Albert.

Rooney joined Johnny at the door, and they walked out into the dimly lit street and into the late November drizzle. Coming to the crossing at Laygate, they made their way to the Chichester, up Meldon Terrace towards the Infirmary, then turned off and walked through a number of short streets until they came to Filbert Terrace. And here even the darkness could not hide the difference of this terrace from its immediate neighbours, for jutting from the foot of each tall house was an iron railing encircling a square of ground inside of which could be sensed rather than seen patches of green, broken in some places by crazy paving, and even bird baths.

It was with definite trepidation that Rooney stood behind Johnny as he rang the bell; and had not Johnny's very ordinariness kept itself apparent in his chattering, Rooney would surely have beaten a stealthy retreat.

'This'll startle her for a start,' said Johnny over his shoulder. 'I usually come the back way.'

As Johnny rang the bell again, the front door was suddenly pulled open to reveal in the dim light from the hall the large bulky figure of a woman.

'Hallo, Ma. I've brought a fellow, a Mr Smith. He's lookin' for an unfurnished room. Come on in.' Johnny rattled on as he crossed the threshold. And Rooney, after a moment's pause, followed him, passing the woman with his head slightly bent.

As the door closed behind him he pulled off his cap.

The woman had not spoken, but she switched on another light, and Rooney, raising his eyes to her and on the point of bidding her the time of day, found his words hanging stupidly on his lips. His eyes became fixed on her head; he could not tear them from it, for it subdued into drabness every colour in its vicinity. Her hair was like a miniature busby, and its colour was that of a freshly scraped carrot. And to Rooney's startled eyes it looked almost afire.

Seemingly not at all unpleased by his scrutiny, Ma returned Rooney's gaze, but her eyes did not stay on his hair, they wandered over him, taking in his thick but well-set-up figure, his fresh complexion, and square blunt face. She smiled.

'Good evening,' she said formally.

'Evening,' said Rooney.

'Well.' She paused as if uncertain of her next move,

23

then added, 'You'd better come in and sit down a minute. You see, my daughter's got her stuff in the room. She's getting married soon, and she's taking it next—'

'I've told him,' put in Johnny, moving towards the second door along the hallway. 'Come on—' He beckoned to Rooney and led the way into the room.

Anything but happy, Rooney went to follow him; then paused to let Ma precede him, which she did with a jauntiness that put him in mind of a young lass and made her appear slightly ludicrous.

The room into which he stepped seemed to him to be packed with people, and Ma, sweeping a plump, jumper-encased arm around it, said, 'This is my family.'

Rooney nodded once to include the three women and two men.

The men with different motions of the head returned the nod, as did one of the women, but the other two fixed on him expressionless stares that immediately put him, as he thought, on hot bricks.

'Sit down.' It was Johnny who pushed a chair towards him. Johnny seemed to be enjoying himself. 'This is me wife, Betty,' he said.

Rooney inclined his head to the young woman who had favoured him with a nod. He had somehow guessed that this one would be Johnny's wife. She wasn't got up so much as the other two – in fact she looked none too spruce, and it surprised him that she was a relation of the others at all.

'Mr Smith has come to see the room,' said Ma. 'I'll just go up and see if I can get in.' Ma turned her eyes on Rooney again. 'My daughter's got her stuff in there, and—'

'I told you,' put in Johnny with irritating emphasis, 'I explained it to him . . . He knows.'

Ma cast a look at her son-in-law that should have silenced him, or at least put him in his place. But what Johnny's place was, Rooney was finding it difficult to understand. If he had been in Johnny's shoes he would have been sitting with his mouth shut, among this lot.

Ma left the room, and Johnny, seating himself next to his wife, asked a question of her in two words, 'All right?'

'All right.' She smiled at him. Then, leaning forward to see past her husband, she looked at Rooney and remarked, 'It's been a nasty day.'

'Yes, it has,' said Rooney.

'Do you work inside?'

'No . . . out,' said Rooney. 'I work on the Corporation.'

'Oh.'

Uneasily now, Rooney realised that he had the entire company's attention. But it was a polite attention. Working on the Corporation could mean anything from Parks and Gardens to . . . dustbins.

Rooney swallowed. 'I'm on collectin' . . . ashbin-man.'

'And likes it,' put in Johnny, thrusting out his lips and wagging his head. 'What do you think of that? Wouldn't change, would you?' Johnny was going on the conversation they had had on the way here, and although it was perfectly true that he wouldn't change his job, hearing it from Johnny made it sound

25

something of a disgraceful admission.

One of the two men sitting by the fire, after looking at Rooney under lowered brows, slowly got to his feet. He was a tall man, thin, with a querulous expression and fast-growing baldness, and, as he made his way somewhat casually towards the door, Johnny looked at him and remarked quietly, 'If she doesn't let that room, Dennis, it'll be ten bob a week off each of us as soon as Doreen goes.'

'Really! You get worse. You're . . . you're past bearing.'

The woman who got sharply to her feet Rooney surmised to be the tall man's wife. She was glaring now across the room at Johnny. But Johnny was in no way intimidated.

'It's true,' he said, 'isn't it?'

'Of course it is,' said Betty, his wife, 'and come off it, our Pauline. If Mr Smith's going to live here he'll soon know how things stand. What d'you say, May? And you, Jimmy?' she appealed to the other couple.

The woman addressed as May made no comment, although her face showed displeasure, but Jimmy, her husband, in a deep base voice, which was in sharp contrast to his delicate-looking face and slight figure, said, 'True. True. But there are ways of approaching these things, Betty. And Johnny always favours the bull-at-the-gap tactics. He delights in it. Makes you feel good, doesn't it, Johnny? Getting one over, sort of.'

'Would you come up now?'

All eyes were turned towards the door where Ma was standing, but Rooney did not rise immediately; he looked towards the bald man, giving him a chance to have his say. But when Dennis turned and sat down again Rooney got to his feet and left the room on the heels of Ma. And as he did so he determined definitely that this was no place for him. He would look at the room, and no matter what it was like he would say he would let her know, and that would be the end of it.

The stairs led up from the right of the hallway on to a large landing with a number of doors leading off, all brown-painted.

Ma walked briskly across the landing towards one of the doors.

'This is the room. It's a front room, and lovely in the mornings when the sun's on,' she said.

Rooney did not point out that that was the least of the attractions he looked for, as he wouldn't be in in the mornings.

The room was packed with a dining and bedroom suite and various oddments, but he could see it was a big room and had a fine fireplace.

'It's nice,' he said.

'Yes, it's a lovely room,' said Ma. 'And cheap.'

'Yes?'

'Seventeen and six a week.' Ma looked straight at him.

Rooney remained silent. He was only paying twelve and six where he was, but of course this was a much better room. Yet likely the rent of the whole house wasn't much more than what she was asking him.

'You'd want me to cook for you?'

'Er . . . aye . . . yes.'

'Well, I'll do that for . . . shall we say seventeen and six? That would make thirty-five shillings a week.

It's very cheap when you think . . . ?'

Ma did not go on to say what she thought, but she stared at Rooney with her round, doll-like, pale-blue eyes. Then, adjusting her skirt and smoothing down her jumper over her swelling breasts to fill in the pause that Rooney was creating, she added, 'I'm sure I'll do all in my power to see you are comfortable. Are you a widower, Mr Smith?'

'No,' said Rooney. 'I've never been married.'

'And you've got your own furniture?' She gave a high-pitched laugh. 'Well, it's about time you were. When Doreen gets married in a fortnight's time she'll be the last of mine; I'll be lost for something to do. Well there it is, Mr Smith. I'm sure you'd be comfortable.'

'Yes. Yes, I feel I would, but I think I'd better tell you I'm on the Corporation . . . collectin' . . . the bins.'

'Oh.' Ma's mouth, wide in a fixed smile, slid to a straight line and remained there for a second before stretching again.

'Well now, are your clothes very dirty? That wouldn't include your washing, not the thirty-five shillings.'

'No. My clothes aren't very bad at all. I change my top things at the depot. And I understand about the washing.'

She moved out on to the landing, and he gave one last look at the room. He could see all his bits here and himself sitting afore the fire of a night-time . . . But that lot down there – he couldn't put up with them no more'n they could put up with him.

'There's the bathroom.' Ma pointed to the door

28

opposite. 'You could have a bath when you wanted one. And that's something . . . the fire's always on in the winter. It's a back boiler.'

'Thank you. Yes, that would be something.' And it would, too, he thought, to have a bath in a house without having to go to the public baths to get clean.

At the foot of the stairs he paused. He didn't want to go back into that room; but he had left his cap there, so he could do nothing but follow Ma again. Immediately, he noticed that the miserable-looking fellow and his wife had gone. But another woman had come into the room. She must have made her entry from the kitchen doorway almost at the same time as Ma and he had come in from the hall, for she was still holding on to the door handle when Ma said, 'Oh! It's you, Nellie. You're late, aren't you?'

The girl turned. At least Rooney thought she was a girl because of her height and the slightness of her figure, until he saw her face, and then he realised that she was a woman. But of what age he found difficult to place . . . she could be anything from thirty to fifty.

'This is Nellie, my cousin,' said Ma.

Nellie inclined her head. And Rooney murmured, 'Good evening,' and found his gaze remaining on her as it had done on Ma. But it wasn't her hair that drew him, but her eyes, large, brown eyes in a small, dead-white face. He had never seen such large eyes in a woman, nor, he thought, such a tired face. He listened to the others greeting her.

'Hallo, Nellie,' said Betty. 'Tired?'

'Yes,' answered Nellie.

'That's put paid to my jumper then,' said May.

29

Nellie shook her head slowly. 'No, it hasn't. I'll finish it over the week-end.'

'Now, our May!' Ma's voice startled Rooney, for it suddenly matched her proportions, becoming large and forceful. 'You know she's got all Doreen's things to finish, and there's only a fortnight, so your jumper'll have to wait.'

'Most things have, for our Doreen,' said May under her breath. 'She's going to feel a draught when she's married.'

'They'll all be done in time.' Nellie had taken off her raincoat, and even to Rooney's uncritical eye she looked drab.

The same thought must have been prominent in the delicate-looking fellow's mind, for he said, 'It's about time you did a bit of sewing for yourself, isn't it, Nellie?'

'Well, are you takin' it?' Johnny's voice cut off Jimmy's, as he addressed Rooney. And Rooney, holding his cap once again in his hands and facing the battery of eyes, could only say, 'Yes. Yes, I'll be pleased to.'

2

MA

Rooney moved on a Saturday afternoon. Sep Tindall did the job, as always; and as he rolled up the lino at one side of the room he laughingly remarked to Rooney at the other, 'I know this little lot as well as me own bits. This is the ninth time I've moved you, isn't it?'

Rooney made no reply; all he wanted was to get the lino into the van and look on Mrs Kate Sparks for the last time. That he was bound to look on her for just once more he knew only too well; she had planted herself in the passage, and she meant to . . . let him have it. He was well acquainted with the signs. She had cried several times during the past week in an effort to get him to stay. She had even said he had encouraged her to think she meant something . . . My God! Women were awful. He sweated at the memory of last night, and he blushed for Kate's brazenness, for Mrs Sparks had made it plain that he would be welcome to the fruits of matrimony even without a ring.

He had confided the whole business to Danny this morning. He could talk to Danny about these things whereas, as much as he liked his other mates, he could tell them nothing personal.

Danny had said some women were made like that and when they reached a certain age, round about the middle forties, they went man mad. Danny thought

33

it was a good job he was moving to this new place, for if the woman had had a big family all the interest she would likely show in him would be of a motherly turn.

Rooney had pointed out to Danny that that was how most of them started, every woman he met seemed to think he wanted mothering. But Danny had insisted that by the sound of things this one was the safest bet yet. And on this point Rooney had agreed with him. Danny had ended their talk as always, 'You look out for a lass, Rooney. Why, man, you're wasting your life, and that of some good woman. Any young lass would jump at you . . . a fine-set-up fellow like you.'

It was all right for Danny to talk like that, Rooney thought, but where did he go looking for a lass? He couldn't dance, not a step, nor could he start from scratch and chat to a strange girl, like some of them did. The only women he could have spoken to were the ones that frequented the snugs and Bottle and Jugs, and he had sworn a solemn oath that never would he pick up with any woman he saw in a bar; he would rather remain alone to the end of his days than risk his father's life over again. It was about the only point on which he thought vehemently. As for being a well-set-up chap, he had no ideas about himself. He had a good strong body, admitted, but his face, he considered, was as plain as a dustbin.

When they moved into the passage it was to find Mrs Sparks's matronly figure filling it.

Sep Tindall stood with the lino on his shoulder, and Rooney, standing at his side, murmured, 'Well, I'll be going, Mrs Sparks.'

'You think you're doin' well for yourself, don't you,' said Mrs Sparks. 'Filbert Terrace! Oh, I know where you're going.' She closed her eyes before resuming. 'And she won't do for you what I did, waitin' on you hand and foot . . . Well' – her head was wagging now – 'if you can afford to pay for Filbert Terrace you can pay me what you owe me.'

Rooney's eyes and mouth stretched, and it was a moment or two before he brought out, 'Why! I settled with you last night.'

'Yes, you did . . . up to last night, Friday. This is Saturday, a new week, and I want a week's money in lieu of notice.'

'But I gave you notice a week last night.' Rooney was looking completely mystified.

'Yes, I know fine well you did, aren't I telling you? And that week was up last night,' emphasised Mrs Sparks. 'You've broken into another week, and I'm entitled to a week's money.'

Rooney cast a swift glance at Sep. And Sep, hitching the lino more firmly on to his shoulder, said very pointedly, 'I'd see her in hell first.'

'Would you?' cried Kate. 'Well, I'll take that lino with me, 'cos if he doesn't stump up I'm keeping that. And just you try to get it out.'

The two men looked at each other. Then Rooney, putting his hand in his pocket, drew out a handful of silver, and picking out five half-crowns he handed them to her.

'Thanks for nowt,' said Kate. Then very reluctantly standing aside she hissed one parting shot at Rooney, 'You big noodle, you!'

35

Safely in the van sitting next to Sep, Rooney wiped the sweat from his face.

'You're well rid of that 'un,' said Sep. 'She's as bad as you've had 'em.'

He started the engine and as the van rumbled down the street he sent an amused, sidelong glance at Rooney and enquired, 'What's it about you, mate, that gets 'em?'

'Aw, shut up, man!' said Rooney with an unusual tartness. 'I don't feel like chaff at this minute.'

'I wasn't chaffing, man, but all the old wives seem to make a set at you.'

'You've said it,' said Rooney. 'Old wives.'

'Well, not so old either. What was she . . . forty-five or so? What's that these days? What's the one like where you're goin'?'

'Past it, I hope,' said Rooney. 'Seven of a family and six grandbairns. She's near sixty and her hair's dyed red.'

'Oh, my God!' Sep gave vent to a gale of laughter. 'A rejuvenated job! It might be the frying-pan into the fire . . . You watch yersel'.'

'Oh, for the Lord's sake, man!'

'All right. All right.' Still laughing heartily, Sep swung the van in and out of the traffic; then through the quieter streets until he stopped at 71 Filbert Terrace. And there, jumping out and running to the back of the van, he had the lino on his shoulder almost before Rooney had time to ring the doorbell.

Rooney had not been near the house since his first visit, and in the daylight it seemed to have lost some of its pomp. The outside needed paint badly and the

36

curtained windows weren't as spruce as many in the lower quarters of the town. But it still had the power to subdue him, for was it not a large terrace house with its own front garden and electric bell on the door, and the letter-box and number in brass?

Mrs Howlett herself opened the door. She was wearing a green woollen dress, and from the lobes of her ears dangled red ear-rings, the shade of which was at definite variance with the colour of her hair. Her lips were rouged and the powder was thick on her nose, making it stand out from her face. But her get-up did not disturb Rooney. If anything, it took away any dread Sep's merriment had aroused, for in the naked light of day Ma looked what she was, a fat old woman, done up.

'Well, here I am, Mrs Howlett.'

'And welcome, Mr Smith, I'm sure. Come in.'

'Do you mind calling me Rooney?' he said shyly as he moved into the hall. 'Everybody does.'

Ma laughed. 'Rooney? It's an odd name, but all right, we'll call you Rooney. And I hope you're here for a long stay, Rooney. Well, you know where to go. Just lead the way now and show the man.'

Quite suddenly at his ease, Rooney went up the stairs. The door of the room was open, and he stood for a moment in pleased surprise. Being empty, it looked even larger that he had imagined it to be, and although all the paint-work was brown it appeared unusually light after the dullness of the stairs and landing. It struck him momentarily that everything in the house was brown.

Sep dumped down the lino, and together they laid it.

But to Rooney's disappointment it did not cover one half of the floor.

Next followed the dresser; then the bed and mattress. And when they went down the stairs for the third time a young girl standing at the foot stared up at them. She could have been termed pretty had her face not been marred at the moment with temper.

'This is my youngest, Doreen,' said Ma, moving forward and taking a firm hold on her daughter's arm. 'Doreen, this is Mr Smith. We are to call him Rooney.'

'How do you do?' Rooney, feeling almost gay, smiled widely. But his smile disappeared and his gaiety vanished when the girl, pulling herself from her mother's hold, flounced round and dashed into the living-room without even a nod.

'Tut! Tut!' Ma clicked her tongue . . . 'Young and silly. She's in a bit of a stew today. She doesn't think she'll have her things ready for the wedding.'

Rooney could not really see the connection, and he felt dampened, but as he returned with a chair from the van Doreen's attitude was made perfectly clear to him, for her voice came in angry tones from behind the closed door, saying, 'Old rubbish! That awful bed. And the whole street watching. And my wedding so near. Doris Taylor and all the lot of them'll be laughing up their sleeves. If you had to let, why take him?'

'Be quiet! Else I'll ring your ear for you. Mind, I'm telling you.' Ma's voice was muted.

'I won't. A binman! What will Harold's mother say? You've bragged enough to—'

The voice was abruptly cut off, and Rooney continued his way slowly up the stairs. His spirits now at low ebb, he went into the room and put the chair down.

Old rubbish. He looked about him. His furniture might all be odd, but it wasn't rubbish, it was good substantial stuff. He felt hurt and experienced a rising feeling of . . . not anger, that would have been too strong a term, but of annoyance. They all acted here as if they were . . . the last word. And although he knew they were a cut above the usual people he lodged with they were still not the last word.

In his daily travels from door to door he had in his own way docketed the classes and, to his mind, they were many and various. There were those who were nothing and didn't care who knew it, and there were those who were nothing and tried to pull the wool over your eyes; then there were those who were something and went to a devil of a lot of trouble to make you recognise it; and then again there were those who were something and pretended they weren't and tried to be all pals together and made everybody uncomfortable; then there was a section you couldn't pinpoint, who dressed like one set and talked like another. Like old Mrs Bailey-Crawford, or old Mrs Double-Barrelled as they called her. She lived alone in a big ramshackle house in Westoe Village, and she ordered you about like a duchess, even though she looked like a tramp. There were all types, and Rooney was for giving them all their due, and the occupants of this house in particular. But to talk the way that 'un had done was to his mind getting too much above herself.

'Can I help you fix anything?'

He turned to the doorway and there stood the little thing with the big eyes.

'Thanks. I'm managing all right.'

'What about your curtains? Will they fit?'

She looked to where his curtains, rolled into a bundle, were lying on the bed. 'These are long windows, six foot six.'

Rooney glanced at the two windows. 'Aye . . . yes . . . well, I hadn't thought. They're not that long. A foot out, likely.'

'Have they got a hem?' She walked to the bed and turned up the edges of the curtains; and after a cursory examination said, 'They'll let down top and bottom. I'll be able to fix them.'

She lifted the bundle up and, ignoring Rooney's protest, she went out saying, 'Grace says there's a cup of tea as soon as you're ready . . .'

'Thanks.' He stood in the middle of the room looking after her. She sounded off-hand, rather curt, but that might just be her voice. It was husky as if she had a cold. But anyway, she was being helpful. He hadn't thought about the length of the curtains. Grace, he supposed, must be Ma's name.

Sep came in with the other chair, saying, 'If you'll give me a hand with the dressing-table and the chest I'll dump your case and the boxes in the hall, and then perhaps you'll manage. I've got another little job I'm going to and I want to finish afore dark.'

'All right,' said Rooney.

When the dressing-table and the Scotch chest had been installed, Sep looked about the room with approval.

'Your things look better here than they've done anywhere. You should be comfortable. And' – he

40

leaned forward, pointing his thumb floorwards – 'I don't think you need fear owt from old red-for-danger. My! there's hair, and your mother bald. Well, never say die. Huh! That's a good 'un, eh?' He nudged Rooney. 'Never say die.'

'Be quiet, man,' said Rooney.

'OK, OK. That'll be fifteen bob. All right?'

'All right,' said Rooney, once more putting his hand into his pocket.

As the van rumbled away Rooney closed the front door. But during this short operation he noticed a definite movement of the curtains in the house opposite. It was as the lass had said, they were all on the watch. In Cartham Street, from where he had moved, they would have been at their doors and the kids swarming over the van, but there hadn't been a sign of a bairn in the street here and not a soul at a door, yet they were on the lookout all right. People were people the world over.

The last box up in the room, Rooney sat down on it and looked about him. It was as Sep had said: his bits looked good here. When the curtains were drawn and the fire on . . . by lad! He smiled to himself. He'd be comfortable.

His spirits were rising again. What did it matter what the lass had said? She'd be gone soon. The old woman was all right, and the little one . . . Nellie. Well, somehow he couldn't quite make her out. She was so quiet, like a mouse. Not shy as he knew shyness, but sort of closed up.

His china arranged on the dresser, his bed made and covered with a bright artificial silk bedspread, his

41

clothes packed away in the drawers, the chairs one each side of the fireplace and his folding table placed under the window, he gave the room a last glance of appraisal before going downstairs and knocking at the living-room door.

'Come in. Come in.'

Diffidently he entered the room, and was relieved to find only Ma and the little one there.

'Don't knock,' said Ma. 'You must make yourself at home. Come and sit down and have a cup of tea. We don't have our meal till six. I hope that suits you. And will you be taking your meals with us, or do you insist on them in your room?'

He would have liked to say, 'In me room, please,' but the word insist put him off. So he said, 'Whatever suits you best. And six o'clock'll do me fine. I've got a little joint and things for the morrow, but after this I'd be obliged if you'd get my stuff in for me.'

'I'll do that,' said Ma, 'and it's arranged then that we'll all eat together. I won't say it won't be a big help, there's so much to do in a house this size. So you like your room now you've got your things in?'

'Very much, thanks.'

'Your curtains are nearly finished,' said Ma.

He looked to where the little one was sitting at a hand-sewing machine rapidly turning the handle. She didn't look up, not even when Ma placed a cup of tea on the corner of the table for her, but went steadily on, one hand pressing and easing the material under the needle like an automatic machine itself.

As he drank his tea Rooney glanced around the room, and the same impression struck him here as in the rest of the house . . . everything was brown. Brown-leather couch against the wall opposite the fireplace, brown table and chairs, brown sideboard, brown-painted woodwork, even a brown carpet, which, like the furniture, appeared very much the worse for wear. The room had a miserable look to him. Perhaps it was the fire; there was so very little in the grate. But then it was a close day. Looking at the fire reminded him to broach the subject of heating.

'Is there any place I could keep a bit of coal?' he asked.

'Well, yes, there's a shed in the yard. Doreen's bicycle's in it, but that'll be going soon.'

'Thanks!' he said.

The machine stopped whirring and Ma asked, 'Have you finished?'

'Yes,' said Nellie briefly, folding up the curtains.

Rooney looked at her in amazement. She had unpicked and done those four curtains in much less than an hour.

'My! You've been quick,' he said.

Nellie made no reply, but in a tone that somehow robbed the words of praise Ma said, 'She does all our sewing.'

'Is it your job?' Rooney spoke to Nellie, but Ma again answered for her.

'No, she manages a drapery shop . . . Bamford and Brummell's, off Green Street, you know.'

Bamford and Brummell's. Yes, he knew Bamford and Brummell's. And its name was the biggest thing about it – it was a little one-window place that sold mainly haberdashery; it was a cheap, poor sort of

43

a shop, thirty years behind the times. As for a manageress, well, he couldn't see the place holding more than two assistants, if two would really be necessary. And as for custom, people had money these days and, he imagined, most of them went to Green Street proper, or down to King Street.

The sudden sound of a door opening in the hall caused Ma's relaxed body to stiffen in her chair and the smile to leave her face, and turning to Nellie she murmured, 'If he comes in here take him back.'

Perplexed, Rooney watched the little one squeeze out from behind the chair and table and make for the door. But before she reached it, it was pushed open and an old man shambled a step into the room. He looked a good age, about eighty, Rooney thought, and the most striking thing about him was the shaggy growth of white whiskers which sprouted from his face at all angles. He was small and slightly bent, but his eyes were bright and alert, and they fixed on Rooney with an almost tangible hold.

'What's goin' on here?' His voice was a thin squeak.

'Come on.' Nellie went towards him and took hold of his arm.

'Leave be, Nellie. Something's goin' on here. Who's he?'

Ma rose, and going to her father-in-law, cupped her mouth with her hands and yelled in his ear, 'Mr Smith. He's come to stay.'

'What? Why can't you speak up? Who is he?'

Ignoring the old man, Ma turned to Nellie. And she, taking a pencil and a little pad from her overall pocket, wrote one word on it, then stubbing the paper twice with her pencil in a precise, definite movement she handed it to him.

Pushing his head back into his shoulders and holding the pad at arm's length away from him, the old man read out the word 'Lodger'.

Rooney gave a conciliatory smile as the fierce old eyes came on him again. 'Don't want no lodgers. Whose house is this, anyway? It's my house.'

'Oh!' Indignation was now being expressed from every curve of Ma's body. She was rearing as she cried, 'Go on to your room!'

'What?'

She pointed.

'Don't order me about. I'm nigh frozen in there. What I want to know is, about this chap.' He pointed a quivering finger at Rooney.

Ma turned her back on the old man and in an aside to Rooney she whispered, 'I'm sorry. Don't take no notice.'

Rooney, not yet used to the technique, looked at Ma and answered reassuringly, 'That's all right.'

'Talkin'. I can hear you. Go on!' Grandpa glared at Ma's bulging back muscles, and on this she turned and yelled at him, miming as she did so by thrusting her finger into her ear, 'Well, where's your ear thing? Where is it if you want to hear?'

'That!' Grandpa's chin was thrust up aggressively at her. 'It's like you, no damned good. I can hear better without it.'

Nellie again took his arm, firmly this time. And his manner undergoing an immediate change, he said with almost childish pleading, 'No, Nellie, I don't

45

want to go back yet, I want to sit here.'

Again Nellie took the pad and wrote one word, finishing it off with a double stab, and again at arm's length he read it. Then throwing the paper on to the table and lowering himself into a chair he muttered, 'Behave! Behave!'

No-one spoke for a moment and, under the gimlet stare of Grandpa, Rooney began to shift uneasily, until he thought of his baccy. Taking his pouch from his waistcoat he opened it and pushed it across the table. The old man continued to look at him steadily for a time before his eyes dropped to the tobacco. There were three short rolls in the pouch, and the old man, touching one, said, 'All this? Do you want me to have all this?'

Rooney nodded. And Grandpa, taking a roll, put it into the pocket of his woollen jacket.

The silence returned to the room, and during it Ma refilled the teacups and also a large chipped cup that Nellie had brought in from the kitchen. It was Nellie who handed it to the old man.

'What's his name?' he asked of her.

Patiently Nellie again wrote on the pad, 'Mr Joseph Smith. Call him Rooney.' And as she wrote Rooney visualised her in the shop continually writing out little bills – stab, stab – stab, stab.

After a long gulp of tea, Grandpa read the slip of paper, then asked pointedly of Rooney, 'Why Rooney if your name's Joe?'

Rooney held out his palms and shook his head and mouthed, 'Middle name . . . mother's.'

'What's he say?' Grandpa turned to Nellie again. But

46

she did not write any more explanations. Instead, taking up the *Shields Gazette* from a chair, she handed it to him, whereupon Ma, making the pretence of poking the fire, exclaimed angrily, 'Now what did you have to go and do that for? You know what he is when he gets the paper. Try to get him back.'

'He won't go yet. He's better with the paper than talking. He'll be all right,' said Nellie, and, lifting up the curtains from the table, she left the room.

Rooney knew that he too should rise and go upstairs, but it was always the way when he got sat down, he found it most difficult to get up again and had to wait for an opportune moment. And that moment, he somehow sensed, was not yet, for Ma was worried over the old boy. Well, she needn't be on his account, he had quite taken to the old fellow.

Somehow he made him feel more at home, sort of levelled things down a bit. He had seen a few like him in his time. The only really happy place he had lived in was with a Miss Cuthbert, and her father was just like this one. He had been a good old fellow really, and when he had died she had got herself married to a bloke who objected to lodgers, and that had been that. So the old woman here need not get herself into a stew about what he might think of the old man. As far as he could see there was no doubt but that this one was an old tartar, and Ma had his sympathy in a way, for by the sound of him he'd take some putting up with.

'Damp-day pains are caused by rheumatism.
For speedy relief, take Thirty Days
Rheumatic Tablets.'

Grandpa read out the advert in a slow, high croak, then added, 'Tripe! Tripe! All adverts are tripe. And it's under Personal an' all . . . It's false pretences.'

Ma groaned audibly, and attacked the fire with the poker.

'First Church of Christ Scientist.
Subject for Sunday: Adam and The Fallen Man.'

'They've got it wrong.' Grandpa looked at Rooney. 'Eve and the fallen man, it should be. There'd have been no fall without her.' His eyes flicked towards Ma, where she was now gathering up the cups. 'Women! They should be smothered at birth . . . Are you saved?'

This question was addressed with startling pointedness to Rooney, and he again spread out his hands, smiled and shook his head.

'Well, you can thank God for that. And don't you be saved. And stop anybody from trying to do it. Women and religion, they drive you barmy. How old are you?'

Although Ma in an aside muttered, 'Take no notice,' she stopped and watched Rooney put up both his hands three times, then one hand with the fingers and thumb spread out.

'Thirty-five?' said Grandpa. 'You don't look it. No more'n thirty. Married?'

Rooney shook his head, and Grandpa stared at him fixedly.

At this point the front-door bell rang sharply, and Ma, after a moment's hesitation, left the room. The old man's eyes followed her; then leaning across towards Rooney, he whispered, 'You be careful, lad. I'm

48

warning you. That scarlet menace'll have you singing hymns afore you know where you are . . . And more'n that . . . Ay, more'n that an' all. You look out. I've known her some years, and I'm tellin' you . . . What brought you here?'

There was the sound of the front door closing, and Rooney indicated Ma's return to the old man with a movement of his head, whereupon Grandpa, taking up the paper again, stared at it, and as Ma came into his view, he read aloud,

'Regent Cinema.
Shields Operatic Society
Annie Get Your Gun
Full Chorus and Dances.'

He sniffed up both nostrils before going on,

'Palladium.
Sitting Bull.
Westoe.
Back to God's Country.
Savoy.
Mightiest Spectacle of the year on the screen.
The Prodigal.'

'Women with no clothes on. Look at them! That's the Bible for you . . . D'you go to the pictures?'

Rooney nodded and pointed to a picture of James Stewart in a Stetson under the heading of 'The Man from Laramie'. 'Cowboy,' he said.

The old man ignored this, and his eyes continued to

roam over the paper. Then he exploded loudly, 'Birthday Greetings! Many Happy Returns! Lot of bunkum! Every week birthday greetings and congratulations to Tom, Dick and Harry. What do they want to stick them in the paper for? Who wants to see them? Who does it matter to anyway, but among themselves, eh? Show off! Daft show off. That's what people do, they show off. Skint and save to show off. No coal. Look—' He pointed to the fire, and Ma, coming swiftly from the kitchen like a tugboat cleaving through the water, went to the room door and called sharply, 'Nellie! Nellie!'

There was a movement in the room above, and then a moment later Nellie came into the room, and without asking any questions she took Grandpa firmly by his arm and raised him to his feet.

'What's up? I don't want to go, Nellie. I'm all right. What am I saying? Nowt wrong.'

'Come on.'

Steadily she led him out of the room, and as the door closed on them Ma sank into a chair and covering the side of her face with one hand exclaimed, 'I'm so ashamed . . . I wouldn't for the world . . .'

As was often the case, Ma did not go on to explain what she wouldn't for the world, and Rooney said soothingly, 'There's no need to worry. I mean, about me. Why, there's nothing to worry about – he's only an old man.'

'An old man! A wicked old devil. Oh . . . !' Ma checked her description, and her voice dropping she ended, 'If you only knew what my life's been like with him . . . what I've gone through these past years . . . I could write a book . . .'

The moment now seemed appropriate for rising, and Rooney rose. 'I'll have to be getting me foodstuff down,' he said. 'And then I'll be going out for the evening. It's time I was putting a move on.'

Ma said nothing, but she looked slightly taken aback, and with puckered brows she watched him depart.

On entering his own room Rooney was amazed to find his curtains up. How, he wondered, had the little one managed it? Even if she had stood on the window-sill he couldn't see her reaching the cornice pole. She wasn't more than five foot two, if she was that.

The curtains made all the difference to the room. Where they weren't faded they showed a soft pink and, being the remains of a good-quality pair, they hung nicely. They were lined and warm-looking. Now, he thought, if only he had a fire on he would have been inclined to stay the night, but as he hadn't and no coal to make one – he hadn't dared remove the small amount of coal he still had left at Mrs Sparks's – he would keep to his usual routine and go to the Dogs.

Ma cooked him the two rashers of bacon and the egg he took down for his tea, and set before it his half-pound of butter, a loaf and a pot of jam. But as he ate he did not feel entirely at ease, for Ma and Nellie were sitting down to small slices of what looked like cold potato pasty. Rooney liked to see a good table, and give Mrs Sparks her due she had been a good cook and ate well herself and always saw that there was some tasty bit for him. Yet Ma here looked as if she could eat her share, for that bulk wasn't sustained, he imagined, on cold potato pasty.

'How,' he asked Nellie after a long uncomfortable pause, 'did you manage to hang me curtains?'

'Oh, it was quite easy. I—'

'She's got a set of steps in her room,' put in Ma. 'It saves lugging them up and down stairs.'

'Well, thanks,' said Rooney.

Nellie did not acknowledge the thanks, but kept her attention on her plate. And Rooney, as he ate, glanced at her from time to time, and he thought that he had never seen anybody so white-looking. Perhaps it was the size and darkness of her eyes that made her face look paler than it really was. Her hair was the same colour as her eyes, dark brown, and could have been nice hair if it had been cut properly. But it looked as if it had been cut round a pot pie basin. She was wearing a shapeless, grey woollen jumper, and, he mused, she could have done with a bit of Ma's bust, for it looked as if she had none of her own. Once, while Ma was refilling the tea-pot in the scullery, she raised her eyes to find his upon her, and hers did not drop shyly away but stared back at him with some defiance, and it was his head that went down and his colour that went up.

Later, dressed in his good brown suit and best cap and with his mac over his arm, he called in the living-room to ask if he could have a key.

Ma was sitting before the fire staring into it, her arms hugging her breasts, and she started and turned to him, surveying him a moment appraisingly before saying, 'Well now, we've only got the one key, but the back door's always open. You could come the back way.'

This to Rooney was a bit of a damper, for it meant that he couldn't go in or out without coming to the notice of whoever was in the kitchen and living-room, but, as usual, he couldn't press his point so just said, 'Well, if that'll be all right with you and I won't be intruding . . . ?'

'No, no, not at all. Are you off to the pictures?'

'No, not tonight. I generally go to Horsely Hill on a Saturday night.'

'Oh!' Ma's expression became blank, and it was evident to Rooney that she was one of those people who weren't in favour of the Dogs.

'Well, I'll be off. So lo . . . Goodbye.'

'Goodbye,' said Ma. 'And you can go out the back way if you like.'

From the sitting-room door he turned on his heel and with unsteady steps crossed the room and went into the kitchen.

It was a fair-sized kitchen but appeared small, for most of its space was taken up with a large table opposite the sink, and odd cupboards flanking the walls.

Nellie was standing at the sink, evidently finishing the washing up, and as he passed her he said, 'Good evening.'

She did not raise her head, but answered, 'Good evening.' And he went out thinking, I can't make her out at all. She's not uppish like that lot the other night, but she's more stiff somehow.

After half an hour at the Dogs, Rooney came to the conclusion that the new place had brought him luck, for he'd had two wins and was richer by three pounds fifteen. Now, as with living, Rooney had a method with his winnings. When he won, which wasn't often, he put two-thirds of it in the Post Office to swell the mounting store that his saving of a pound a week was making. The other third he would put on his favourite the following week. But tonight he felt a bit reckless, not quite himself at all, and in a sudden flash of devil-may-care he decided to risk the lot, and not on the favourite but on a bit of an outsider. That he had gone and done a real daft thing he was certain when he saw the dogs lined up; and even when they were off, bounding after the uncatchable hare with Tarantella lying third, he was bitterly regretting his impulsiveness. And then in one great, inspired spurt, Tarantella was home by a head.

He took off his cap and crushed it in his hands, breaking the peak, which showed how deeply he was stirred, for it was a new cap. Four pounds was the most he had ever won, and now to win thirty or over, just like that. What if he put the lot on the next race? No. No, that was a fool's game. He knew when to stop. And he wasn't going to put a third of this on next week either. He'd buy a suit with that third, and start in the usual way again, making ten bob his limit.

Pushing through the crowd, he collected his money and made his way outside the ground, carrying with him thirty-three pounds more than when he had entered.

On the bus from Westoe to Laygate he looked out on the shops, and he felt a little regretful that they were all closed for he had the desire to buy something for somebody . . . but who? Ma and the little one? No, he mustn't start that. No, something for Bill's bairns. Toys, or sweets, or something.

From Laygate he made his way to The Anchor, and

was a bit surprised to find only Bill occupying the MPs' corner.

'Fred not been in?' he asked. 'Nor Albert?'

'No, nor likely to,' said Bill. 'You missed somethin' the day, not comin' in.'

'Did I?' said Rooney. 'Well, I was moving me things, as you know. What's up?'

'What's up? What isn't up!' Bill threw off the remainder of his drink, drew his finger across his upper lip and began, 'It was like this. We called in as usual, and were sitting just here when a chap comes up and says he'd like a word with Albert. Well, they go to the door. And weren't there a minute when Albert comes back. White as a sheet, he was, and wouldn't say nowt for a minute. And then he ordered a glass of whisky. And then another as quick as lightning. And then he opens up. Apparently the fellow had tipped him off – his wife's goin' round with a coloured bloke.'

'A coloured bloke?' repeated Rooney in a slightly shocked tone.

'Aye, from across the water. And they usually cross over in the ferry about two o'clock, the fellow said. By! lad, I've never seen anybody as mad as Albert. Although he knew fine well she was carrying on night after night at different dance halls he had done nowt about it, until he knew the bloke was coloured. "What's the bloody difference?" I said, trying to quieten him. "He's just another bloke. They're all the same under the skin." But it was no good trying to reason with him; it was as Danny said, "All black boys are oor brothers until they want to marry oor sisters or make a pass at oor wives, and then they're not even human beings."

Well, off he went . . . Albert. And we felt a bit uneasy. So the three of us decided to go home, have our dinner, and be at the ferry round about two. And it was as well we did. There he was, at the corner of the market place, in a doorway. We kept out of sight for a bit. And then they came, her done up like a doll, and this black bloke. Fine-looking chap, mind, I will say. Albert didn't wait, he went right in. Man, did that dark boy looked surprised, but he would've knocked the daylights out of Albert if we hadn't interfered and pulled him clear. It was all over in a minute, and her and the bloke had cleared off afore the bobby showed up. We said there had just been an argument, and he told us to get moving.'

'What'll happen the night,' asked Rooney, 'if she comes back?'

'She won't. D'you know what he did when we got him back home?'

Rooney shook his head sadly.

'Took the poker and smashed everything he could hit. Look' – Bill pushed up his coat sleeve to reveal a great black-and-blue weal – 'that's what you get when you try and stop a fellow with a poker. Danny got a welt on the shoulder. And he nearly knocked Fred out altogether. He's got a lump on his napper the size of a turnip.'

'Where's he now?' asked Rooney.

'Danny took him to his place. Best place he could be. Mrs D.'ll see to him. But boy, it's been a day! You've missed something.'

Without further comment Rooney went to the counter and ordered two pints. The glow of his winnings had dimmed somewhat. These four men with whom he worked were a sort of family to him. What happened to them affected him. He became filled with a sadness, and at the same time a strange feeling of relief and thankfulness that he wasn't in the heart-breaking, temper-trying, pocket-clearing state of matrimony, for being the kind of fellow he was, he felt sure that had he tried to pick a lass she would surely have turned out like either Bill's, Fred's or Albert's wife, not Danny's.

When Rooney returned to the corner, Bill remarked, 'You looked pleased with life when you come in. Got some place to suit you at last?'

'It wasn't that, although the place is all right,' said Rooney, 'but I had a win the night.'

'Aye?'

'Aye. Over thirty pounds.'

'No!'

'Aye, I did.'

'Well, I'll be damned! . . . By God, you're a lucky bloke, Rooney.' Bill leant across the table and pushed his pug face nearer to Rooney's. 'Do you know that? Do you ever realise just how lucky you are? Nowt ever happens to you, nowt bad.'

'I don't know so much. You try keeping clear of women who are out to get your blood.'

'Aw, that! If it was me I'd treat it as a pastime. But you are a lucky bloke. We all say it. And now thirty quid! Well' – Bill leant back and stuck his feet out – 'you can pay for all the drinks the night.'

'I'll do nowt of the sort,' said Rooney. 'Things'll be as usual. But here' – he put his hand in his pocket –

'here's a quid for the bairns. Give it to the missus to buy the bairns something. And mind, give it to her. I'll ask the bairns on Tuesday.'

Bill smiled slowly, then took up the note from the table.

'They'll get it. And thanks, man . . . What do you say we go along to Danny's and see how things are?'

'Aye. Just as you like. It's dead here the night without the pair of them.'

Having finished their beer in one draught, they left The Anchor and walked to Eldon Street. Here the houses flanked the main road which ran into Tyne Dock. It was broken here and there by long streets shooting off into drab sameness. Yet about most of the windows and doors of this main road was a sparkle that shone through the lamplight and defied the dust and muck from the docks beyond. If the painted window-sills, polished doors, bath-bricked steps were any indication of the interior of the houses, then most of them in this street would have been little palaces. And Rooney thought they were, for he judged every house with a bright exterior on Danny's, And yet he didn't often go to Danny's, for it unsettled him somehow. And now when Mrs Danny opened the door and the cream-painted passage formed a setting to her neatness, the old feeling, that could have been envy, returned.

'Oh. Come in. Danny thought you might be round. Oh, hallo, Rooney.' Her greeting was full of sincerity. 'Where've you been all this time?'

'Dodging women, Mrs D.,' put in Bill. 'That's all he does. He spends his time dodging women.'

'Go on with you.' She pushed them along the

passage and into the kitchen. And here Danny rose from his chair.

'Hallo.'

'Hallo,' they both said.

'He's gone back home,' said Danny.

'No,' said Bill.

'Yes,' said Mrs D. 'But he's comin' back . . . he promised. Sit down.' She pushed chairs forward. 'He felt he must go and see if she turned up. But he'll be back. Now I know you've both been drinking beer, but would you like a cup of tea?'

'No thanks. No thanks, Mrs D.,' they replied together.

The conversation centred around Albert and what line he should take. And as words repeated themselves and as the same thing was said over and over again with hardly a variation, Rooney's eye and mind wandered and took in the kitchen. This was the kind of place he would give his ears for. It was alive with colour and brightness. Not that the furniture was anything to crack on; there wasn't a piece as good as his dresser here – but it was the way Mrs D. had things set out. And the light paint everywhere. And the bits of brass. And the hanging plant on the corner of the mantelpiece, with its green leaves flowing down the pink-ground wallpaper like a picture to be seen in some fashionable magazine . . . She had everything lovely . . . Then he put a rein on his thoughts. Even if he ever managed to get a house it might never look like this, for he was no hand at arranging things. He could put a bit of paint on, but it had taken more than paint to make this room look as it did.

'So you've moved again, Rooney, Danny tells me?'

'Aye. Again, Mrs D.'

'When are you goin' to get married and move to a house of your own?'

'Aw!' Rooney moved his head from side to side. Then shyly he brought out, 'The truth is, Mrs D., I'm waiting for somebody like you.'

There was a burst of laughter, and it included Rooney's, for he was amused and as surprised as any of them at his own gallantry.

'Ah! He's learnin'. What d'you think, Danny?' said Mrs D.

'I think he's a damn fool,' said her husband. 'And I'm tired of telling him.'

'Oh, I don't know so much,' said Bill. 'Lucky, I would say. Do you know he won thirty quid the night?'

'No!' said Danny.

'Oh, I'm so glad,' said Mrs D. 'And mind you look after it, Rooney.'

The conversation turned and turned again. And at ten-thirty, when Albert had not put in an appearance, Rooney and Bill rose to go. And as Mrs D. led the way to the front door, Rooney stayed behind for a moment and stuck a note in the leaves of the hanging plant.

'Here! What you doin'?' said Danny.

'It's just a bit to get some flowers or something for herself,' said Rooney.

'You start doing that with everybody you meet,' said Danny, 'and your thirty quid'll soon go. You get dafter, you know. But thanks all the same. And she'll put it to good use and be as pleased as punch. But I wish you'd have some sense.'

Outside and having parted from Bill who lived near by, Rooney, making his way to Filbert Terrace, thought, Danny's right. I wouldn't have much left if I went on like that. Yet the pleasure he had got from making the two gifts stayed with him, and the desire also to buy something for somebody still lingered. The quicker he got the money into the Post Office the better, he told himself. He didn't know what was the matter with him the night. It was likely the result of a funny day, him moving, then winning that money, and Albert's do. It would be just as well when Monday came and he got back again into the old routine.

When he entered the living-room, Ma was sitting exactly where he had left her. It could have been that she had never moved since he went out. The little one was at the machine, her arm moving like a piston, her fingers pushing at a mass of grey material. She did not raise her eyes or give any greeting whatever. But Ma's greeting, covering a number of points in one breath, dispelled any feeling of awkwardness Nellie's attitude might have caused him.

'Ah, there you are. Have you had a nice night? Now do you want any supper, or have you had it? I was just saying I'd leave you something out in future so we wouldn't wait up. And you could make yourself some tea.'

'I don't want anything the night,' said Rooney. 'I've been to a friend's house and had a bit of supper. Thanks all the same.'

As he spoke he threaded his way across the room, quietly, as if he might disturb someone. And at the door he turned and said, 'Good night, all.'

'Good night,' said Ma. 'And I hope you sleep well.'

The little one said nothing. And if he hadn't remembered her gentle handling of Grandpa and the old man's evident liking for her he would have considered her at this moment the worst of the bunch.

He was just dropping off to sleep, his mind sinking into the layer where, to use his own term, daft thoughts struck him, where he sometimes heard himself reciting bits of poetry from his schooldays and where he sometimes saw himself doing the most extraordinary things, such as leading a lass down a fine staircase and on to a ballroom floor, or walking down a road dressed up to the nines in a trilby and wearing gloves, and a lass on his arm . . . or even kissing a woman on the palm of the hand – that was the daftest bit of all and the one he experienced most often. It was just starting, this one. There was the hand, palm upwards. He could see the lines on it; and it was lying in his big fist. And there he was, getting nearer and nearer to it, when the most odd thing happened . . . somebody swore. It seemed to be the owner of the hand. 'Hell!' it said. 'Damn and blast! Damn! Damn!' The hand leapt away from his palm and made a thumping noise.

Rooney was wide awake, staring into the darkness. From behind his head came the sound of a soft thump! thump! as if someone was beating their fists into a mattress. He raised himself on his elbow and looked towards the wall. That was funny. He'd been dreaming. Yet that thump, thump, that wasn't in his dream.

Then to his amazement he heard the sound of sobbing, low, smothered sobbing. It did not last for

62

long, yet he waited, wondering what he'd hear next. But there was no further noise. And when his elbow got the cramp he lay down again.

Who was next door? He couldn't imagine Ma lowering herself to use such words, or yet her daughter, who fancied herself. That only left the little one . . . He must have been dreaming. Yes, of course he was dreaming. Who could she have been swearing at? But he hadn't dreamed that he heard someone crying – no, he hadn't dreamed that.

It was some time before he went to sleep, and when he did he dreamed he ran off with Albert's wife, and she was a coloured woman with white hands, which just showed you, he told himself the next morning.

3

THE BEADS

On Monday morning, Bannister, the foreman, came up to them in the depot and, addressing Danny, said, 'You're to take number four rear-loader the day and hook on a trailer for the waste paper. And by the way, there's been a complaint sent to the office that some bloke from your district refused to pick up a box of paper and a bag of rags.'

Danny looked round at them, and they looked back at him blankly, almost stupidly. 'Hardly makes sense,' said Danny. ''Twould be cutting off wor nose to spite wor face.'

'I'm glad you see it that way,' said the foreman.

'There was that iron bedstead and flock mattress. But I told you about that,' said Danny. 'We couldn't get them on at the time and I told her to contact the office.'

'No, this wasn't beds or mattresses. But what you blokes have got to remember is it's all salvage.'

He turned away and Fred, looking around the great open sorting room, said, 'Salvage! Salvage! You get sick of the bloody sight of it.'

Rooney's gaze followed Fred's, but the conglomeration of stuff did not disturb him one way or the other; he was so used to seeing old John Crawley on the paper press that the surprising thing would have been if he had not seen him there. Sometimes they would return with the loader five times in one day to drop the salvage before going on to the controlled tip to dump the refuse, and each time old John would be stuffing the paper into the press, switching on the machine and adding another two-hundredweight bale to his stock. Ned Harvey would be doing the same with the rags; Jack Llewellyn would be sorting metals, aluminium kettles and pans, lead from iron; Tom Paisley would be stacking mattresses or bundling up the threadbare remains of mats and carpets, or doing the brain-softening job of packing feathers; Con Rainton would be sorting the woollen rags from the cotton and spreading anything wet out to dry; while a number of young lads would incessantly be tearing up cardboard boxes to feed old John's press; and all working in a through draught that almost wiped the lugs off you.

It was all part of the pattern of the job, and it did not affect Rooney, only sometimes to make him think, By! who'd think there was money in this muck? For he, like every other man dealing with the collecting and sorting of the refuse, knew just what money there was in the salvage part of it . . . they received quite a bonus from the Corporation after their wages had been paid, the maintenance of the lorries seen to, and other expenses connected with the work were paid. So naturally they made themselves conversant with the prices. Every man Jack of them knew the current price of each material, at times discussing the rise and fall of these prices in the manner of stock-brokers. For instance, it was to be regretted that wool was at the moment only bringing a hundred and fifty pounds a ton, compared with three hundred just after the war; rags were fetching thirty pounds today; paper eight; where copper would bring two hundred and seventy-five pounds, brass bedsteads and bicycle frames brought the handsome sum of two pounds ten. There was seldom much copper kicking around, so, as Danny said, if you didn't pick up paper and rags it was cutting off your nose to spite your face. Besides, there were so many blokes rag-, bottle-, and paper-collecting in the town to sell to the private firms that they'd run miles to get the stuff. More than once Rooney himself had been approached by chaps to see if he'd drop stuff, particularly wool, on to their barrow for a back-hander. But that he considered would have been a mug's game, although Bill argued till he was blue in the face with Danny that material thrown into the dustbin was classed as abandoned material and was therefore nobody's property because the dustbin belonged to the householder, who had thrown away the stuff that was in it. Danny would always come back and say the lorry was the property of the Corporation, and once the stuff was in it the Corporation was responsible for it, so if it cut one way it also cut the other. If the Corporation were to be held responsible for the refuse then it should be classed as theirs.

The top and the bottom of it was, Rooney thought, there was more in muck than met the eye.

In the garage, they all made for number four, and Fred, pulling himself up into the driver's cab, sang softly in a ragman's call, 'Any rags, bottles, or bones? Any rags the day? Any rags for ruddy rubbystone?'

Climbing up beside him, Danny chided, 'It's not

69

funny, Fred. I don't want any complaints about our lot.'

Rooney, Bill, and Albert got into the loader's cab immediately behind, and Bill, tugging his cap farther on to his head, muttered, 'Salvage! You'd think wor lives depended on salvage.'

'It pays wor wage,' said Danny.

'Who paid wor wages when it all went in the incinerator? We had to be paid then. They've got to have us.'

Danny, speaking over his shoulder through the let in the dividing partition, said, 'You'd grumble in heaven, Bill. You're young yet. You should have been on in the days when we were known as scavengers and classed below the muck we moved. They don't think much of us now, but they thought a damn sight less of us then. Long shovels and open carts it was in them days, and the stink would knock the devil down. No dustbins. You don't know you're born, lad.'

'I wouldn't have worked on the job in them days, Danny,' said Bill in a somewhat quieter tone.

'No, perhaps you wouldn't, Bill, but there was no pick and choose then . . . we had to eat.'

There was a strong reprimand in Danny's voice, and Bill became silent. But Rooney thought, Nor would I; I wouldn't have worked like that, not even for to eat. The job now was still dirty and unpleasant, and you were often soaked to the skin, and in the frosty weather your hands almost froze to the bins, but if you were strong and liked outdoor work the job was bearable; if you weren't so strong but stuck it like some did, it broke your health and your heart.

The lorry swung out of the yard, across the town, and up to Westoe Fountain; then into Westoe Village itself, which was but another section of Shields, the good-class section. Once the place of residence of shipbuilders and big business men of the town, now many of the big houses were turned into offices. Still, Westoe Village managed to retain its superiority.

The first two hours went by without a word from Albert, and Rooney, who was paired off with him, found the time a little trying. He felt that if Albert would let off steam in some way he would feel a lot better. He was saying as much to Bill as they tipped their respective bins into the container when Albert's voice was heard from the end of a long sidewalk that served as the tradesmen's entrance to Honeycroft, the home of Mrs Bailey-Crawford.

'He's talking all right now,' said Bill; 'you'd better go and see what's up. Likely having a row with the maid. Anything female will do for him to get his teeth into at present.'

'Can't be a maid,' said Rooney. 'That's old Double-Barrel's place. She's got no maid now.'

'So it is,' said Bill. 'By lad! Don't say he's goin' for her.'

Rooney, leaving his empty bin by the grass verge, hurried down the tree-lined sidewalk, past stables as big as a house, and across the brick and grass-strewn yard to a glassed-in covered way, where stood Albert, pointing to the bin. His face was red and his voice high with anger.

'You report me? It's me that'll do the reportin'!'

'How dare you speak to me like that! Go away this

71

minute, and take that bin with you. And I promise you you'll pay for your insolence.'

The old lady was standing in the kitchen doorway, and as usual she looked like a bundle of rags tied together. Her white hair was hanging loose from a couple of pins, and her face looked as if it hadn't been washed for a week. Yet she held her tall, lean body as straight as a ramrod.

'What's up?' asked Rooney.

'Look at that,' said Albert, pointing to the bin. 'Full of wet muck. Wet tea-leaves on top of all that stuff, and it's running out of the bottom.'

'Get away this minute! And take that bin with you,' ordered the old lady.

'I can refuse to lift it in that state.'

The old lady's face darkened even further. 'Get out of here at once!'

'Aye. I will an' all. And you can do what the hell you like with your bin.'

Albert, turning away, cried to Rooney, 'Come on.'

But Rooney did not immediately come on. He looked at the bin which was certainly in a mess, and he looked at the old lady, and quietly he said, 'Don't worry, I'll see to it. But, you know, you shouldn't put wet stuff in.'

'It's a bin, and I'll put what I like in it. And I'll report that man immediately.'

Looking at her, Rooney thought, She will an' all. He didn't like any trouble among the gang; there was enough in the yard at times, and if Bannister got any more complaints from this end he could become unpleasant and Danny'd be the first to get it in the

72

neck. He pushed his hair back before replying, 'I wouldn't do that, mum. He's not usually like that. You see, he's in a bit of trouble.'

'Trouble? What trouble?' demanded the old lady.

'Well –' Rooney looked at his boots and said under his breath, 'It's his wife . . . she's left him.'

'And a very sensible thing to do. Who'd put up with a man like that? Daring to speak to me in such a fashion! Because I'm alone they think they can do what they like. But they can't . . . You'll take that bin.'

It was an order, and Rooney said, soothingly, 'Yes, mum, I'll take the bin.'

With a jerk from his wrist on the handle and a lift from his hand at the bottom he swung the dustbin on to his shoulder as if it was a pail, and as he did so he was thankful for his leather jerkin.

At the van, Albert challenged him. 'What you go and do it for? The likes of her! Who does she think she is? Her day's past, and a damned good job, too.'

'Aye,' said Rooney. 'But it'll save a lot of trouble, man.'

'Trouble be damned! There should be more trouble,' cried Albert, stamping away.

Rooney returned down the walk and put the bin under the covered way. The old lady was in the yard now and she watched him in silence. And as he passed her on his way back he suggested again, 'I wouldn't put no more wet stuff in, mum.'

'I'll put in what I please. You only call when it suits you; weeks go by before you collect.'

'Oh, mum.' Rooney smiled, as if at an irritated child.

'We come if we can get in. But sometimes your gate's locked.'

She made no comment on this. So saying, 'Good day, mum,' Rooney departed, thinking: Poor old wife, living in that great place alone. He did not voice the opinion of the gang as to why she should be allowed to live there when the place would house four families comfortably – to him, old Double-Barrel was of a class that had always lived in big houses. Nor did he envy her any part of Honeycroft, for it did not fit in with his idea of a home. What he wanted was a little house, something he could manage. That place would be a headache to anybody, even the Council, he thought, for the whole roof needed retiling and the bricks pointing, for a start.

At the bottom of the road they stopped, and Fred and Bill, together with Rooney, gathered on the kerb. This was the spot where they usually had their break, after which Fred would wind up the van end to make way for more dirt.

Rooney had taken up a pole and was distributing the refuse more evenly, so that Albert could get his last binful on, when Bill said softly, 'Hold your hand a minute. What was that?'

Leaning over, he pulled from among the indescribable mess a battered cardboard box, in which a galaxy of colours was dimmed by ashes and clots of what could have been porridge.

'Beads, and bairns' things . . . look.' He picked up some little bricks in one hand. 'They're bonny, they're painted with real little pictures, look—' He rubbed at them. 'They'll do for the bairns.'

74

'Better watch out,' said Fred. 'Remember Hughie Foggarty.'

'What's that got to do with it?' said Bill. 'I'm not going to sell the damned things, these are only bairns' bits. I'm havin' them, and to hell!'

Rooney himself could not see the harm in it. As Bill said, he wasn't going to sell the stuff, or anything like that. If a chap took stuff for that purpose he deserved all he got. But these were just beads and things; and well, after all, they'd been thrown away.

As Bill pocketed a rubber doll, a little monkey on a stick, and the bricks and beads, Rooney pushed the rubbish still farther back, exclaiming, 'I think there's some more here, Bill. Red beads. Look!' He raked them forward towards Bill, and it was at this point that Fred warned them in a whisper, 'Look out. Here's Danny.'

Danny had always been dead nuts on them picking up anything. Long before Foggarty got pulled up, Danny would say, 'Now none of that, it's not worth the candle.' And so Bill abruptly finished his scrambling and turned away.

Rooney had the beads under his hand. They looked nice beads in spite of them being all messed up. They were on a chain of some sort, and it seemed a shame to push them back among all the muck, when they'd please some bairn. With a quiet movement he covered them with his fist and unobtrusively pocketed them.

Now that Albert's tongue had been released, it seemed impossible for him to control it. Walking half a dozen paces each way in front of the lorry, he stormed against his wife and the world that dared to

75

give foot-room to Negroes, and women in general.

Danny motioned to the rest of them to let him carry on, and the fact that Albert carried on for the rest of the day contributed to Rooney's forgetting to hand over the beads to Bill. That, and one or two other things he had on his mind, the main one being that before he went home he had to make a purchase.

At four-thirty he left his mates at the depot, and making his way to King Street he started to look round. And it was before a high-class gentlemen's outfitters that he finally stopped and saw in the window what he wanted. It took him some time to enter the shop, for to his mind his working togs were not in line with what he was after, but had he gone home and changed the shops would all have been closed, and he would have had to wait until the week-end. And he couldn't wait till then to go to the bathroom. And he wasn't going to risk another look like he got yesterday when he met that madam on the landing, with just his trousers on and his galasses hanging down. He'd been having a bath when he ran into her, and she'd looked as shocked as if he'd been naked. She was in a dressing-gown, they all wore them. The old woman made the breakfast in hers. And this morning he had seen the little one draped in a thing that made her look worse, if anything, than she really was.

In the shop, an assistant stepped forward and said, 'Can I help you?'

'I want a dressing-gown.'

There was a moment's pause while the assistant took in Rooney from head to toe.

'Yes, sir. Have you any particular colour in mind?

How about this?' He went to a stand, where a red-patterned, artificial-silk dressing-gown draped a headless man.

'No, not like that,' said Rooney. He didn't want to look like a Chinese mandarin. 'Like the one in the middle of the window.'

'The mushroom-coloured one? Yes, sir.'

There had been no price on the dressing-gown, and when the assistant laid it on the counter and Rooney saw its thick, tartan-lined interior, he thought, I've done it now. I should have asked him what it was first.

'How much?' he said.

'Eight pounds nineteen and eleven. It's a lovely gown, beautiful quality.'

Eight pounds nineteen and eleven. Nine quid! It would have to be beautiful quality . . . why, he could get a suit for eight pounds nineteen and eleven. He looked towards the headless man, and the assistant said, 'That's very good value at seventy shillings. And we have others, thicker, a mixture of wool and cotton. But I think this will be more your size, sir. It allows for breadth, where the cheaper ones don't, and your shoulders are' – he smiled congratulatorily – 'pretty broad.'

Rooney remained dumb, staring at the dressing-gown. He couldn't have a suit and this an' all and put twenty pounds in the bank. But did he need to put twenty pounds in the bank? If he hadn't had the win he couldn't have done it. 'I'll take it,' he said.

'And anything else, sir? Pyjamas? Shirts?'

Pyjamas. If you had a dressing-gown you'd have to have pyjamas, he supposed. He never wore anything in bed; winter and summer he slept . . . blank.

He bought two sets of pyjamas.

'Slippers, sir?'

Lord! He groaned inwardly. He had slippers, but they were felt ones, and they certainly couldn't stand up to this rig-out. He bought slippers, leather ones with lamb's-wool lining, and left the shop fifteen pounds lighter, telling himself he was barmy, but accompanied by a feeling of recklessness touched with excitement. If his coal had come – he had asked Harry Baker on his way to work to be sure and drop him a couple of bags in – then he would get dressed up and sit in expensive comfort afore the fire . . . By! lad, eh? He shook his head and laughed at himself. What would the chaps say if they knew! Phew! He grew hot at the thought.

As he opened the kitchen door of No. 71 he was immediately aware that there was company, for from beyond the closed door of the living-room there came the sound of voices, and the high-pitched note of a child squealing, 'Just let me have one more look. Just one more. Yes! Yes! Mummy.'

He took off his coat and his boots, and put on his slippers which he had left in the corner, and with the parcel under his arm, he entered the room.

'Oh! I didn't hear you come in. You're late. I thought you weren't coming.'

Ma was seated at the table, and across from her was the wife of the miserable-looking fellow Dennis, and the young, stuck-up piece, Doreen. And by Ma's side was a thin, pert-faced child of about six, who stopped her chattering to stare at Rooney.

'Good evening.'

Pauline had the grace to answer, but Doreen continued her meal in silence.

'I've got your pie all ready,' said Ma. 'Will you . . . ?' She paused as her grand-daughter cried, 'I'm going up to look just once more.' The child had slipped from the chair and was now at the door.

'You're not! Come here. Be quiet. We're going home in a minute,' said Pauline, with calm preciseness.

The child, ignoring her mother, appealed to Ma, 'Oh, Gran, can I? Just a peep. Say yes.'

'Go on then,' said Ma. 'And don't be a minute, mind. Now as I was saying –' She turned to Rooney. 'Oh, she's a chatterbox, I don't know where I was. Oh yes. Will you have your tea now or get washed first?'

Although he would, in any case, have said, 'I'll have a wash first,' he felt that Ma had a way of placing her words so as to make you do what she wanted. And she evidently didn't want him to sit down with her two daughters. Well, she needn't have worried.

'I'll be down later,' he said.

'Very well.'

As he mounted the stairs, Doreen's voice came up to him as it had done on Saturday, and he heard her say quite plainly, 'How can you be so smarmy with him! He's like a big gorilla.'

He stopped dead, and the heat from a wave of unaccustomed anger covered his face. Gorilla! By! lad, he'd like to take his hand and smack that one's face.

It was such an unusual thought for him that he was upset as much by it as by the remark that had caused it.

A light streaming from the room next to his own lit

the dark landing, and as he passed the open door he saw the child standing beside a single bed, and on the bed, propped up by a pillow, was a doll. The room was small, but even its size could not take away the impression of bareness, for all he could see in it was a corner hanging wardrobe, a small chest of drawers, and a bed. As he went into his own room his anger was lifted a little, for the fire was on and his curtains drawn, and his chair arranged before the hearth. The picture it made eased the hurt of the stinging words, yet as soon as he had put down the parcel he went to the dressing-table and surveyed himself. His shoulders admittedly were big, and his body perhaps over-thick, but his face wasn't even dark, it was fair-skinned, and he had a good skin, if nothing else. His sandy-brown hair was a bit unruly and wouldn't stay put for five minutes, but he had seen worse. He had no false ideas about himself, but . . . gorilla!

Before opening the parcel he went across to the bath-room and had a good wash. Then, once again in his room, he gently lifted the dressing-gown from its wrapping and tried it on.

Standing again before the mirror he stared for a long while at his reflection. Then his grey eyes gave himself an appreciative twinkle. By! lad, who would have believed he could have looked like this. It was the colour – mushroom, the fellow had said. Or was it the cut; easy, but fitting snugly like an old boot? . . . And that one saying 'gorilla!' Oh! he'd like to show her . . .

A scream, suddenly rising through the floor from the living-room, startled him out of the rare act of self-approval, and he stared downwards.

It came again. And then again, but now through a confused babble of voices. And when it continued, he went swiftly to the door, and opening it, listened. It was the child, and it sounded as though she had been scalded or something. He heard a door open and the voice of the old man muttering, 'What's all this? What's goin' on?' Then the muted voices from the living-room seemed to explode into the hall, and he made out Ma's above the rest, crying to the old man, 'You get yourself back! . . . As for you, you'll end up in the asylum.'

'And who'll put me there? She's not having it, it's mine.'

He was surprised to hear the little one speaking.

'Kathie . . . leave go! Do you hear? All this fuss about a bit of a doll.' It was the mother's voice. 'Really, Nellie; you're beyond me.'

Then Ma's voice came again, outdoing them all, barking with finality, 'The child's goin' to keep it! What is it, anyway, but a clouty doll? You can make another. You're going bats . . . you and your dolls!'

There followed a quick, odd silence, during which even the old man's tongue was still. Rooney moved forward to the top of the stairs, impelled by more than mere curiosity. Then very distinctly he heard the little one say, with quiet yet piercing emphasis, 'If I don't get it, I don't put in another stitch . . . not one.'

The silence took hold again, until it was broken by Doreen's pseudo-refined tone: 'Give it back to Aunt Nellie, Kathie.' Another silence – then, 'If you don't, I won't have you for my bridesmaid, mind . . . I'll get Aunt Betty's Doris. That's who I'll get.'

No more words, but the sounds of movement, and before he knew what had taken place, Nellie was on the stairs below him, and there was nothing for him to do but to pretend to be on his way down.

He stood on the top stair to let her pass, and as she came abreast of him he stared at her, fascinated. In the dim light she looked like a young girl of seventeen or eighteen hugging a child. The doll was dressed up in a white lacey thing, like a christening gown, and her hand was covering its head, pressing its face into her chest.

She was not aware of him until she was close upon him, and then she lifted her head for one brief moment, and the pain he saw in her face caused a feeling of pain in himself as if he were witnessing the baiting of an animal or small child, and he wanted to cry out to her, 'Don't be hurt like that, whatever it is.'

He watched her run across the landing and into her room, and after her door banged he waited for a moment before softly returning to his own room. He felt bewildered . . . he couldn't make it out. He didn't know what to think. She must set some store by that doll. Perhaps she'd had it since she was a bairn . . . The picture of her face came back to him. He'd never seen anybody in his life with such sad eyes. And they could be lovely eyes, he thought, if she was happy.

He took off the dressing-gown and hung it on the back of the door, put the pyjamas away and the new slippers on; then sat down and waited until he heard Doreen come upstairs. When her door closed, he went down to the living-room. The mother and child were gone, the old man was not to be seen, and Ma was clearing part of the table. She went into the kitchen and returned with his meal before she spoke.

'I'm so ashamed. I'm sure you couldn't help but overhear that terrible carry-on.' She put the dish on the table, then threw out her arms. 'And all for nothing, absolutely nothing! It makes me so ashamed. We never have rows in the house, I can't stand rows.'

'Oh, it's all right,' said Rooney. 'Families always have dust-ups. It's all right.'

'It's not all right, Rooney. Not at all.' Ma placed her two plump hands flat on the table and leaned towards him. 'Can you imagine a grown woman making herself a doll? And just because a child takes a fancy to it, going on like she did? Between you and me she's a trial . . . a great trial. What with her and him' – she motioned with her index finger towards the right-hand-side wall – 'life isn't worth living at times.'

Rooney was never very curious about people, but there were a number of questions he would have liked to ask Ma, but all he could say was, 'It's better to have a family to quarrel with than no family at all.'

Ma looked at him hard for a moment, and after straightening and adjusting the back of hair, she said, 'I suppose there is something in that.' She allowed a pause to follow before going on, 'But when you try to make people feel one of the family and you get nothing but ingratitude it hurts. Do you know I've had her since she was ten? After her mother died I took her in – her father had died years before. My Queenie was nine at the time, and I had a boy ten and one eight, and three younger girls. But I didn't hesitate. She was one of the family – I treated them all alike – I didn't make flesh of one and fish of the other. And this is what I get. And'

– she drew in her chins as she stared at him – 'you've seen her, the sight of her. She gets worse. She doesn't trouble. Now, there are my girls – you've seen three of them. Do they look like her? And my Queenie . . . no-one would believe there's only a year between Queenie and her. You haven't met my Queenie yet. She lives in Roker. I go over there once a month. She's got a beautiful place, modern house, everything really up to date. And a lovely garden . . . They keep a gardener. Her husband's manager for a large wholesale firm.'

Ma delivered this information in short staccato gasps, then sat down. And there was another pause. She had folded her hands on her lap, and was staring into the fire. She seemed to be thinking of her eldest daughter and her grand house, and Rooney did nothing to disturb her reverie but went on quietly eating.

He was telling himself it was a good shepherd's pie, as good as any he'd tasted, when Ma suddenly exclaimed, apropos neither of rows, nor of Nellie, Queenie, or beautiful houses, 'Do you go to church at all, Rooney?'

It was such an unexpected question that Rooney swallowed, almost gulped. 'No, I'm afraid I don't.'

'You're no denomination?'

'No.'

'Have you ever thought about it?'

'Well, I can't say I have . . . No, to be honest, I haven't.'

'Well, it's never too late. I'm Low Church myself, and I find it such a help. I've been sustained all my life through the Church. I've sung in the choir since

I was a young woman, at the same church, St Jude's, Francis Street.'

'Oh.'

'You must come in some night to one of the fellowship meetings, they'd be pleased to welcome you, they're all so friendly and chummy.'

Rooney ate hurriedly. 'It's very kind of you. Thanks all the same.' He began to sweat. If it wasn't marriage or money they were after, it was to get you to God. You were never safe.

'Well' – Ma rose – 'I'll have to be making a move. We're starting tonight, practising for the carols. There's just over three weeks to Christmas. Doesn't time fly? I'll have to get ready, not that I feel like going out tonight. Are you going out, Rooney?'

'Yes. Yes, I'm meeting a friend.'

He'd had no intention of going out, but he wasn't going to leave any loopholes that might lead to him being roped in for a meeting. With a certain amount of irritation he thought there was always something to spoil an enjoyable evening. He'd got a good book to finish, a good cowboy yarn. Moreover, he was feeling tired . . . he'd done some humping in one way and another during the day.

The room door was pushed slightly open, and Doreen's voice came from behind it, saying, 'I'm off, Ma.'

'All right, dear. Give my love to Harry.'

There was no response to this, only the banging of the front door.

With an apology for leaving him, Ma left the room. And Rooney, having finished his meal, took the dishes

85

into the kitchen and washed them up. He was in the process of drying them when Ma appeared again, dressed, as he termed it, up to the eyes. She was wearing a fashionable, heavy grey tweed coat with a deep roll collar and a close-fitting brown felt hat. He was set wondering how she had managed to get all her hair underneath the hat, but she had, and the result was, in his opinion, a turn for the better. And as he watched her preening herself before the little mirror at the side of the sink, he thought, The old girl fancies herself, and no mistake.

'I'll be in before you, I suppose, about half-past nine.' She spoke to him through the mirror; then turning towards him, she smiled. 'Is your fire all right?'

'Oh! . . . Yes. I forgot to thank you for lighting it. It looked grand when I came in . . . homely.'

'I'm so glad. It's nice to have a man in the house to do things for – you know, Rooney, you put me in mind of my eldest son.' Ma looked down. 'He was killed in the war.'

'I'm sorry,' said Rooney.

'It was the second cross God laid on me – but He also gave me the strength to bear it. Well –' Ma managed to smile brightly. 'Well, I must be going. I'll be seeing you. Ta-ta.'

His reply would have been 'Ta-ra,' but it would have sounded a bit too familiar by half, so very politely he said, 'Goodbye.' His only reaction to having been placed in the exalted position of resembling Ma's son was to make him think, She makes me hot under the collar.

He went upstairs and reluctantly changed all his

86

clothes. The fire was burning brightly, the room was warm, and the chair was calling to him . . . Damn! Why must he go out? There was no must, he could just say he changed his mind. But he was supposed to be meeting a fellow.

'Nellie! Nellie! Open the door.' For the second time that evening he was startled by a voice, the old man's this time, and coming from the landing.

There followed series of raps, and his voice again: 'It's me. It's only me, Nellie. Can you hear me?'

The rapping became louder, and for a moment a disturbing thought crossed Rooney's mind. Of course she could hear him, if she could hear at all. He recalled her face again, and as he did so he went out on to the landing.

The old man turned to him. 'Oh, it's you. She won't answer. Push the door open and see if she's all right.'

'She might be asleep,' said Rooney softly.

'What?'

Rooney shook his head.

'One of these days she'll do something. She'll drive her to it. Come on, push the door.'

Rooney was relieved of the trying necessity of coming to a decision by the opening of the door and Nellie appearing, her face no longer white but red from crying.

'You all right, Nellie?' The old man spoke tenderly.

'Yes.' She nodded her head and then catching sight of Rooney she pulled the door closed behind her. Then, taking Grandpa gently by the arm, she said under her breath, 'Come on.'

But Grandpa did not move under her guidance;

instead he put his hand to his left side, then reached out and supported himself against the wall. Now that he was relieved of anxiety his strength seemed to have failed him, and he muttered, 'Let me get me breath, Nellie.'

Her back to Rooney, Nellie waited a moment. But the old man made no effort to relinquish the support of the wall, and his breathing became even more laboured. 'I'll . . . I'll have to sit down, Nellie.'

'Bring him in here,' said Rooney, pointing to his door.

Nellie seemed to hesitate. She glanced towards the stairs: then easing the old man from the wall, she gently propelled him past Rooney into the room.

Rooney pushed the big chair forward, and with a sigh the old man sank into it. Then bringing the other chair up to the fire, he said to Nellie, 'Sit down.'

Without a word she sat down and took hold of Grandpa's hand, and after a moment the old man smiled at her. 'Long time since I did them stairs, Nellie.'

She nodded.

He looked at the grate full of glowing coals; then his head moved slowly about, taking in the room. 'You're comfortable,' he said. 'Lovely fire.' He held out a hand to the grate. 'I used to have a fire like this when my missus was alive. But not for years now. Nellie' – he turned to her, seeming to forget Rooney's presence – 'why don't you do it, like you were going to? Get some place, and take me.'

She shook her head.

'In the right place I'm good for a few years yet. Me

breath going is only because of the stairs – why! look at a week gone – I went out, didn't I? By!' he laughed, 'that put her into a stew, to find me been out.' His voice became quiveringly eager. 'We could do fine, Nellie, on our own.'

Again she shook her head, and Rooney realised she hadn't her pad with her and knew it was no good answering.

'Then why don't you go off yourself? – don't mind me. I've told you time and again.' He looked up at Rooney. 'They've used her all these years, workin' for the lot of them. And that one will drive her off her head yet. Look what she did over Queenie.'

As if she had been shot to her feet, Nellie was standing. 'Come on.'

'No, Nellie. Let me stay a minute,' he pleaded. 'All right. I won't say no more. Just' – he disengaged her hand from his arm – 'just let me sit here a minute, near this fire.'

Nellie turned her back on the old man and looked at Rooney. 'I'm sorry,' she said.

'That's all right. What's there to be sorry for? He can stay as long as he likes. It's nice having him – he's company. Sit down.' He touched the back of the chair, then added softly, 'There's nobody in. Doesn't matter where you sit, does it?'

She looked up into his eyes, staring into them. And he did not drop his gaze from hers when she said, 'Do you think I'm odd . . . mad?'

'That's daft talk,' he said emphatically.

'Is it? . . . No . . . I know what I would think if someone went on as I do . . . not speaking. You mustn't mind me not speaking when . . . when Grace is there. You see . . . Oh!' Her head drooped, and she swung it from side to side. 'It's no use trying to explain, it would all sound so silly.'

'There's no need to explain anything.'

She raised her head again, but turned her eyes sideways, looking towards the dresser as she spoke. 'About the doll. I must have seemed like someone demented to you. But you see, you can't keep anything. I know it was only a doll, but—' She brought her teeth sharply down on to her lip and stopped.

And he, affected by her embarrassment, rubbed his hand over his chin. 'It's all right, I understand,' he said.

He didn't understand; he understood nothing; he couldn't understand the people in this house, nor the things they did. Why Ma could be religious and treat the old man, there, as she did. For there was another side to the old boy, he could see, and he was beginning to think that Ma had asked for all she had got from him. Nor did he understand about the doll. Not for anyone to get into such a stew as the little one here had done.

He was surprised to realise that he had not yet been in this house three days.

'I'll go down now, Nellie. I'd better get to bed.'

Together they went to him and helped him to his feet, and as they walked him to the door he began to tremble. He was going to have a worse job getting down the stairs than he had up, Rooney thought. And so, on the landing, when the old man paused again, he said, looking at Nellie, 'I'll carry him.'

'Can you?'

90

He smiled quizzically and added, 'He's no heavier than a dustbin.'

It wasn't a smile that came on her face in answer to this comparison but a soft, relieving light that was closely akin to it. It was the first time, as he put it, that he had seen her let up.

After a 'Here! Here! what you up to?' the old man relaxed against Rooney, and in a matter of seconds was sitting in his own room.

The sharp contrast from the bright warmth of the room above with this one struck Rooney immediately. But nothing could be done, he saw at once, about arranging the furniture into comfort, for there was too much of it. It lined the walls, piece touching piece. Sideboard touching wardrobe, wardrobe touching dressing-table, and that close-pressed against a large dining-table. Chairs in a double row, and the bed, full-sized, sticking out into the room.

'I'll get him a drink,' said Nellie, and when she had gone the old man beckoned Rooney's head close to his.

'Here!'

'Yes?' said Rooney.

'Do you go in a pub?'

Rooney nodded. And Grandpa, pushing two trembling fingers into his waistcoat pocket, brought out half a crown. 'Could you get me a drop of hard?'

Rooney nodded again and took the half-crown.

'On the quiet, mind. Don't let her know . . . the other one. Nellie gets me a drop at the week-end, but I'm all of a dither the night and need a glass. The other one would see me dead first. And she collars me pension. Half-crown, that's all I get, and me baccy coupon. Bad 'un, that. Hypocrite. She would have had me in the workhouse . . . Harton. Aye, she would, but for Nellie. And she's treated her cruel. You don't know, lad.' The old man shook his head. 'I could tell you some things, but Nellie gets vexed. But she's gonna get a shock one of these days, that 'un is. And this is my house, the rent book's in my name. I came here when I was first married. Fine house I had. Happy an' all. I had the best wife in the world. And then my only son had to go and take her! Of all the women he could have had he had to go and take *her*. And she led him a life. Pushing him from one job to another, trying to live big. An upstart, that's all she was. D'you know something? I was glad when he died. Aye, I was. It's an awful thing to say, but I was. For he was at peace. He was a quiet lad, and if it hadn't been for Nellie, I'd have been with him long since. You'll get me that drop, will you?'

Rooney mouthed, 'Aye, yes,' nodding the while. And when Nellie came into the room, he went upstairs, put on his mac and cap, and went out. It must, he thought, be many a long day since the old man had bought any whisky himself . . . four-and-six a glass, it was now. He paid nine-and-a-penny for a quarter-bottle, and when he was once again in the house he waited in the living-room until Nellie should come in.

She must have heard him, for she came out of the front room immediately and said, 'He shouldn't have asked you; I'd have gone.'

When he handed her the bottle, she looked at it. 'He only gave you half a crown, didn't he? You mustn't do this. Once you start he might expect it to go on . . . he's old.'

92

'That's all right,' said Rooney.

'I'll give you the rest of the money.'

'No, it's on me. I had a win on Saturday, I'm flush.'

'It's very kind of you.' She looked up into his face, and repeated, 'Very kind,' before turning away and going out.

He stood in the room feeling at a loss. He didn't know whether he should go out again or go upstairs. He could go upstairs and say truthfully, should the old girl ask him, that he had been out. He decided on this course, and in the room he donned his new dressing-gown, took up his *Dawn Came to Benders Creek,* and sat down before the fire.

But the combination of the fire, the dressing-gown, and the book had not the soothing effect they would have had an hour earlier. For one thing, he thought he'd been a damn fool over the dressing-gown. What did he want to go and pay all that money for? The three-pound one would have done just the same, and suited him better because he wouldn't have minded messing it up a bit at that price, but with this one he'd have to watch out how he used it. Anyway, why had he let himself be driven to buy a damned dressing-gown at all? Dressing-gowns weren't for the likes of him.

It had been a funny night. All this to-do starting from a doll. But the little one appeared different altogether when she got talking to you; the stiffness went and she didn't look so lost and sort of alone like. It was a funny house this and no mistake. He didn't think he'd been in a funnier. Why had she wanted so much to keep that doll? He couldn't work it out. Unless she wanted it because she hadn't got a . . . He checked his thoughts

93

and moved uneasily; but his mind had touched on bairns and refused to be jolted away from the subject in any rush, so he wondered how Bill's bairns had received all the junk their da had stuffed into his pockets, which immediately reminded him of the beads. They were still in the inner pocket of his coat, and that was hanging up in the kitchen.

He was out on the landing before he realised he was about to go downstairs in the dressing-gown. Well, that's what it was for, wasn't it?

Almost defiantly he went into the room. Nellie was at the machine, and she looked up as he came in and her eyes stayed on him, and the surprise showing in them made him feel hot.

He pulled the cord tighter about him as he crossed the room, and when he was abreast of her he stopped and asked, 'Do you never leave that machine alone?'

'Hardly ever.' She smiled wistfully. And he said with sudden daring, 'Why don't you leave here, as the old man says?'

Her eyes dropped to her hands, and it was a long moment before she said, 'It's too late now.'

He could find nothing to say to this, but stood looking at her. After an awkward pause, she said softly, 'Twice I was ready to go. The first time just before the end of the war. I had got a house and everything. And then Wallace, her eldest son, was killed. That was two, in just over a year. She was ill . . . I couldn't go.'

'Was her man alive then?'

'No. He died in nineteen-forty. There was no money from any of them – her husband died of TB, and the boys were married. If we had gone, Grandpa and I, it

94

would have gone hard with her. And then later, when things were better, I was going to leave again.' Her head moved downwards now, and she shook it. 'Things hold you and you find you can't. You hate to stay and you're frightened to go . . . It's too late.'

He was quite at a loss for any suitable reply. The only thing he could think of was the old tag, 'You know what they say, it's never too late.'

She did not take this up but started the machine again, and self-consciously he moved away into the kitchen, and going to his coat he took out the beads.

Now that he could look at them, he saw to his disappointment that they weren't really beads, not beads a bairn would like. There were only six of them, and each was hanging by a little chain from a main chain. And it didn't look like a chain either. The whole thing was stuck up and it would be impossible to make out what it was until he washed it.

Taking it to the sink, he ran the tap on it, and finally had to use the nail-brush to get the dirt out of the crevices. Then, having dried it on a towel, he laid it on the table.

Well, it didn't look much, although the stones shone nice and red. The chain affair looked like pieces of roughly battered tin with holes punched in them; it certainly wasn't of much value. It wasn't gold, and it didn't even look like silver . . . tin, he thought, probably Woolworths. And yet not Woolworths, it was too old-fashioned for them. Anyway, he decided, he'd give it to Bill the morrow. Yet as he held it in the palm of his hand he thought, it isn't a bairn's piece. The stones were bonny and it would likely show up on a jumper.

95

His head turned slowly towards the kitchen door – it might cheer her up.

No, by gum! – the necklace was thrust into his dressing-gown pocket – he was starting none of that. Although he was sure she would be the last person in the world to get wrong ideas, being so sensible like, he wasn't going to take any chances.

As he entered the room again, she stopped the machine and asked quietly, 'You won't say anything, will you, about Grandpa and tonight?'

He looked a trifle hurt as he replied, 'As if I would.'

'I know. I didn't think I need ask . . . But I'm always a little afraid.'

Always a little afraid. That was the main thing about her. He hadn't been able to pinpoint it before, but the impression she gave off behind that tightness was of being afraid.

'Well, you needn't be afraid of anything I'll say.'

The machine started again, and awkwardly he went out and up the stairs, and as he went he thought, I wish I'd never come to this place. And he asked himself why should he think that at this particular time, for this evening he had talked to a woman more freely than he could ever remember doing before.

4

THE WORM
WITH THE
ELEPHANT'S HOOF

During the next two weeks Rooney became well acquainted with the routine of the house. For instance, he knew that Ma's nights out were Mondays, Tuesdays, Thursdays, and Sundays. In fact, Sunday she classed as her day off. She went to church in the morning and again in the evening. Friday nights were given over to the family. He would have supposed that the little one's nights off would have been Wednesday, Friday, and Saturday, but, apart from Wednesday night, she stayed in the house. It would have been more correct to say she stayed at the sewing machine. And the time she spent there didn't seem to satisfy Ma, for there had been a shindy last Wednesday before she had gone out.

He wondered where she went on this one evening, and Ma, expounding on the selfishness of people, told him. She went to the Literary Society. Knowing there was piles of sewing yet to be done for the wedding, she had gone to the Literary Society. Could he understand it?

No, he couldn't. But not in the way Ma meant. He had thought she would have gone to the pictures to get away from the drabness of her days. But a Literary Society – it sounded dull and stuffy to him. And he never saw her reading. Well, as far as he could see she never had any time.

But her taste in pleasure had somehow put a new slant on her; and furthermore, what he couldn't understand was that he himself no more than Ma took to the idea of the Literary Society. Yet in the little one's defence, he said to himself, She's not uppish. But this Literary Society seemed to have suddenly swung her away out of his orbit, out of the category in which he had placed her.

Doreen's wedding was to take place on Saturday morning. There was to be a wedding breakfast held in an hotel in King Street; then the couple would leave for Edinburgh for two days. Because of this wedding Rooney had done more thinking around the term 'class' than he had done in his life before. Doreen had never spoken to him, but she had shown him plainly and in no tactful way that she considered him an unsuitable appendage to the family, and that the house had certainly lost caste in harbouring him. He knew she was nowt but an upstart, but just how much he didn't know until he'd had a talk with Johnny in The Anchor last Friday night. He had thought the bloke she was going to marry must be somebody well off, but when he learned he was a tally man, a door-to-doorer, he had thought, By hat! she's got something to stick her neb up about. And he was surprised that he should feel angry about this; and his reactions further surprised him when scorn was added to his anger on hearing that the actual wedding garments were being hired . . . satin gown, trailing veil, morning suit an' all . . . By hat! he had thought again, she's an upstart all right. To his mind the hiring of clothes was equivalent to wearing second-hand things, and because every day he saw so much rubbish he had never been able to bear the thought of second-hand clothes; even though he knew that half the clothes he saw in the shops were the finished product of rags, it made no difference. And on this point Johnny heartily agreed with him. But he added, 'It's fashionable now, man. Ye don't wear somebody else's cloes until ye're somebody, or trying to be.'

On Friday nights, when the gang, as Rooney called Ma's family, were assembled as usual in the kitchen, he would make his way out of the front door, avoiding them en masse, and so the only other members of the family he had encountered since that first evening were Pauline, on the night of the doll rumpus, and on one occasion, Jimmy, the fellow with the deep voice. He had seen him coming out of the Town Hall, where he worked, and although there had been quite some distance between them, and Jimmy could have gone on his way without acknowledging him and it wouldn't have seemed like a cut, he had raised his hand in salute and smiled across the distance, and Rooney had gone his way, thinking, Well, he's human, anyway.

And now it was Monday and the wedding was almost upon the house. Ma was in a dither, worked to a stand-still, as she put it. Even the choir practice had to be forgone tonight so she could go with Doreen and help her fix the curtains and fittings in the new flat, for, as she said to Rooney earlier, if she didn't go, Harry's mother would be along, and as much as she liked her she had no taste, yet was adamant in having her own way.

On this remark Rooney had resisted looking around the room, for he could see little evidence of taste here; not that he knew a lot about such things, he admitted to himself, but this room was so drab it even affected his stable spirits after he had been in it for any length of time.

After the door banged behind Ma there was quiet in the house except for the whirring of the sewing machine, which could only be distinguished by its faint irritation on the silence. Rooney had two fresh books. He had come across a new avenue of supply. It was in a shop in Eldon Street. Danny had put him on to it. 'Why don't you try for your books there,' he had said, ''stead of trailing right up to Boldon Lane? She only charges twopence a time.'

'Why pay twopence,' said Fred, 'when you can get them for nowt at the public library? Isn't that what we pay rates for?'

'Do you get your books there, Fred?' Danny had asked with a twinkle.

'I've no bloody time for reading,' said Fred. 'He's so lucky, he doesn't know he's born.'

Rooney thought of what Fred had said as, with his feet on the fender and a book on his lap, he stared into the fire. Aye, he supposed he was lucky. At least, he knew what he was coming home to. Fred or Albert didn't; and Bill knew a little too well. Yes, he had a lot to be thankful for.

The book promised to be a good one, but somehow he couldn't get into it, for his thoughts kept straying – the posses and the shooting could not hold his interest tonight and he found himself thinking, She'll go on turning that machine until she's an old woman. He could see her down the years becoming a little, shrivelled brown moth, but still turning the handle, sewing for another generation and its weddings.

He had been staring into the fire for some time before he realised the machine had stopped; and he found himself waiting for it to start again. When it didn't, he tried to read. But his concentration wavered, and quite suddenly he took up the coal scuttle and went downstairs.

Nellie was sitting in the armchair, her head back and her eyes closed. Her face was not its usual white but a grey mottled hue and he stared down on her for a moment before asking, 'Is there anything the matter? Are you bad?'

She opened her eyes but did not look at him.

'Are you all right?' he asked.

'I've . . . I've been a little sick.'

'Sick?' he repeated. 'Can I get you something?'

'No. I'm all right now.'

'You don't look it.' He put down the scuttle. 'Let me get you something. I always keep a drop of whisky in, in case of a cold.'

'No. No, thanks.' She checked his departure by sitting up.

'It would do you good.'

She shook her head. 'I never take anything.'

'Well, I'll make you a cup of tea.'

He did not wait for her consent or refusal but went into the kitchen and put the kettle on the gas stove. When he returned she had her elbows on her knees and was supporting her head on her hands.

'You should go to bed.' He stood some distance from her. 'Why don't you?' he asked. 'Look. Go on – I'll pop the drink outside your door.'

When she did not reply, he glanced at the machine, and his voice rising, he said, 'It's all that sewing – you're never done. Can nobody else work that thing?'

The sight of the machine annoyed him, more than annoyed him. He had a swift, startling, almost over-powering desire to chuck it out of the window. The desire itself disturbed him, even frightened him a little, and he rubbed his hand over his face.

Nellie raised her head and said slowly, 'I'm all right now.'

'You don't look it.'

He went into the kitchen again, and after a few moments returned with the tea.

'If you'd let me put a drop of whisky in it . . .'

'Thank you, no,' she said hastily.

He stood on the hearth-rug watching her as she sipped the tea, and when the colour of her face did not change, he said, 'It's nothing to do with me, but I think you've about had enough. You're never done.'

She sighed, and shivered; then, turning slowly side-ways, she looked into the fire. 'I had enough a long time ago.'

The few words were like a long, revealing confi-dence, bringing them together. Suddenly he felt he wanted to help her, that he must help her, and he found himself for the first time in his life offering someone else advice: 'I'd make a break if I were you. Why don't you? You've got a steady job, haven't you?'

'Steady job!' She made a harsh sound in her throat.

'You don't have to be told what Bamford and Brummell's looks like. And it's worse in than out.'

'But couldn't you leave there?'

'No. No more than I could leave here. There comes a time when you get frightened to move.'

He wanted to say, 'Oh, that for a tale!' but he suddenly looked at himself. Why had he not tried to make a move? Away from the bins, anyway. Why? Because he felt at home in his job, of course. No, it wasn't really that. It was because, in the back of his mind, he was uncertain of being able to tackle another job. He could have been charge-hand by now or even foreman if he had done a bit of pushing. He knew more about the work than most of them, but he had never been able to see himself giving other fellows orders.

'Thanks. I feel better.' She handed him the cup. Then, looking again into the fire, she said, 'Sometimes I wonder what we're here for, what it all means. Just living.' She brought her eyes up to his, and as he had no immediate answer to such a question he turned slowly red.

'You're happy, aren't you? I mean in what you do.'

'Well—' He moved his feet and rubbed his hand up the side of his cheek. 'I wouldn't say I'm happy about it, but I don't grumble. There's thousands worse.'

'Yes, I suppose that's a way of looking at it. There are thousands worse off than me, too.'

He wanted to say immediately, 'Not much, these days,' for, as far as he could see, lasses and women had gone mad – with dancing, drinking, and clothes. Drinking among the young folk in the town was so bad they were writing about it in the papers. He would put a stop to women drinking altogether, if he had his way – forbid them the bars, especially the young ones. It put years on them. Yet it wasn't drink that had put years on this one. He had a strong curiosity to know how old she really was. He would have liked to say, 'How old are you, anyway?' but he checked this, yet could not stop himself probing with, 'Why don't you get out more? You're young yet.'

Her eyes seemed to leap up to his. 'Young! . . . Do I look young?' It was a challenge.

'Well,' he said, 'you're . . . you're not old.'

'No, I'm not old. But you're frightened to say how old. I know. I won't ask you to guess how old I am . . . I'll tell you. I'm thirty-four.'

'Thirty-four!' He was quite unable to keep the surprise from his voice. But then, he had thought she could be anything between thirty and fifty. Yet now, looking down into her face, into those great brown eyes, he could well imagine he was looking at a young lass. Her face had that odd effect on you. Sometimes it looked so young that the rest of her appeared incongruous, for about her body was the straight shapelessness of an old sack.

Suddenly, to his deep concern and embarrassment, she began to cry. The brown of her eyes was blotted out, and in a moment her whole face was hidden from him as she turned it into the corner of the chair.

'Aw,' he said. 'Aw, don't . . . don't take on. What have I said? . . . You don't look thirty-four, more like twenty-four. If you . . .' He was about to add, 'got yourself done up,' but, again, tactfully changed it and said, 'If you had a mind you could be younger than any of them.' And thinking back to the four women of the family he had already seen, he thought, And there might be some truth in that an' all.

His hand went out, and for a moment hovered over her arm, but just in time he withdrew it, halted by two distinct views of such an action as a comforting pat. She might imagine he was taking a liberty, and he, off his own bat, didn't want to start anything. Remembering Kate Sparks, he thought, By lad! no.

Thinking he heard the back-yard door click he turned and looked towards the kitchen door. If that was Ma coming in he'd make himself scarce. It wouldn't, he felt, do this one any good if he was found talking to her, and her crying. But when there was no corresponding click to the outside kitchen door, he sat down, pulling his chair opposite to Nellie's.

'Look,' he said, bending towards her and nodding to her hidden face, 'if I was you, you know what I would do?' He never remembered afterwards what it was he was going to advise her to do, for when Ma's voice struck him from the doorway, crying, 'Well!' he left the chair in one guilty spring, which brought him round to her and Nellie bolt upright.

'Well!' said Ma again, giving to the word so much meaning that guilt weighed Rooney down, and he stuttered, 'She's . . . she's been . . . been bad.'

'Bad!' Ma glared from one to the other.

'She was sick,' said Rooney. 'I was just passing through for some coal.' Why, he wondered, should he have to explain his movements, and why should he feel like this, guilty? It was as if he had been caught in an act of some kind. He had been doing nothing. It was the way she had yelled that 'Well!'

He looked into her flaming eyes – the blue had deepened until it was almost black. He watched her tear off her hat, her eyes still on him, and saw her hair spring from her head as if it was alive, like a picture he had once seen of a woman with snakes for hair.

Lad! she was wild. But why?

Nellie was on her feet now. She had stopped crying and had dried her swimming face, and in a flat unemotional voice she addressed Ma without looking at her. 'I had a bilious attack. I don't feel well, I'm going to bed.'

Ma made no response but watched her leave the room. Then turning to Rooney, she said for the third time, 'Well!'

'Well,' he answered, pulling the cord of his dressing-gown so tight it caught his breath, 'it's as she said, she was sick. And she did look bad. I thought she was going to pass out.'

Ma seemed to be making an effort to get hold of herself. She tugged her jumper down viciously all round her; then with her back turned to him, she said, 'She plays for sympathy, she's always sorry for herself – she's eaten up with self-pity. I'm just warning you. She had what she calls a love affair years ago, and she's never let herself get over it. The man never intended anything, but she made a lot out of it . . . I'm just warning you.'

'Warning me?' he repeated. 'Well, I can tell you straight, you've no need to do that.' And picking up the empty scuttle, he went hastily out of the room, ignoring Ma's rapid and conciliatory comments.

In his own room, he stood rasping his hand across his chin. Lord above! What was the matter with him anyway? Why did he always run into these situations?

The evening was spoilt. He couldn't read or settle down. He couldn't even sit staring peaceably into the fire. So he went to bed.

It was around half-past twelve when he heard the thumping sound again. And as he listened, he thought, The best thing for me to do is to get out of here, and quick. And if she doesn't get out an' all, she'll snap.

It was on the Wednesday morning that the letter came. The previous morning, Tuesday, no-one had spoken to anyone else, and he had gone to work thinking, There's nothing for it but to get moving again; I couldn't live there in that atmosphere anyway. But on his return home last night Ma had been her usual gay self, and with one exception everything had been the same. Ma hadn't gone out, but he had. He had gone to Danny's and talked the whole thing over with him and Mrs D.

When he said the little one worked in Bamford and Brummell's Mrs D. had exclaimed, 'Why! I know her – she's worked there for years. A nice little thing. I remember her when she was just a young lass. Bonny she was, as light as a fairy. She's not the size of six-pennorth of copper, is she?'

'No,' said Rooney. 'Five foot two, I should say.'

'That's the one.' said Mrs D. 'I haven't been in the shop for years though. And she's still there? Fancy.'

After two hours of chatting and various cups of tea Danny had offered his advice, which was to stay put for a while, and to take everything the old 'un said about the little 'un with a pinch of salt.

And then the letter had come. It was part of the morning routine that Nellie did the step and the front-door brass, and it was generally while she was doing this that the postman came. As a rule she brought the letters through when she was taking the pail to empty. She would drop them on the corner of the table where Ma or Doreen could flick through them should there happen to be more than one. This morning, the procedure was as usual. There were four letters, and Doreen, coming out of the kitchen, made straight for them. She picked out two; then with no small surprise she exclaimed, 'Why! This one's for you, Nellie.'

'Me?' Nellie put down the pail and came back to the table; then taking up the letter she turned it slowly over then back again. Doreen and Ma were watching her, and Rooney, just at the end of his breakfast, felt his interest to be as keen as theirs. It was evident to him that her letters, like those he received, were very few and far between.

'Aren't you going to see who it's from?' asked Doreen, her curiosity making her more civil than usual.

Nellie looked towards her before taking a knife from the table and slitting open the envelope. The letter, whatever it contained, was short, and, as she read, her neck took on a pink tinge, which spread to her face and over her eyes. It was the first time Rooney had seen colour in her face other than when she had been crying.

Ma went to the table and began to gather up the plates, and from there she asked casually, 'Who's it from?'

'That's my business.'

For all Ma's size her movements could be swift, and she swung round now with the agility of a young woman. 'Don't you speak to me like that!'

'Then don't ask questions.'

Rooney watched Nellie walk to the bucket and pick it up; then stand stock still with it in one hand and the letter in the other, looking towards the kitchen door. Then as quickly as she had picked the bucket up she put it down again, and turning slowly about she looked straight at Ma. But what her eyes said only Ma could read. But Ma did not say a word until the sound of Nellie's door banged overhead. And then, addressing a mystified Rooney, she exclaimed, 'Now I ask you! Was there any call for that? It's likely just an advert.'

'It wasn't an advert,' said Doreen under her breath.

'How do you know?' asked her mother.

'I don't. But didn't you see her face? I've never seen her look like that. It wasn't an advert.'

'What else could it be? She hasn't had a letter for years, eight or more.'

Ma's face looked pained as she said to Rooney, 'Every now and again I have this business. Look at the other night about that doll . . . Oh! you don't know.'

'Ma!' Doreen checked her mother, making Rooney conscious of his presence. 'There's no need to go into that.'

But Ma had no intention of being silenced, and she exclaimed to her daughter, 'Why should I keep my mouth shut? Rooney should know all there is to know, else she'll play on his good nature. She's odd. Her mother was the same, although she was my own sister.

She went to the devil with pride . . . men and money, that's all she thought about. She married a waster. She thought he had money, but she was sucked in . . . Oh, I could tell you some . . .'

'Ma!' The syllable was significant of Doreen's total disapproval of her mother lowering herself to take the lodger, and such a lodger, into her confidence.

Rooney relieved her of any further anxiety on this point by rising, but he looked her full in the face before saying, 'It's all right, I'm going.' He wished that he was a different kind of chap, ready with his tongue. He would have, at this moment, liked to level half a dozen words at her which would floor her.

That Doreen was now getting it he could hear as he went upstairs. He had just reached the landing when Nellie came running out of the bathroom, actually running, and more so than ever now she looked like a young lass.

At the sight of him she stopped, and, pushing the wet hair back from her brow, she came towards him, so close as almost to touch him, and straining her face up to his she whispered softly, 'It may not be too late after all.' Then darting away she went into her room. And he went into his, to stand blinking down at the dead fire and untidy hearth.

What did she mean, it might not be too late? Did she mean that she was contradicting what she had said last night, that it was too late to make a move? It was that letter. There was, as that 'un downstairs had said, there was something in that letter.

He left the house in a thoughtful mood, and he found himself wishing it was half-past five and he was coming in again, for he had a mounting curiosity to know about the letter. He gave himself a few guesses. Perhaps the fellow who had given her the go-by had come back again. Or perhaps she had won the pools. No, it couldn't be the pools – the chap would have come to the door. And yet not if she had stated she wanted to keep her name secret. But there were no pools done in that house. Perhaps she had been left some money by a rich relative. But she had no relatives, nobody in the world, Ma said. No, the most likely guess was that the fellow had turned up again – that look on her face seemed to point to it being a fellow . . . it had wiped the years off her in one go.

It had rained all morning. Fred had the toothache; Bill couldn't open his mouth unless he swore; Albert did not open his mouth at all; and Rooney, never the one to lead the conversation, remained mute. So it lay with Danny as usual to ease the situation. They were finishing their bait in The Anchor, and Danny, taking up last night's evening paper from the table, remarked to Rooney, 'See that about old Double-Barrel?'

'No,' said Rooney. 'Is she dead?'

'Dead? No. Her place has been robbed.'

'Go on.'

'Aye, it says so here. I saw it last night.'

'When?'

'Monday. They broke a window and got off with quite a bit of stuff, silver mostly. It says here' – Danny read – 'some George the Third silver, cruets, a canteen of cutlery, a complete tea-service, two gold watches, and some jewellery.'

'Good luck to them. Why the hell should she have all that stuff!'

'A collection of snuffboxes,' continued Danny, ignoring Bill's remark, 'Nankin China and twenty pieces of . . . Severs.'

'What's Severs?' asked Rooney.

'Damned if I know,' said Danny. 'Probably the name of the china.'

'They should have cleared the bloody house oot.'

'You'd have run the paper van round to help them if you'd known, wouldn't you, Bill?' put in Danny, laughing.

'Aye, I would an' all. There's the old bitch with twelve rooms, if she's got one, an' all to hersel'.'

'Well,' said Danny, with patient toleration, 'I don't suppose she's very happy in them, not on her own.'

'Then why doesn't she move to some place smaller? There's too many like her.'

Danny swallowed the last two mouthfuls of his dinner before saying, 'If you was born in a house, Bill, and married out of that house, and if you lived nearly all your married life in it, and your son was born in it and your man buried out of it, well, I suppose you'd want to die in it yersel'.'

'Is that a fact?' asked Rooney. 'Has she lived there all that time?'

'Aye, she has,' said Danny. 'And I'll tell you something else . . . me mother was kitchen-maid there when she was a lass. And the old girl then was a bright spark, riding, dancing, and all the rest.'

Rooney had last seen Mrs Bailey-Crawford on the Monday morning. Albert had said, 'You go down to that 'un. I'm not goin' in there, for if I do I'll give her a mouthful.'

The bin had been in the same condition as it had been the week previous, and he was standing looking down at it when she put her head out of the scullery window and barked, 'If you don't take it I'll report you.' Then she had screwed up her eyes and exclaimed, 'You're not the other one.'

'Mam,' he had said, 'I told you last week you must keep the bin dry, ashes and stuff.'

'I'm not putting the tea-leaves down the sink.'

He wanted to suggest that she should drain them, but looking at her old face, the flesh wrinkled, sagging and half washed, he had summed up her condition to himself with, She's past it, poor old soul. And as he emptied the bin and saw the quantity of tea-leaves he thought that she must have been bathing herself with tea. Now recalling the sight of her at the window, there was nothing left to suggest that she had ever ridden or danced, or even that she had ever been young.

'Has she no family left, no-one?' he asked of Danny.

'Aye. She has a son. I don't know whether she has two or not, but I know she has one. He was something in the war, and he married a Frenchwoman. And as far as I know, he lives over there.'

'That's the moneyed lot for you,' said Bill. 'Let their old folk rot. I wouldn't see me mother in a mess that one's in. Something should be done. It's months since she had any help there.'

Danny let out a roar. 'For an ordinary puzzle-headed mule, let me have you, Bill! I bet the next thing I hear, you'll have taken the side-loader up there and have carted her down to your house.'

'To hell with you, Danny!'

'Same section to you, Bill . . . Come on.'

With the exception of Albert, whose face these days wore a perpetual scowl, they all got to their feet laughing, and as they made their way out into the road and towards the depot three young lads on their way to school passed them, kicking a small football from one to the other along the gutter. The tallest of them, putting all his weight behind his foot with the intention of lifting the ball high over the heads of his chums, drove it straight into the side of Albert's head. Had this incident happened a few weeks ago, Albert would have cried, 'Aye! aye! Is that your game?' and would have kicked the ball sky-high himself. But now, his face contorted with fury, he dived at the young lad and having seized him by the collar was raising his hand to cuff him when Rooney grabbed him by the arm.

'Steady on, Albert, man. He didn't mean it.'

'Leave go of him,' said Danny, pulling at the other arm. 'What's got into you? Leave go!'

The boy, once released from Albert's grip and recovering a little from his fright, backed away from the men and joined his pals. Then running to the end of the street, they turned and in a concerted shout yelled, 'Hit one of your own size, you dirty muck pusher, you! . . . MP! Muck pushers! MPs! Mucky muck pushers!'

The men walked on, silent now. Albert was wiping the clarts from his cheek, but the look of fury still remained.

Inside Rooney was a sore feeling, as if some part of him were aching. Albert would have struck that lad, and hard; and he solid and sober. He didn't seem to be in his right senses . . . he wasn't. And all through a woman, and her no good. Why did he bother his head? . . . The soreness became touched with a slight feeling of humiliation. Those kids calling them muck pushers! Whenever kids shouted after them it always brought on this feeling. Not that he was ashamed of his job, he wasn't; yet, on the other hand he knew it was nothing to be proud of. Then why didn't he get out? He could, nobody was stopping him. There were the pits, the shipyards, the factories, all calling out for more men. He stuck, he supposed, because he liked working outside. And somebody had to do this job, hadn't they? Bill had a theory that in a hundred years' time the people who would be drawing the highest pay would be those who did the dirtiest work. And so the bin men would come into their own then. But it wouldn't do them much good then, would it?

He glanced at Albert. He was a nice bloke, really, not like he looked now. But this business made him feel a bit ashamed for him. That's what being married did to you. It was as they all said, he himself had a lot to be thankful for.

Then, sitting in the loaders' cab, as the van swung into Fowler Street, Rooney saw the little one. She had just stepped out from a doorway, and with her was a man. The question of whether he was 'the man' did not arise, for he was an old fellow. But what struck Rooney as being strange was not that she was in the centre of the town when she should be either in the shop or at home for her dinner, but that she was laughing, with her head back and her mouth stretched wide. And why the sight of her laughing with an old fellow should make him feel more depressed he was unable to answer. And he thought, What's up with me? I've got the hump these days meself, without being married.

It wasn't until he almost reached Filbert Terrace that evening that he remembered it was Wednesday. Wednesday was half-closing day. That could account for the little one being in the town, but it still didn't account for her being merry. Merriment and the little one didn't seem to go together somehow.

As soon as he entered the back door, the kitchen door was pulled open and Doreen, after ascertaining who it was, withdrew sharply. And as he was taking his boots off, Ma came in saying, 'It's been a dreadful day, hasn't it? Are you very wet? You'll be glad to get in.'

'Yes, I am,' he said. 'But I'm not wet, I changed me things at the depot.'

'I got a neck of mutton for you today and made some broth with it. Is that all right?'

'Yes . . . fine, thanks. Nothing could be better the night.'

'Is it still raining?'

'Yes. Worse than ever.'

Ma was going back into the living-room when she paused, closed the door, and came over to him, and under her breath said, 'You get about the town, Rooney. Have you seen anything of Nellie on your travels?'

She did not await his answer, and he had time to think as she continued, 'She went out as usual, but came back at ten. Ten, mind you. And wouldn't say what she wanted. She went upstairs for a minute. And we haven't seen her since. And it's Wednesday. She's always in by ten past one.'

He wanted to keep clear of this, whatever was in the wind, so he said, 'No, I haven't seen her.'

Ma drew in a deep breath which expanded her already large chest to alarming dimensions before muttering between her teeth, 'And so much to do.'

She flounced out of the kitchen, and Rooney followed her into the living-room. Doreen was sitting by the fire sewing. She looked anything but happy, and as he passed her on his way upstairs he thought, Well, it's a change, anyway, to see somebody else with a needle.

After washing and changing he went downstairs again, and he had hardly entered the room before Doreen gathered up her sewing and made to leave. She was on the point of making some remark to her mother who was seated at the table when the back door clicked, and she turned and stood waiting for the door to open. Ma had risen quickly from the table, but she didn't wait for the door to open. Pulling it wide, she cried, 'Where d'you think you've been?'

There was no answer from the kitchen, and Rooney, although he was facing the door, could not see past Ma, but he could imagine the little one slowly taking off her wet things.

'Do you hear me! Where've you been? Everybody worried to death.'

'I've been to the pictures.'

There followed a silence, during which Ma turned

and with popping eyes looked at Doreen, and as Nellie came into the room she stood back and surveyed her as if she wasn't sure she had heard aright.

'That's a dirty trick!' said Doreen.

'What?' Nellie said this word softly, with a sort of quiet enquiry as she turned towards Doreen.

'All my things to be finished; and only three nights left. And you going to the pictures! You've never gone to the pictures before on a Wednesday.'

'No,' said Nellie, still quietly, 'I haven't. But I've turned over a new leaf.'

'What's up with you?' cried Ma, who was evidently finding it impossible to understand this attitude. 'What you should do, as I've said before, is to see a doctor.'

'Very likely,' said Nellie, still quietly.

'It's spite . . . spite!' cried Doreen, her voice breaking on tears.

'Spite?' Now Nellie swung round on her, no longer calm. 'Spite? You dare say it's spite! I've sewn nearly every stitch you've worn for the past ten years, and every night for weeks past I've sat at that machine and sewn and sewn and sewn. Spite! How dare you say it's spite?'

Her face had lost its new serenity, and the old white tight look was back. 'Have you ever asked yourself why I should sit there and sew for you? Do you pay me for it, with even a kind word? No, you've been led to expect that I am here just to serve you all, to make whatever you want. It wasn't your fault in the beginning, but you've been old enough for years now to think for yourself . . . Well, now you can sew for yourself. Your dresses are finished, and if you want to disport yourself in lace house-coats and fine lingerie you can sew them, and if you're too busy that's just too bad. You should have married a man more fitted to your ideas of luxury.'

'You're possessed, that's what you are. You've become possessed!' cried Ma.

'Yes,' said Nellie, now turning on her. 'Yes, I'm possessed. Possessed of courage, and it's a wonderful feeling.' She stared at Ma, and Ma stared back at her, but this time she did not speak. Her lips were moving, forming words, but no sound came.

When Ma did not voice her thoughts, Nellie gave a look that could have held scorn before turning from her and leaving the room.

'The little cat!' cried Doreen. 'The old cat! Would you believe it! Her!'

Ma, still temporarily speechless, sank into a chair; then slowly she lifted her eyes to Rooney and with her face crumpling, she said, 'I ask you.'

Rooney tried to keep a level expression, but what he really wanted to do was cheer. By lad! it had been an experience to see the little one standing on her feet. He wouldn't have missed this for worlds. Talk about a worm turning – she had turned all right.

'Stop it, Ma!' Doreen was no longer in tears, and as she chided her mother for hers, saying, 'Instead of crying you want to find out what it's all about,' Rooney too thought, Aye. There was something behind this courage, something big, big enough to make the little one into a new creature, or at least to make her brave enough to resurrect her old self. Whichever it was, he felt it was something unusual.

'Will I help meself to me tea?' he asked.

Ma, deep in her troubled thinking, replied absent-mindedly, 'Yes. Yes.' Then rising hastily, she exclaimed, 'No, no, I'll see to it – you've been out in this all day.'

As her mother went into the kitchen, Doreen sent a furious glance after her, and grabbing up her sewing and muttering something under her breath that Rooney could not catch, she left the room.

To Rooney's surprise, Ma was strangely quiet all during the meal, and he guessed that she was more than a little disturbed. It was not until he was finished and leaving the table that she spoke, and then her voice was tearful again.

'All this upset and the wedding so near. I don't know what I'm going to do.'

Her talking did not seem to require an answer, and Rooney went upstairs, glad to have escaped so easily.

He had not been in his room more than ten minutes before he heard Nellie come out of hers and go downstairs. Then came the sound of Grandpa's enquiring croak; and after a few minutes Ma's voice penetrated up to him. And when at one point it rose to the pitch of a scream he heard the front door bang, and he knew that the little one had gone out again. And for the moment he felt as frustrated as Ma. Somehow he had hoped that he would have had a word with her, and she would have cleared the mystery up, for had she not almost confided in him this morning? There would be no further chance the night . . . perhaps in the morning he would know.

But in the morning, Nellie was not to be seen. She did not get up and take the pail and do the front, and it looked when Rooney left the house that she wasn't going to work either, for she hadn't yet put in an appearance. It also looked to him as if Ma was going to have a seizure.

It was not until eight o'clock that evening that he saw the little one. She had not come in at tea-time, and this had caused Ma's bulges to become filled with volcanic fury. She was no longer tearful, but ready to burst with frustrated curiosity, ascribing Nellie's attitude to madness, badness, frustration, complexes, and spite. But becoming calm for a moment, she had enquired if Rooney were intending to stay in this evening. When he answered yes she said she wanted to slip out to Betty's and couldn't leave the old man alone in the house in case he went out on his own, as he had done a few weeks ago and brought himself back in a taxi, for which she'd had to pay; or set the house on fire, which he had nearly done last year. But she wouldn't be long, she assured him; she didn't really want to go out at all, but she just had to, for it had been arranged that she – whom he took to mean the little one – was to take Saturday off to see to Grandpa while they were at the wedding. Somebody had to stay behind, and so she must go and try to persuade Betty to come now. There was the tea to be laid and things seen to, as Harry's people were coming back here in the afternoon. Oh, the trouble that one had caused! Nellie, he had been given to understand, had upset the whole blooming apple-cart, and it seemed a bit odd to him that it should be the one in the house who was of the least importance who was having the greatest effect.

Grandpa seemed to sense when Ma was out, for

shortly after she had gone Rooney heard his door open and him going into the living-room. Fearing lest the old fellow did get up to anything, he went downstairs.

The old man was turning up the cushions of the big chair, and when Rooney's legs came into his view he glanced up and exclaimed, 'Where's the paper? . . . Where's Nellie got to? She always brings me the paper. That one's gone out. Good riddance! Did you see what she gave me for tea? Wouldn't feed a rabbit.' He straightened up and his bright old eyes darted from side to side before he beckoned Rooney to him with a quick wag of his finger; then in a gleeful whisper he said, 'Summat's up here, eh? Nellie's turned at last. She didn't go to work the day. By! I'm glad I've lived to see it . . . I nursed Nellie as a bairn . . . I know her and she knows me. She's good, is Nellie. She's a cut above any of God-forsaken Grace's lot, and I say it although they're me own grandbairns. Do you think they come in and see me? No. And never slip me a penny. Except Jimmy. Jimmy's all right – May's man. He's the only one who has ever let on I was alive. Jimmy's all right; I like Jimmy. Too damn good for May . . . Now where's Nellie got to? She said she'd be in.'

Rooney shook his head, and the old man asked, 'You going out? Will you get me a drop? I've got the money. Quarter-bottle, like you did afore.'

Going to the sideboard Rooney took a pencil and paper from a coloured-glass fruit dish and wrote, 'Not the night. Get you one tomorrow.'

'Tomorrow?' said Grandpa dolefully. 'Could be dead by then. I'm so cold and she won't give me no coal but what hardly dirties the bucket . . . Oh, where's Nellie got to?'

As if in answer to his plea the back door clicked, and a second later Nellie came into the room. She was dressed as usual, but she didn't look as usual – she was almost gay. She was carrying a parcel and some magazines.

'Hallo,' she said.

'There you are,' said Grandpa. 'I've hardly seen you the day. You're looking bonnie, Nellie.' He went up to her smiling, all querulousness gone, and patted her cheek. 'Aye, you're looking bonnie.'

She smiled back at him and pointed to the parcel, then turning to Rooney, she said again, 'Hallo. Everybody out?'

'Yes,' he said. 'Been enjoying yourself?'

She drew in her breath; and as she let it out again, she said, 'Yes. Just that.'

She put the parcel on the table and opened it, drawing the old man near her to observe the process. And the wrappings undone, she revealed to his delighted gaze two sets of woollen underwear.

'My!' Grandpa's eyes glittered as he fingered the vests. Then lifting up the long pants, he said, 'Them's wool, Nellie.'

She nodded, smiling.

'By lad!' He danced the pants up and down. 'Heavy.'

She nodded again, laughing happily.

Rooney looked at the garments. They were wool all right, real wool. He knew wool when he saw it. He often wished he could afford a couple of sets like these for the winter. But each of these pieces would cost about three pounds, if not more.

'Come on.' Nellie lifted up the things from the table and beckoned the old man with her head. And as they went out Rooney asked, 'Have you had your tea?'

'Yes,' she called back from the hall. 'But I could do with another cup.'

His brow puckered as he went slowly into the kitchen. She was different somehow . . . there was an airiness about her that was strange and not a little disconcerting.

The tea made, he took it into the living-room, but it was some time before she came out of the old man's room, and he said, 'It'll be cold by now.'

'It doesn't matter . . . I had to get him settled.'

She poured herself out a cup, then sat down at the table, sipping it in silence. After a moment she pulled one of the magazines towards her and flicked over its pages.

Rooney stood, uncertain what to do. His legs would not carry him to the door, nor could he sit down. Suddenly she looked up at him.

'You're wondering what it's all about, aren't you?'

'No,' he lied. 'It's your business. The only thing is I'm glad you're looking happier.'

'It's odd.' She turned and looked at the magazine again. 'You think you're dead and then a miracle happens, a miracle all to yourself, and you suddenly become alive. It's a frightening experience at first, when you know you're capable of feeling other things besides sadness . . . and . . . and resentment, and to know that you are no longer afraid.' She looked up at him again. 'You don't know how I hate this house' – her voice was deep in her throat now, husky, almost harsh – 'the brown, dampening deadness of it. When I have a house it will be like this —' She flung the pages quickly forward, then back, and said, 'Like that.'

She twisted the magazine round towards him, and he bent over the table and looked at a picture of a room out of some swell house, all shining with period furniture and glowing chintz.

'Colour . . . I'll have piles of colour. No old stuff, unless it's good – I like the modern stuff.' She was talking like an excited girl – a girl who had just become engaged, a girl who was going to build a home – and as she went on he became strongly aware of his bits in the room upstairs. If she was going in for this kind of furniture she must take a very poor view of his stuff. He was sharply affected by this and found himself rearing in defence of his possessions. They would do him, they were good solid pieces.

'Do you like it?' She was still looking at the picture, and he was bold enough to say, 'Not for meself, I don't. That room doesn't look used somehow. But,' he added, 'for some folks it'd be all right.'

'Home is where the heart is.'

'What?'

'Nothing . . . Do you know' – she gazed up into his face, now quite close above hers – 'I've talked to you like I haven't talked to anyone for years . . . years and years. It's all right' – she quickly straightened up, putting out her hand in a defensive but reassuring movement – 'you needn't be nervous. I'm – not after anything.'

'I'm not nervous. What makes you think that? And who said I thought you were after anything?' He was finding himself to be quite indignant.

Nellie smiled, a small tight smile. 'Grace would leave no doubt in your mind about that. Grace is the eternal mother and the eternal girl, and she imagines everyone else is the same.' She took a deep breath again. 'But now things have changed she's going to have something to think about.' She turned her face from his, saying, 'Oh, so much . . . as much as I can possibly give her.'

Again she flicked over the leaves of the magazine and he went and sat down slowly at the other side of the table. He knew for a number of reasons that he should go upstairs, the main one being that if Ma found him here there'd be fireworks. But there'd be fireworks in any case . . . he could see that.

'Do you like that?' She had pushed the magazine round and towards him again, and he looked down now upon the full-page picture of a fashionably dressed woman. She was wearing a blue tweed suit and holding open with artful effectiveness a top coat, the colour of his dressing-gown. But that which immediately drew his eye was the necklace the woman was wearing on top of the matching-coloured jersey. It was almost identical with the one he had upstairs.

He did not answer her question but said eagerly, 'See that necklace, she's wearing? I've got one exactly like it.'

Nellie, leaning over the table, looked at the necklace. 'Have you? It's nice. It's costume jewellery. And you've got one like it?'

He sat back and laughed. 'Aye, yes. And it's funny

seeing one like this. Look, I'll get it and show you.' He rose quickly and went out, and was back within a few minutes. 'There.' He put it on the table on top of the book. Then with some disappointment he added, 'Well, would you believe it, it isn't really like it, except the red beads hanging down and the colour of the tin.'

Nellie picked the necklace up and after looking at it for some time she said, 'It's a lovely thing . . . It's old.'

'Do you think so?'

'Yes. It's silver filigree work.'

'Oh, I shouldn't say it's silver.'

'I think it is. There should be a stamp somewhere. And it is like this one' – she pointed to the magazine – 'only prettier.'

'You have it.'

'What!' Her eyes darted up to his.

'It's no use to me . . . I can't wear it.'

She dropped her gaze to the necklace lying over her hands, and when she raised it to his again her eyes were soft with gratitude. 'Thank you, Rooney.' It was the first time she had spoken his name, and it added to his feelings of excitement and awkwardness.

'That's all right,' he said. But having said it, he felt at a loss what to do, so he sat down again. No sooner was he seated, however, than the yard door clicked, and he was on his feet in an instant. Then looking at her in embarrassment for a second he made for the door, saying, 'I'd better . . .'

He did not finish, but she took it up and said, 'Yes, you'd better . . . And thanks, Rooney.'

He was hot as he went up the stairs, not so much for having done such a foolish thing as to give a woman a necklace but far more for his ignominious retreat at the sound of Ma. And in his room, he thought, I hate this scurrying, as if I'd done something or other.

His eyes moved over his furniture. The lot, he supposed, wasn't up to much if you were comparing it with the stuff in the magazine. But who was comparing it? It was good stuff, and suited him. He sat down. She must have come into a bit somehow or other to be thinking of furniture like that, but he was no wiser than was Ma as to where she had got it.

Suddenly Ma's voice filled the house. He could not make out what she was saying, but the fury of her feelings came up through the boards. The living-room door must have been pulled open, for now he heard her crying, 'Don't think you'll hoodwink me, I'll find out.'

There came the sound of Grandpa's door being opened, then closed, then silence.

Rooney continued to gaze into the fire. He hoped that the little one would give Ma 'a good run for her money' and keep her guessing. But it disturbed him somewhat to find that he hoped she would not keep him guessing.

On Friday evening, the wedding eve, Rooney was greeted by Ma almost on the back door-step. Would he have his meal up in his room as the living-room was full? Queenie and her man had arrived earlier than expected, Pauline had brought the children round, and Doreen was in a state.

Yes, that was all right, he assured her with relief.

Very well then, she would bring it up to him.

He wanted to suggest that he came down for it, but

that would mean coming among them again, so he refrained.

The living-room was full of people and chatter, and the chatter, to Rooney's painful embarrassment, died away on his entry.

Ma came in behind him, then pushed round him to the fore, and, with the attitude of a collector showing off a treasure piece and with the accompanying emotion in her voice, she presented her daughter Queenie.

Queenie inclined her head, which was but a younger edition of Ma's, and in an ultra-'refeened' voice said, 'How do you do?'

'How d'you do?' said Rooney, unconsciously giving the correct reply.

'And this is my son-in-law Tim.'

Rooney looked at the big fellow and nodded; and the big fellow nodded back. And, thought Rooney with some comfort, he looks about as happy as I do when among them. His impression of these two was that they were dressed to kill . . . he was wearing a pepper-and-salt tweed suit and spanking great brogues, while she was decked out in a blue corded velvet suit. The man, although well over six feet, was flabby, running to fat, with more than a suggestion of a paunch, which was all out of place, Rooney considered, in a fellow who didn't look forty. He had straight black hair and a heavy blue jowl, and was handsome in a way. But for all his largeness there was something about him that seemed to belie it – he looked . . . cowed. Aye, that was the word.

As Rooney, with feet that seemed to have doubled in size, picked his way out of the room, he met May

131

coming in. She smiled at him and said, 'Hallo.'

In his surprise he almost let her pass without answering, but managed to say, 'Hallo. It's turning cold.'

'Yes. Yes, it is.' She smiled at him again before closing the door.

Well, that was heartening – he hadn't seen this one since the night he first came here. Perhaps living with Jimmy had done something for her after all.

When Ma brought his meal up, she seemed in no hurry to return downstairs. 'Did you see their car?' she asked softly.

'No,' he said, 'I didn't.'

'No. Of course; you came in the back way. You'll see it when you go out the front . . . It's a beauty. Over a thousand he paid for it. Queenie picked it . . . Do you think my Queenie's like me?'

'Yes. Yes, I do.' This was definitely the truth.

Ma tilted her head, as if looking into a mirror. 'Yes, she's like me. I can see myself all over again in her.' She paused in her reminiscences and looked down into the fire.

Rooney looked longingly at his dinner, with the steam spreading away the heat.

'Well' – Ma recalled herself – 'we're just as old as we feel, aren't we?' She smiled widely at him, and blinked her eyelids with a coyness that added to her years and made her somehow pathetic.

'Aye, that's true,' he said.

'Now I'll leave you to your dinner. I hope all this noise doesn't disturb you.'

'Not at all,' he said.

'It'll soon be over.' Ma sighed. 'I'll be lonely without Doreen, she's such a comfort.'

Rooney failed to see it, but he replied politely, 'Aye.'

'Now—' Ma looked hastily about her and, as if getting back to business, said, 'You're all right? Everything comfortable? Get on with your dinner then.'

Left to himself, Rooney got on with his dinner, quickly washed and changed, and let himself out of the front door. And yes, he thought, it was a spanking car all right, one of the latest. And it set him thinking that if that pair had so much money why didn't they look after the old girl, so she didn't have to let? But it was generally the way – the more some folks had, the less they did.

There was no-one in the MPs' corner when Rooney arrived in The Anchor; but Johnny was at the bar.

'Hallo,' he said. 'Squeezed through the mob?'

'Just about,' replied Rooney.

'Full house, the night, eh? Our Queenie and Big Tim there yet?' he asked, mimicking Ma.

'Yes,' said Rooney. 'It seems they've arrived.'

Johnny took a long drink. 'By, she gets me goat, that one. Going to hell with swank. And how that big swab dare come back there I don't know . . . But he's soft, soft as clarts. And as miserable as hell. Queenie sees to that. But to my mind he's getting his deserts. I bet he's rued the day he let Nellie go. By lad! I bet he has.'

'Nellie?' Rooney, about to order his drink, paused and turned to Johnny.

'Of course, you wouldn't know nowt about it. Queenie pinched him off Nellie, her and the old girl.'

133

'That big fellow?'

'Aye, that big fellow. That's part of what done it – him being big and Nellie little. Scoffed the lugs off him, they did . . . never let up – all the time. And Queenie buttering him up and slobbering over him on the quiet. And the old girl . . . Oh! the old girl – how she worked on that business.'

'But was he engaged or something to the little . . . to Nellie?'

'Sort of. He was a traveller what called at Bamford and Brummell's. That's how he met Nellie, just after the war. It appeared they had been going strong for nearly two years afore she let on to Ma. It would have been better if she'd never brought him back there at all. Ma had Queenie and him tied up within six months. It was a "give me child a name" job – she had one in the oven.'

Rooney ordered his beer and one for Johnny, paid for them, and sat down. So that was it. But why had she stayed there all these years? Why had she slaved at that machine for them? Why hadn't she stood up to them all and got herself somebody else? There were better blokes, surely, than that big soft goof. Why hadn't she showed them? But she hadn't . . . she had, to use Ma's words, let herself go.

The thought came to him from nowhere that Ma hated her, with a deep hatred. Very likely she was a weight on her conscience, the shabby sight of her being a constant reminder of her own connivance in breaking her life.

Rooney had not touched his beer when he asked, 'Why has she stayed there?'

134

'Beats me really. But I suppose it's the old man . . . she was always fond of him, and he dotes on her. Ma would have had him put nicely away behind the iron gates long afore now but for his pension. And without Nellie he'd have been a damn sight better off there. But give old Nellie her due, she's looked after him.'

But the old Nellie was gone . . . things had changed since Wednesday. 'Have you been there this week?' Rooney asked.

'No. But Ma came dashing round last night and went on about Nellie something chronic. Says she's going barmy. They'll both go barmy, if you ask me. This wedding's goin' between Ma and her wits. Well, here's one who's not losing half a shift the morrow. Not for Miss Doreen, I'm not. And there won't be a lick of hard, not so much as a smell. Shabby wedding, eh? Ginger beer and buns!'

He threw off the remainder of his beer, and rising, said, 'Well, here I go to be sniffed at. But it doesn't affect me. You know summat?' He leaned towards Rooney. 'I like these Friday nights. Wouldn't miss 'em for the world. I get one or two in on the quiet . . . So long. Be seeing you. I suppose it'll be a long session the night.'

'So long,' said Rooney.

Later, when Bill, Fred, and Albert arrived, the conversation swung from the Chief Constable getting the liquor licence stopped at the Christmas British Legion dances to the latest news of the union affairs in the *GMW Journal*. Albert made no contribution to the conversation, not even to comment that all dance halls should be closed; and Rooney, for the most part, sat quiet. For he couldn't get Nellie and the big fellow out of his head. He kept thinking, Poor soul, poor soul. And the more he thought 'Poor soul' the more his dislike of Ma grew.

'Come on, Brother Rooney,' cried Fred; 'snap out of it. The old wife after you now?'

'Oh, be quiet, man,' said Rooney.

'All right, Brother . . . !'

'Brother!' put in Bill. 'All this brother business. You're talking like a bloody journal. It gets up my nose. It strikes me as if we were a lot of bloody communists . . . Comrades and brothers! Brother this, Brother that.'

'Well, they've always done it,' said Fred.

'They've always done lots of things they shouldn't have,' answered Bill. 'When I hears some of them on the platforms calling us Brothers when they want their own way, I think, Brother, me Aunt Fanny! I'm telling you this – the trade unions plus the Labour Party's in a brother of a bloody state, and if one or t'other doesn't soon do something, Brother, we'll be extinct.'

Rooney suddenly laughed. You couldn't help but laugh at Bill. He never stayed on one subject long enough to get anywhere. But as the evening wore on and the conversation jumped from Labour to Tory via the trade union, Rooney found himself possessed of the feeling that could only be termed as boredom. He often had it in a lesser degree when Danny wasn't present in the company. He now found the one-sided talk of Fred and Bill more than a trifle wearing, so nearly half an hour before closing time he rose, saying, 'I'll be off, fellows.'

'What? You going, mate?' Even Albert protested.

'I've got a thick head. Cold or something comin', I think.'

'Take a glass back with you,' said Bill, 'and have it hot. That'll sweat it out of you. I thought there was something up with you the night.'

'I've got a drop in,' said Rooney. 'I'll do that . . . So long.'

'So long,' they said.

It was a calm night, a bit nippy, with the sky high and star-sprayed, and as he walked through the almost deserted street – the bars and the pictures had not yet turned out – Rooney found, not a little to his surprise, that running through his mind were words that the little one in her misery had spoken.

'Sometimes I wonder what we're here for,' she had said. 'What's it mean . . . living?'

His eyes lifted to the sky, far away and impersonal, not understandable.

Aye, what did it mean . . . living? For himself, did it mean going on like this, year in, year out, never able to get a house, living in somebody's room, feeling neither particularly happy nor sad, clinging to his bit of furniture, evading women, meeting the fellows in The Anchor, going to the Dogs? . . . Well, the Dogs hadn't done him badly, had they? . . . But that wasn't the point. Well, what was? . . . Oh, he didn't know. All he did know at this moment was that he didn't want to go through that blooming room tonight. Nor did he want to encounter Ma, or any of her family.

Because he was so averse to passing through the

room, he went to the front door, hoping that he might see someone leaving and so get in that way. But No. 71 was fast closed, and to ring the bell would assuredly bring Ma. So he skirted the terrace, went down the back lane and into the yard.

The buzz of talk reached him even here, and when he opened the kitchen door it flooded on to him. Betty, May, and Pauline were in the kitchen washing up, and their earnest conversation stopped as they greeted him with varied hallos.

'Hallo,' he said. 'Busy?'

'Yes, busy,' answered Betty.

Pauline, with a tea towel in her hand, went into the kitchen, and Rooney heard her say, 'It's . . . it's Mr Smith.'

The buzz of conversation lessened, and Betty asked him, 'Would you like a cup of tea?' But without waiting for his answer, she went on, 'If I know anything, you wouldn't.'

'Surprise you if I said yes, wouldn't it?'

She laughed. 'By, it would.'

'Well, good night.' He nodded to May and her, and together they answered, 'Good night.'

When he went into the room, he saw at once to his dismay that, with the exception of Doreen, all Ma's lot were there, and their men, Johnny, Jimmy, Dennis, and the big fellow, Tim. Queenie was lolling in one armchair and Ma sat opposite her in another. But Ma wasn't lolling, and she didn't entirely look her bright, breezy self.

'You've got back in then?' she said.

He did not answer the obvious statement, but

returned Jimmy's and Johnny's nods. Dennis did not nod. The big fellow said, 'Hallo.'

Rooney did not answer this greeting; in fact he made a point of ignoring the salute, and the man.

When he was almost at the door, Johnny, as if they had not met earlier, said, 'Had a good night?' And Rooney, looking over his shoulder to give a brief reply, halted both his words and his departure, for the back door had clicked open and a very audible gasp was coming from the kitchen – a gasp which said, 'Nellie!'

What the gasp indicated, Rooney had no idea, except that it concerned the little one. She would soon come into the room and she would have to look at that fellow and his wife and see in her, materially at any rate, all the things she had missed . . . and that wasn't counting what she might still feel for the bloke. Even with her new defence she would probably feel it pretty bad. He wondered when she had last seen him – they must have met during the past eight years. And how did the big fellow feel about the shabby little creature she had become?

His hand was on the door knob when Nellie entered the room, and the gasp, like sound carried over a long distance, was repeated.

Rooney's lips parted and his head lifted backwards in surprise. There she stood framed in the doorway. He knew it was her by her eyes, but they were the only instantly recognised thing about her, for she looked, as he phrased it, as near as dammit to the woman in the magazine she had pointed out to him last night. Only the colour of the clothes was different. Her costume was a dull brick colour, and her coat the flecked yellow brown of an autumn leaf, and on the back of her head was fitted a tight velour hat, matching the colour of the costume. And her hair . . . her hair made Rooney gape. Gone was the pot-pie-basin cut. He couldn't imagine that there had ever been one, for it now lay in shining careless quiffs on her brow and about her ears. And if this wasn't enough, her face was made up, really made up. And to bemuse him and everyone else further, she appeared taller by an inch or two. Two other things struck him, one pleasurably, the other with dismay. First, he noticed she was wearing the necklace, and secondly, she was drunk. Well, if not drunk, pretty far gone. He was too well versed in seeing a woman in drink to make a mistake. He prided himself he could practically tell how much they were carrying from the film in their eyes. Never before, even remembering the torment caused by his mother, had a woman in drink hurt him as this one was doing. And as Ma gave her usual war-cry of 'Well!' he heard a new and unused voice crying from within him, 'Aw! no, Nellie, you shouldn't have done that. Why had you to go and do that? Aw! Nellie.'

He could have cheered her for slapping them all in the face with her fine get-up. But to get drunk . . . she had spoilt it.

'In the name of God!' It was Johnny. 'Why, Nellie! Well, I'll be damned!' He was on his feet, as was Ma. The others were all sitting upright in their seats, showing different expressions of incredulous amazement; while behind Nellie, in the kitchen doorway, stood Pauline, Betty, and May.

Slowly, Nellie returned their gaze. One after the

140

other, she looked at them . . . all except the big fellow. She did not turn her head in his direction although his eyes were fixed upon her. Then with her head cocked to one side, a little smile on her face, and moving circumspectly, she crossed the room. Her intention, Rooney saw, was to pass through without speaking.

But Nellie had counted without Ma, for, like a prancing hippopotamus, Ma bore down on her, and grabbing her by the arm, swung her about.

'You! . . . You hussy!'

There was the immediate sound of a ringing slap as Nellie's hand came in sharp contact with Ma's fleshy arm. 'Don't you touch me!' Her voice was thick and uncertain, and it caused Ma to step away from her.

Unlike Rooney, Ma was not versed in the effects of drink, but the combination of Nellie's voice and the smell of her breath was patent proof of the horrifying truth, and that Ma was truly horrified was evident, for she was temporarily derived of her voice. When, with an effort, she regained it, she gasped, in a whisper, 'You're drunk.'

'Not quite.' Nellie's voice was quiet again; there was even a touch of laughter in it. 'No, not quite. He assured me that you couldn't get drunk on four ports and two advocaats. That's all I've had . . . four ports and two advocaats. Have you ever had advocaat?' She poked out her head towards Ma. 'It's nice . . . thick . . . custard with a kick. No, you've never had advocaat.' Her voice rose sharply on a bitter note. 'Vitriol's your drink.'

'It's made your old gig-lamps shine anyway,' put in Johnny quickly. 'Have you won the pools, Nellie?'

'No. No, Johnny, I haven't won the pools.'

'No!' Ma cried, her face almost purple, 'but I'll tell you where . . .'

'Be quiet, Ma!' Stepping quickly to her mother's side Pauline took hold of Ma's arm. 'Don't upset yourself. As for you' – she turned to Nellie – 'if you had to show off your finery and your emancipation, you could have picked some other time.'

'Why?' It was a blunt if slightly fuddled demand.

'Why? You know why. The wedding and everything.'

'Oh, the wedding!' Nellie's eyebrows moved up and her nose moved down. 'I wasn't asked to the wedding. So . . . so I can sleep in the morning . . . I wasn't asked to stay back and look after things in this old mausoleum . . . I wasn't even told to do it . . . It was just taken for . . . for granted . . . Nellie's there. Nellie's always there . . . Wedding? I've worked for months for that wedding, like I did for all your weddings. I sewed for that young upstart—'

'You dare call—' Ma was prevented from descending on Nellie by both May and Pauline.

'Yes, I dare!' Nellie lessened the distance between them by stepping forward. 'They're all upstarts, every one of them, thanks to you. And thanks to you they've looked upon me as an unpaid servant for years. You've done a lot of harm in your time, Gracie Howlett, but the greatest harm you've done is to them . . . what you've turned them into.'

'I hope you're not including me, Nellie?' It was Betty who, although she used a smarmy tone, was, like Johnny, trying to make light of the situation.

'Yes, you an' all. If you're human you've got

Johnny to thank . . . And he isn't much cop, when all's said and done.' The last was uttered by way of an afterthought.

'Well, I'll be damned!'

Rooney could have laughed aloud at the sudden change in Johnny's countenance, but his attention was turned towards Nellie again. She was pointing to Jimmy with an unsteady finger. 'There's the only one among you who's any good . . . Jimmy . . . him. He's the only decent one among you. The only one who thinks. You think, don't you, Jimmy?'

If this remark had been addressed towards Rooney, however merited, he would have become suffused with embarrassment, and it was with something akin to envy that he saw Jimmy smile and say easily, 'Well, now, Nellie. To the last I'll say, Yes, I try to, although it isn't always easy. And I will return your compliment and say you're looking very nice tonight, Nellie. In fact you're what they would call a . . . smasher.'

Jimmy leant towards her as he said this as if he were addressing a soothing remark to a child, and with almost childlike enjoyment Nellie's face lit up for an instant, and her lips were parted to speak when Ma's voice cut in, not loud this time but weighed down with an emotion that could only be classed as venom.

'Smasher! Whore, more like it. I know where you've got your money. I went to the shop. Miss Tanner knew nothing. But I met old Brummell, and he couldn't look me in the face. None of his business, he said. He's been living with a woman for ten years, and now he goes and leaves her for you! An old man, sixty-seven if he's a day . . . You dirty—'

'Ma! Ma! Be quiet.' The request came from several quarters of the room.

'I won't be quiet. Let me be!' She flung off her daughters and faced Nellie.

Nellie did not move, but glared up at Ma, her face drawn and tight, the old Nellie under the make-up. Then, as if something was tickling her from inside, her body slumped, and with a swift movement she turned from Ma and with both hands on the table she leant over it and very gently began to laugh.

It was the most painful sound Rooney had ever heard. It did not touch on mirth, and held neither joy nor gaiety, nor even ribaldry; it had an empty, lost sound, that made him want to go to her and lead her from the room.

'Laugh . . . That's it, laugh! You! You . . .' Ma resorted to her Bible and brought out, 'Harlot!'

The laughter rose, and Rooney, finding it unbearable, was being impelled from within to do something and was actually on the point of moving towards her when Jimmy signalled to his wife, and May, going to the table and gently pressing her mother aside, said, 'Come on, Nellie. Come on up to bed.'

With unnatural suddenness, the laughter stopped, and when Nellie turned and faced the room again it was as if she had laughed herself sober. Hitching her coat up on to her shoulders, and ignoring May's hand, she looked at Ma and said, 'Your detecting got you so far but not far enough. It isn't Mr Brummell – I turned down that offer a long time ago, for I felt with a little effort I could do much better for myself should I feel so inclined . . . What do you say, Tim?'

She had moved her head quickly round, and Rooney, looking at the big fellow, found it in his heart to be sorry for him. His face was a reddy purple, except for his lips, which appeared bloodless and dry. And his tongue began to flick over them as Nellie, moving from the table towards the door, came nearer to him.

The room became quiet; even Ma's spleen was forbidden voice for the moment. Within a foot of him, Nellie stopped. Nor did the big fellow drop his eyes from hers when she said, 'It's eight years gone Wednesday since we last spoke, Tim . . . Far too long, isn't it?'

'Really!' Queenie was standing erect and indignant. 'This has gone beyond everything.'

'Oh!' Nellie put up her hand and softly patted the air. It was a pat that ignored Queenie as a whole and pushed her forcibly into her place. 'Don't, as your mother would say, take on, please. Should anybody feel indignant it should be me. What do you say, Tim?' They were still staring at each other. 'Wouldn't you think they would all be rejoicing to see me in the money?' She smiled with one side of her mouth. 'I'm sure you'll be happy, because now I'll be off your conscience, and you have enough to put up with without that.'

'Get her out before I . . .'

Rooney watched the scuffle to keep Ma in hand. But neither the scuffle nor Ma's voice seemed to have the slightest effect on Nellie. It was as if she heard neither, for looking deep into the shamefaced eyes of the big fellow, she said: 'I've always had one advantage over you, Tim . . . I've been a free-lance. Even in my misery I was a free-lance.' On this she turned from him; and Rooney, stepping quickly aside, let her out.

She went past him with her head up, giving him no sign of recognition. And he stood in the doorway watching her mount the stairs while the room to his side became a bedlam.

'By God! Who'd believe it? And to turn on me, and me always sticking up for her.'

'Stop crying, Ma. Look, you'll be ill. And there's tomorrow, remember.'

'Well, thank God Harry and his people aren't here.'

'I'll throw her out. I will, I will.'

'All right, Ma. All right. Only stop crying.'

'"And the worm when it turned had an elephant's hoof."'

'Oh, for God's sake stop your clever quotations, Jimmy. Just because she said you could think.'

'All right, Queenie. I'm sorry if my quoting upsets you. But it was very nice of her to realise it . . . Don't take it so badly, Tim, it's life.'

'He's not taking it badly. And you shut up.'

'Now, Queenie, that doesn't go with all your accoutrements. And what about letting Tim speak for himself?'

'She's nothing but a prostitute! She admitted it, didn't she? And to think, all these years and what I've done for her.'

'There, there, Ma.'

'Where are you going?'

The big fellow, his face now devoid of colour, went quickly past Rooney and out of the front door without answering his wife, and Rooney, moving quietly, made for the stairs.

In his room he stood with his cap between his hands looking towards the wall at the head of the bed. The babble of voices coming up to him was not more confused than were his feelings, for only a small part of him was now in sympathy with her. That she had planned her entry he was sure. And he should now be waving a flag for her. But she'd got drunk, or pretty near it. And to him that had taken something out of her act of retaliation. He did not name it dignity. If she had come in, dressed up to the nines as she was, and with a few cool words, as they would have done on the pictures, passed through the room leaving them all flabbergasted, that would have done the trick. Her dressing up and staging her entry had been something like the pictures anyway, but she failed to carry it through. The big fellow had likely deserved all he got. But, by God, he had looked awful. Drunk or sober, she had certainly carried that part out all right – she couldn't have hit him harder or better. Yet somehow or other he now felt sorry for the chap. One part she hadn't done very convincingly. That was about the old fellow. Her laughter had not the effect of denial as she intended it should, but appeared to him a poor cover-up. She had perhaps been taken off her guard by Ma's knowledge.

He threw his cap on to a chair, and having pulled off his clothes got ready for bed. But he did not go to bed. The bed was too near the wall that separated him from Nellie and he did not want to think any more about her or of her business. She had got herself fixed up and his pity would not be called upon in the future.

He sat before the fire, his feet stretched out on the hearth, and as time went on the voices became more subdued, rising only once when he guessed Doreen had come in.

He heard the car starting up outside, which meant the big fellow was back; then voices from the street, one in particular, Dennis's high reedy tone. And he remembered with some surprise that he had been about the only one who hadn't opened his mouth during the do, yet he had looked the most astonished of the lot of them. Of the bunch, it was that bloke Dennis, Rooney thought, he disliked the most.

He was still sitting before the fire when he heard Doreen and Ma coming upstairs, and he put out the light in case Ma, when sanity should return, would mention his extravagance. But he still sat on. The fire-light glowed darkly on his dresser, and his pieces of china responded with their usual glints. The glass trinket set from his dressing-table, after trebling itself in the mirrors, sent silver streaks across the lino. The brass knobs of the bed twinkled at him, saying, 'Come on, man, don't be a damn fool.' His bits all spoke to him, bringing their usual comfort, and he rose thinking, Aye, well, I wish her luck. And no doubt she'll need it with an old bloke like him. And I hope she gets some comfort out of her fancy furniture. It did strike him that she was becoming compensated for an antique with more antiques, but he was in no mood for jests.

He made his way to bed, telling himself that he was definitely going to make a move from here, but until he could get away he'd move his bed to the other wall.

5

THE BASHING FEELING

The movement in the house started early – it was the unusual sound of a fire being raked that woke Rooney, and he looked at his watch – it said ten minutes to five. And try as he might after this he couldn't get to sleep again. The consequences were that he lay tossing and turning until, a good half-hour before his usual time, he made himself rise and get ready for work.

He had a thick head, like he sometimes experienced at Christmas when he went over his allowance and took on a drop too much.

For no particular reason, or so he told himself, other than that he had woken too early, he found himself in a devil of a temper. The appearance of the whole room irritated him; the electric light seemed to be starkly glaring, showing up his bits as no light had shown them up before. And it crossed his mind that his bed looked a monstrosity. As he combed his hair before the mirror he was surprised at the sight of himself. His mouth looked set and his eyes dark, and his whole expression vaguely reminded him of Albert.

Downstairs, somewhat to his surprise, it was a subdued Ma he met. She made no comment on his early appearance, but poured him out a cup of tea without a word, and while he was drinking it she went into the kitchen and fried his bacon and eggs. And when she placed his meal before him she took herself a cup of tea and then sat down at the corner of the table and, staring down into the steam rising from the cup, she asked, 'Well . . . now, what do you think?'

He chewed on his food before saying in a voice that sounded to himself almost a growl, 'It's no business of mine.'

Ma nodded at the steam. 'No, I suppose not, but you can't help thinking. Nobody can. An old man, and with a name like he's got. He's been living with this woman up Harton for years. And he has a wife in Harrogate . . . I'm so ashamed. Well, she won't stay here . . . she'll go.'

As Ma took a quick sip of her tea, Rooney thought, She'll go all right – there wouldn't be much point in the whole business if she didn't.

'The wickedness of her! And to come in like that, drunk, like . . . a . . . a . . .' Ma refrained from repeating last night's denunciation and substituted 'Hussy'. 'And all the upset. She did it on purpose . . . Oh, she did it on purpose all right.' Ma shook her head slowly from side to side as she corroborated her own statement. 'Don't you think she did?'

The point-blank question caused him to move uneasily, and without looking up from his plate, he said, 'I'm having nothing to say in the matter.'

'Well, you're right there. But as I said, you can't help thinking. And you thought a bit last night; you were as astonished as any of us.'

That she should have noticed his reaction surprised him. She should, he thought, have had enough to think about without taking in how he looked.

'And to go on to Tim like that. He didn't know where to put himself, did he? She would make anyone believe who didn't know that she had really meant something to him. And she never has; they were only friendly . . . Look at the size of him to her. It would have been grotesque. They were like Mutt and Jeff, the long and the short of it.'

She could go on until she was tired here, Rooney thought, and she would never convince him other than what Johnny had told him and what he himself had surmised from the big fellow's face. He had been going to marry her all right, and if the truth were told he was now damn sorry he hadn't.

A movement on the landing caused Ma to get quickly to her feet. She had momentarily forgotten the great day. But the sound of Doreen made her bustle sharply about, saying, 'I don't know where I am this morning. Oh, she's got a lot to answer for, that one. God is slow, but He's sure.' Her voice became ominous. 'As she is sowing so shall she reap. And I'll see her brought to her knees in the gutter yet!'

For the moment it shocked Rooney to realise that she could couple God with her innate desire to see the little one brought low; it seemed to him now that in some odd way she had derived a satisfaction from the drab, colourless creature that Nellie had become, and had experienced some form of pleasure in keeping her like that.

Covertly glancing at her as she darted between the kitchen and the living-room, he came to the conclusion that there were some folks who were past understanding. A man or woman could be jailed for assault, for robbery, for defamation of character, yet a woman like Ma, a regular churchgoer and a woman who, he had to admit, had done all in her means to further the welfare of her family, could slowly and painfully strangle one of her own kind while professing to be doing her nothing but good; but when the victim escaped, as the little one had done, she could become so consumed with the desire to see her brought low that she would stop at nothing to achieve this end.

Rooney's mind up to now had not been used in trying to explain the intricacies of human nature, and he was finding the process rather trying. He could come to no conclusion or cut-and-dried explanation of the social behaviour he was now encountering in this house. All he could say to himself was, Some folks should be fetched up for what they do.

But seeing the cupidity of Ma did not put the little one in better focus. If she had to go on the loose why hadn't she done it years ago? Why had she waited till now? Yet it was undoubtedly the pressure of life in this house of late that had driven her to it.

'I won't see you at dinner-time,' said Ma, as he went out, 'but I'll leave everything ready. Betty's coming round. She'll pop it in the oven.'

'You've no need to bother,' said Rooney; 'I can get my meal out. I should have mentioned it sooner.'

'Well, I won't say that won't be a help. We'll leave it at that then . . . you'll have your dinner out. Once this is over we'll be back to our own quiet life again.'

He did not wait to hear more, but saying 'Good-bye', he closed the door. Quiet life! Not if he knew it, he wouldn't. There'd be no quiet life for him there. The young one and the little one gone would leave him alone with her. And Ma, he was beginning to feel, was a very uncertain quantity. It could be mothering, marriage, or getting him to God, any one of the three, or all of them . . . he wouldn't put anything past her. No, no. He was bolting, and as quick as possible.

Walking through the rows and rows of streets, he thought, Surely there's some place for me where I won't meet trouble.

These houses were mostly of three rooms on the ground floor and four rooms on the upper, and each floor was classed as a house. And these were the more spacious kind! In Alice Street and thereabouts there were only two rooms on a floor. But each one appeared to him like a palace, and he wished that a miracle would happen and he could get one.

His desire for the accomplishment of this miracle was as fervent as another man's to win the seventy-five thousand pounds' pool; and in the depot, where he met Danny, and with hardly any preliminary, he voiced this to him yet again.

Danny, looking hard at him, said, 'Trouble?'

'No,' said Rooney. 'I just want to get away from there.'

'Who is it, the old one or the . . . ?'

'Neither. I just want to move.'

Although he had already told Danny about the little one, he found he could not pass on the latest developments. He could no more have said 'She's gone on the loose' than he could have talked of his own mother's lapses.

'Why, man, I don't know what to make of you.'

Danny rubbed his nose with the side of his finger. 'Well, in any case, whether you stay or go Mrs D. wants you to come to wor place for Christmas.'

Rooney smiled. 'I'd like that, Danny. Thanks . . . Thank her.'

Bill and Fred joined them and, after the usual cursory greetings, they stood together waiting for Albert. And when at last Albert put in an appearance, hurrying across the yard towards them, Danny muttered under his breath, 'Aye, aye! Something's happened here, an' all.' There was a sheepishness about Albert that was unusual, especially since lately his whole attitude had been one of aggression, and Bill, never able to keep his observations to himself, remarked, 'Pinched the cat's milk, Albert?'

'What! No.' Albert lit a cigarette, then looked from one to the other. And after a long, sustained draw he remarked with forced casualness, 'I'd better tell you. I'm . . . I'm going to give me notice in.'

They stared at him. A chap didn't give his notice in just like that. It brewed up for a long time. He threatened it, he talked about it. Then one day he did it and no-one was really surprised.

'Got another job, Albert?' asked Danny.

'I'm goin' in the pits.'

'The pits! Well, I'll be damned! After the big money?' said Bill.

'Why not?'

'Why not at all,' said Bill. 'But I thought that, like the rest of us, you preferred to meet your number above the gutters.'

'When me time comes I'll go, and not afore.' Albert

turned away, and after a quick glance had passed between the others they followed him.

It was not until the middle of the morning, while in the privacy of a long tradesmen's entrance, that Albert, able to contain himself no longer, said, 'She's come back, Rooney.'

Rooney stopped in his tracks and asked slowly, 'You're taking her?'

His eyes following his hand, Albert dusted down his jacket. 'She's turning over a new leaf.'

Albert was now surveying his feet. 'She won't stay in Shields . . . we're goin' to Darlington. I've got some relations there; they're letting us have a room until we get settled. I can't tell the others; you could tip them off for me, if you will. They'll say I'm daft, barmy, but it's me own life.'

Side-tracking the main issue, Rooney said, 'But you always hated the pits when you were down as a lad, Albert.'

'I'll get used to 'em again. And me money'll be double what it is now, that's the main thing.' He looked up. 'I'll miss the lot of you. But you more than any of them . . . we've been good mates. But' – his mouth and eyes became hard as he turned away – 'nothing or nobody matters. I'll work in hell if it's goin' to make things right.'

Rooney walked behind him up the path, through the gate, and out on to the road. What was it that got into a man that would allow him to take back a woman after he knew she had been with other blokes, coloured an' all? What was there to measure the torment of knowing your wife was like that against the torment of wanting

157

her back in spite of it? . . . The emotions bred of living were beginning to worry Rooney. If it should happen to him it would drive him mad. But he was consoled that it wouldn't happen . . . he would never be eaten up with the passion or whatever it was that drove men to do what Albert was going to do. Again came the consolation that if he had missed any of the transient joys of marriage, he had also missed the more concrete woes.

On top of this came the uneasy thought that things were going to change and change quickly. Albert going, Danny due for his pension next year, and with a new charge-hand they would likely be changed all round. Nothing would be the same. And when he came to consider it, the change had already begun, because nothing had been the same since he went to Filbert Terrace.

At twelve o'clock, after Albert had departed and before they dispersed from the depot, he told the gang the news. Bill swore long and loudly, as Rooney had thought he would. Fred said, 'Well, he'll have no sympathy from me. He deserves all that's coming to him.' Danny, quiet as usual, remarked, 'I guessed it was like that. Mrs D. won't be surprised either . . . she said that's how it would be. Well, it's his life.'

Although it was bitingly cold, the sun was shining as Rooney made his way home, and he was vindictive enough to be thinking it was more than that Madam Doreen deserved, and that it would have served her right if it had snowed and hailed.

Betty was in the kitchen when he went in, and she greeted him affably. 'Oh, hallo,' she said. 'I was hoping you'd be in shortly. Are you going to stay long? I've lit your fire.'

'Well,' he considered, trying to arrange in his mind just how long he could stay in without running into Ma and the party on their return, 'well, I'll be going out about three.'

'Oh, I'll be back before then . . . I just wanted to pop home to see to Johnny and if everything's all right. I won't be half an hour. It's only because of Grandpa . . . She's in, but I wouldn't ask her anything.'

Rooney was quick to notice this change in Betty's attitude. Nellie had become 'she' – not so much, he considered, if at all, because of her lost virtue but because of her remark last night to Johnny. It was a case of prick a husband and you stab a loving wife.

'I'll just slip my things on. I won't be long. I'll be back before they are anyway. They'll be here shortly after three. They're going to take the wedding presents straight to the flat, then call at Harry's place.'

She had put her coat on and departed before he went upstairs; and as he made his way to his room, he hoped, with a surprising urgency, that he would get there without meeting . . . her. Like Betty's his pseudonym for Nellie had changed . . . she was no longer the little one, a name that had its birth in pity, but 'her', and he gave no reason to himself for the meaning of the change.

Before going to have a wash he sat down before the fire. It was burning brightly, and the hearth looked neat and tidy and his bits once again looked good to his eye. And he should have felt relaxed and at ease; but he felt neither. He was wishing fervently that he was out of

159

this, yet at the same time he wished that there was not lying before him the search for a new home.

No movement whatever could be heard in the room next door, and he tried to keep his ears from straining to hear some sound by thinking, I have enough on me own plate.

She was likely sleeping off her hangover, and if he knew anything, her head would be feeling as if there was a shipyard riveter inside it . . . her not being used to it.

It was after two o'clock when he went across the landing to have his wash. Back in his room, he was fastening the collar on a clean shirt when a tap-tap came on the door. He turned from the mirror and stared towards it for some moments. Then, one hand on the still unfastened collar, he went to the door and opened it.

Nellie was standing there, dressed as she had been last night. He imagined that when he next came across her he would see her slightly cowed, or at least shamed, but the Nellie before him was in neither of these admonished states; she looked – the only word he could think of was pert.

'Hallo, Rooney.'

He swallowed, brought the other hand to the aid of his collar, then said, 'Hallo.'

'I would like a word with you.'

He blinked at her while trying to push the stud through the hole.

'Are you shocked about last night?' she asked quietly.

He let an end go. 'It's none of my business.'

'Oh!' Her pertness vanished, and she cried with a

mixture of irritation and bitterness, 'Don't say it like that, as if I was still of no consequence.'

'Well, it isn't, is it . . . no business of mine?'

She looked hard at him, and as she did so she seemed to become deflated, and the old Nellie came back into her voice as she said, 'You are shocked because I staged it all, and came in drunk . . . I had no intention of coming in like that . . . I wasn't really drunk, it was because I'm not used to it. I thought I'd have a glass of wine to . . . to give me courage. And then I had another. I didn't think you could get like that on port wine.' She waited a moment and continued to look up at him, and he said lamely, 'Well, yes . . . you can . . . and badly.'

'I had intended just to walk in and through them and leave them guessing as to where I had got my things.'

To leave them guessing. She was pretty hard-boiled about it. He ignored the thought that she should have intended to do just what he himself had imagined would have been a most effective entry and exit.

'Did I act silly . . . talk a lot?'

'Well, you said enough.'

'I feel I did too, although I can't remember everything clearly.' Her eyes dropped. 'Only yelling at Grace, and . . . and what I said to Tim. I'm sorry I spoke to him like that. I shouldn't have done it. But it's been burning in me for years. And yet now, today, it seems as if it doesn't matter any more, that it has never mattered. I can forgive Tim, and I'm even sorry for him, but I can't forgive her. What she did was calculated and cruel . . . not Queenie, her mother I mean. Queenie just went where she was pushed . . . she'd never have carried it off on her own . . . Tim and I were to have been married. I suppose you guessed that?'

He did not reply immediately. And when he did it was not to say yes or no, but to ask a straight question. And to his own surprise he asked it angrily. 'Why did you stay on here after, then, if she did all that to you?'

'I stayed because I was afraid to go.' She said this boldly, making it a statement of fact. 'The only other person in the world I have ever felt belonged to me, other than Tim, was Grandpa . . . I needed somebody, I even needed them.' She flung her arms wide, taking in the rooms that had once been full of her relatives. 'I wanted to belong somewhere, to have people to call my own. If I had gone then, I think I would have jumped in the river. We shouldn't be left to face things alone. I didn't feel capable of living without some kind of love . . . Grandpa gave that to me, and still does.'

'I'm sorry; I shouldn't have asked.'

'Yes, you should. It's all right.'

'Well, what'll happen to him now, when . . . when you go?'

It was a long moment before she said, 'When I go, he'll go, too.' She pulled the strap of a new brown leather bag back and forward through her hands before adding, 'I . . . I only came because I . . . I felt I owed you some kind of explanation.'

His fingers became agitated on the collar again. 'You owe me nothing. Why should you? You don't need to explain to me, it's none of my business.'

She suddenly brought her eyes up to his, fixing them on him intently, forcing him to look back into them, and as he did so he saw her face change, and she became again, in spite of her fine rig-out and make-up, the old Nellie he had seen on the first Saturday he came here, stiff, buttoned up.

'You . . . you believe—' She paused, her hand to her head. 'I've been trying to remember all morning what she said last night about . . . about Mr Brummell. I can only remember—' She paused again, before adding harshly, 'Do you believe that there is something between Mr Brummell and me?'

What could he say? To say, 'Yes, that's about it. You gave yourself away when you tried to laugh it off,' would be to hit her as hard as Ma had done.

Viciously now, he pulled on his collar, tugging at both ends, his chin stretched up and out. And as he was bringing the ends together her laugh struck him as suddenly as it had done last night. The tightness had vanished, and she looked gay, recklessly gay. 'I don't believe you do . . . not really. Stop pulling at that collar for a minute, will you, and listen to me; I want to tell you something. I don't want any misunderstanding with you, Rooney, at least. Here, let me fix it for you and be done with it.'

Before he could step back and ward off her hands, she had reached up and, taking the two ends of the collar from him, was fastening them together with the stud. 'There!' She patted the achievement with two quick gestures similar to those she used after writing Grandpa's notes.

The patting hit his Adam's apple and caused him to swallow. Worse than that, he almost choked, for looking over her head towards the stairs he saw Betty's half-startled, half-shocked face looking at them.

Following his gaze, Nellie swung round, and her

163

colour rose, outdoing the rouge on her cheeks. Then, moving slowly away, she muttered something which sounded to him like 'More evidence'. But still the unexpected sight of Betty did not cower her, for she marched boldly towards the stairs, tucking her bag under her arm to enable her to draw on her gloves as she did so.

Betty had now mounted to the landing, and, looking at Nellie as she passed, she said pointedly, 'You're making up for lost time, aren't you, Nellie?'

Without pausing in her walk, Nellie replied, 'Being your mother's daughter, Betty, it would be unnatural for you to think otherwise.'

Quickly and quietly Rooney closed his door, and standing with his back to it he took in air, filling his chest and expanding his stomach. If that had been Ma, my God!

But no doubt she would get to know, and then . . .

He touched his collar. Never before had a woman fixed his collar. What had made her do it? Trying out her hand? Pert? Yes, that's what she had become. And he didn't like it; he preferred her as she had been, miserable. Yet the little one was still there. But why had she tied his collar? He could feel her fingers on his neck yet. When Ma did get to know . . . He jerked himself from the door. Blast Ma, and all her works! What had Ma got to do with it, anyway? She was becoming an obsession. What kind of a bloke was he to be frightened of a fat old woman?

He quickly put on his coat, grabbed his cap and mac, and went downstairs. Betty was in the hall. She did not speak, but her eyes spoke for her. And he stared back into them defiantly. He had, he considered, put up with enough; he wasn't going to be cowed by the lot of them and made to feel he was up to something when he wasn't.

He could hear Grandpa's voice coming from the front room, and guessed . . . she was in there. That she might come out and leave the house with him spurted his departure, and he hurried down the street. And not until he was at a safe distance did he slacken his pace. Then a not entirely irrelevant thought struck him. If the man was sixty-five or so, and she took Grandpa with her, it would be like an old-age-pensioners' home. The thought was not funny. A lover of sixty-five and a charge of nearly eighty? . . . No.

He stopped dead in the street. She wouldn't do such a thing. If she was taking the old fellow, then it wasn't Brummell she was going to. Anyway, she had just denied it. But that it was some man he could not doubt; though it must be as she had said last night, that she had done better for herself than Brummell.

She had been about to explain it all to him. She had said she didn't want him to misunderstand, and had seemed anxious that he shouldn't. Yes, when he came to think of it, she had.

He walked on slowly now. If he hadn't left the house like a frightened hare, she might have come out and caught him up.

He was pulled up sharply by his cautious self that had been somewhat neglected of late. What was he thinking now? Did he want to get involved in this business? No, no, of course he didn't. Well then, he'd go for a walk round the market, then to the pictures, and finish up at the Dogs; and keep minding his own business, and let her keep her explanations to herself – he was going to be no recipient of confidences, of how she had got herself a man, one who could rig her out like a fashion-plate at that.

He walked round the market, then went to the pictures. But he didn't go to the Dogs – he went straight to The Anchor. He had considered going to Danny's, but he knew that once he got there and started talking the whole business of . . . her might slip out. And more than that might slip out – things inside himself. Oh! he wished to God he had never set foot in Filbert Terrace.

Neither Fred nor Bill was in the MPs' corner. He hadn't expected to see Albert there, but before he had been sitting down a few minutes he saw Johnny come into the bar and look straight towards him. But he didn't immediately come over – he ordered his drink first; then slowly crossed to the corner, carrying the pint mug in his hand. And when he reached the table he did a strange thing. Strange for him anyway. He did not greet Rooney straight away, but stood looking down at him over the mug of beer.

'Hallo,' said Rooney. 'What's the matter with you?' He did not speak too affably, for he was thinking illogically that if it hadn't been for this fellow he would have known nothing about Filbert Terrace, Ma, her family . . . or Nellie.

'Nowt's the matter with me, lad.' Slowly Johnny sat down, put his beer on the table, and with the back of his hand dabbed the point of his nose. It was in no way intended to be a cleansing process, but apparently to engender thought, for Johnny now gazed into the space between Rooney and the bar proper, and became lost for a time in contemplation. When he did return to his surroundings, he startled Rooney with a quick demand. 'Well, let's hev it,' he said.

'Have what?'

'Aw! now, look, man . . . I'm on your side, even after the way she turned on me last night. She was tight and we all say things when we're tight.' Johnny took a drink from his mug, then looked at Rooney again from beneath his brows, and what he saw made him say, 'Now look, you needn't get on your high horse.'

'Have what?' repeated Rooney again.

Johnny straightened up in his chair, took hold of the sides of the table, and pushed his elbows out. 'It's no business of mine, it's got nothing to do with me, but you must admit I took you there.'

'Damn well I know you did! But what you getting at?'

Johnny's brows drew more closely together and his face took on a surly look. 'Why you trying to come the high hat all of a sudden? Betty saw you.'

'Saw me what?'

'Well, if you must have it in plain words, necking on the landing with Nellie. It didn't strike her till later. And then she put two and two together. She said all along it wasn't old Brummell.'

Rooney had always known just what type of a fellow he himself was . . . he was the placid type. His nerves were steady; he did not get het up about the things men usually got het up about, politics, religion, unions, and women; yet he wasn't without his emotions – his two brief love affairs had called up other feelings that could be described as stirrings of the blood. But when the stirrers of his blood had disappointed him his reactions had not driven him to any strong measures; perhaps they had strengthened his affection for his furniture and his own company, but that was all. In his own quiet way he sometimes compared other people's reactions to his own, and found them wanting in control. It was nothing to see two young fellows fighting outside a dance hall over some lass; it was nothing to see two grown men, well in their forties, as he had done a short while ago, come out of the Winter Garden, walk side by side to the nearest back lane, and then proceed to bash each other's brains out. He had walked unsuspectingly behind these two and had been one of the blokes who had helped separate them. As far as he could gather their wives had got mixed up, and he had thought, Fair enough . . . have it out. But why had they to make a holy show of themselves in the street? And now, with his hand gripping a large fistful of Johnny's collar and the blood pounding in his head as if he had been standing on it, and a desire to bash this fellow's face in filling every pore of his body, the old placid Rooney was struggling for dear life against this wild animal that was in possession.

'Give over, man! What in the name of God's got into you?' It was Bill pulling at him.

'Leave go! Do you hear me? Leave go!' This was Stoddard, the manager, at the other side of him. 'Leave go! Come on now, leave go. Whatever it is, talk it out. I want no fighting in here . . . You of all people, Rooney! I'll believe anything after this.'

The red mist was clearing and he was seeing Johnny's startled countenance more clearly. He released his grip, and Johnny, although he was standing on his own feet, seemed to drop quite a distance to the floor.

'There, now,' said Stoddard, patting Rooney's arm. 'Sit down. Well, I've seen some things in me time from behind this bar, but nothing that has surprised me more . . . There now' – he went on patting – 'let up, man . . . relax. You want something stiff, eh? What about a whisky?'

Rooney did not reply. But Bill said, 'Let's have three. I think this bloke's more in need of one than anybody . . . No, sit down.' He pushed Johnny back into the chair. But Johnny, recovering himself now, shook off Bill's hand and rising on not very steady legs went to the counter without again looking at Rooney.

'You could have knocked me down with a side loader,' said Bill, 'when I come through that door and saw you holding that bloke by the throat. What was it? . . . He's the fellow who got you the digs, isn't he?'

Rooney swallowed and blinked. Then taking a deep breath he leant against the back of the chair and closed his eyes. He felt suddenly very tired, as if he had been swimming and gone too far out.

Stoddard came to the table with the drinks, and Rooney took the glass from his hand and drank the whisky in one gulp; then he shuddered, closed his eyes again, and said, 'Give me another.'

It was a full fifteen minutes later when Bill, in some exasperation, exclaimed, 'Well, for the love of Mike! let's have it. What was it all about?'

'If you must know,' said Rooney, staring down into the sovereign gold of yet another whisky, 'he accused me of keeping a woman.'

169

Bill sat back. 'Keeping a woman? . . . You? . . . Well, are you? All right! All right! Don't start on me.' He pushed his long arm out, warding off the look that Rooney levelled at him. 'You late starters don't know when to stop. But if you was, it would be the first damn sensible thing you've done in your life.'

'You don't always talk like that.' Rooney did not raise his head, just his eyes. 'You're always growling about being tied.'

'Who're talking about being tied? You can keep her without being married, if that's how you want it. And as for being tied, there's worse states, I'm thinking, for you're never out of trouble, free as you are. I used to envy you, you know, Rooney, but you've run into more bloody hot water through evading women than the lot of us have encountered with all our wives put together, and that, to my mind, includes Albert an' all. Why don't you get hooked? You'd only have one lot of trouble then. And you'd know which street you had it in. So far you've nearly covered the bloody town. It's none of my business, but . . .'

Bill left the 'but' in the air, finished his drink, and said, 'What you havin'?'

'The same.'

Bill said nothing but raised his brows as he went to the counter. It was Rooney's fourth and the night was young. He had never known him to take more than two, except on New Year's Eve. In fact, his sticking so rigidly to the rules he had set down for himself had irritated the gang on more than one occasion. That was, all except Danny. But, then, Danny was a bit of an old wife at times . . .

Rooney drank steadily until ten o'clock, and when he finally got to his feet his legs were afloat. But, he assured himself, he wasn't drunk. No, he wasn't drunk. If he could keep his feet on the floor he'd be all right.

The wooden floor of the bar was kind to him. Possessing some magnetic quality, it attracted his feet from out of the air to it, but once outside, the cold, hard, greasy pavements began to play tricks on him, and nothing would convince him but that some damn fool on the road gang had set the paving stones at different levels. Leaning on Bill's shoulder, he endeavoured to explain the situation, yet he knew this to be a waste of words, for Bill was drunk and he was taking Bill home.

Tentatively he stepped out, hanging on to Bill, and when he tried to speak he again came to the conclusion that somebody had been up to something, for all the words in his head were tied into knots. There were lots of things he wanted to talk about. About life and marriage and women. It was all in his head – he had never imagined he could think such things. Gradually the cold night air undid the knots, and the words began to flow in long, quick-moving lines through his brain. He could see the sense of them as they passed, although many of them were strange, highfalutin words which he had only read and never spoken and which filled his mouth so much when he tried to speak them now that he choked on them and coughed.

At one time during the journey home he could have sworn he was walking down King Street with a lass on his arm and feeling so happy he wanted to sing. Until Bill swore, and he knew it was Bill on his arm and he was taking him home because he was drunk.

'For God's sake if . . . not . . . not for your own, keep your trap shut else the old girl'll not let you in. Come on! Come on!' Bill tugged at him.

He didn't like being tugged . . . he resisted.

'I'll leave you here, mind. Here at the gate, mind. I'll ring . . . the bell. Look – get this. I ring the bell, she'll open the door and you . . . you make a clean crack for the stairs. Get me? Come on.'

'Gracie, Gracie, gie me your answer, do . . .'

'For God's sake, man, don't start singing now. Where's the bloody bell?'

Rooney heard Bill say 'Evenin'.'

He heard himself say 'Evenin''; then lifting his foot over the step, which had risen higher than any paving stone he had yet encountered, he stumbled past Ma and into the hall, shouting '. . . 'Night, Bill.'

The door banged, cutting off Bill's final farewell.

Rooney was too far gone to appreciate the look on Ma's face, but he saw her skip . . . like . . . like – his mind told him what she skipped like – like a water buffalo to the room door and close it.

'You're like a . . . a water . . .'

'Go on! Up those stairs.' Ma's voice came in a sibilant whisper from the depths of her stomach. 'How dare you come into my house in this condition!'

He looked at the line of words passing through his mind and discarded buffalo for hog. 'Hog,' he said, 'wa . . . ter hog!'

'Get upstairs this minute . . . or get out!' It was a petrifying hiss, but it slid off Rooney.

'Out? . . . Me furniture.'

172

Suddenly he was seized by what appeared to be a herd of water hogs and propelled bodily to the stairs and up them. The hazardous climb was over in a twinkling – it seemed as if he had flown. He was on the landing . . . there was his door. But he was going to it himself – no woman was going to push him about. With a jerk he threw off Ma's hands and made a straight line for his room. But through no fault of his the line swerved and he banged into Nellie's door, and as Ma pulled him back the door opened and through a veil of mist he saw the little one.

Ah, there she was . . . she was the cause of all this. She had put her hands on him. Pert, that's what she was.

'You!' he began. 'You . . .' He was jerked away and Nellie left his vision, and the next second he was in his room, lying back in his chair with Ma standing over him.

'You move out of here again tonight and I'll have you thrown into the street. Do you hear me? . . . Mind, I'm warning you . . . you move.'

Silently Rooney stared back at her, until her face disappeared. The door closed and he turned his head towards it. His nose twitched like a rabbit's and his face became contorted as he grabbed at words now moving much more sluggishly through his mind.

'Bossy bitch! Who . . . she . . . talking to? Walrus face! Not move . . . out of here? I'll show the fat old dyed . . . dust-bin.' He reached the door and pulled it open. His mouth too was open, ready to shout.

'Go on, get in. Get in now.'

He was back in the room and in his chair again, and

Nellie was by his side. 'Don't talk,' she said softly. 'Don't, Rooney, that's a good fellow, don't talk.'

She seemed to be pleading with him, and he, not unchivalrous even in his drink, whispered back, 'No . . . all right. She's an old cow.'

'Yes. Be quiet now. Let me get your collar off.'

'No, no, you're not. Don't you touch me collar.'

'Please,' she entreated. 'Lie back and don't talk. There now' – she pulled his hands away from his neck – 'you'll feel better with it off.'

He did feel better with it off. 'Nellie . . . tell me sumthin' . . . Will you tell me sumthin'?'

'Yes.'

'Leave me shoes alone' – he tried to stay her hands – 'I wan' you . . . tell me sumthin'.'

'Be quiet . . . don't talk now.'

'Aye, now. Yes, now.'

'In the morning.'

'Albert's wife . . . Albert's wife went . . . went off with a nigger, an' . . . an' he . . . he took her back . . . You went off with . . . No! No! Get by. Leave me coat alone . . . No!'

'Sit up till I get it off.'

He pressed harder back against the chair.

'Rooney, listen to me.' Her hands were holding his face. 'Listen to me, will you?'

Her hands felt nice. He tried to look up at her, but he couldn't see her face any longer, for it kept coming and going, coming and going. When for a brief second he did see it, it brought the queerest feeling to him, the queerest feeling . . . he wanted to kiss it as he did that lass's hand in his dream. It was funny . . . funny. He

174

began to laugh, a deep, low, rumbling sound. The laughter rolled about inside him.

'Sh! Rooney, please. Please listen. Listen to me. I spoilt things for them downstairs last night – please don't you do it tonight. Try to understand.'

It was something in her voice like the sound of crying that got through to him, and he whispered, 'All right. All right . . . Let me be. Go on.' The lines of words were becoming more difficult to see and grasp and he could hold on to none of them. He wanted to sleep. He lay back but was pulled upright again.

'Come on, get on to the bed; you can't lie there all night. Come on . . . up! Up!'

He was on his feet, rolling like a top-heavy ship.

'Take your coat off. There . . . that's it.'

With an effort he reached the bed, and with a heavy relaxed flop fell into its billows.

Her hands were on him, covering him up. She touched his face again, bringing words back into his mind.

'Nellie . . .'

'Yes?'

'Nellie . . .'

'Yes. Go to sleep now.'

'I'll be like Albert. It woon't . . . it woon't matter what . . .'

'All right. Go to sleep.'

'Nellie . . . Nellie, in the morning . . . I want to talk . . . to . . .'

'Sh! Sh! Go to sleep now,' she whispered; and he went to sleep.

6

AND WHATSOEVER THINGS ARE PURE

In the deep dark of the night that had pressed its blackness into his head Rooney woke feeling past description. For some time he did not realise where he was, and to find himself in bed, still in his trousers, added to his confusion. In a thick daze he got up, supporting his head the while, took off his clothes, had a long drink of water, then flung himself back into the bed again. Thought was painful, so with his face half buried in the pillow he went to sleep again.

The room was in dim light when he finally awoke, but the sun was shining outside, for a bright golden strip from the side of the curtain lay across the dressing-table. Thinking was still painful, but he made an attempt at it. What had happened last night? He could remember seeing Ma in the hall, but from then his doings remained blank.

He looked at his watch. It was half-past ten. He wanted a drink . . . a strong cup of tea. The desire for a strong cup of tea got him out of bed.

He held his head in his hands. God, but he felt awful. Why had he got like this? He had been tight before but never with this after-effect. It wasn't worth it; it wasn't worth the candle; all the drink on earth wasn't worth feeling like this. He'd give it up . . . he could if he liked, he only drank for company . . . God in heaven! his head was going to burst.

He dragged on his dressing-gown and switched on the light, but the glare hit his eyeballs like a spray of acid, and he switched it off again. He'd have a wash . . . a bath. He'd have to before he went down, for if he looked anything like he felt, he looked pretty awful.

He was going round in circles trying to find his towel and soap when a tap came on the door . . . Ma . . . my God in heaven! couldn't she wait until he could think?

He let her knock again before going to the door and pulling it open. Nellie stood there with a tray in her hands, and she was smiling with a sort of mischievous smile that did nothing but irritate him in this moment.

'I thought you might like a strong cup of tea . . . I had to wait till she went to church. Feeling awful?'

'A bit,' he said. 'Thanks.' Then, 'Oh, thanks. I've been praying for this.' He took the tray from her, but to his concern she did not turn away but, putting out her hand, switched on the light and walked into the room saying, 'I'll light your fire . . . I'd have a bath if I were you.'

He looked at her already kneeling on the mat. The tray was still in his hands. Funny how she repeated his thoughts.

He poured himself a cup of tea, and then another, before asking the question that was foremost in his mind. 'What happened last night? Did I . . . ?' He paused, not being able to name whatever type of rumpus he had caused.

She looked up at him over her shoulder, her eyes still

merry. 'You did. It's becoming a habit, me one night, you the next.'

'I kicked up a row?'

'No, not really.'

'How did I get upstairs? I can never manage stairs when I'm . . .'

'She pushed you up, or dragged you or something. Anyway, she got you up.'

His face began to burn. 'Did . . . did she come in here?'

'Just to see you were safely in.'

He let out a long-drawn breath, then said, 'In any case I'll be for it.'

'You're not afraid of her?' Nellie's brows drew together.

'No, no.' He didn't know whether he was lying or not. 'But I don't want any trouble with her.'

Nellie rose from her knees, the pan of ashes in her hand. 'I don't think you need worry. She'll likely forgive you and read you a lecture . . . she won't miss the chance to try and reform you.'

He gave a weak smile. 'That'll be as bad.'

They looked at other, like conspirators against a common enemy. Then they laughed.

They were still looking at each other when she asked, 'Who is Albert?'

'Albert? Did I talk about him?'

'Yes. And his wife.'

'Oh.'

'She went off with a Negro.'

'I told you that?'

She nodded, smiling tenderly at him.

181

'When you're drunk you can't mind your own business . . . I'll have to watch out. It's a fool's game anyway.' He wanted to add, 'And don't forget that.' But what he said was, 'What else did I say?' But having said it he found himself suddenly afraid of knowing, so added quickly, 'I'd better have a wash. Thanks for the tea; it . . . it saved me life.'

The ash-pan in one hand, the tray in the other, she went out. What had he said last night? And how did she know what he had said, if it was Ma who had brought him upstairs and pushed him in here? He looked slowly around the room, and his eyes came to rest on the dressing-table. On it lay his collar and tie. The tie was folded in four, and reposing on the top of it were his studs. He had never folded a tie in his life.

At the foot of the bed stood his shoes, side by side, unfamiliar in their military position. His coat was not over the back of a chair but on a hanger on the back of the door.

The heat from his face spread over his body. She must have . . . put him to bed.

Clamping down on further thought, he went to the bathroom.

Nellie was proved right about Ma's attitude, for when Rooney put in an appearance downstairs, round about one o'clock, she did not go for him but with a pained expression she surveyed him across the length of the room. Then, as if she were admonishing a favourite child, she said, 'Rooney, I'm surprised at you.'

He moved uneasily and strained his neck out of his collar.

'I'm surprised at meself . . . I'm sorry for coming in like that.'

'Well, I hope it's not going to happen again, Rooney.'

'No,' he said, 'it won't.' He did not add, 'If it does, you won't see it.'

He wished now that she had gone for him and given him notice; it would have saved him a lot of trouble in the long run.

'Well?' Her bust rose with a great intake of breath. 'We'll say no more about it then. I hope things are going to settle down . . . everyone seems to have gone mad at once. Come and have your dinner so that I can get cleared away. That one hasn't done a hand's turn . . . I came back to find everything just as I left it. She can afford to eat out now that she's in the money . . . on the ill-gotten gains of sin.'

Rooney hadn't heard Nellie go out, and the knowledge that she was gone made the house more alien to him. In direct contradiction to this he was experiencing a mounting feeling of irritation towards her . . . She had been going to explain things to him yesterday. Why hadn't she? And then this morning, when she'd had the chance, she had said nothing, nothing that threw any light on the subject anyway. But hadn't he made up his mind that he didn't want to know? Oh, blast everything!

'There.' Ma put his meal on the table. 'I've had mine. But I'll sit down a minute, because I feel there's a need to talk to you.' She lowered herself slowly into the chair. 'You know, Rooney, you're like my own son and I don't want to see you . . .'

No; he just couldn't stand this, not at the present moment he couldn't. So he didn't sit down, but with forced courage faced her, saying, 'If you don't mind I'll . . . I'll take it upstairs. Me head's splitting, and I'm no company to meself or anybody else.'

Ma's surprised look also held a touch of indignation. Her lips pursed and her whole face tightened, bringing a group of lines from her nose that made her mouth appear corrugated.

'Well! If that's how we feel, very well. But we must have a talk, and soon. And we'll both feel better for it.'

This was no request but an order.

He escaped with his dinner. But in the privacy of his room he found what little appetite he'd had for it had vanished, and he sat before the fire smoking, his mind not on Ma now but on Nellie again, out eating with the fellow.

About four o'clock he heard some members of the family arrive for tea, and this gave him the needed impetus to get ready and go out. Fifteen minutes later he reached the hall, when, as if he had been awaiting him, Grandpa's door opened.

'Hallo, there,' said the old man. His eyes were twinkling, and his whole manner jovial.

'Hallo,' said Rooney.

'Going out?'

'Aye.' Rooney nodded.

'So am I . . . the morrer. Nellie's getting a taxi and taking me out. All round the places I know. Cleadon, Frenchman's Bay, right to Sunderland . . . Have you seen Nellie?' This was a whisper.

Again Rooney nodded.

'Ain't she bonnie? Just like when she was a lass. Come into some money, Nellie has . . . Has she told you? She's had some money left her.'

Rooney shook his head.

'She will. She's happy now. Doesn't she look grand?'

The room door opened and Pauline came out into the hall, where, ignoring Rooney, she said briskly, 'Come along, Grandpa, come along.'

'Now you leave me alone, madam. I'm just havin' a word . . .'

Rooney made his escape, but he could still hear Grandpa's protests after he had closed the iron gate behind him.

What, he wondered as he walked along the streets which Sunday seemed to strip of people and make desolate, would the old fellow's reactions be when Ma informed him just how Nellie was getting her money? He'd likely hit her, as he himself had been going to hit Johnny when he suggested it was he who was supplying it . . .

He reached Fowler Street when this thought came to him, and although it did not stop him in his tracks, he turned aside and stood looking into the window of a sweet shop piled high with Christmas attractions. That had been the start of it, he could remember it all now . . . Johnny coming across to him and saying . . . What had he said? That he had been keeping Nellie.

A faint echo of his rage returned. He had wanted to strangle Johnny. But why had he felt like that, like . . . like this . . . this churned-up feeling inside, wanting to bash somebody? He was as bad as Albert. But it was Albert's wife that had made him like that – he

185

himself had no wife to get worked up over.

He looked at his reflection in the shiny cover of a box, expecting to be confronted by a different being, but he looked the same as ever. Yet he wasn't the same, and he knew it. He'd have to pull himself together and get away from that house as soon as possible, and in the meantime keep clear of the little one, and let her keep all the explanations to herself. It was none of his business, anyway.

He was turning briskly from the window when he though of Ma and the element of forgiveness in her attitude; and his decisiveness vanished and worry settled on him again, for knowing Ma, he knew that there would have been no touch of forgiveness for him had she been made aware of the tie incident and his resulting handling of Johnny. That retribution was something surely to come.

Groaning audibly, he went to the pictures, and there, watching the effects of a sizzling sky on a stretch of yellow sand and a pair of uninhibited lovers, he wished he could have gone back a month, for then, in comparison, life had been an easy uncomplicated affair. There might have been Kate Sparks and others like her, but they had aroused no battling tendencies; their impact had not touched his character or his heart. As his mind spoke this word, the sizzling lady on the screen suddenly burst into song. 'Climb up the Garden Wall,' she sang to an opposite number who, apparently, had been getting along quite well without having to attempt this Herculean feat.

Tripe! Rooney stood up, pushed through a row of glue-eyed, hypnotised Sunday escapists, and came out into the dark streets again. But he did not make his way to The Anchor. Instead, hoping to evade an encounter with Ma, he returned home, for he judged that she would still be at church. Arriving in the yard and seeing no light in the kitchen or the living-room, he felt he was in luck. But between closing the door and groping for the switch he was thrown into a state almost of agitation by the sound of Ma's voice coming either from the hall or from Grandpa's room. That Grandpa was also in the thick of it he soon knew, for the old man's treble was at its highest.

'Tell her to get out, would you! You can tell nobody to get out of here. The house is in my name, on the rent book. You're the one that'll get out . . . And me furniture . . . don't think you'll get that. Or me insurance policy either – it's hers. Ah! I've put a sneck on your neb, me lady. You wait and see.'

'You old devil!'

'Old devil, am I? I can hear you, I'm not so deaf.'

'Be quiet! Go on in . . . Yes, yes, go on now. I'll be there in a minute.'

Rooney was surprised to hear Nellie's voice – he could just hear it and that was all, it was so quiet and level.

There was the sound of a door closing, then Ma saying, 'You little liar! You've tried to hoodwink him, telling him you've had money left you. Who have you got that I don't know of who would leave you money? Nobody . . . Well, I told him . . .'

'Yes, you would. You told him it was old Brummell, didn't you? But let me inform you, Grace, you are mistaken.'

187

'I'm not mistaken. Don't think you can pull the wool over my eyes – I saw his face when I asked him where you were. And you seem to forget you told me yourself he'd tried his hand.'

'I know I did, but that was years ago. But I tell you again, it isn't him . . . Brummell! I wouldn't let that man within a mile of me.'

For no accountable reason Rooney felt his spirits rising, for the words, so quietly and softly spoken, held the quality of truth, and that this had got over, even to Ma, was revealed in her next question.

'Are you denying it's a man?'

During the long pause that followed, Rooney's spirits remained stationary; then, as Nellie's voice, still quiet, came to him, they took a rapid downward descent.

'It would be stupid to deny anything, for you would believe what you want to believe. Yes, there's a man. Are you satisfied? I'm in love with a man. Now that will give you something to rake over in your twisted mind! I'm in love. A state you've never been in in your life, Grace. That's why you could never bear to see me happy. The happiest time in your life was when I was in the depths, when nobody noticed me, only as an object of pity. Oh, I've known almost your every thought and mood for years. You hated my mother because she got the man you wanted. You didn't love him, but you thought he had money. What you did to me through Tim was in your estimation, rough justice, and you would never have taken me into this house in the first place had it not been for the few pounds that went with me and which you claimed in lieu of my keep. But what does it matter now? . . . Yes, there is a man. I'm in love, I have money, and there IS A MAN!'

The silence descended again, and Rooney had a picture of them facing each other, their minds fighting without words through their feelings. Then Nellie's voice again, a little louder now, saying, '"Think on these things." Saint Paul to the Philippians, chapter four, verse eight. I remember you stopping me going with the rest to the sands because I couldn't repeat that verse, word for word. It's ironical when you think of it, you of all people to make me learn that. "Finally, brethren, whatsoever things are true, whatsoever things are honest, whatsoever things are just, whatsoever things are pure, whatsoever things are lovely, whatsoever things are of good report; if there be any virtue, and if there . . ."'

He heard her step on the stairs and her voice getting fainter . . .

As he let himself quickly and quietly out again, a laugh followed him like a husky echo, but full of composure, so full of composure that it transcended Ma's loud howl of raging words. But Ma, nor nobody else, could rattle her any more for, as she had said, she was in love, she had money, and a man.

Feeling more depressed than he had ever felt in his life, he went to The Anchor.

7

THE LETTERS

It was on Monday evening that Ma showed Rooney the flowers.

'Look,' she said, before he'd hardly got in the door. She was pointing to a large cellophane-wrapped bunch of tousled-headed chrysanthemums lying on top of the sewing machine. 'They came for her this afternoon. "Does Miss Nellie Atkinson live here?" the boy said . . . Miss Nellie Atkinson!' Ma's chest expanded. 'Look, a card on them, too. And a letter.' She jerked her thumb towards the mantelpiece. 'That came at dinner-time . . . Do you want any more evidence?'

Rooney's eyebrows seemed to spring apart. 'Me want evidence? I don't want evidence – it's nothing to do with me.'

'But you don't believe she's up to anything, do you? Oh, I know. I wasn't born yesterday, nor the day before that. I know all about it; she played on your feelings and she told you such a tale . . .'

'She did no such thing. And look here, Mrs Howlett. This is none of my business, it's no concern of mine, and I don't want to have any say in the matter. And what's more, I don't want to hear anything more about it . . .'

'You needn't shout, Rooney.' Ma sounded distinctly hurt.

'I'm sorry, I'm forgetting myself. But once and for all, I want nothing to do or say in . . . the little . . . in her affairs.'

'Very well.' Ma's head wagged. 'I was only pointing out to you for your own good. I know you, and you could be taken . . .'

'Damn it all!'

'Mr Smith!'

He was past being affected by her indignation; he was disturbed, upset, all to pot. As he put it, he didn't know where he was, except that he was in this damned house.

He went upstairs, changed, and went out without his tea.

The following morning, Ma brought another letter in from the hall and placed it conspicuously against the clock. But she needn't have done that; he knew who it was for, although he did not look towards it.

The same thing happened on Wednesday. But on Thursday morning Ma threw the letter on to the table, almost to the side of his plate, and he had to check himself from exclaiming, 'Now, look here!' But he and Ma were barely speaking, and he was beginning to wonder which was causing the greater strain, listening to her or not listening to her. As for Nellie, almost the same situation existed there. On Tuesday evening she had come out of her door just as he was coming out of his. She was wearing a different hat and coat and her face was done up. She had said 'Hallo', and he had answered briefly, 'Hallo.' Then she had stood before him, saying, 'Grandpa's had a wonderful day. You know where we've been?' She had not finished, but looking into his face she had smiled, a funny little smile, and added, 'Oh, is that how it is? I'm in your bad books now.'

'Why do you say that? Why should you be, it's got nothing to do with me?'

'I know, I know . . . it's got nothing to do with you. Nothing's got anything to do with you. Look, Rooney.' She had strained her face up to his and whispered, 'I'd like to talk to you.'

As he looked down on her, he could hear her voice coming through the days and nights as it had been doing since Sunday, saying, 'I'm in love, I have money and a man.' And to her request, he replied briskly, 'I'm busy, I'm seeing a pal.'

She had let him pass and precede her downstairs, and in the street he had protested volubly to himself. It wasn't fair, her being able to put him in the wrong like that. Looking as if he'd hit her. What did she want? She'd got everything now, she'd said so herself. And then those letters and flowers. The bloke must be an unusual type to send her flowers, either old, like Brummell, or . . . a foreigner. There were dozens of white women married to Arabs an' such. God in heaven! what was he thinking about? And anyway, what did it matter to him what she did? Or how many letters or flowers she received.

Now the letter was lying by his elbow, and his eyes slid sideways to it. The writing, like everything about this affair of hers, was odd. It was like script: Miss Nellie Atkinson. . 71 Filbert Terrace. . South Shields. .

Why is it that out of the morass of mannerisms

peculiar to an individual one scarcely perceivable motion should impinge itself on the eye of the onlooker and from its small unconnected self create its creator?

Rooney sat staring, fascinated at the envelope, and slowly he was telling himself that if what he was thinking was right there was something fishy here. What did it mean? What could it mean? He threw his mind back to the first time he had seen Nellie take a pencil and a pad from her pocket and write 'Lodger' and go da-da with the pencil, making two dots after the word. He could remember thinking along the lines that it looked a very precise and definite action from such a nondescript person. And there staring at him from the envelope were two dots after Atkinson, two after Terrace, and two after Shields. He knew there was a correct way of addressing an envelope. There was a comma at the end of each line, and at the finish you put a full stop. There might be two people who would put two full stops at the end, but would they do so at the end of each line?

He left a good part of his breakfast uneaten, and in a bewildered state went out to work. It just didn't make sense. Why should she write letters to herself? Yet why not, if it was going to make Ma wild and give her something to think about? . . . But there were the flowers. Well, if she had sent the letters, she could have sent them an' all. But what about the fellow?

During the following hours he had to stand a lot of chaff from Bill because of his more than usual silence. Bill had already made the events of Saturday night into an epic; the whole depot knew that Rooney, that quiet-looking chap with the sandy hair, had nearly killed a bloke in The Anchor because the bloke had asked him the ordinary conversationary question, Was he keeping a woman? And the journey home through the streets Bill had turned into a rip-roaring pantomime in which Rooney had become a cross between a ballet dancer and a mountain goat.

But, make what effort Bill might, the pantomime stopped at the door of '71', for Rooney refused to be drawn as to what he could remember once he had got inside the house.

All this had happened six days ago, but Bill was still playing on it, and by five o'clock Rooney was hating the sound and sight of him. For not even under Danny's cautionary admonition of 'Let up now' had he ceased to tease and mickey him. He had teased and mickied him before, but with no adverse effect; in fact he had enjoyed it, for better than most he could stand a laugh against himself. But the subject of Saturday night, like a constantly scratched pin-prick, was turning into a sore, and it was all he could do not to round on Bill and cry, 'Shut your mouth else I'll shut it for you!' So by five o'clock he was glad to escape from the depot, in case he should create another epic.

He was walking out of the gate with Albert, and Albert was confirming his own views by saying, 'You stand too much. It's your own business, I know, but if he doesn't let up you want to let him have it,' when a voice to the side of them said, 'Hallo.'

'Oh, hallo.' With some surprise Rooney looked at Jimmy.

'Just finished?'

'Aye. Yes.'

'I'm going your way.'

'Oh . . . well . . . This is me pal, Albert Morton. This is . . . I don't know your name, just Jimmy.'

'Fairbairn.'

The men nodded, and a few yards farther along the road Albert cut off from them saying, 'So long. I'll be seeing you.'

'So long,' they both answered. And then continued in silence for some way, until Jimmy, turning to Rooney, said, 'I don't know what you're thinking but I'm not here by chance, Rooney.'

'No?' It was a question.

'No. I want to ask a favour of you . . . It's about Nellie.'

My God! Rooney did not voice this expression, but waited.

'I suppose it's none of my business and I should let things slide, but I just can't. The fact is they are determined to get to the bottom of this affair of hers. I won't say I'm not intrigued myself, but there's a great difference in that to spying. The fact is they're having her followed.'

'Followed? Who by?' Rooney's step had slowed.

'Oh, the great moraliser, Dennis. Also Ma is determined to get into her room. Nellie has kept it locked since this business started. There's been a great rake round for keys. Oddly enough Nellie's is the only bedroom door that's got one . . . You'll be wanting to know what all this has got to do with you.'

Rooney pushed his hair under his cap. 'Yes, I am a bit.'

'Well, it's just this! I want you to tip her off. It's

impossible for me to catch her, but you're on the spot . . . Would you?'

After a moment's pause he said, 'Yes . . . aye, I'll put her wise.' There was no need for him to debate about this. The thought of that long, slimy bloke spying on her brought on him the urge to hit out again. 'What'll I tell her . . . just what you said?'

'Yes. You can't do anything else. And tell her to burn anything of importance.'

Aye, thought Rooney, that would be the main thing. It wouldn't matter if they found out if there was a fellow and who he was, but it did matter if they found out that the letters didn't come from a fellow at all . . . that's if they didn't . . . Oh, he didn't know what to think.

'I've always been fond of Nellie, and she's had a hard time of it. I don't need to improve your knowledge of Ma, do I? It's been pretty grim watching Nellie going downhill these past few years, especially when one remembers what she used to be like . . . in spite of Ma. But now she's taken on a new lease of life.' Jimmy gave a deep chesty chuckle. 'Sin, to use Ma's term, can be very rejuvenating, don't you think?'

Rooney did not offer his opinion on this but asked, 'When does he intend to follow her?'

'That I don't really know. It could be tonight or any time. It was May, my wife, who told me about it at lunch-time. They've decided it isn't Brummell. All I know is that Dennis has appointed himself Ma's lieutenant and proposes to go there straight from the office and follow Nellie when she leaves the house. Apparently she goes out between half-past five and seven. It's a dirty business and it's got my back up. If she doesn't want to say who the man is that's her affair, and under the circumstances I shouldn't imagine she'll want to divulge who he is, for he's almost sure to be an old fellow or somebody married who will be as anxious as she is to keep the thing dark.' Jimmy paused. 'It puzzles me though how she has met either type with enough money to float her in the style she's adopting, for she wouldn't open her mouth to a man, not even those in the Literary Society. It was myself who got her to join that, unknown to Ma, of course. I happened to go in one evening and she was reading, for a change, and we got talking, and I told her I thought she'd find it interesting. At least she'd find some companionship there. I used to be in it before I joined the Archaeological Society. I know all the members there and not one of them fits the picture.'

Rooney liked this fellow. Like Nellie, he felt he was the best of the bunch, but it perturbed him to find that even he was creating, to a certain extent, the . . . the bashing feeling within him. Discussion in any form of Nellie's morals was erupting a new and decidedly disturbing side of himself which he did not want or like but could not disregard.

'You don't mind me asking this of you?'

'No. No, not at all.'

'I'm glad . . . Do you think they're a queer lot . . . Ma and them?'

'I do, damn queer.' This was said so quickly and definitely as to cause Jimmy to laugh outright.

'After thirteen years, you've either had to get used to them or do a bunk. I myself don't happen to be one of Ma's favourites. One thing of deep regret to my

200

mother-in-law is that I've given her no grandchildren.' He inclined his head towards Rooney confidentially. 'Believe me, I've purposely refrained from this indulgence, fearing that heredity would out and I'd be confronted with miniature Ma's for the next twenty years or so. My sense of humour, which I've had to cultivate assiduously as a shield against Ma, could not have stood up to it.'

Rooney laughed. This Jimmy, he could see, was a fellow who could talk, and liked it, but he was a decent bloke all the same.

'I'll leave you here.' Jimmy stopped before they reached the main thoroughfare. 'If you can't find the opportunity to have a word with her perhaps you would pop a note under her door. Would you?'

'Yes, I suppose that would be the best thing,' said Rooney, 'for there's not much chance of conversation there.'

'All right then, I'll leave it to you. And thank you . . . it's good of you to bother.'

'It's no bother. So long.'

'So long,' said Jimmy.

Although she couldn't hope to go on indefinitely keeping everything up her sleeve, the thought that the truth might be brought to light by that individual, Dennis, maddened Rooney. Not that it was any business of his, it wasn't, but the least he could do was to put her on her guard. His step quickened, as much as he told himself from a desire to keep warm as to get home, for it was beginning to freeze hard.

His approach to Filbert Terrace was from what he called the bottom end, and to get to the back lane he had to pass the front street. The terrace was no better lighted than any of the surrounding streets, and figures walking twenty yards away were hardly discernible, but he checked his step and peered through the dim light when, from half-way along the terrace, he heard a gate shut and saw a slight figure merging into the distance. He stood peering up the street. Was it her? Well, if it was, he should catch her up; there mightn't be an opportunity like this again.

He went up the street, hurrying now. But he still couldn't be sure if it was Nellie, for the figure ahead was hurrying too.

There was a bicycle leaning against the railings of No. 71 and he had gone but a few yards farther on when he heard the door open. He did not turn to see who was coming out, but pulling up the collar of his mac and tugging his cap farther on to his head he cut across the road. The figure ahead was now walking into Deans Road, and as she passed a lamp post he saw that it was Nellie all right. He did not look behind him until he was about to turn the corner of the terrace, when a quick glance told him what he already suspected. The tall hurrying figure was Dennis and he was pushing the bike.

Nellie was almost opposite him now on the other side of the road. Rooney watched her pause at a bus stop and look back up the street, before moving on again. Then quickly, as if changing her mind, she recrossed the road and was walking within a few feet of him. He slowed his pace, for he was now in a quandary. If he were to speak to her here Dennis would imagine he had solved the problem – it would all tie up very convincingly with Betty's story. He didn't want that. But what, he wondered, would be Dennis's next move if she got on a bus. Follow it until she got off, he supposed. That was what the bike was for. Without implicating himself he could not see what his own next move should be . . . She must not get on a bus, for he too would have to get on it, and he would not escape Dennis's eye. An idea came to him. Waiting until he came to a quiet stretch of the road, he self-consciously moved nearer to Nellie, but still keeping behind her he said softly, but definitely, 'Nellie . . . don't turn round. It's me, Rooney. Dennis is behind us; he's following you.'

She had given a start and had almost stopped at the first sound of his voice; but after a moment her step quickened.

Passing her without turning his head, he murmured, 'Make for the park, round the bottom, into Stanhope Road.' Then he hurried on briskly ahead. And as he heard the sound of her heels tap-tapping behind him, he thought, I'm daft. What's it got to do with me? It would come out sooner or later, anyway. But the thought of Dennis slinking behind made him add, Well, not this way, if I can help it.

Coming out of Stanhope Road he was confronted with the question, Where next? Automatically he turned right, making for the direction of Tyne Dock. But as he neared the top of Stanhope Road, he thought, This could go on for ever. He had constituted himself leader of this evasive action, and he wasn't, he knew, cut out for a leader. No brilliant escape tactics filled his mind. Nor were there any byways around here where a

203

man with a bike could not follow. He had already made sure that Dennis was still following. He went on, down the slope past St Peter and Paul's church to the foot of the Tyne Dock station bank, and it was here there occurred to him an idea that might be classed as strategic. Farther on was a very steep incline; it branched off the pavement and doubled back towards the station, and at the top was a piece of open ground connecting with Hudson Street and another entrance to the station. If Nellie were to go up to the station bank, under the arch, and up the steps to Hudson Street, there would be nothing to stop Dennis humping his bike that way and keeping her in view. But if she went past the station bank up the incline and on to the dimly lit land she could, if she were quick, turn either right and go down the station steps, or left and into the Crown Picture House. And Dennis would be unable to tell which way she had gone.

When he neared the station bank he stopped and fumbled in his pocket, pretending to feel for a cigarette, and as she came abreast of him he said, 'Go farther on, up the incline, and run. Go into the Crown.'

She did not pause now, and when a little way along the street she reached the opening off the pavement she turned sharply, and like a puff of wind went up the slope.

Rooney walked steadily on past the incline. But in order to see what Dennis was up to now he looked from side to side under the pretext of crossing the road and he saw Dennis's long legs carrying him and the bike up the slope at a surprising pace. And he estimated that if Nellie was to cross that patch of land and get down the street to the Crown, then she'd have to be going some.

He himself was almost running when he came out into the bottom end of Hudson Street and made his way back to the picture house. There was no sign of Dennis, but there was the sound of a train leaving the station, and he wondered if Dennis was watching it and thinking Nellie was on it.

At the door of the Crown he paused. He had often come here when he lived in this neighbourhood, for he had felt more at home here than in the flashier places in Shields. Upstairs was comfortable, and he had been on speaking terms with the manager. He looked down at himself. He couldn't go in like this. But there was nothing for it, he'd have to if she was in there waiting for him.

Feeling hot now for a number of reasons, he walked into the little lobby, and there she was, standing well back from the door. She was looking now neither amused nor pert, but her face showed deep concern and a touch of the old sadness. He went slowly over to her and when they confronted each other neither of them seemed to have anything to say. When Nellie did speak, it sounded to him a silly thing to say at the end of a chase.

'You've never had your tea yet, have you?'

'That's all right' – he rasped his prickly chin with his hand – 'I've a better appetite for it now.'

'It was good of you, but how did you know?'

'Jimmy met me coming out of work and asked me to give you the tip off what Dennis was up to. I saw you leaving and made to catch you up when that . . . he came out of the house, with pretty much the same idea.'

She linked her fingers together, then pulled at them as if straining to get them apart. 'I wouldn't have believed Dennis would do such a thing.'

'Well,' he went on, still rasping his chin, 'I suppose they're all curious.'

She looked quickly about the little hall. A few people were at the box office, but they hadn't reached there without having eyed them first.

'Do you think we could go outside now?'

'I wouldn't risk it if I were you, not for a bit anyway. I'd go in and see the picture, or some of it.'

'I want some place to talk to you.'

He remained silent.

Her voice was scarcely audible when, looking intently up into his face, she asked, 'Do you believe I'm living with a man . . . Brummell or any man?'

His eyes fell from hers to his boots. She was placing him on a spot. He felt a quick rising irritation and he wanted to say, 'I'd rather have you say you were outright than have you standing there lying to me.'

'I'm not, Rooney. Won't you believe me?'

'Look,' he lifted his head again, 'I didn't do it intentionally, but I heard what you said to Ma last Sunday night.'

Her eyes screwed up and she repeated, 'What I said?'

'Aye. Yes. You don't want me to tell you, do you?'

The colour mounted to her face and her head drooped.

'Yes, I remember. And it's quite true, all of it . . . but I'm not living with him. Rooney, it's difficult for me to make you understand.' She raised her eyes suddenly to his face. 'Look, meet me tomorrow night and I'll give you proof, will you? I can show you the proof. You remember that first letter I got?'

Letters. That was another thing. And then trying to open her door . . . Lord, why had he got himself into this? How could he put it without hurting her? How could he say, 'Stop writing letters to yourself?'

'Letters,' he cut in. 'That reminds me. Jimmy says that Ma means to get into your room. She's been raking round for keys.'

He had to turn his eyes away from her face. Her hand was on her lips, patting them like a child in distress. 'Could they find anything?' he asked lamely.

'Yes . . . No. Not unless they've got a key to the drawers . . . I'd better get back. I've been silly . . . foolish.' She drew in her breath and tried to recover herself; then added, 'But what can she find? Nothing. Only . . . Oh!' She joined her hands together again, and he said, 'If I was you I'd not send . . . well, what I mean is I'd get the fellow to stop . . .'

'There's no fellow,' she said quickly, almost harshly; 'haven't I told you! And don't look like that as if I was the world's worst liar. Anyway, he didn't send me the letters. Oh, dear God!' She moved her head from side to side, then patted her mouth again. 'If you weren't you, I could tell you everything. But I can't, I can't bring myself to.'

He could not understand what she was really driving at, but he could believe her when she said the letters hadn't come from a fellow. He could believe that all right, and he said so. 'Don't worry yourself about that,

207

only don't keep it up . . . the writing. I mean.'

He knew before her eyes began to widen that he had said the wrong thing.

'I mean . . . well, what I mean is . . .'

'You mean,' she whispered, 'you know that . . . I . . . I . . .' Her humiliation filled the vestibule. She seemed to become smaller with it; and her clothes lost their touch of class as her body slumped within them.

'It's all right, don't take on like that.' He was talking to her bent head, and he watched her shiver as she whispered, 'But how . . . how did you know? How could you?'

'Watching you write notes to the old fellow. You always made two dabs with your pencil at the end of a line. I saw them on the envelope. I'm no detective, but it just struck me, that's all. One of those things. It seemed, well, sort of part of you when you did it. I didn't think I had noticed it until I saw the dots.'

'O . . . o . . . oh!' She was groaning audibly. 'I was mad, but I wanted to give her something to think about . . . I . . .'

'Look. Come on. Aw! don't cry . . . not in here.'

'You must think I'm not all there . . . insane.'

'Don't be daft. Now look, don't give way like that. Go on in and see the picture, that's your best plan.'

'No, no.' Discreetly she wiped her eyes. 'I must go back, just in case . . . I never dreamed they'd try and get into my room.'

She turned her back on a group of people entering the door, then very softly she asked, 'Will you meet me tomorrow night?'

208

It was a long moment before he answered, 'Yes, all right. Where?'

She seemed to consider, then said, 'I don't know. Here, at the bottom of this street. At . . . at seven o'clock.'

'All right.' He nodded. 'At seven. Go on now, and I'll let you get in first. I'll say I've been doing overtime.'

She looked up at him, not only into his eyes, but at his hair, which was as usual, he knew, sticking out from beneath his cap; at his collar, and lastly his rough, red, blunt hands. Then without saying a word of farewell, she turned abruptly away and walked into the street, leaving him very conscious of himself and the eye of the cashier upon him.

What should he do now? He'd have to pretend he was waiting for her coming back, then slip out.

This is what he did do. And once in the street, he began to retrace his steps the way he had come, but leisurely now, giving her time to get well in. Outside the back door of No. 71 he hesitated long enough to rehearse his piece.

'Sorry I'm late,' he'd say. 'Had to do a spot of over-time. If . . . if you don't mind I'll take me tea up; I'm in a bit of a hurry the night to get out.' And he would be too, for the less he saw of Ma from now on the better.

There was no-one in the kitchen, or in the living-room, but when he reached the hall Ma came hurrying out of Grandpa's room. She looked agitated, and exclaimed, 'Oh, I thought it was Dennis.'

She took her apron and wiped the sweat from her face. 'He had a seizure . . . upstairs. I was all on my own until Dennis came in. He's gone for the doctor.'

She made no reference to Nellie, but he could hear a movement in the room, and knew she was in there. He could also hear the sound of the old man's laboured breathing.

Ma made no mention of his lateness but went into the kitchen, and he went slowly up the stairs. And as he washed and changed he wondered what had brought Grandpa upstairs. He would know Nellie was out, for she always went into him before leaving the house. Yet it wasn't likely he could have heard Ma at Nellie's door, for he was as deaf as a stone. Or was he? Perhaps he wasn't as deaf as he made out.

Rooney returned to the living-room, and, as Ma set his meal before him, Nellie came from the kitchen carrying a kettle of hot water. Her face under the make-up looked bleached. She did not look towards him, but he knew she was aware of him.

The door had hardly closed behind her when Ma exclaimed, 'Brazen piece! Gallivantin', that's all she does. She's brought this on, telling him she was going to take him away with her! Took him out in a taxi, weather like this an' all. She's got a lot to answer for . . . Is your steak all right?'

'Yes, thanks.'

'You were late.'

'Yes, I had to work overtime.'

The back door opened and Ma got to her feet. 'That'll be Dennis,' she said.

She went into the kitchen, and Rooney, reluctantly leaving the last piece of a very tender and well-cooked steak, went quickly out of the room and upstairs again, for it wouldn't do, he told himself, to meet that bloke face to face the night.

A little while later a ring at the door bell and the subsequent bustle spoke of the doctor's arrival. After ten minutes the front door closed again and the house became quiet.

As he sat before his fire drawing quick puffs on his cigarette he found he was anxious to know just how bad the old man was. But he refrained from going downstairs until he felt absolutely sure he would not meet up with Dennis. So when he again entered the living-room it was to find Ma preparing to go up to bed.

She looked him up and down as he stood in the doorway.

'I just wanted to know how he was,' he said.

'Oh! The doctor says he could last weeks . . . it's his heart. You never know . . . She's making herself a martyr, sitting in there.' Ma bounced her head towards the wall. 'That won't do much good now. She's to blame . . . she should never have taken him out.'

'Perhaps it was him climbing the stairs.'

'The stairs! What do you mean?'

'Well, you said he had the seizure upstairs.'

'I said no such thing, you must have been dreaming!' Ma's face showed a purple tinge. 'It was in the hall he had it.' She turned her back on him and gathered up a small clock from the mantelpiece, a glass of water from the table, and her glasses and prayer book from the sideboard, and saying stiffly through pursed lips, 'Good night,' she left him.

If anything could have proved that she had said the old man had had the seizure upstairs, this, Rooney thought, was it: to leave himself downstairs with Nellie, the dangerous woman.

Having waited a while to make sure that Ma was well in her room, he tip-toed to the front-room door and gave the gentlest of taps.

After a moment it was opened by Nellie, and he saw that she was no longer the Nellie of Friday night, nor yet the one of tonight, nor any Nellie he had seen, for her face was twisted and drawn with anxiety.

'How is he?' he whispered.

She shook her head. 'Very ill.'

'He'll likely get over it?'

She shook her head again. 'No, not this time . . . he's going.' She seemed to find talking difficult, and he stood at a loss what to say. But as he looked at her he knew he couldn't leave her here alone all night, with no-one to turn to should anything happen.

'Look,' he whispered, 'I'll be next door. I can sleep just as easily in a chair. Just give me a tap if you want me.'

She did not refuse this offer, but murmured, 'Thanks, I'd be grateful.'

Using some duplicity he went upstairs, none too quietly. Then after waiting a while he descended again in his stockinged feet, carrying two blankets and a book, and having settled himself in the armchair he proceeded to read to keep himself awake.

He had no idea at what time he had dropped off to sleep, but when he felt the tapping on his arm he woke, feeling cold and cramped.

'Will you come in? I . . . I think he's going . . . I can't hold him up.'

He was on his feet in a moment, and still only half awake he followed her into the room.

If he had never before seen a man die he would have known that Grandpa was coming quickly to the end of his time. Following Nellie's directions, he put his arm under the old man's shoulders and raised him up on to the pillows.

Grandpa's cheeks were hollowed and moving like bellows as he fought for breath. His eyes were fixed on Nellie, and between his gasping he made several efforts to speak.

'What is it, dear? What is it?' She hovered over him tenderly.

Again he made an effort, and his mouth formed a word, but no sound came. Then lifting one trembling hand he motioned with it towards a chair.

Nellie turned her head and said, 'Your coat? All right, I'll get it.'

She left his side and brought the coat to him. And when she laid it on top of the bedcover his hand fell on it and rested there for a moment. Then with an effort he pulled at one side of it and exposed the lining.

'Something in your pocket?' Nellie took a number of small pieces of paper and a calendar from the pocket and spread them on the bed, but the old man did not look at them. He waited a moment, and then put his hand into the pocket again and his trembling fingers pulled back the torn lining, and as he did so his eyes looked into Nellie's. And she, following his hand with hers, put it down the lining and pulled out a letter.

As if at the end of some great physical achievement, the old man sank into his pillows and rested now.

213

Rooney looked at the letter lying in Nellie's hands. It bore her name in large scrawling letters on the envelope: 'For Nellie Atkinson.' And as she went to put it into her pocket the old man's hands moved again, and she said, 'You want me to read it now?'

Struggling for breath, he brought out 'Aye.' And Rooney, from the other side of the bed, watched her slit open the envelope and take out two sheets of paper, and, holding them in one hand while with the other she held the old man's hand, she began to read.

She must have covered half the page when he saw her eyes lift. They were wide and staring. He watched her mouth fall slack as if in amazement. She sat on staring ahead at the row of furniture against the opposite wall. The old man's hand moved in hers, and she brought her gaze slowly to the letter again. And as she came to the end of it Rooney watched her head droop lower, and still lower. Then with a choking cry she was on her knees by the side of the bed, her head buried in the coverlet, her arms across the old man.

'Oh, Grandpa! Grandpa!'

His hands moved on her head and he spoke her name. 'Nellie.'

She raised her anxious face, and as the old man touched it Rooney felt he could not bear to witness any more, for never in his life, not even when his father died, had he felt like this.

Quietly, he went out and into the living-room, and for something to do he put the kettle on, and stood over it, waiting for it to boil. When the tea was made he poured out a cup and took it into her. She was sitting on a chair now, her face buried in the pillow beside that of the old man. And Rooney saw that he was dead.

Putting down the tea he went to her and, placing his hands beneath her arms, took her from the bed saying, 'There now. Come into the other room. Come on now.'

Her body hung limp in his hands. Her back was to him, and she swayed as she looked down on the old man. Then turning swiftly about she stood with her face buried in her hands, her sobs shaking her body.

It was the most natural thing in the world for him to put his hands on her shoulders and bring her to rest against him, and as he stood in the furniture-cluttered room and looked over her head to the slumped form of the dead old man on the bed he knew that he was experiencing the strangest moment of his life, for in him was a tenderness, such a tenderness that softened the whole of life, the whole world even.

When she drew herself away his being became empty, and as she dried her face he asked, 'Will I go and get her up?'

She shook her head, then said brokenly, 'I'll lay him out myself.'

'You can't do that.' His tone was shocked.

'Yes. Yes, I can. He wouldn't want her to touch him.' She looked up at him through swollen eyes. 'Would you give me a hand?'

'Yes.' He did not hesitate in complying with her request, but nevertheless he did not relish the task, and as the business proceeded he relished it less. But overweighing this was his admiration for the capability, the deftness, and, overall, the patient love which she brought to this last rite.

Grandpa had died at five minutes to three, and at half-past four he lay dressed for his last journey in the long shirt and stockings he had kept by him for years for this purpose. The room was left as tidy as it could be made, and on the bedside table Nellie had placed the flowers that had arrived in cellophane, and she had lit one ordinary candle. And when the electric light had been switched off Grandpa's face took on a happiness that the gentle glimmer of the candle seemed to draw from within him. And Nellie, after standing looking down on him for a moment, closed the door and went out with Rooney into the living-room.

As if now at a loss what to do, she sat on the edge of the chair and looked at the low embers of the fire. Her face was composed, but her eyes held so much sadness that he found it almost painful to look at her. He stood on the hearthrug, seemingly at a loss, too; then feeling that he must say something he brought up the topic of common irritation.

'She's going to get a surprise,' he said. 'It's a wonder she hasn't been down afore now.'

Nellie did not immediately answer, until the movement of his feet seemed to attract her attention, and then she said, 'She sleeps heavily. And her surprise will be in more ways than one . . . Would you read that?' She withdrew from her pocket the letter she had taken from Grandpa's coat.

He hesitated. 'You want me to?'

'Yes.'

He took the letter from her and having unfolded it slowly began to read.

'Nellie,

'I never was much of a hand at letter writing, but I want you to know one or two things. First, I want you to know that apart from my Elsie you've been the best person on earth to me. And if I'd been left to that 'un's mercy I'd have been dead years since. I hate her, Nellie, I've always hated her, and I've died hating her. It's always been my great fear that she'd get a penny of mine. If she had thought I had anything she'd have had it out of me years ago. You didn't think I had anything either, did you, Nellie? It's twenty-five years ago since I got the compen. for losing my two toes and the shock that knocked me deaf. That one thought we had gone through it. Both Elsie and me made her think that. But we hadn't. We spent a bit, but we put the rest by. We didn't believe in banks, so we kept it hid in a box screwed to the bottom shelf underneath the chest of drawers. You would have had to turn the whole thing upside down afore you could see anything was there. And it's been there for years. All the hundred and eighty-four pounds. And lately it got to worrying me, for although I'd left a letter saying you was to have it I got frightened of that 'un claiming her lot to be next of kin and doing you out of it. I had thought of giving it to you. But knowing you, you would have spent the lot on me, and I didn't want that, as I'm past enjoying anything but a good fire . . . and I can't get that.

'Well, Nellie, I thought and thought, and then I got an idea. I took the money and went out one day and went to Mr Pomphrey, the solicitor who fought my case years ago, and told him what I wanted. I wanted you to have the money, anonymous like, and for him to say you were to spend it and have a good time. But there was one condition: you had got to leave that shop. And he was to send you the letter on your birthday. And I asked him to get in touch with the insurance company and for them to pay you me insurance. There was a big snag here, as I wanted no letters sent, and I had to go back and sign a form for the insurance. I didn't feel too good that second time going out, and I got a taxi back. And Nellie, it did me heart good to see her face when she seen I'd been out again, and to make her pay for that taxi. Well, Nellie, you got the money, and it's made you young again, and the fun and enjoyment it's given me watching you will last me the remainder of me time.

'I'll be gone when you read this, Nellie, and there'll be nothing to keep you here any longer. Get away, away from her, Nellie. And you're to have me furniture, the solicitor knows. I told her you were going to take me away, but I knew I would never leave this house again, not alive anyway. Now, Nellie, you're not to worry. Take care of yourself and know that you were the only bright spot in my weary days since I lost Elsie.

'God bless you, lass, and send you happiness, for you deserve it.

'Grandpa.'

Rooney sat down. He was bemazed. It was incredible. All this business about a man keeping her. Even when he knew the fellow hadn't sent the letters he himself had still thought there was one. Talk about circumstantial evidence, and giving a dog a bad name. Well, this would just show you.

He sat on, looking at her, the letter still in his hand, and pondering; and it came as something of a shock to him that even now when he knew where the money had come from it made no real difference to the state of affairs, for hadn't she admitted herself that there was a fellow. By! the old man had started something when he played Fairy Godmother to her Cinderella, and not only to her but to himself, for he doubted if the tight-compressed little one could have brought him, even with his pity for her, to the state of unrest the present Nellie, the outcome of Grandpa's strategy, was doing. But there was one thing sure: she was going to miss the old fellow more now than she might have done had she not known of his kindness.

'Well, now you know.' She was still staring into the fire, and she spoke without turning her head.

He could find nothing to say.

'And me thinking the money came from Mr Bamford.' She shook her head derisively at herself.

'Bamford?' he repeated.

'Yes, Bamford, the other partner in the shop. He's older than Brummell. He used to manage the Wallsend one. They've got six shops altogether, and years ago when I was going to leave he came over himself and asked me to stay on. He gave me five shillings rise and told me if I kept things going he would not forget me. A year ago Brummell and he dissolved the partner-ship. I . . . I thought because of the condition that I should leave the shop that it was he who had arranged for me to have the money to spite Brummell. And I wasn't averse to spiting Brummell myself, because he's a pig of a man.' She made a derogatory sound in her throat and her lip curled slightly. 'What a gullible fool I've been! Just as if a close-fisted devil like him would give me anything. I don't suppose for a moment I ever crossed his mind again, only when I wrote, as I frequently did, to say yet again that the assistant had left . . . No-one in their right senses would have stayed there all those years. As Grace so often has kindly implied, I'm not all there, I'm odd. And I must be, stupidly odd.'

'You're no such thing.'

'Well, looking back now, I don't see myself as possessed of any powers of reasoning at all, for, lonely or not, I should have broken away. At least I should have got a new job. I could have done that . . . Well, now I've got to get one.'

Yes, he thought, a hundred and eighty-four pounds at the rate she had been spending this past week wouldn't last very long.

'What are you going to do?' he asked.

She rocked herself slightly. 'I don't really know. I've been looking round. There's plenty of work in factories and . . . and the big shops, but' – she put her hands between her knees – 'I've worked practically on my own for so long I'm scared of going among crowds. And I wouldn't like factory work anyway. I'll get a sewing job of some kind . . . Oh, I'll get a job.'

'You're leaving here, then?'

'Yes, that's one thing I am doing, as soon as Grandpa's gone.'

'Nellie,' he leant towards her, 'if there's anything I can do to help you, I'll do it . . .'

'Thanks, Rooney.' She glanced up at him. 'You don't know how much you've done already. If it hadn't been for you . . . well' – she moved her head – 'I don't know what I would have done.'

'I've done nothing yet. Look, Nellie.' He bent still nearer. 'I would like to ask you something just to get things clear.'

'Yes, Rooney?'

'Well, it's like this . . .' He was stuck. Her eyes were on him, waiting, but he couldn't say, 'Is there another fellow as you said, or have you just been making him up an' all.' This wasn't the time or place to ask a thing like that. It would really be indecent, and the old man lying dead next door and her in the state she was. He straightened up. 'It'll keep. I'll talk about it later.' He stood up and her eyes followed him, and at this moment there came the sound of a door opening overhead.

'Here she comes,' he said.

Nellie rose slowly and faced the door, and Rooney, who was only a foot away from her, did not lengthen the distance between them but waited, as she was doing, for Ma to enter.

They heard her step on the stairs; then the front-room door opening; and still they waited. Fully two minutes passed before she appeared in the living-room doorway and that she had received a shock was evident.

Rooney had a swift and laugh-inspiring picture of the old man standing outside himself with his thumb to his nose as she looked down on his recumbent remains.

'You think you're clever, don't you?'

Nellie made no reply; and Ma turning her glare on Rooney demanded, 'And what are you doing down here?'

'I've been here all night,' said Rooney quietly.

'What!' This bold answer evidently took Ma further aback. 'You've what? Well, there'll be a stop put to this, and I'm telling you.' She bustled past them. 'I'd thank you, Mr Smith, to keep out of the household concerns.'

'I asked him to stay with me.'

'Oh, you did, did you?' Ma turned with her usual agility. 'Whose house is this anyway?'

'It was Grandpa's, and, if I choose, it is mine now, furniture, insurance policy, and the rent book. He has left all he had to me. You can contact Mr Pomphrey, the solicitor. He will tell you everything you want to know.'

If Ma had had a seizure there and then Rooney would not have been surprised. He saw that she was finding breathing difficult, and no words would come to relieve her congested feelings. Although he could not rake up a spark of pity for her, yet he could no longer stay and witness her discomfort, so, with a small nod to Nellie, he went out and up the stairs to his room.

8

THE EFFECTS OF LOVE

The first thing Danny said to Rooney on his arrival at the depot was, 'You look under the weather. You all right?'

'Yes, I'm all right,' said Rooney. 'A bit tired . . . been up all night . . . The old man died.'

'Oh. Sorry to hear that,' said Danny. 'Sudden?'

'Yes, a bit.'

'I always think death around Christmas time seems worse somehow, puts a damper on things. And have you noticed that all the accidents seem to gather around this time an' all?'

'Cheerful Charlie Chester,' said Bill, mounting the cab. 'Come on, man, and let's gang and meet an accident, it's never been my policy to wait for things to come to me.'

This quip brought a smile even from Albert, and Rooney, pulling himself up beside him into the loaders' cab, thought, Funny, he's happy again.

Rooney found himself watching Albert covertly most of the morning, for he was intrigued by the air of suppressed excitement about him. Today was Albert's last day on the job and tomorrow he was leaving the town. Perhaps it was the prospect of a new start, or . . . having her back again. Well, whatever it was it was making him easy to work with, just like it used to be.

But that wasn't much good, seeing it was his last day.

The loader had stopped opposite Honeycroft, and Rooney asked, 'You going to pay your last respects to old Double-Barrelled, Albert?'

'Not likely,' said Albert. 'I want to finish quiet.'

'Go on, man,' said Fred. 'She might give you a Christmas box if she knows you're leaving.'

'You talking of Christmas boxes?' said Bill, coming up with a bin on his shoulder. 'Wait a minute . . . I bet you don't cap this one.' He tipped the contents of the bin into the loader. 'She—' He nodded towards a house hidden by a tall hedge, and mimicking what was to his mind a superior tone said, '"There you are," she said, "and will you be good enough to remove the rubbish near the gate?" . . . You know what she offered me? Threepence!'

'No!'

'Aye, she did.'

'What did you say?'

'What did I say? I said, "Thank you, missus, but you'll be needin' that afore me, and we can't take on all that junk, we're nearly full, there's other folk's dustbins to be emptied."'

They all laughed, and Danny said, 'Well, you know, Bill, if everybody you met the day gave you threepence you'd have a bit. You must admit some of them won't even give you a kind word.'

'Aye,' said Bill. 'Well, she can keep her bloody threepence, and I can tell her what to do with it. Great big hoose like that an' all. Why, they never offer you threepence in Dock Street.'

'No, that's why they're still living in Dock Street,' put in Fred.

They dispersed laughing, and as Rooney went down the sidewalk of Honeycroft he thought he would have had to take the threepence rather than hurt the woman's feelings. Yet the act of receiving any kind of present always put him on edge, for he had never been able to accept a gift gracefully . . . he liked giving, but hated receiving. Why, he had never worked out.

When he reached the yard he was surprised to find not the old woman at the kitchen door but a man, a round tubby individual with a pointed beard and almost bald head, which brought back to his mind Danny's description of the son who lived in France. This fellow looked French all right, and when he spoke the impression was confirmed, for his English had just a trace of something different about it. His tone was polite, even chummy, not a bit like the old girl's.

'Hallo,' he said. 'I wonder if you'd mind taking this stuff?' He pointed to a pile of cardboard boxes and old clothes lying under the covered way.

Rooney looked at the salvage. It would mean holding up the loader until he came back and collected it, and some oaths from Bill for getting behind, but it was dry stuff, and the fellow was a nice civil bloke.

'I'll be back for it,' he said.

'Is he going to take it?'

The door the tubby fellow had pulled to behind him was jerked out of his hand, and there stood the old lady.

'Oh, that one will take it,' she said; 'he's all right . . . it's the other one. If you had been here and heard him you would . . .'

'You go in, Mama, it's too cold out here.'

The little fellow's voice was coaxing, and to Rooney it sounded funny to hear a grown man calling his mother Mama.

When he returned and was gathering up the stuff the man came to the door again and extended his hand towards him palm downwards.

'Oh, that's all right, sir.'

'Good lord!' The ejaculation was full of surprise, and the only reason for it that Rooney could see was that he had hesitated in putting out his hand. The man stood looking at him as he rammed the rags into the boxes.

'Cold job?'

'Yes, a bit, sir.'

'Perhaps you could help me about getting rid of some stuff. I'm clearing out the top rooms. There's two brass and iron beds and two mattresses dropping to bits with moth, and a stack of other stuff. It's no use to anyone; would your people take it?'

'Yes, yes, they'll send a lorry to collect it for you. All you need to do is to phone the cleansing superintendent. The only thing is you'll have to get it down and stacked, say in the yard here.'

'Oh, I'll manage that. Thanks, I'll do that. They'd come within a few days, would they?'

'Yes. You tell them you're in a hurry to get cleared, and they'll meet you, I'm sure.'

'Lance!' The door was jerked again, but this time the little fellow held on to the knob.

'Lance. I forbid you to dismantle those rooms.'

The little man pulled a face and winked, and Rooney, laden with the boxes, went across the yard smiling to himself as he heard the fellow say, 'Now, Mama.'

Mama. It was laughable, but he seemed a nice bloke. He didn't envy him his job with the old girl, though, yet somehow he thought he'd be able to manage her all right . . . Mama's attacks were likely to bounce off that round, stolid body of her son.

It was when they were having their break at the end of the road that he showed them the half-crown, and he did it more to cause a bit of fun than in any form of show-off, for it was agreed among them that what they received they stuck to. Pooling tips had years ago brought up some dissatisfaction, as it had been suspected that all donations had not found their way into the common purse. No-one had been accused, but four of them had felt that it was odd how Fred was always unlucky.

Albert was the first to comment, he having been at grips with the old lady. 'Well, I'm damned!' he said. 'She gave you that?'

Rooney nodded – it was more of a joke when it was supposed to have come from the old girl.

'It's that bloody soft-soap look he wears,' said Bill. 'Makes all the old wives go for him. From Monday I'm partnering you, lad. Round Christmas, anyway. I'll rattle the bin lids and you stick near the back doors and smile at the dames. If you do your stuff properly we'll get enough to get a television.'

'Who'll get the television?'

'Me,' said Bill.

'I thought you would,' laughed Rooney.

'Take some smiles to draw out half-crowns,' said

Danny. 'Yet the old girl used to be pretty open-handed at one time, but she's had to draw in her horns these last years . . . Well, come on, let's get going . . . this won't get you your television, Bill. It's a watch I'm wanting meself.'

With back-chat and laughter they spread themselves out again, and for the rest of the day they were all merry, seeming to make an effort to send Albert off with pleasant memories. And at four-thirty, when Albert shook hands all round, he looked as if he were genuinely sorry to be leaving them. And to Rooney as they walked together out of the gates for the last time, he repeated what he had said earlier, 'I'll miss you, man.' And he added, 'There aren't many blokes like you about, you know . . . easy to get along with.'

Alone and walking homewards, his head down against the cutting wind that spoke of snow, Rooney was finding that his liking for Albert went much deeper than he had imagined. Perhaps it was because Albert had shown his own liking for him. There might be something in that. Yet he hadn't imagined that Albert, or any other fellow for that matter, considered him other than an ordinary bloke. And anyway, that's all he was, and he knew it. But it gave a chap a bit of a lift inside to hear something like that. That's how Nellie must have felt when she thought her boss had remembered her services – sent her all gay and carefree . . .

His mind was back on Nellie; it really hadn't been off her all day, but he had made his work keep it layered down. But now he'd have to think of her . . . he wanted to think of her and what he was going to say to her. But – he pulled himself up – what he had to say must wait

230

till after the funeral; he couldn't talk about such things until this business was over. And anyway, what he'd better set his mind to during the next couple of days was to find some place to live, and quick.

Before he entered the back door he knew there was company, for the buzz of conversation reached the yard. Committee, he thought, to debate Nellie getting the policy, and whether a rent book could really be left to anybody. And they certainly were going at it, he considered when he entered the kitchen. The door leading to the living-room was closed, but he could distinctly make out Danny's high-pitched voice and that of his wife's, but as he changed his shoes he was a little surprised to hear Jimmy's deep tone, too, and the broad twang of Johnny. They hadn't lost much time . . . must have come straight from work, the lot of them.

His opening of the door seemed to cut off their voices, for no-one spoke as he entered the room. Then Ma, from her position in front of her daughter and the three men, turned and confronted him, saying 'Well!'

It was no new addition to her vocabulary, and it left Rooney thinking, Aye, well, what's it about this time?

'You've got an eye-opener coming to you.' Ma's voice seemed to be dragged from the depths of her chest, and each word was ominous.

Oh my Lord! was she going to start on him in front all of these?

'You took her side, didn't you? I always knew you were gullible. But I warned you.'

'How was he to know,' said Jimmy, 'any more than the rest of us?'

'What should I have known?' asked Rooney quietly.

Ma's head came forward like a charging bull about to gore its victim. 'That she was a thief!'

Rooney said nothing to this but stared back into Ma's infuriated face.

'She's one of a gang . . . she's a thief.'

'Nellie?' Rooney felt his nose expanding as his lips stretched, allowing for the incredulity in his voice.

'Yes, Nellie! She was in on the robbery at the house in Westoe, the Bailey-Crawfords' house.'

Rooney looked towards Jimmy, and he nodded sadly and said, 'Yes, it's hard to believe, but they've been here and taken her.'

'Taken Nellie?'

'Taken Nellie,' mimicked Ma.

'What did I tell you?' said Johnny, turning and spitting into the fire.

Rooney looked sharply at him. It was evident that Johnny had it in for him and that he had spilled the beans to the old girl, and Ma's next words left no doubt in his mind.

'I'm giving you notice, Mr Smith, I'm having no improper carry-on in my house.'

'Don't worry,' said Rooney quickly. 'I'm going. I was going to give it to you. And as regards improper carrying-on, I'd better warn you to be careful what you say.'

'Warn me! I've got proof. And you're welcome to her when she comes out of jail. I always said it would be either jail or the asylum. Sending flowers to herself! Did you ever!'

'She never sent flowers to herself.'

'She did.' It was May speaking, and Rooney turned sharply and confronted her.

'How do you know?'

'I happen to have been told by the proprietor of Portal's when I went in to order our wreath. I gave her this address, and she said she knew it as the boy had brought some flowers here during the week, and she described who had bought them.'

'After you asked her.'

May's face tightened. 'This matter concerns our family.'

'She likely wrote the letters to herself as well, for there's nothing in her room, only this, and she had no time to clear anything up today.' Ma snatched up a piece of paper from the table, and with her lip curled back read:

> 'You taught me things I never knew;
>   The fascination of your sandy mane,
> Spun from the sun itself into golden strands,
> A lair for my hands,
> Your hair.
>
> Your neck,
> Tight, firm, forcing its strength against your collar in
>   corded bands . . .

'Licentious twaddle! Did you ever!'

Slowly Rooney's skin began to burn as the five pairs of eyes were levelled at him, and only in time did he stop his hand from going up to his head. Their eyes were moving from his hair to his neck, but he could see that Ma was only now approaching the conclusion that the others had already arrived at, and as he watched the purple tinge creep into her face Jimmy began to laugh, a deep rumbling sound as usual, and it distracted attention from Rooney for a moment.

May said tartly, 'It's neither the time nor the place, Jimmy, to practise your sense of humour.'

Jimmy sat down. 'I can't help it. He knows what I'm laughing at, don't you?' He nodded towards Rooney.

Rooney did not answer. Jimmy was likely thinking of his request asking him to put Nellie on her guard, and he was no doubt now thinking that it was he, Rooney, who had written Nellie the letters. Over a thing like that you would either have to laugh or get blazing mad. He was blazing mad himself; he was filled with such an anger that he was shaking with it. And it wasn't only against this lot, but against Nellie . . . pinching, stealing! My God! Jewellery an' all. That's where she had got her money . . . What was he thinking? What about Grandpa's letter? Yes. Aye, there was that. But what was a hundred and eighty-four pounds these days, especially the way she had been spending; and out of a job and looking up swell furniture.

'You've been taken for a ride.' It was Johnny's voice, thick with satisfaction.

'Well, mind you're not taken for one, and in an ambulance.'

The aggressiveness inside himself startled him. For two pins he would have laid Johnny on his back.

Sensing this, Johnny retreated behind the armchair,

234

and now Dennis's voice took up where Johnny had left off.

'You won't be able to afford her ruby necklaces unless you find another appointment.' Each precise word carried a sneer.

Rooney had always wanted to hit this bloke – it had dated from that first meeting – but in the act of swinging about he stayed his hand. 'What did you say?'

'You heard; I have no need to repeat it.'

Rooney advanced a step. 'Say it again. What did you say about a necklace?'

Dennis stretched his neck out of his white collar. 'I said that you won't be able to buy her one, not like the one she was wearing.'

'What kind of a necklace?'

'A ruby one. I've told you.'

'Yes. And the brazen piece has been sporting it for days,' cried Ma. 'Daring to wear it . . . the nerve! If that Mr Crawford hadn't seen her in King Street and recognised it and followed her here, she would have got off with it. Likely gone on.'

'Six beads hanging from fil . . . from a sort of tin affair?' cut in Rooney, still staring at Dennis.

'For your knowledge, the tin, as you call it, was old silver.'

'But they couldn't take her for that.'

'Why not? It was part of the stuff they're looking for.'

'It wasn't! It isn't!' He swung about, looking rapidly from one face to the other. 'I gave it to her.'

'You?'

'Aye, me.'

'You gave it to her? Where did you get it?' This came from all quarters at once.

'Never mind; I gave it to her.'

'You're lying.'

Dennis delivered this flatly and with authority. 'She's one of a gang. I know, for I trailed her.'

'Yes, you trailed her. And you trailed me an' all. All through the park, up Stanhope Road, and she dodged you up the bank, near the station, didn't she?'

Dennis's face was a study. He looked comical with surprise.

'You sneaking rat, you!' Rooney moved nearer.

'What! How dare you! How dare you speak to me like that! You forget yourself. All I can add is that Nellie's let herself down much further than I'd imagined . . . an ash-binner!'

As Rooney's fist crashed into his chin, Dennis's feet shot up as if he were demonstrating a backward dive. He fell straight across Jimmy's knees; and in a moment the room was filled with a bedlam of cries and exclamations of horror.

'My God!'

'You beast, you!'

'What did I tell you?'

'You've killed him!' cried May.

Rooney, rubbing his fist up and down the front of his waistcoat, cried back to this, 'It would be a damn good job, too.'

He knew that he would never have spoken like that to a woman if he hadn't been possessed, but he knew he wasn't himself – far from it, for he was possessed by

236

a pulsing life that was speeding up his thinking and his actions and loosening his tongue. He could have set about the lot of them in this moment, Ma an' all. Oh yes, Ma . . . he'd love to land one at Ma.

He pulled himself together. He must be going barmy . . . he'd better get out.

The same thought was in Ma's mind. 'Leave my house,' she cried, 'before I call the police.'

'I'm leaving your house, don't worry,' he barked back at her. 'But I'll be back for me things the morrow.'

'You'll find them on the street.'

'You do, if you dare!'

He seemed to be towering over her. 'You touch one piece of my furniture and I'll have you up. I will, mind, if it's the last thing I do. It's about time somebody told you just how far you can go. Mind, I'm warning you.' He pointed at the astonished and seemingly paralysed Ma.

He moved away towards the door, past Johnny and Jimmy as they assisted the groaning and bemused Dennis on to a chair.

May, turning from her husband's side, like an angry vixen, cried at him, 'This is what comes of taking a . . . a scavenger' – she used the old disparaging title – 'into the house! You're a low, common . . .'

'Aye, all that,' he cut in sharply, 'an' more. But there's one thing I'll tell you: I'll have to drop a bit to come down to this family's level.'

He went into the kitchen, banging the door behind him, and there, rapidly changing into his coat and shoes again and stuffing his old slippers into his pocket, he left the house. But once outside, in the dark of the back lane, he paused and wiped the sweat from his fore-head. What had come over him? He had never had a row like that in his life. He'd never knocked a man down before; nor had he ever felt the blood racing through his brain as it was now, nor had his thinking been so keen . . . Nellie . . . they'd taken Nellie because of the necklace. But how? Why? Why hadn't she told them where she had got it?

He didn't have far to go for that answer. She thought he had pinched it and was shielding him . . . Oh, Nellie!

What was he to do? He asked this of himself as he stood in the main road. He could go to the police and say he gave it to her, and that he'd got it out of the bin. But would they believe him? Wouldn't it be better if he went and saw the son and explained to him what he thought had happened – that the old girl, his mother, must have thrown the necklace away that day with all the rubbish, and when her jewellery and stuff was stolen she had imagined it had been taken then. It must have come out of that box with the bairns' toys . . . The toys! That was an idea . . . Bill's bairns might still have the toys. If Bill came along with him and said he'd picked up the toys for the bairns at the same time as he himself had taken the beads, then they would be more likely to believe him – or should he go by himself?

He stood pondering beside a lamp-post. My God! Just what should he do? If Bill came with him and became implicated, it might mean them both getting the sack for helping themselves. And Bill couldn't afford the sack. Every now and again somebody had to be a guinea pig and provide a test-case, and like as not they'd make this one, for there had been one or two rumpuses lately over totting . . . But there was still Danny: he'd go to Danny; Danny would know what to do.

9

THE CHAMPION

When Mrs D. opened the door, he almost pushed past her, saying, 'I'm sorry for disturbing you, but I've got to see Danny.'

'Yes. Well, come in,' said Mrs D., laughing now at his back as he went along the passage. 'Is something wrong?'

Danny turned from the table, with his fork holding a melting-looking piece of buttered finnan haddock paused halfway to his mouth. The fork went to his plate again, and he asked, 'What's up, man?'

'Everything, I think,' said Rooney.

'Nothing that a cup of tea won't better,' said Mrs D., going to the hob for the teapot.

'You know Nellie, the one at the house? She's been I . . . I . . . locked up,' he stammered in his agitation.

'Locked up!'

'Aye. They think she took the necklace – a ruby necklace.'

'A ruby necklace! What necklace?' Danny pushed back his chair.

'Here, drink this up,' said Mrs D.

Rooney took the tea without the usual acknowledgements. 'What was stolen from the Bailey-Crawfords' place. But I gave it to her.'

'Look,' said Danny, 'drink that tea and then start at the beginning.'

Rooney took only a short sip from the cup, then put it down and rubbed his hand tightly over his mouth.

'It's like this. Some weeks since, I was pushing the muck back when I saw a box full of bairns' toys and beads. Bill took these for the bairns, and I saw a necklace affair and pocketed it, meaning to pass it on to Bill later. You see' – Rooney's eyes flicked downwards – 'you came on the scene. And then it slipped me mind. And after I'd cleaned it up, it didn't look a bairn's piece, so . . . so I give it to her . . . Nellie. Well, when I got in the night, the house is up in arms. They'd been and taken her . . . the polis. If she'd said where she'd got it, they would have been an' collared me afore now, but she must have kept mute, thinking I'd pinched the thing.'

'Well, I'll be damned!' Danny leant back in his chair and shook his head. 'I've told you, this is what comes of totting. I've told the lot of you time and again.' He stood up and reached for his pipe off the mantelpiece. 'Now we're in a hell of a fix. You and Bill'll be for it in some way. As for me, who's supposed to be in charge of the damn lot of you, I'll be up on the carpet.'

'But they were only bairns' pieces, man.'

'Bairns' pieces,' said Danny. 'Bairns' pieces be damned! Ruby necklaces!'

'Aye. But don't you see, she must have thrown it away with the old toys.'

'The only thing I can see,' said Danny, 'is that this is going to cause a bit of a stink, whichever way it goes. What do you propose doing now?'

244

Rooney had come here to Danny thinking that he might supply a solution, but now, to his own surprise, he laid out the plan of action that he had himself thought of earlier. 'I was for going to Bill's to see if there's owt left of the bairns' toys, and taking them to the fellow . . . the son, and asking him if he recognised them, and telling him how I came across the necklace.'

'Yes,' said Danny, 'you could do that.' And taking the action further, he went on, 'You could say that you took the bairns' toys an' all; that would cut Bill out, for you never know where this might end. He's got six bairns where you've only got yourself.'

'Yes, that's true,' said Rooney. 'Yes, I've been thinking about that. I'll say I picked up the lot.'

'Where's me coat?' said Danny.

'Where you going?' asked Mrs D.

'To Bill's.'

'But your tea, Danny.'

'That can wait . . . Come on.'

'I'm sorry, Mrs D.,' said Rooney.

'That's all right,' she said. Then laughing, she added, 'Oh, Rooney, you do get into fixes. Never mind' – she patted his shoulder – 'I'll come and visit you in jail. And look . . . leave those slippers here.'

He handed her the slippers as he smiled weakly. 'There's many a true word spoken in a joke, Mrs D.'

With the exception of Nancy, the eldest child, who let them in, Bill and his entire family were seated around the small table in the living-room. Bill rose, wiping his mouth, asking, 'What's up? Don't tell me it's Albert again, and the black fellow's back.'

'No, it's not him,' said Danny. 'Can we have a word with you?'

'Aye.' Bill looked at his brood. 'Come on. Get that stuff golloped up and get outside with you.'

Five pairs of eyes fixed themselves, first on Danny, then on Rooney, but there was no sign of golloping.

Bill signalled for his wife, who, with utter complacency, was eating a meat pie. 'Get them moving.'

'They've just started,' she said. 'Can't you go into the other room?'

Bill's face took on a slight tinge of colour as he retorted, 'No, we can't.'

'Here a minute.' Danny, taking Bill by the arm, moved towards the front door, and there, in a low voice, he roughly explained the situation.

But if Danny saw reason to keep the matter from the children, Bill did not, for coming back to the centre of the room, he cried, 'Now look, Danny, it's a sore point with me. I've said afore and I say again, what's chucked away belongs to nobody.'

Oh, my God! thought Rooney. He's not going to start on those lines now.

'That's all very well,' said Danny, 'but a woman's been pinched.'

'That's too bad, and it should never have happened, because stuff that's been classed as abandoned material—'

'Look, Bill.' Rooney quickly forestalled a debate on Bill's ideas of the moral rights of refuse. 'All I came for is to see if you've got any of the bits left, to help me prove they were picked up altogether.'

Bill turned to his wife. 'Those blocks and beads and

things I brought for the bairns, where are they?'

'Oh' – she rose leisurely – 'what's left of them should be in the bottom of the cupboard. Get down, Nancy, and look.'

Nancy got down. 'The monkey's broke,' she said, 'but the blocks are here.'

'There were beads . . . lots of beads,' said Bill.

Nancy stood up, saying nothing, but her hand went protectively to her none-too-clean neck, where hung an assortment of different-coloured and -shaped beads.

'Look,' said Rooney, 'I'll buy you a fine strap for Christmas . . . pearls.'

'Will you?'

'Yes, I will, honest.'

Slowly, Nancy pulled the beads over her head and handed them to Rooney. Then going down on her knees again, she gathered up the bricks and the monkey.

'I'll say I picked the lot up together and later passed them on to you,' said Rooney to Bill.

'You'll say nowt of the sort; I'll stand by what I did, and I'll maintain what I said . . . Once in the dustbin—'

'Aye, we know all about that, man,' impatiently put in Danny. 'But what about the court that recently took the view that the blokes on that particular corporation were stealing 'cause they picked out some lead from the loader?'

'I know all about that,' said Bill, 'but that was different . . . it was in the depot. And once it's in the shed it's Corporation property, but not afore.'

'You're splitting hairs, Bill. You take my advice and let Rooney do as he wants.'

247

'No bloody fear!'

'Be nice if you lost your job.'

Bill turned to his wife, growling, 'Damned good thing if I did! It'd make you go out and get some of that lazy fat off you.'

Mrs Stubbly seemed in no way put out, but Rooney thought, This is marriage: and his mind made to leap away from the subject. But he stayed it. There were other marriages – Danny's for instance, and many more like it.

'Well, what do you propose doing?' Bill turned to Rooney.

'I'm going to take these things up to the house and show them to the son. He seems a decent bloke . . . I saw him this morning. And perhaps the old woman will remember that the necklace wasn't with the other jewellery. Perhaps she'll remember . . .'

'Aye, it is perhaps. Sounds a daft scheme to me. And that old girl always struck me as being up the pole a bit. She'll not be able to remember what she did or when she did it.'

'Not a bit of it,' put in Danny. 'She's all there.'

'Well, have your own way about her,' said Bill, 'but if you take my advice' – he had turned to Rooney – 'you won't go near the house. Go to the polis station right away. If you go and see this fellow first, you could be brought up for intimidating witnesses or something.'

'Intimidating me grannie's aunt!' said Danny shortly. 'There's been no case yet. Look, Rooney, it's up to you. How do you feel about going to the station?'

How did he feel about it . . . and everything else? He felt terrible.

'If you go to the fellow you'll still have to come back to the station,' warned Bill, ''cause remember, it's in the polis's hands now.'

Yes, he thought, there was that in it: he'd still have to face the police.

'Well, what's it to be?' asked Danny.

'I'll do as Bill says, I'll go to the station. But you needn't come, or Bill.'

'Go on, get moving.' Danny gave him a shove. 'Come on, Bill.'

'You won't forget me pearls, Mr Rooney?' called Nancy as they went out.

'No,' said Rooney. 'I won't forget your pearls.'

'For a bloke who has nowt to do with women,' said Bill as they hurried down the street, 'you manage pretty well . . . you get into more scrapes than a Hollywood film star.'

'Never mind talking of women,' said Danny. 'What we've got to make up our minds about is what Rooney's going to say.'

'That's simple,' put in Rooney. 'I'll just say I picked the stuff out of the loader and gave it to Bill's bairns later.'

'You know you'll likely be in for it from Bannister, and maybe the office?'

'Aye, I know all about that. But there are plenty of other jobs. I won't starve. Anyway, a change will do me good. Best thing that could happen, I think.'

Both Danny and Bill looked at him. But he did not answer their looks, for he was at the moment concerned with himself. Aye, perhaps it would be the best thing that could happen. What did it matter if the Corporation did give him the push? There were the shipyards, the mines, the factories. He'd get a better job, and, like Albert, make more money . . . and for almost the same reason.

'What says you get ten years?' said Bill, as they entered the police station.

'Don't joke, man,' said Danny.

Rooney said nothing, until they were in the main office, and there it was he who answered the duty officer's enquiry as to what their business was.

'I'd like to see the inspector, please. It's . . . it's about a woman you locked up the day. She was wearing a necklace, a ruby one . . . I know where it came from.'

The policeman looked from one to the other, then said, 'Take a seat, will you?'

They did not sit down but watched him go out. And when he did not return for some minutes Bill, looking about him at the various notices on the walls, said, 'Gives you the willies, don't it? I'd swear me mother's life away to get out of here.'

Again Danny cautioned him: 'Be quiet, man!'

The policeman returned, and with him a sergeant and another man in plain clothes. The sergeant looked hard at Danny and said, 'Macallistair, isn't it?'

'Yes, sergeant.'

'Well now' – he looked at Bill and Rooney – 'what can I do for you?'

'It concerns me,' said Rooney.

'Yes?'

'You took Nellie, Miss Atkinson, up because she was wearing a necklace the day. She never stole it, I gave it to her.'

After a long stare at Rooney, the sergeant said, 'What's your name?'

'Joseph Rooney Smith.'

'Just a moment.' The sergeant walked to a door, knocked, then entered the room.

The policeman at the counter was now dealing with a man wanting to know whether a fountain pen he had brought in two months previously had yet been claimed. The plain-clothes man was casually examining articles in various cubby holes, and Danny, Bill, and Rooney stood stock still waiting.

The door at the far end of the room opened again, and the sergeant appeared in the doorway, saying, 'Come in here, will you?'

One after the other, they went into the room, and the inspector sitting at the desk looked up at them.

'Which of you is Joseph Rooney Smith?'

'I am.'

'You want to make a statement?'

'Yes, sir. I want to tell you how Miss Atkinson got the necklace, and where I got it.'

'Go on.'

Rooney went on, surprising himself with his lucidity. But when he had finished, the inspector did not seem at all impressed, or convinced. He looked across at an officer sitting writing at a table at the opposite side of the room; he looked at Bill, then Danny; he looked at the beads, blocks, and the broken monkey reposing on his desk; and finally he looked at Rooney.

'You say you took these things out of the lorry. Have you any proof of this?'

'Yes . . . No.'

'No? . . . No proof?'

Rooney stopped himself from glancing towards Bill. He hadn't thought about proof. In a few words these blokes could twist you about till you didn't know which end of you was up or what you had said.

'That's a pity.'

Bill shuffled from one foot to the other.

'Mrs Bailey-Crawford, she would recognise them, and remember when she threw them away,' said Rooney. 'They're likely the son's toys. He might remember them, an' all.'

The inspector stared at him, then said slowly, 'Yes, you might have something there. But it would have been better if you had . . .'

'He has got proof.' All eyes were now on Bill. 'He never took them things, I took them for me bairns. And Danny here' – Bill's head jerked sideways – 'Danny's our overman, he was coming to the loader and he's dead nuts on us touching stuff, so I stuffed the bits in me pocket, and Rooney, seeing the red beads, pocketed them an' all. He meant to hand them over to me for the bairns, but he saw they weren't a bairn's piece, that's about it.'

The inspector again said nothing for a moment. Then he asked, 'Why didn't you say this at first?'

Rooney cut in just as Bill was about to speak. 'Because he's got a big family, sir, and we'll likely get pulled over the coals and I didn't want him to get into trouble or anything. If it hadn't been for me taking the necklace there'd have been none of this. These' – he pointed to the table – 'are only bairns' bits and no use to anybody. You can see that, sir.'

The inspector moved the blocks about with the point of his finger, and without raising his eyes said, 'You know there was quite a lot of plate and jewellery taken from the Bailey-Crawford residence?'

'Yes, I knew there had been a burglary.'

'When did you pick up the necklace?'

'Oh, it was afore that.'

'How long before?'

With the eyes of the others upon him, Rooney stood considering. 'It was on a Monday. I moved to my digs on a Saturday. Yes, it was on a Monday. It would be November . . . November the twenty-first.'

'Are you sure of this?'

'Yes, sir; I'm sure.'

'Well, we'll be able to check this with Mrs Bailey-Crawford. She'll remember when she threw the stuff away.'

'Let's hope so.' Bill's forefinger travelled the length of his nose.

'What?' The inspector's mild blue eyes were on Bill. 'Why do you say that?'

Bill moved his feet, then his shoulders, and then his head. 'Well, it appears to me the old girl's a bit 'centric. If you're to go by what she stuffs in her bin she must brew about six pounds of tea a week. Her bin's always full of wet tea-leaves. She lives on tea.'

The inspector's eyes lingered on Bill for some moments. Then without making any comment on this information he addressed Rooney. 'You know, of course, we'll have to go into all this?'

'Yes, sir.'

'Have you anything further to tell me?'

'No, sir, nothing. I've told you everything, and the truth . . . Sir?'

'Yes.'

'Will you be able to let Miss Atkinson out now?'

'Well, we can't do that at the moment, Mr Smith.'

Rooney's heart took a painful plunge downwards. 'But, sir, I . . . I swear it was me that gave it to her.'

'Why do you think she didn't say so when she was questioned?'

'Because . . . because, sir, she must have thought I'd pinched it, and . . . and . . .' The words, 'and she was shielding me', seemed to assume an almost sacredness, and he found it impossible to utter them. He knew that were he to speak them, the meaning that he dared not allow himself to recognise would fill the room and would be reflected from the five pairs of eyes as knowledge to be laughed at.

Yet without him going further there came an amused light into the eyes of the inspector, and a quirk to his lips as he asked, 'You know Miss Atkinson well?'

'No . . . that's . . . well, only four weeks.'

Bill coughed, and Rooney, without looking at him, thought, If he makes any funny cracks I'll hit him

'Well, Mr Smith, we'll have to contact Mrs Bailey-Crawford.'

'Yes, sir.'

'And I don't think there's any need for you two to stay.' The inspector was now looking at Danny and Bill. And it was with something akin to disappointment in his voice that Bill said, 'But it was me what took the bits.'

'Well, that's a matter for the Corporation. We'll

contact you if we need you. Leave your names and addresses in the office.'

Both Bill and Danny turned and looked at Rooney as the inspector continued, 'But we would like you to remain for a short while, Mr Smith.'

'Yes, sir.' Rooney now sounded distinctly nervous, and Bill, unable to suppress a wisecrack even within the portals of the police station and the inner sanctuary itself, said, 'Well, so long, mate; see you in Durham.'

'Will you come along to us when you come out?' asked Danny, when they were once again in the outer office.

'That's heartening,' laughed Bill. 'When he comes out!'

'For God's sake shut up, Bill!' Danny turned away, saying, 'We'll expect you, lad.'

Rooney nodded, and when he saw them pass through the doorway a tiny feeling of panic assailed him.

'Take a seat,' said the policeman from behind the counter.

Rooney took a seat, and as he did so he glanced at the clock, and was amazed to see it was only a quarter to seven. He had seemed to have done so much and experienced so many different emotions since leaving work that he could not credit that it had all happened in under two hours.

The pendulum of the wall clock swung slower than that of any clock he had ever seen, and its hand took much longer to move from minute to minute. This was borne out when, after listening to the policeman answering the telephone numerous times, dealing with the report of a lost child, a purse theft, and an almost tearful boy giving notification of a stolen bicycle, the clock struck seven.

It was almost on its last stroke that the door opened and Mr Bailey-Crawford entered. At the sight of him, Rooney half rose from his seat, then sat down again. The little man looked towards him, but without recognition, then went straight to the counter where he gave his name. A few seconds after the policeman had spoken into the phone, the office door opened and the sergeant came out, and when Rooney saw him take Mr Bailey-Crawford in, he felt as if he was witnessing the retirement of the jury and that their verdict of guilty was a foregone conclusion. He had thought old Double-Barrelled's son a nice bloke, but no bloke appeared nice inside here if he was on the other side of you, so to speak. He could understand now Bill's saying that a fellow could be made to half swear his life away . . . And Nellie; what in the name of God had she felt like when they brought her in? And what was she feeling like now? She was somewhere in here, likely in a cell. God in heaven! He got to his feet, and as he did so the policeman glanced up, and he went over to him.

'Miss Atkinson – you know, she's small . . . slight, the one they brought in the day – where will she be? Is she in a cell?'

The policeman looked down at the counter and wrote something on a pad before saying, 'She's all right.'

'But is she in a cell?'

'They're not as bad as you think.' The policeman smiled.

Rooney rubbed his mouth, then turned his back on the counter and the policeman. This fellow was likely a Shields bloke, they were all likely Shields blokes, but they were all as foreign as men from another planet. He'd go barmy if this went on much longer. He could understand now why fellows made jail breaks . . . there was something constricting even in the look of this policeman, although he seemed civil enough.

'Will you come in here a moment?'

'What? . . . Oh.' Rubbing his lips, one over the other, he went once again into the inspector's office. And now Mr Bailey-Crawford did recognise him, and his friendly tone when he said, 'Oh, it's you,' somehow lightened Rooney's burden.

'Yes, sir.'

'Well, we didn't expect to meet here, did we?' His manner was light, almost jovial.

'No, sir.'

'Mr Bailey-Crawford recognises these toys, Mr Smith,' said the inspector.

Rooney's muscles relaxed and the tightness left his jaws.

'But we haven't as yet ascertained when they were thrown away.'

'Oh.'

The little man's head went back and his beard wagged. 'My mother will undoubtedly remember that. In fact, I could almost name the day myself. It would be when she received my letter saying that I was positively not coming to England again until she made up her mind finally to leave the house and go into a flat, or home or something. Last year she had me over here

257

five times on stupid pretexts . . . maids leaving, the odd-job man dismantling the greenhouse and making off with it.'

The inspector checked the jovial flow with a laugh. 'I remember that. But now, if we may see her, and the date tallies with that given by Mr Smith, we can then dispense with him.' The inspector looked at Rooney.

'Thank you, sir.'

'Can we see her tonight?'

'Yes, yes, of course. And I can well believe now that the necklace was thrown out with these things – she has never valued it. It belonged to my grandmother, and it was because I had seen her wearing it so often that I recognised it when I saw . . . the person wearing it. That's a point.' Mr Bailey-Crawford turned to Rooney. 'Why didn't she say you had given it to her?'

'We have been into that, Mr Crawford,' said the inspector quietly, rising.

'Oh.' The little man's eyebrows moved upwards.

'Sir.'

'Yes?' The inspector's mild eyes appeared kindly as they rested on Rooney. 'About Miss Atkinson. If the dates tally, can she come out?'

'Yes, if the dates tally.'

There seemed to be still some doubt in the inspector's mind, and his mild tone brought a sickness into the pit of Rooney's stomach, as he went on, 'There is a point that needs clearing. Perhaps, you, being a friend of hers, can throw some light on it. Miss Atkinson has recently been spending quite a bit of money. She has no known income and she has left her employment, so her aunt, Mrs Howlett, tells me. When

Miss Atkinson was asked where she got the money, all the information she would proffer was that it had been left to her.'

'Yes. Yes, it had.'

'Oh.'

'By her grandfather. Well, not her real grandfather . . . Mrs Howlett's father-in-law . . . He thought the world of her, and she him. I read the letter myself.'

'Well, why didn't she say that?'

'She wouldn't want Ma, that's Mrs Howlett, to know. They never hit it off. But you can easily tell if she's speaking the truth there by the solicitors who did the job for the old man. Before he died he went to them and got them to send her all he had.'

'Who was the solicitor?'

'Pomphrey & Mears . . . Mr Pomphrey.'

'Oh well, we can easily check on that in the morning.'

'In the morning!' Rooney both sounded and looked aghast. 'Do you mean you're going to keep her here all night?'

'Now, now, Mr Smith, this isn't the Dark Ages.'

'No. No, I know, sir, but if you knew what she's gone through all these years living with Ma . . . Mrs Howlett. I've only been there four weeks, and it's nearly turned me white. Nellie's good, she's a good woman, she's —'

'All right, Mr Smith. Now don't you worry. Would you like to come along with us now?'

'Yes, sir.'

'Come on then.'

Outside, Rooney got into the back of the police car with the sergeant, while the inspector sat next to the driver. Mr Bailey-Crawford had driven off in his own car, and within five minutes they were on the drive of Honeycroft, and, as he stepped in through the front door, Rooney could not help but ponder on the strangeness of life, for who would have thought this morning when he moved the bin that this evening he would be going in by the front door with the police?

'Come in here,' said Mr Bailey-Crawford, ushering them into a large room that reminded Rooney of Grandpa's, so crammed was it with furniture.

'We would like to see your mother alone for a moment,' said the inspector.

'Yes, yes, of course.'

Left alone in the room, Rooney stood by a massive, deeply carved table, and glanced about him. It was evident that the whole place was in need of a duster, yet it looked lived in, for a large coal fire was blazing in the grate and a small table holding a tray with a tarnished silver coffee jug and two cups on it stood by a much-worn leather chair. At another time the furniture would have caught his interest, but now it brought up no comment in his mind other than that it might be grand stuff but it was much too big. How long, he wondered, would it take the old girl to remember? What if she couldn't remember, or if she swore she hadn't thrown it away?

There was a commotion in the hall, and the door was thrust open.

'All this fuss about nothing! Why couldn't you come to me at first?'

'Now, Mama.'

'Be quiet! You treat me like a half-wit . . . Why

couldn't you find the people who stole my Sevres and my Georgian silver?'

As the old lady stamped across the room, Rooney thought that she looked a bit different from when he had seen her last, for her hair was not hanging about her face but was now in looped strands, neatly coiled on her head, and she was dressed in blue velvet. It looked an old-fashioned dress, the skirt trailing on the ground, but she no longer looked the poor old wife he had felt sorry for, but a noble old woman, and much more awe-inspiring.

She stopped for a moment at the sight of him, and, as her son had done earlier, she exclaimed, 'Oh! it's you.'

'Yes, mam.'

'And it was you who picked up the necklace from out of the dustbin?'

'Yes, mam.'

'You were a fool. That necklace has caused more trouble in this family than enough. It belonged to my husband's mother – she was a hateful old harridan. That's all she left me, and she put a curse on it.'

'Mama!'

'Be quiet!' She rounded on her son. 'She did. Doesn't this prove it, getting this man into trouble and locking up a woman? I did not throw it away by mistake, I threw it away to get rid of it . . . as I threw away all your things that I'd cherished for years, because you don't know your duty as a son. Sit down!' This was to Rooney.

Slowly, and with his eye on the inspector who was standing in the doorway, Rooney slid into a chair.

'And don't stand in that door. Come in or go out, I hate draughts!'

Much to Rooney's amazement, the inspector did as he was ordered, and was followed by the sergeant, who closed the door gently after him. The old lady seated herself by the fire. Then after allowing a pause, she looked straight at the inspector and said, 'Now that this stupid mistake has been rectified I feel that there is an apology owing to this man.' With a somewhat theatrical gesture, she indicated Rooney with a sweep of her arm.

Rooney, not daring to look at any one of them, said, 'That's all right, mam.'

'It isn't all right. Hasn't this woman, this friend of yours, been put in jail? It's Freda they should have put in jail. But you can't find Freda, can you?'

When the inspector did not answer, she went on, 'Freda was too clever for you . . . she planned her work. She must have had every piece in this house worth anything checked. And now she's most probably in somebody else's house, busily checking there. All she had to do was to dye her hair again.'

'Mama, be quiet.'

Rooney glanced covertly at the inspector. He was smiling; he even seemed to be enjoying the old girl. But when he spoke, there was no trace of amusement in his voice, only a certain deference. 'You're likely right, mam, but we do our poor best.'

'That's a very good word for it.'

The inspector cleared his throat. 'We must go now. Goodnight, mam. Are you coming, Mr Smith?'

'Yes. Yes, sir.' He rose hastily, then turning to the old lady, said, 'Good night, mam.'

'Good night, and don't let them frighten you.'

'No, mam. Good night.'

In the porch and out of hearing of his mother, and between a laugh and a sigh, Mr Bailey-Crawford said, 'I wish I was back in France.'

The inspector smiled. 'I can see you've got your work cut out. When are you returning?'

'As soon as I can find somebody to look after her. She just flatly refused to leave this house, and I can't get anyone to live in. I've even offered the old coachman's house rent free with added baits in return for some small services for her. But can I get a couple? No. They all want the rooms, in fact offer rent for them, but as for doing anything in the way of domestic help, it seems to horrify most of them.'

'Yes, it is a problem. But at least we've solved one tonight. Yours, Mr Smith.'

The inspector had a way of turning a conversation, and Rooney was brought back from a startling prospect that had suddenly been conjured up in his mind by Mr Bailey-Crawford's remarks.

'Yes, sir. Is everything all right now?'

'Well, we'll go back to the station and then we'll be able to tell you. Good night, sir. I'm sorry we've put you to so much trouble.'

'Oh that's all right. I'm glad it's been cleared up. Well, good night . . . Good night, Smith. Sorry about everything.'

'Good night, sir.'

In the car once more, the inspector began to laugh, and to no-one in particular he said, 'I bet that old girl leads him a life. His garret in Paris must appear like paradise after a weekend at home.'

'He's a painter, sir, isn't he?' said the sergeant.

'Yes. Becoming quite well known too, in more ways than one . . . divorced three times.'

'Oh yes? Well.' They both laughed. And Rooney thought, That's it. I couldn't place him, with him being so free and easy, and chatty. But if he's an artist . . .

Once more they went through the main room and into the inspector's office. And there the officer behind the desk rose and handed the inspector a typewritten paper.

Rooney watched him as he read. He watched the slow movement of his hands as he folded the sheet in two and put it on his desk, saying, 'There, then, that's that.'

Rooney waited.

The inspector sat down and joined his hands, resting them on the desk.

'Well, everything seems in order now, Mr Smith. Mr Pomphrey has vouched for Miss Atkinson as to where she got her money. I may want her to meet Mr Pomphrey tomorrow, just a matter of mutual recognition, but I think we can safely say that every-thing is all right. I'll just have a word with her before she goes.'

Relief made Rooney giddy. 'Thank you, sir.'

'Go with the sergeant now and you'll see Miss Atkinson in a minute. And if I may advise you, close your eyes when you see a ruby necklace in future.'

Rooney smiled sheepishly. 'You bet, sir. If I see the Crown Jewels in a bin, I'll cover them up. Good night, sir.'

264

'Good night, Mr Smith.'

He felt almost gay as he went into the main office, but as the sergeant left him with, 'I won't keep you a minute,' a wave of shyness filled him with painful confusion. What would he say to her? How could he thank her for trying to shield him? Would she feel bitter?

But whatever her reactions would be, there was one thing he knew for certain: for him, life was changed, nothing would ever be on the old humdrum level again after all this set-to. Sitting before strange fireplaces, surrounded by his bits was going to be devoid of even comfort now, for his furniture had suddenly become meaningless. It was most disturbing, but he really didn't care if he never saw it again, unless . . .

There she was, looking more like a child than ever against the blue largeness of the sergeant. Her face was white like it had been when he first saw her, and although her expression was strained her eyes held no bitterness. He moved slowly towards her.

'Hallo, Nellie.'

'Hallo.'

He could hardly hear her voice.

The inspector appeared behind her in the doorway. He looked jovial; the sergeant looked jovial; the policeman behind the counter looked jovial; the man and woman standing before the counter looked interested. Rooney buttoned up his coat, stretched his neck out of his collar, and said, 'We'd better be getting along.'

Nellie's eyes drooped as she moved from the shelter of the sergeant to his side.

'Good night.' It was Rooney's final word.

'Good night,' they all said together.

He opened the door, and Nellie passed out before him into the corridor. In the lobby there was a maze of doors and corridors, but without hesitation or touching her he led her to the main entrance. Only let them get outside of here and they would talk . . . he would talk. Never before could he remember such an over-whelming desire to talk.

He opened the outer door, and there, at the foot of the steps, was the street. And for a moment it looked wonderful, until from out of the shadow of the lamp-post moved two figures, Danny and Bill.

Swearing had never been a form of expression with Rooney – he had always told himself he left that to Bill – but now he was in a good way to outdoing even Bill. Why had they to be here at this particular moment? This was the time for him to say what he had to say: he was full of words and his mouth appeared oiled for their flow.

'By, mate, we thought they'd pushed you along the line. Evening, Miss.' This from Bill.

'We had to come back, lad. Just a bit worried. How do you do?' Danny inclined his head towards Nellie. 'You've had a bit of a nasty do, Miss.'

'It was an experience.' There was a little smile in Nellie's eyes.

'I'd say,' said Bill. 'And how did you come off?' he asked of Rooney.

And Rooney, feeling all churned up inside and wishing Bill in the warmest region he knew of, answered, 'Oh, it's a long story. And . . . and she's tired, she wants to get home.'

Nellie looked up at him. And in her eyes he saw a touch of anxiety that had once been their permanent expression. 'I can't go back there tonight . . . I couldn't face them tonight. Tomorrow I'll have to go and see to Grandpa, but tonight I'll get a room somewhere.'

Rooney looked down into her face. 'Come back to Danny's place with us. She can, can't she, Danny?'

'Yes. Aye, the wife's expectin' us.'

As if Danny and Bill were not there, Rooney held her eyes and entreated softly, 'Mrs D.'s nice, you'll like her.'

'It's kind of you.' She meant this for Danny, but her eyes stayed on Rooney's until she turned and moved away.

Rooney walked by her side, with Danny and Bill behind, and without further words they cut up a side street and into the market place, and from there took a tram. And when they alighted in Eldon Street, Rooney did something that surprised himself still further. Pulling Bill to one side, he said, 'Will you mind, man, not coming along with us now? She's gone through a bit the day, you understand?'

Bill's look did not convey his understanding, but it showed how deeply he was offended. 'Well, if that's how you feel. I only came because I didn't want to see you in a mess.'

'Yes, I know, man. And it was good of you, and I'll not forget it, and I'll tell you about things the morrow.'

'To hell with the morrow!'

267

'Good night, Danny.' It was Bill's only salute, and showed the extent of his pique.

Blast! thought Rooney, as Bill marched off. Yet it was far better that he should take the pip than be given the chance to start his wisecracking in front of her the night. Somehow it had become a matter of importance that the folks she met who were connected with him should be nice, and a bit refined like: and, to his mind, there was nobody further removed from this description than Bill, or better fitted for it than Mrs D. But, had he been allowed to get going, Bill's patter would have swamped Mrs D.'s refinement.

Mrs D. greeted Nellie as if she were an old friend, and straight away offered her her solace for all ills, a cup of tea. And although she talked as she trotted back and forth, setting the table for a meal, her patter did not seem to put Nellie at her ease. There she sat, in the armchair at one side of the fireplace, relieved of her hat and coat and looking, to Rooney's eyes, more lost than ever. Guilt weighed heavily upon him. It was being shut up in that place that had done this . . . pushed her back to where she was before she had got the money.

Alone with her, Danny having gone into the backyard to get some more coal and Mrs D. being occupied in the scullery, he smiled at her, and said, 'They're nice, aren't they? I've known them most of me life. They're the best friends I've got.'

'Yes.' To him the syllable had a funny cracked sound, his smile faded. She continued to look at him, then, to his utter consternation, she began to cry. In almost as much distress as herself, he watched her gripping her throat as if to cut off the sound trying to escape, and he rose hastily, exclaiming in a helpless fashion, 'Don't, Nellie, don't!' His hand went out to her shoulder, but instead of a tentative touch quietening her distress, it acted as a spring for its release. Her face now buried in her hands, the sound of her sobbing filled the house and brought Mrs D. from the scullery.

'There, there, that's the best thing you could do. Just cry it out, hinny. And you know what I think?' Mrs D. was holding Nellie to her now. 'Bed. Bed'll be the best place. And in the morning you'll feel a new woman. There now, there now.'

'I'm . . . I'm so sorry.'

'There's nothing to be sorry for, lass. Have another cup of tea. Pour one out, Rooney.'

As Rooney hastily did as he was bidden, Nellie said between gasps, 'It's . . . it's the kindness. You're . . . all so kind.'

'Kind? We've done nothing yet. Here now, drink this.' Mrs D. took the cup from Rooney and continued, 'I'll fix the couch in the front room for you. It's fitted Rooney, so it'll fit you all right. There now, that's better.' She stood back from Nellie as she drank the tea, and turning to Danny, who had come back into the kitchen, she said, 'Give me a hand, will you?'

'Aye. I'll just wash me hands.'

Two minutes later Danny followed his wife out of the room, and Rooney slowly and deliberately pulled up a chair to face Nellie. He took a deep breath, pulled at his collar, and opened his mouth. But to his utter consternation the oiled words filling his brain refused to flow. He knew now what he wanted to say – aye, he

269

knew all right – but there they were, sticking in his throat. He could have said them pat at the police station, for the glow of high adventure was still on him then, and Nellie had just been snatched, as it were, from danger. But now things had simmered down and the words just would not come.

'I'm sorry I went on like that,' Nellie said softly.

'That's all right.'

'I suddenly felt' – she handed him the cup, then clasped her hands tightly in her lap before adding – 'so lost . . . of not belonging anywhere. That awful feeling of aloneness. You know?'

This was a good enough cue, but he couldn't take it, for he suddenly thought of Mrs D. and Danny next door . . . what if they should come in in the middle of what he had to say. That'd be worse than never starting at all.

'It's . . . it's the loss of Grandpa,' he said, 'making you feel like this.'

'Yes, that's it, I suppose.'

'And . . . and being in that place all day. Were they awful?'

'Oh no, they were rather kind. But the place was awful. Something about it.'

'Why . . . why did you do it, Nellie?' He leaned slightly forward. And she looked down at her hands, and her voice was small as she said, 'You had been kind to me, it . . . it was nice to be able to do something for you. At least I thought I was doing something. But it's like Grace says, I'm a fool.'

'You're not . . . Her!' At the sound of Ma's name, his new self erupted to the surface again, making him feel

as he had done earlier in the evening, capable of
conquering the world . . . if it was only with his fists.

'By!' he said, 'it's a wonder I didn't hit her an' all the
night.'

Nellie's head came up. 'You hit someone?'

'Dennis.' There was a quirk to his lips and a sly smile
in his eyes. 'It was a nice feel.'

'Oh, Rooney.'

The gentle chiding made him lower his head.

'He went out like a light.' His eyes lifted and met
hers, and their glances held and mingled as he went on
sheepishly, 'I'm a bit scared of going back; I might be
tempted to try it on again . . . with Ma.'

'Oh, Rooney.' The little smile broadened; then
suddenly died away, and making a small movement
with her head she said, 'I'll have to go back; I'll have to
get my things. I saw the undertaker about Grandpa this
morning. They're burying him on Tuesday. I must get
my things away before then . . . I couldn't go back after
he's gone.'

'What are you going to do, I mean, after?'

'I'll get a job.'

'Nellie . . .' He moved on to the edge of his chair.
'Nellie, would you mind doing a job like . . . like service,
looking after someone?'

She was staring at him, her face soft now and full of
shy youthfulness. Gently she answered, 'No, I
wouldn't mind, Rooney.'

He watched her lips as they rounded his name. He
had never heard that daft name sound so sweet.
He swallowed and moved restlessly. 'Well . . . you
know the . . . the old lady who owns the necklace, Mrs

271

Bailey-Crawford . . . well, her son wants somebody just to keep an eye on her. And they can have the coachman's house. The son was telling the inspector the night. Would . . . would you take it?'

He watched the brightness fade from her eyes, and when she said, 'Yes,' her voice was flat and heavy with weariness.

'I just thought,' he said lamely, 'it might suit you.'

'Yes, yes it would. Oh yes, I'm sure it would.'

He saw that she was making an effort. She was tired out; he couldn't expect her to appear over the moon about anything the night, anyway.

'I'll have to find some place for meself, an' all. Later on, I'm going along to the chap who usually moves me. I'm putting me things in store with him until I look round.'

There fell a silence between them, and he was almost glad when Danny and Mrs D. came out of the front room.

'There then, it's all ready when you are.' Quite abruptly, Mrs D. took hold of Nellie's arm and raised her to her feet, saying, 'Come along, my dear.'

'Good night,' said Nellie quietly.

'Good night,' said Rooney.

'Good night, Mr Macallistair, and thank you.'

'Good night, lass. And sleep well.'

Danny watched his wife and Nellie out of the room; then going to the mantelpiece, he took up his pipe, knocked it on the hob, and exclaimed, 'Well, you didn't get it over then?'

'Get what over?'

Danny turned round. 'Rooney, I'm not given to

swearing, but I'm going to say now, you're a bloody fool. I thought after you had the spunk to push Bill off . . . Oh, what's the use!' He turned to the fireplace again.

The colour mounted to Rooney's hair. They had been in there waiting, listening . . . his two friends. He pushed back his shoulders and buttoned up his coat, but all he said was, 'I'm off to the phone.'

Bloody fool, was he? Now, remembering the almost dead look on Nellie's face, he supposed he was. 'Would you like to look after someone?' he had asked. But Danny and Mrs D. listening! He wouldn't have credited it. What if he had asked her? The sweat ran down his face at the thought.

10

AS YOU WERE

At half-past nine the following morning Rooney walked out of Danny's with Nellie, feeling a variety of emotions, not the least among them, irritation. And this against Mrs D. of all people. She knew he had to be at the Bailey-Crawford's house afore ten, and there she had been, for the past half-hour, with Nellie in the front room. Natter, natter, natter. He had listened to her voice going on and on until he had positively begun to dislike the sound of it. His restless night, spent rolled up in blankets on the mat, had not fortified him for today, and now he was feeling at an acute disadvantage walking under the cold hard sunshine with Nellie, and her got up in her best.

On the other hand, Nellie seemed to be fully recovered. In fact, her whole manner was a trifle disconcerting. She seemed almost like she was when she had first come into the money, except for the pain of Grandpa's loss still in her eyes.

He said, for the second time that morning, 'I feel I should have gone back to seventy-one and changed.'

'Oh, you look quite all right. And I doubt whether you'd have got in. If she guessed it was you she'd have pretended to be asleep.'

'Yes, perhaps you're right.'

They boarded a bus and sat in silence until they came

277

to the Fountain, but when they had alighted Nellie said, 'It'll be odd if I get this place, for I've always had a longing to live in Westoe.'

'You have?'

'Yes.'

He quickened his step, almost causing her to trot alongside him. It would be just like the thing, wouldn't it, if someone had stepped in afore them. But the son had said last night on the phone that he'd be only too pleased to see her, and that if his mother took to her it'd suit everybody . . . Still, you never knew.

'There, that's the house . . . the top of it, behind yon trees.'

'It's big.'

'Yes, and it's in a mess inside . . . I'd better warn you.'

'Oh, that won't matter.'

'Well, here we are.' He rang the bell, not of the back but of the front door, as he spoke; then smiled at her. And she smiled back at him. And somehow he felt better.

'Oh, hallo, Smith. Come in. By!' Mr Bailey-Crawford stopped Nellie as she passed him, 'you're small, aren't you?'

'Yes, I am rather.'

'Make me feel quite a giant. Look, come into the kitchen, will you? I'll tell my mother in a minute.'

When they were in the kitchen and the door closed, he looked hard at Nellie, saying, 'You're a surprise, you know. I had imagined some great bustling dame' – his eyes slipped to Rooney – 'someone who could manage mother. Well, not exactly manage her – no-one will do that, I'm afraid – but . . .'

278

'I'm used to looking after people. I've seen to my . . . my grandfather for years.'

Mr Bailey-Crawford laughed. 'He, I feel, wouldn't come up to my mother. I'd better warn you she's rather a tartar; I don't want to give you the wrong impression. Smith here has met her.' He turned to Rooney. 'She's no docile old lady, is she?'

'Well, sir, no . . . But I rather took to her.'

'Yes, that's funny, for she likes you too. Well, now, Miss . . . ?'

'Atkinson.'

'Well, Miss Atkinson, there's not a great deal of money in it – two pounds a week and the coach-house free. It will make a nice flat, but it wants seeing to. But if you shouldn't like sleeping there alone you can sleep in the house . . .'

'And who, may I ask, is going to sleep in the house? Didn't I tell you to let me know when she arrived?'

The old lady, aided by a silver-topped cane, sailed into the kitchen, immediately filling the room with her presence and bringing on it a silence. She fixed her gimlet eyes on Nellie. And Nellie returned the look quietly but unsmiling.

'You're small . . . you look like a child.'

'I'm quite strong, madam.'

'Have you been in service before?'

'No, madam.'

'Then how do you know you can do what is required?'

'I can but try . . . I have looked after my grand-father . . .'

'I don't want to be looked after.' The old lady

279

glanced fiercely at her son. But what retort she was about to make was checked as a pain attacked her leg, causing her to wince. Whether her son or Rooney would have dared to aid her to a seat cannot be known, but Nellie did. Quietly she put her hand on the back of a dusty wheel-back chair, and turning it about, placed it near the old lady.

Mrs Bailey-Crawford stared at her for a moment before sitting down. 'How old are you?'

'Thirty-four.'

'You don't look it. What's your name?'

'Nellie. Nellie Atkinson.'

'Hm . . . Well, let's get some points clear.' She nodded her white head briskly. 'I'm not in my dotage. Also I might inform you there are no more valuables left in this house to steal. Moreover, no matter how nice you are or what you do, you'll be left nothing in my will, for I have nothing to leave . . . but this old house, which will be turned into flats the minute I'm gone.'

Rooney's heart sank; he lowered his eyes away from Nellie . . . she'd never stick the old girl.

'What do you consider the most important thing in a house?' The old lady's voice sounded like that of an army commander.

'Warmth.' Nellie's tone was full of deep sincerity as she made this statement, and Rooney glanced up to find her looking at the old woman with the kindly light in her eyes that she had kept for Grandpa, and he thought, with surprise, she likes her.

'What are you two to each other?' The old eyes flicked between them, and as Rooney searched wildly to give an answer, Nellie replied quietly, 'Friends. We're friends.'

'Pity; I'd have liked him round about. It's a nice coach-house; he could have done odd jobs.'

Rooney's colour had reached his hair when the son took pity on him. 'I'll show Miss Atkinson the rooms, Mama, and let her decide.'

'She can't sleep over there all alone, she'll have to sleep in.' There was a command in both voice and eyes. But Nellie replied quietly, 'I'd prefer a . . . a flat, madam, if I may?' The small wrinkled eyes and the large brown ones held. Then the old lady's switched away. 'Very well. Go and see it. You won't like it; the rain comes in, and the fire smokes . . . Go on . . .' She waved them all out.

In the yard Mr Bailey-Crawford wiped his perspiring brow. 'You see what I mean?' he said.

'No,' said Nellie, with what to Rooney appeared to be alarming frankness. 'I only see that she is old and very lonely and' – she paused – 'so vulnerable.'

The little bearded man stopped and looked at her before saying, with something of a shamefaced look, 'Yes, perhaps you're right. I hope you decide to stay. She took to you, although you mightn't think it. I should stay with her, but I can't, and she won't leave the house.' Quickly he turned away and moved on ahead of them to the coach-house.

Here he unlocked the door by the side of what appeared to be a converted garage. 'Mind,' he warned, 'the staircase is dark and a bit cobwebby.'

The staircase leading to the rooms above was dark and cobwebby, but when they stepped from the top of the stairs directly into the centre of a large room they both stood and stared about in surprise, for windows on two sides flooded the room with light, and on the side opposite the courtyard they looked directly on to a roof of tangled trees that had once been the orchard.

'This could be your living-room. There are two other room, but the unfortunate thing is they all run out of each other. The last is the kitchen . . . through here . . . This is the bedroom—' He stopped in the second room. 'It is a fine view, that is if you like trees. In the spring it's a picture. And here's the kitchen. It's not bad really, although it doesn't look much at the present moment. The water has been coming in a bit.' He pointed to the corner above the sink. 'It was a stopped gutter, but I cleared it. I think you'll find it all right now.' He addressed his remarks to Nellie, and Rooney stood back from them, looking about the kitchen. There was an open range, besides an electric stove; the sink was good and the floor was covered with red lino. The room only wanted a coat of paint to make it look grand. It was large enough for a couple of easy chairs and a good-sized table . . . and a dresser.

'Well, there it is.' Mr Crawford now looked from one to the other. 'Do you mind if I leave you to have a look around?'

'No, no, not at all,' said Nellie.

'Call in when you're finished.'

'Thank you.'

As they heard his steps going down the stairs they turned to each other, and Rooney was the first to speak. 'It's fine, isn't it?'

'Yes.'

He couldn't make much of her reply. And when, abruptly, she moved out of the kitchen and through the centre room into the big room, he followed her, thinking, She's not taken with it; it's not modern enough for her. And he recalled her enthusiasm for the furniture in the magazine . . . He watched her walk to the window and look down into the garden for a moment, before turning to face him. There was almost the width of the room between them now, and suddenly, there was the width of the world, of taste, of temperament.

'It's not very modern,' he said quietly.

'No,' she said, 'it's not.'

There came a dull hurt ache beneath his ribs. He was filled with a sadness that almost made him sick. To him the place was wonderful, like a palace dropped from the sky and come to rest on the treetops, but to her . . . it wasn't modern. It just showed how different people could be. The ache became an acute pain. No two people could make a go of it, thinking like that. She was different. Hadn't he known she was. That night in the kitchen with the magazine, he knew then that she aspired to things, things that he would never possess, because he would never want them.

He made himself say, 'Perhaps you could make it do until you look out for something else?' His voice was as cold as his heart now.

'Yes, perhaps I could . . . Rooney?'

'Yes?'

'Are you blind?'

'Blind?'

'Yes, blind . . . Or don't you want to see? Can't you

283

see I don't want a modern house . . . or anything? All I said about modern furniture that night was just talk, don't you know that? I love your brass bed, and your chairs and your dresser, and everything you have, don't you see? . . .' Her voice dropped to a whisper, but a clear whisper. 'All I want is you, Rooney.'

The floor dragged at him, staying the wild leap of his body to her, but the space between them widened, making room for what he had to say, what he must say. Even in this moment, his cards must be put face up on the table.

'There's one or two things you've got to know, Nellie. I'll never be other than I am. I've had to face it – I've no ambition. All I want is to stay put, in the same job; to know that I'm safe. Yesterday I thought I wouldn't mind changing, but I would. What's more, I'm like all them back in seventy-one . . . I'm ignorant. I could never keep up with you, or go to your Literary Societies and things.'

'Oh!' Her voice cracked on the exclamation, cutting off his flow, and her great brown eyes sent the tears flooding over her face. Yet in the same instant she threw back her head and laughed. 'Literary Societies!' Then moving only one step towards him, she whispered across the distance, 'I want you to stay put, never to change . . . never . . . your outlook, or your furniture, or anything about you, ever.'

For a moment she became lost to his sight.

'Don't you want me, Rooney?'

The last words brought her into focus again. She was only a few steps away from him now. There she stood, like a young girl, her white face even whiter and her eyes even larger. His throat swelling, his heart pounding, he thrust out his arms, and pulled her against him. And as she smothered her crying in his shoulder an uplifting feeling of wonderment filled him, and her words came back to him: 'What are we here for? What does it all mean?' Well, he knew now.

THE END

THE NICE BLOKE

Catherine Cookson

PATHWAY

For Mr R. G. Wilson
Another nice bloke

Contents

Dig in the soil of a quiet
man and you unearth the savage.

I

HARRY BLENHEIM

The Nice Bloke

He sat encased in frozen terror aware of people passing
him and the looks they cast on him as they went into
the Court. The terror had been rising in him since he
awoke at four o'clock this morning. It had brought him
out in sweats, hot and blush-making like a woman in
the menopause; it had dropped him into baths of cold
perspiration where his teeth chattered and he had to
grip the bed head to steady himself. But now all his fear
was at a standstill; it had frozen during this waiting
period and he was grateful even for this respite because,
gathering force as it had done since he entered the
Court-house, he knew that if it rose just a little further
he would go berserk.

His eyes unblinking, he stared before him and again
asked himself why he was here, how had it come about?
How had it happened to him, Harry Blenheim? He was
a nice man, was Harry Blenheim. He didn't have to be
big-headed to know that was the general opinion of
him. It had been his own opinion up till a few months
ago, at which time he had been full of self-respect.

When he looked in the mirror he liked what he saw;
not exactly a good-looking fellow, but, as his wife had

once said in her far back loving, laughing days, his was a face full of character, with the kindest brown eyes God ever made. And then there was his voice, deep, what they called musical. And it was musical, because he could sing. It was the singing that had made him a successful business man. It was odd when you came to think about it, but it was true. They had taken him out of the Sunday school and put him in the choir because of his voice, and in the choir he had chummed up with Tony Rippon, and that was something, because the Rippons were from the top end of Fellburn and he was from the bottom end.

When his voice broke, it broke well and he became a tenor. It was after he had sung solo with the church choir on the television that Esther Rippon had singled him out. He hadn't taken to her very much at first and nothing might have come of it, but Tony died and she seemed inconsolable.

Mr and Mrs Rippon hadn't been elated when he and Esther became engaged. He was working then as a junior clerk in the Rates Department and his prospects, although secure, were very, very dull. And that was how Mr Rippon saw them too, and, as he said, something would have to be done. And he did something; he got him set on in the firm of Peamarsh, of which he was then a junior director.

On the face of it Peamarsh's was a small wholesale chemists firm, but once Harry entered it he realised it had a finger in every pie in Fellburn. There were five directors, and they were all out to monopolise, most of all their youngest director, Mr Rippon.

Harry had never really liked Mr Rippon, even before

he married his daughter. As for Mrs Rippon, he whole-heartedly disliked her. He saw her as a psalm-singing, sanctimonious prig, and he only hoped Esther wouldn't take after her. Esther didn't; at least not altogether.

Esther was nineteen and he was twenty when they were married and life, even with its pinpricks in the form of Mr Rippon, promised good. And for sixteen years it kept its promise, more or less, until hell had opened and swallowed him. But hell had been a private hell. The public had only got wind of it a month ago when he had tried to kill his father-in-law. He hadn't quite succeeded. He wished he had. Knowing what the consequences would be, he still wished he had.

He blinked once and looked around the wide corridor as if in search of a friendly face. Even at this moment he would have been glad to see Esther, but Esther was the last person he was likely to see. Nor would he be likely to see his sons, John and Terry. Then there was Gail . . . Oh! Oh, Gail.

He hadn't seen his daughter for weeks. Esther had packed her off somewhere, and she said that if it lay with her he would never clap eyes on Gail again.

Esther blamed him; she blamed him for it all, not her father, oh no, not her father, that dirty old licentious beast . . . But that was exactly what Esther had called him, himself, wasn't it? Not a dirty old licentious beast, just a dirty licentious beast. Well, he wouldn't have that. He told her he wouldn't have that; what he had done didn't deserve that title. He had made a mistake as many a man before him. He had been weak, and he had paid for his weakness. He was paying for his weakness at this moment as he waited for his name to be called to be brought to justice for what, as one paper stated, was the worst case of its kind Fellburn had ever known.

'It shouldn't be long now.'

He looked at his solicitor who had just moved away from the barrister. His face wasn't friendly. A month ago he had called him Peter and he had been Harry to him. They were both members of the Round Table; they played golf together, and it was they who saw to the organising, each Christmas, of some stunt for bringing in money for parcels for the old folks. They had been buddies, Peter Thompson and he, yet when the balloon went up Peter had been reluctant to have anything to do with the case.

Nor had he any hope of leniency from the judge. Callow was one of the old school. He wasn't nick-named Horse-whip Callow for nothing. At a talk he had given to the Round Table dinner he had indicated that a great deal of crime was due to people moving out of their class. 'And don't let us forget it,' he had said; 'there is as much class distinction today as there ever was, and rightly so.' As one member had remarked later, old Callow was a ghetto-minded old sod, and if he had his way no-one would be let out of his district.

Harry knew that he himself had been let out of his district so to speak. Let out from the bottom end of the town and into the top end, and that people were remembering. It didn't do, you see; leopards didn't change their spots. And it wasn't only the people from the top end who were remembering, those from the bottom end were, too. That's what you got for being

300

an upstart and trying to climb; they said, 'But it wasn't really his fault, it was his grannie's. Mary O'Toole was a pusher. She had pushed him into the choir and then into the rate office, and he should have had the sense to be grateful and not try his luck.'

But there were two from Bog's End who didn't think like this: Janet Dunn and her son, Robbie. And, as if his thoughts had conjured them up out of the air, he saw them standing before him. They said nothing, neither of them, they just stared at him. And he returned their stare, his gratitude for their presence making him speechless. When young Robbie put his hand out and touched his shoulder he wanted to grab it and hold it, as he would have held John's or Terry's had they been there with him at this moment, but he resisted the impulse and just continued to stare gratefully at Janet as her eyes asked, 'How did this happen to you, how?' And as if she had spoken aloud he shook his head slowly. He didn't know, he didn't know, it was just one of those things that started at an office party.

One

It was snowing heavily when he reached home. At the top of the drive the house greeted him with lights in all the downstairs windows. He could see the Christmas tree in the drawing-room. It was bare yet; they would start decorating it tomorrow.

The snow excited him. He hoped it would lie over Christmas; it was some years since they had had a real white Christmas. He went to the boot and took out a largish parcel and wondered if he would get it into the house without Gail spotting him.

When he opened the front door he was met by warmth and the sound of voices coming from different directions, Janet's from the kitchen raised in protest against Terry – he must be pinching something again – John's voice from somewhere in the cellar, yelling, 'Mother! Mother! I can't find them. What did you say they were in?' Then Esther coming from the morning-room and looking towards him, and lifting her hand in greeting before she shouted down to the floor, 'The old green box in the corner, the right hand side of the boiler.'

He was about to slip into the cloakroom and deposit

the parcel until he could take it upstairs when a cry from the landing brought his gaze upwards, and there stood Gail. She stood poised for a moment; then, taking the stairs two at a time, she was in front of him before he could escape. 'Hold on! Hold on! You'll have me over, you big horse.'

As she reached up and kissed him she cried, 'It's snowing, it's snowing and it's going to lie.'

'All right, all right. It's snowing and it's going to lie. Let me get my things off.'

'What's that?' she was whispering. 'Coo. It's a big parcel. Who's it for? Me?' She dug her finger between her small breasts, and he said, 'You! Of course not.' Then bending his head quickly down to her he whispered, 'Your mother.'

'Oh, what is it?'

'I'm not telling you; you'll give the show away.'

'Honest, I won't, I won't.'

'It's a set of frying pans.'

'Oh, Dad!' She pushed him, and he drew her to the side of the curtain that bordered the passage leading to the loggia and, his voice low, he said, 'Do you think you could get it up into the attic without her seeing?'

'Leave it to me,' she said. 'You do an evasive tactic and leave it to me.'

He left it to her to see that she hid her own Christmas box. He could imagine her reactions on Christmas morning when she saw the fitted dressing case that she had admired in Pomphreys months ago. Esther had been against him getting it. She considered it too sophisticated for a girl of fifteen, but he considered that Gail needed something sophisticated to help her over her present stage of plumpness. His daughter couldn't as yet see her plumpness as a prelude to beauty, but he could. He knew that in two or three years' time she'd be breath-taking. In a strange way she had inherited all the good points from Esther and himself; Esther's height, her pale complexion; his own brown eyes and his hair, but whereas his hair was a sandy nondescript colour, hers, though of the same thick strong texture, was a tawny shade.

If he had been asked what made life worth living for him he would have answered airily, 'Oh, a number of things'; his wife, his home, his family. But deep in his being, where no question penetrated, the truth lay, and the truth was that it was his daughter and she alone that answered that question.

He had been proud when his first child was born and that a boy, but he had experienced no feeling of wonder until Gail had been put into his arms, and then it was as if a miracle had been performed for him alone. He had no longer believed in miracles. He had sung of miracles in choirs and concerts for years; miracles had been ten a penny. And then Gail happened to him.

Esther had, at first, been jealous of his feeling for the child; then the next year Terry had come, and things balanced themselves out. She had John and Terry, and he had Gail. Sometimes he had felt guilty about his almost utter lack of feeling for the boys and had tried to rectify this by being more friendly towards them. Yet with the insight of children they had gauged the parental balance of his affections. That was why, he had surmised, they had teased and tormented Gail until she was able to stand up for herself.

His wife came towards him now. 'I thought it would hold you up,' she said.

'Another hour and the way it's coming down and it might have.'

When he shivered slightly she said, 'Go in the drawing-room, the meal won't be more than fifteen minutes.'

As he went into the room John's voice came up through the floor again, bawling, 'I can't find it, Mother.' And he heard Esther exclaiming impatiently, 'Leave it! Leave it! That'll be the day when you're able to find anything without it jumping up and hitting you.'

There was a big fire roaring in the open grate. The room looked comfortable, colourful and lived in. He sat down on the couch and stretched out his feet, and all of a sudden he had a longing for a drink. That was the only thing that was lacking in his home life . . . well, perhaps not the only thing, but something that became an irritation at a moment like this, a moment when he wanted to relax. But Esther was firm that no intoxicating drink of any kind should enter the house. This was one of the standards she had brought over from her mother.

He often wondered how his father-in-law had managed over the years to cover up the smell of liquor on his breath. He didn't do it with scented cachous or mints; he must have had some special formula because he had come into this very house, his eyes hazy with whisky yet not a smell from him, and Esther had never suspected a thing. When her father was gay and he talked loudly and laughed a lot, she put it down to a business success. In a moment of weakness, once she

305

had admitted that his manner embarrassed her at such times. He had, on this occasion, stared at her amazed, wondering how such an astute woman could be hoodwinked. But there were none so blind as those who did not wish to see. It would have been unthinkable to Esther that her father should take intoxicating liquor on a Saturday night, then on Sunday walk with stately step up the aisle to his pew, not paid for any longer but definitely reserved for himself and his family.

The sound of congenial commotion now came to him from the hall and he heard Esther say, 'Why, Robbie, it's beautiful, but you shouldn't, you know you shouldn't,' and a thick voice answered in airy tones. 'Why shouldn't I, Mrs Blenheim? Why shouldn't I?'

'Harry!' He hitched himself up straight on the couch and looked towards the door where Esther was entering the room carrying a square box. 'Look what Robbie's brought me for a Christmas present. It's too much I'm telling him.'

He got to his feet as she came towards him and looked down at the highly polished foot square box inlaid with mother-of-pearl. 'What is it?' he said.

'A workbox. Look at it.' She lifted the lid to disclose a tray of small compartments with inlaid tops and pearl knobs, holding strands of coloured silks and boot buttons studded with coloured glass. 'It's got everything,' she said. 'Look!' She put it down on the couch and lifted out a tray to disclose beneath more compartments holding small bobbins of thread, needles, pins and all the accoutrements necessary for a Victorian lady's needlework.

Harry lifted his eyes to the young man standing by

Esther's side. 'It's an exquisite job, Robbie,' he said. 'Where did you pick it up?'

'Oh, you know . . . I get around.' Robbie laughed and his thin parted lips showed a wide set of blunt looking white teeth.

Harry laughed back into the face before him, the face that yelled out its inheritance.

Some Jewish faces were distinguished only by the shape of the nose but every feature of Robbie Dunn's face proclaimed him to be a Jew. His skin was thick and of a slightly greasy texture; his eyes were round, keen looking and black; and his hair was thick, straight and black. His face was long and if it had followed its structural design would have ended in a pointed chin, but here it levelled itself out, leaving the jaw square, which in a subtle way emphasised the whole.

Robbie Dunn, at nineteen, was only five foot six and a half, but he was thick set, and if when he spoke, he had hunched his shoulders and stretched out his hands, the onlooker wouldn't have been surprised; but when he did speak his voice surprised most people because he spoke with the idiom of the working-class Tynesider.

Robbie Dunn, like most of his race, had a business head on his shoulders and was out to make money. He was both calculating and discerning. There were in him two strong and overpowering emotions: one was gratitude even for the smallest kindness, the other was hate for even the smallest insult. He had brought Esther Blenheim a present but it was out of gratitude to her husband, because it was Harry Blenheim who had helped his mother when she had needed help most, at the time when she was left without a husband, mother or father, all three being killed in an old car that should never have been on the road. And it was this man who had given him ten pounds to get started. He hadn't loaned him ten pounds, he had given it to him.

Robbie now stood looking at Esther as she went into ecstasy over the box. Then his eyes came to rest again on Harry. He liked Harry Blenheim. He was a nice bloke, a good bloke was Harry Blenheim. If he told the truth he was the only one he liked out of the whole bunch; except perhaps Mrs O'Toole, the grannie. He wondered why he didn't cotton on to Gail because she had always been nice to him, but he had the idea she was tarred with the same brush as her brothers.

'It's a beautiful thing, Robbie,' said Harry now, 'but as Mrs Blenheim says' – he nodded towards Esther as he gave her her full title, which he always did when speaking of her to either Janet or Robbie because she had made this a stipulation of the association between them and the Dunns – 'it would bring a good few pounds today. It's real Victoriana.'

'Dare say,' said Robbie nonchalantly; 'but I only paid fifteen bob for it. Honest.' He nodded. 'Fifteen bob in a village yon side of the river, down by Washington way you know. But I've cleaned it up a bit since I got it. There was a bairn playing with it on the steps of a house, pulling all the buttons out. I went straight up and knocked on the door and said, "That's too good for a bairn to play with, Missus, I'll give you ten bob for it." Quick as lightning she said, "You'll not, you know." "All right," I said, "fifteen." "I'll take it," she said, an' whipped it up out of the bairn's hands and

308

set it screaming, and I didn't linger to do any comforting but made off with me box, and here it is.'

They were all laughing now. Robbie could spin a yarn. He'd always had the power to make Harry laugh. His tales very seldom enhanced him, they were nearly always told against himself, which was clever Harry thought, as it tended to make people like him rather than otherwise.

Harry had not the slightest doubt that Robbie would one day get where he wanted to go, and he would take pleasure in climbing the obstacles that were set up against him. And he was aware inwardly that Robbie hadn't to go any further than this house to find barricades being erected against him. But as he had told himself before, it was as well to ignore them. Young men garnered wisdom as they garnered years, at least he hoped that this would happen to his sons, especially his eldest.

Gail came running into the room now, she rarely ever walked anywhere. She was saying loudly, 'Gran's starving, and she's not the only one.' Then she broke off and exclaimed, 'Oh, hello, Robbie . . . Coo! what's that? Who's that for?'

'It's for me, madam,' her mother said, inclining her head slowly towards her daughter. 'And remember that.'

'Oh, isn't it sweet!' Gail was fingering the tiny bobbins of thread. 'Did you bring it, Robbie?'

For reply he jerked his head, and again she said, 'It's lovely.' Then looking at her mother she remarked bluntly, 'You won't use it, Mother.'

Esther Blenheim closed her eyes and pressed her lips

together and assumed annoyance before she said, 'Well, if I don't use it, Miss, I can assure you you're not going to get the chance.'

'Oh!' Gail flounced now. 'It'll be mine some day.' She grinned at her father, and as her mother exclaimed on a high note, 'Really!', Harry Blenheim burst out laughing again.

It was at this moment that John came into the room. He stopped just within the door and surveyed the group; then said sullenly, 'Gran's waiting.'

John Blenheim was seventeen, as tall as his father, and as fair as his father was dark. All his features and colouring were those of his mother. His appearance in the room changed the whole attitude of the group, even Gail stopped her chattering.

As Esther now said, 'We're coming, we're coming,' Robbie Dunn walked down the room towards John Blenheim, and the nearer he approached him the shorter he felt, but he kept his eyes on him, and the tall boy returned his stare. It wasn't until Robbie was at the room door that he said in a casual way and over his shoulder, 'I'll wait for me mother if you don't mind, Mrs Blenheim. It's pretty rough out; I had to leave the car on the main road.'

'You've got a car now?' Gail's voice was high as she pushed past him into the hall before confronting him squarely.

He looked at her for a moment in silence, then said, 'Aye, I've got a car.'

'You don't mean the van?'

'No, not the van. I've still got the van, but I've got a car an' all. And I'll tell you somethin' else.' His glance

310

now swept from Harry Blenheim to his wife, then to their son before it returned to Gail, and again he allowed a silence to elapse before delivering his news: 'I've taken a shop the day, in Pine Street off the Market.'

The silence was engendered now by amazement. It went on and on until Harry Blenheim said quietly, 'You've taken a shop in Pine Street, Robbie?'

'Aye, Mr Blenheim, a shop, I'm goin' in for antiques.'

Harry shook his head slowly. At fifteen Robbie Dunn had started with a fruit barrow. He had given him the money to get going. He had only kept on fruit for six months, then had taken a stall in the Market, a cheap-jack stall selling tawdry souvenirs and throw-outs from the warehouses, a stall at which John had once said only mentals or dim-wits would leave their money. When he was sixteen he had gone in for second-hand clothes. But that didn't last very long; there were too many at that game, at least in the Market. And then he had taken up the white elephant trade. Going round the jumble sales he had collected enough bric-a-brac to fill his stall and when it went in almost a day he said he knew that this was the line he had to follow, and he had done so assiduously for the last two years. He had made enough money on a Wednesday and a Saturday to provide him with a van and to pay three women on a Saturday to do the jumble sales. And now, here he was saying he had a car and he was taking a shop in Pine Street, and rents in Pine Street were to be reckoned with. He had to hand it to him, he had push. He only hoped that John, in his way, would show as much

311

initiative when the time came. He dismissed the doubts that rose to the surface of his mind and said, 'Does your mother know this?'

'No.' Robbie grinned now at Harry. 'I was keepin' it for a sort of Christmas box for her, but . . . but somehow it just came out.'

It came out, Harry knew, because he wanted John to hear it. It was odd about the feeling between his son and Janet's son. They had never hit it off from the first moments they had come into contact when Robbie was seven and John was five. The feeling between these two boys had worried him at times. It was a feeling that was not the result of association; it had been from the beginning a feeling that stemmed from a deep elemental knowledge of an old hate, a hate that was beyond their consciousness, a hate that went far back down into the back of time but which was held to the present by a gossamer thread of awareness – racial awareness.

Janet Dunn came into the hall now. She looked at Esther Blenheim and said, 'Mrs O'Toole's getting restless,' and Esther said, 'All right, Janet. And look, don't you stay, you get off with Robbie here. I suppose you've seen this wonderful present he's brought me.' Without waiting for Janet's comment she went on laughingly, 'I'll enlist the battalion to see to the dishes. But anyway, you get yourself off now. And Robbie wants to talk to you, he's got something to tell you.'

Janet Dunn looked towards her son. Her eyebrows were raised in enquiry, but her face held a blank look, giving nothing away. She said flatly, 'That'll be the day when he hasn't got something to tell me.' The remark too was flat, seemingly holding no meaning except to convey that this mother was used to her son's chatter; yet when they exchanged glances there passed between them a language that only they could read, and Robbie gave a hick of a laugh and turned away and walked across the hall and through the door that led into the kitchen, and the Blenheim family went into the dining-room, there to be met by Mary O'Toole, Harry Blenheim's grandmother.

'Is nobody hungry in this house except me?'

'It won't be a minute,' said Esther Blenheim, going down the length of the room to the hatch at the bottom.

Taking her seat by her great-grandmother, Gail leant towards her and said under her breath, 'You've got a tapeworm, Gran.'

'Watch it! Watch it!'

This remark sent Gail off into high peals of laughter and she leant her head against the old woman's arm and hung on to it. She loved her great Grannie O'Toole; she was more with it than some of her own pals. She said, 'Watch it! Watch it!' just like Tivvy on the ITV said, 'Watch it, pigeons! Watch it!' Oh, her grannie was wonderful.

'Sit up and don't be silly.' Her mother's voice, coming at her from behind, brought her upwards in her seat. 'And make yourself useful; serve the potatoes.'

As Gail went round the table with the vegetable dish Mary O'Toole looked at her grandson and said, 'It's a terrible night; I hope you're not going out again.'

'I'll have to, worse luck,' Harry replied as he set about ladling the stew out of a casserole dish. 'I've got to relieve Peter Thompson at eight o'clock.'

'What! you're going to do Father Christmas?' It was

Terry speaking now, his voice cracking on a laugh. Terry was short and promised to have the build of his father, but his colouring was that of his mother and his brother, John, and what he liked above all else was to raise a laugh. His father, looking at him, said heavily, 'Why can't you keep your tongue quiet!'

'You're not going to play Father Christmas on a night like this!' Mrs O'Toole's thin body was erect in her chair. 'Are you mad? Standing around for hours like Johnny-cum-canny; you want your head lookin' . . . Why don't you do something about it, Esther? He'll get his death, sitting in an office all day, then going and standing in the Market till God knows what hour . . .'

'Gran!' The word fell deep, admonishing, and Mary O'Toole closed her eyes against her daughter-in-law's voice and listened to her own inward one saying, 'In the name of God will I ever get used to it.' Five years she had been under this roof now and it had been pleasant enough, oh, she had to admit that. Esther tried her very best, her Christian best – aye, that was the word, her Christian best – but she only had to hear God, damn or blast used and then she came all over starchy. She had the power to make you feel like a child who had wet its knickers, and her at seventy-five, it wasn't right. One of these days she'd let fly and she'd swear for ten minutes and not use the same word twice. Begod! if she didn't.

Janet Dunn, putting the last dish on the table, said to Esther, 'I'll be off then'; and Esther, smiling up at her, said, 'All right, Janet. And thanks. Elsie should be back in the morning. If I don't see you again before the holidays, a Merry Christmas, Janet.'

'Yes, yes, a Merry Christmas, Janet.' They were nodding all round the table, all seemingly oblivious that Janet did not keep Christmas, but she answered, 'The same to you. The same to you,' before going out.

'That was daft,' said Terry.

'What was?' asked Gail from across the table.

'Wishing Janet a Merry Christmas.'

'I can't see what's daft about it,' said his mother; 'we always do.'

'That doesn't make it any the less daft.' Terry had an impish grin on his face now and he turned it towards Gran O'Toole, saying, 'Does it, Gran?'

'I suppose not,' said Mrs O'Toole. 'But it's courtesy like, and she's a nice woman is Janet Dunn, sensible. And have you noticed' – she swept her glance around the table – 'she's got a presence about her, a dignity.'

'Some dignity!' They all looked at John now, and he finished putting some food in his mouth before ending, 'Working at an all-night café. Some dignity.'

'There's never anything undignified about honest work, John.' There was a strong reprimand in his father's voice.

'Honest! The Dunns? Huh!' John jerked his head backwards. 'That sharp-shooting little squirt, honest.'

'JOHN!'

'Well, he is. How's he come by a car so soon?'

'By hard work.' His father was leaning towards him over the edge of the table. 'He's turned his hands to all kinds to make a living and worked from early dawn until late at night. You don't know you're born, so I don't want to hear any more of it.'

They were all looking at Harry now. It was rarely

they heard him talk like this, rarely saw his face set as it was at the moment, and his manner aggressive.

'Oh, I should have known better than say a word against him.' John's voice was a mumble now. 'Better to keep your mouth shut altogether about the Dunns.'

'You needn't keep your mouth shut about the Dunns. Talk as much as you like about them, only be fair. Robbie never had your chance but by the time he finishes . . .'

'Yes, yes, go on, say it.' John's head was up, his chin out. 'He'll get farther than me, that's what you mean, isn't it? . . . The dirty little Jew boy.' His chair scraped back on the polished floor, and as he rose to his feet to leave the table Esther said, 'Sit down, John, and have your meal and no more of it.'

Now also on his feet, Harry silenced her with a wave of his hand and, confronting his son, he said harshly, 'You use that term ever again, my boy, and I don't care how old you are I'll give you a hiding. You understand?'

John stared for a moment longer at his father, then swung round and dashed out of the room.

As Harry resumed his seat a door banged overhead and they all started eating again, Harry and Esther, Gail and Terry slowly, but Gran O'Toole, munching rapidly, one mouthful hardly swallowed before she took on another, threw into the embarrassed quiet one of what Gail called 'Gran's tactless bombs'. 'If he had half the brains of Robbie,' she said, 'and with the advantages he's had he wouldn't be going to the Technical School next year, he'd be working for one of those big Universities . . .'

As Harry stopped eating and bowed his head deeply

on to his chest, Esther's knife and fork clattered to her plate at the same time as she exclaimed in hurt indignant tones, 'There's one thing we can always rely on you for, Gran, and that's your loyalty to the family.' And on this she, too, left the table.

'What have I said? What have I said?' Gran O'Toole looked from Harry to Terry, and then to Gail, and Gail, as truthful as her great-grandmother, answered, 'The wrong thing as usual, Gran, the wrong thing, and at the wrong time.'

'I wish you a Merry Christmas, I wish you a Merry Christmas, I wish you a Merry Christmas and a Happy New Year.'

'Shut up! Shut up, boy!' Harry now barked at his younger son. 'There's a time and place for everything.'

Terry applied himself again to his food. Gran was already applying herself, but Gail looked at her father, where he sat with his head resting on his hand staring down at his plate, and she thought, 'He likes Robbie. He likes him better than he does John, I'm sure he does, and it isn't fair really.'

It was quarter-past eleven that same evening when Harry returned to the house. He felt frozen to the marrow in spite of the double whisky he'd had. He and Tom Vosey had paraded round the town centre for two and a half hours and collected the almighty sum of one pound, eight and threepence. Was it worth it? He could have put the one pound, eight and threepence into the fund and had the benefit of a night at home, and without the prospect of flu looming up before him.

On the kitchen table there was a tray set, and on the

stove a pan with some milk in it. He didn't want to be bothered making coffee – he would have welcomed it if it had been ready – all he wanted was to climb into bed and get warm, but he reminded himself he'd had whisky and it would be on his breath even though a half-hour had elapsed since he had drunk it, so he'd better make the coffee.

The coffee made, he had just sat down by the side of the table when the kitchen door opened softly and Gail came tiptoeing in. 'I heard the car,' she whispered. 'You're late. Did you get much?'

'One pound, eight and threepence.'

'Oh, the mean beasts. You took over five pounds last Christmas Eve.'

'It was a fine night and people were out. Only mad dogs and fools would be out tonight.'

'You're not a fool.' She came close to him and rubbed her face against his cheek, and he put his arm around her and hugged her to his side, and when she sat on his knee her shortie nightdress and dressing gown rode almost up to her thighs. But she didn't pull them down, her mother wasn't here to chastise her. Looking at her father's weary face, she said, 'It's been a rotten night.'

'I'm sorry; I'm to blame I suppose.'

'Half and half,' she said candidly.

'Thanks.'

'Well, you said it. And, you know, you did go for John.'

'He shouldn't have used that term about Robbie.'

'But Robbie is a Jew, Dad.'

'There's nobody disputing that fact, but would you

like to be called the dirty little Englisher. And what's more, when people like John use terms like that, what can you expect from other boys? It's about time that kind of thing was quashed, good and proper. People don't seem to learn ever.' He shook his head slowly; then went on, 'Robbie's a good boy. What he does he does for his mother. I think his one aim is to make enough so that she won't have to work.'

'But Janet likes work, she told me she does. I asked her only yesterday wasn't she tired after getting up at half-past five in the morning to get to the café, and she said no, she was used to it. I asked her wouldn't she like another job and she still said no; she said the hours had always been convenient, half-past six till half-past eleven. They were convenient when Robbie was at school so she could make his dinner. He would never stay for his dinner she said. She said the job gave her a lot of time to herself and she doesn't mind coming and helping mother when Elsie's off. So you see, she doesn't mind work.'

'That isn't the point, at least how Robbie sees it. Anyway, it's a pity it happened. And at Christmas too. It's bound to mar the atmosphere. Did he go out?'

'Yes, he went to the club. But he was in before ten, and he wouldn't have any supper, not even a drink. Mother was worried, but Gran went in to him.'

'Gran?' Harry raised his eyebrows and jerked his head quickly as he said under his breath, 'Gran should stay out of this; she's caused enough trouble. Trust Gran.'

'She didn't mean it; it just comes out. And you know, it's funny, she can manage John. He takes things from her that he wouldn't from anybody else and she tells him the truth to his face. If I was to say half the things to him that Gran does he'd scalp me.'

He said to her now, 'How long has your mother been up?' and she answered, 'Not long. She looked tired. Grandfather came in. He's not coming for Christmas after all, he's going to his friend in York. He said he's ill and wants to see him. It's the one he was in the Army with, I think. Mother was disappointed about that and all. He brought a lot of parcels. They're up in the attic.' She hunched her shoulders and smiled at him.

'Come on,' he said, tapping her leg. 'To bed.'

She walked to the end of the table, then turning and looking at him where he was putting the tray on the draining board she asked, 'What are you going to do about John? If it isn't cleared up he'll sulk all over the holidays and it'll be frightful. He can you know, I mean sulk for a long time.'

'You leave John to me. Go on, get yourself up.'

She made four tripping steps and came back to him and flinging her arms round his neck, she hugged and kissed him. Then in a manner that was individually hers she drooped her head to one side and smiled gently into his face and whispered, 'You're nice, Mr Blenheim. As a certain Gran O'Toole would say, you're a nice bloke.'

'Go on with you.' He rapped her buttocks smartly once and she ran towards the door her hands on her bottom. Then again hunching her shoulders, she adopted a stealthy attitude and crept out into the hall . . .

Esther was sitting up in bed reading when he entered

the bedroom. She didn't put down her book but looked over the top of it as she said, 'You're late.'

'Yes.'

Dutifully she now asked, 'How did it go?'

'One pound, eight and threepence.'

'One pound, eight and threepence!' She clicked her tongue twice, then asked, 'Did you have a hot drink?'

'Yes.' He began to undress, and she said nothing more until he was in his pyjamas and standing by the side of his bed. She laid down her book then and asked, almost in the same words as Gail had done, 'What are you going to do about John?'

He had a sudden and unusual desire to turn on her and cry, 'I'm going to let him get cold in the grease he got hot in,' but that would mean that her face would tighten, then her eyes would take on that hurt look, and when she spoke there'd be that slight tremor at the end of her words, which indicated the effort she was making to remain calm. Esther laid great stock on remaining calm. All the books she read, especially last thing at night, were to aid calmness. Waldo Trine's 'In Tune with the Infinite' was her second Bible. Daily she imbibed its philosophy. He had once said to her, jokingly, 'I bet you could repeat that book backwards,' and she had taken his remark as censure. His thoughts darting off at a resentful tangent now, he said to himself, 'She even took the damn book on her honeymoon, and the second night she sat up reading it.' He shook his head at himself. He was tired, weary. That business with John had upset him, together with the lack of Christmas spirit emanating from the citizens of Fellburn. It was ludicrous, but if he hadn't stood outside each of the three pubs that lined the Market Square it would have been three and threepence he would have collected, not one pound eight and threepence. So much for Christian charity. God! he felt tired and irritable, all at cross-purposes with everything. It wasn't only the business of John, he had felt off colour lately. Some of the joy had gone out of life; there was a sameness about it. Why? Oh well, it was his age he supposed. They all said it happened to you as you neared forty. Looking at it squarely he'd had a long run for his money. He'd known contentment for years, and that was taking into account the frustrations of the bedroom too. He glanced now at Esther. She was looking at him. Her fair hair was smooth and shining. She hadn't a wrinkle on her skin. She didn't look thirty-seven, she didn't look the mother of three children. She was wearing a pink brushed-nylon nightdress; on someone else, like Gail, it would have looked cosy, cuddly, but on Esther it only looked warm and sensible.

He sat on the edge of his bed. He wished Esther was cuddly. He wanted to go to her now and snuggle down beside her and feel her arms going about him. He imagined her pulling his head down, pressing it in between her breasts. He imagined himself pushing the cuddly nightie up to feel her flesh. He wanted comfort. Lord, how he needed comfort at this moment, wifely comfort, motherly comfort, mistressy comfort. The lot combined. His mouth was working and his hands moving against each other. He was sickening for something; the cold had got into his bones. He could see himself in bed with flu over the holidays . . . 'What?'

'I said are you going to him . . . John?'

322

He stood up and looked at her. She was a good woman, Esther, a good mother, a good wife . . . But what made a good wife? There must be various opinions on that one. Some men had their wives every night, two and three times a night so he understood. Huh! From once a week, Esther had regulated it to once a month. But that was only up till Terry was born. From then it was once every time she felt like it, and Esther very rarely felt like it. It must be four months now since he had lain with her. He was only thirty-eight; he felt no different from what he had felt at eighteen. He wasn't, he supposed, what you'd call a passionate man else there would have been hell to pay, but he was human, natural; and besides he was considerate. He had always been considerate with her, too damned considerate.

'What are you standing there for, like that? You're shivering. Either get into bed or go along and see him and get it over with.'

He turned from her and went to the wardrobe and took out his dressing gown. He was putting it on as he went out on to the landing.

Harry opened his son's bedroom door and went into the room. The light was on and the lower bunk was empty. Terry turned from his back on to his side and looked from the upper bunk at his father. He looked wide awake as if he had been waiting for him coming. He said under his breath, 'He's in his study.' He motioned his head towards the wall and the boxroom that his mother had turned into a workroom for his elder brother and given it the title of the study.

Harry put his hand out and ruffled Terry's already

323

unruly head, saying, 'It's time you were asleep, isn't it?'

Terry chuckled, then laughed softly before he asked, 'Did you take much?'

'A mint, one pound, eight and threepence.'

'Coo! Could they spare it?'

'That's what I've been asking. It wasn't worth it, was it? I mean standing out there all night.'

'No, I should say not. Are you cold?'

'I was, but it's wearing off.' Again Harry touched his son's head. Terry was a nice boy. His character was akin to Gail's, kindly, thoughtful, just the opposite from John's. Who did John take after? Not himself; nor yet Esther. His grandfather? Perhaps, for Dave Rippon had his own particular form of sulks.

'Get to sleep now,' he said as he went out.

He did not knock on the door next to the bedroom but opened it quietly and paused as he saw his son sitting at the small desk in the corner of the narrow room. The boy did not turn his head to look at him. He had likely heard his voice from the other room and was waiting for him. Perhaps he had been waiting for him all evening. This wasn't the first occasion when his son had remained stubbornly silent until he had gone to him and, if not actually apologised, made his peace. He stood by his side now looking down on his hair, but he had no desire to put his hand out and touch it as he had done a moment ago with Terry.

'Time you were in bed, isn't it?' he said.

There was no reply from John, no movement whatever.

'I'm sorry about tonight; we were both a bit hasty.'

Still no reply, no movement.

'I know you don't like Robbie. I know you're an entirely different type from him, but that's no reason to call him names.' Harry saw his son's jaw work, first to one side and then to the other, before his teeth came hard down on his lower lip.

'It's Christmas and this is no time to have quarrels or disagreements. Your mother's worried. Shall we forget it?' He put out his hand now and gently touched his son's shoulder; then, before the lack of response should make him angry, he turned about, saying, 'Come on, get to bed. It's well past midnight.' He paused at the door without turning round and added, 'Good night.'

He didn't even expect an answer to this, for this was John acting according to pattern, but tomorrow morning things would be as they had been before the incident at this evening's meal.

Esther was lying down when he returned to the room and she didn't speak until he had got into bed and put the light out, and then she said, 'Good night,' and he answered, 'Good night.'

He hadn't kissed her good night for more than five years now.

It was almost half-an-hour later when he heard her give a genteel little snort which meant she was asleep, and he turned on his side and put his hand under his cheek and lay staring wide-eyed into the darkness. And it came to him that he was lonely.

Two

'Good morning, Mr Blenheim.'

'Good morning.'

'Good morning, Mr Blenheim.'

'Good morning.'

The female voices of the packing staff chorused through the outer office of the first floor of Peamarsh's.

When Harry passed a little cubicle where an elderly man was sitting at a desk on which there were three telephones, he paused for a moment and said, 'Good morning, Mr Hogg'; and the man stood up quickly, saying, 'Oh, good morning, Mr Blenheim. And it is a morning, isn't it? How did you manage to get the car in? Mr Waters has just phoned to say he can't get his car out of his gate and if he could he wouldn't dare risk it down the hill.'

'Oh, I carried mine,' said Harry laughing, and Mr Hogg laughed too.

He was the only man in Peamarsh's who gave the outer clerk, as the man was called, the title of mister. To the other members of the staff, according to their positions, he was Hogg, Charlie or Dogsbody; the last, mostly from the men in the packing departments on the ground floor and in the basement.

Before he entered his office he had to pass a glass partitioned room which housed four typists and was given the glorified term of pool. The members of the pool this morning weren't sitting industriously at their desks but gathered together in the middle of the room looking at something that one of them held in a small square box. A shadow passing their window brought their heads round apprehensively; then seeing who it was they smiled and nodded and mouthed, 'Good morning, Mr Blenheim.' And Harry nodded back to them.

An engagement ring in that box, he bet; likely belonging to the tall blonde, Miss Rice, wasn't it. Yes, Miss Rice. Well, he hoped she'd keep house better than she took down dictation. He'd had her once when Ada was off sick. Which reminded him; he hoped Ada was in this morning. Although there wouldn't be much work done on the premises today, he had one or two things he wanted to get off, but if that cold of hers hadn't eased she would have likely taken his advice and stayed in bed.

She had. His office was empty when he entered and the door to the little cubby-hole which was his private secretary's domain was closed. It was always open for the first half-hour of the day while she bustled backwards and forwards from his desk to hers.

He had hardly got his coat off when the phone rang. He picked it up and heard his father-in-law's secretary, Miss Bateman nicknamed The Paragon, say, 'Mr Blenheim?'

'Yes.'

'This is Miss Bateman speaking.'

'Yes?' he said again.

'Miss Cole has phoned to say that her cold has got worse and she won't be in this morning.'

'Thank you, Miss Bateman.'

'I'll send someone from the pool.'

'Very well. Thank you.' He almost added laughingly, 'But don't let it be the blonde, she'll be very preoccupied today.' But he was dealing with Miss Bateman, and so, instead, he said, 'There's no hurry, I haven't got much to go off.'

'Very well, Mr Blenheim.'

He put the phone down and walked to the window. It was coming down harder than ever now; he couldn't see the clock on Howard's, the jewellers, across the street. If it wasn't for the party this afternoon he would have those letters off and get home while the going was good, for if this kept up till dinner-time all cars, those that had got in, would be bogged down.

He had just seated himself behind his desk when there came a tap on the door and he said, 'Come in.' And when he saw Jim Whelan enter the room, he exclaimed on a surprised note, 'Why, hello! What's brought you indoors without being dragged? Sit down, sit down.' He pointed to a chair.

Jim Whelan was known as the outside man. His title was appropriate, for most of his work dealt with estimates and valuations. He was not quite a chartered accountant, not having stayed the course long enough to pass his exams; he was not quite an estate agent and valuer, having no private business of his own; but he was a bit of both, and a number of other things besides.

He had been with Peamarsh's for thirty years and Harry had the idea that the longer he stayed the less he liked it. As he had once said to Harry, 'It was all right when they stuck to their own line but now you don't know where you are.' Recently he had been dangerously loud in his condemnation of the firm when they had spread out another tentacle and embraced the building trade. Acting as middle men, they secured contracts, then passed them on, raking off a healthy percentage in the process.

'Something on your mind, Jim?'

'Yes, there is.' Jim Whelan settled himself opposite Harry, then leaned forward and said, 'You remember about two months ago I did an estimate on that job for Halliday, the man who took over Benson's garage down Cromwell Road?'

'Yes, yes, of course I remember; I dealt with it. It went through here.'

'Do you remember what the price was, the one I quoted?'

'Let me see . . . well, I can't say offhand, but just a minute, I can get it for you in a tick.' As he made to get up Whelan said, 'You needn't, only to confirm it. It was six thousand, five hundred for having the garage extended, the car park made, ladies' room put up and so on.'

Harry screwed up his eyes before saying, 'That's right. But what about it?'

'Then why was it raised?'

'Raised?' Again Harry was screwing up his eyes. 'To my knowledge it's never even been confirmed, I mean by Halliday . . . Wait a minute.' He got up quickly and went to a cabinet by the side of the window and, opening a drawer, he flicked through some files; then pulling out a folio he said, 'Here it is, a copy of the estimate, six thousand five hundred.'

'Did you send that out?'

'No, I don't send them from here, not now, they go from the next floor, Rippon's office. It's a new arrangement, since they started on the buildings and contracts.'

'Well, look at these figures, will you?' Jim Whelan now handed a sheet of paper across to Harry. 'I've taken them letter for letter from the correspondence that was sent to Halliday. The typist there's my niece. We got talking and this is what came out of it.'

Harry looked down at the paper in his hand and read: 'Peamarsh's estimate to Halliday for work on garage, etc., seven thousand two hundred and fifty pounds. Lovell's estimate to Halliday for work on garage, eight thousand pounds.'

Harry stared at Jim Whelan and said slowly, 'Lovell's? What's Lovell's got to do with this? We only took them over a month ago. We haven't started doing anything under their name yet, I mean nothing new, we're only finishing off the jobs that were already in hand, at least the contractors are. What does it mean?'

'It means that somebody sent an estimate from the firm of Peamarsh to Halliday quoting in the first place seven hundred and fifty pounds more than the reasonable price, and at the same time they've answered Halliday's letter to Lovell's firm asking for an estimate from them too. How was the poor bugger to know that Lovell's was Peamarsh's and some clever Jack was

330

working off one against the other on him?'

'I can't believe it. And the risk!'

'Risk. What do they care about risk when there's lucre involved? They were out to show how much cheaper Peamarsh's could do the job and at seven hundred and fifty above, what I put in at that. And my estimate of six thousand five hundred was leaving them a warm profit, I can tell you.'

Harry looked grimly down on the figures on the paper; then drawing in a deep breath he said, 'Leave this to me, will you?'

'Yes, I'll leave it to you, Harry. But mind you, I want this straightened out; I don't like to see people taken for double suckers. Single suckers yes, it's happening every day, but this is a bit much.'

'I'll see to it right away, Jim.'

'Will you give me a ring?'

'I'll give you a ring.'

'So long, Harry.' Jim Whelan got up and made for the door. And he had reached it before Harry said, 'So long, Jim.'

When he was alone again, Harry sat staring down on the evidence of jiggery-pokery. He didn't need to ask himself whose work this was, he knew. He had a father-in-law with what was called a business head. But business head be damned, he wasn't going to get away with this. For his own peace of mind he must see that he didn't. Over the years he had closed his eyes to one piece of chicanery after another, but there was a limit.

He took the lift to the top floor and stepped straight on to a thick pile, cherry-coloured carpet. This was

331

Peamarsh's directors' sanctum. There was a wide oak-panelled corridor with two doors on either side. The name plates on the doors said: 'Mr Arthur McMullan'; 'Mr Tom Vosey'; 'Mr Frank Noland'; the fourth door said 'Gentlemen'. The corridor opened into a hallway studded with more doors. These were named: 'Mr Graham Hall'; 'Mr Peter Waters'; 'Mr David Rippon'. Another door had on it the simple statement 'Board-room'.

He thrust open the door marked 'Rippon'. Miss Bateman was sitting behind her desk. She looked up and said, 'Oh, Mr Blenheim, I was just going to ring the pool.'

'Oh, that's all right, Miss Bateman. As I said there's no hurry, I just want a word with Mr Rippon.'

'He was on the 'phone a moment ago. I'll see if he's free.'

She pressed a button and listened, and said, 'He's still on but I don't suppose he'll be a minute. Take a seat, Mr Blenheim.'

It was all very formal; it was always formal with Miss Bateman. He could call his own secretary Ada, but he would never dream of calling Miss Bateman, Marie.

Miss Bateman was a power in Peamarsh's. Before the building had been reconstructed and the top floor given over to the directors Miss Bateman had run the staff, and this included the men in the packing depart-ment, and now, not because she hadn't time, but solely because of the situation of her office, her domain of power reached only to the floor below, where she continued to wield it firmly; except over Ada Cole, who, having worked in Peamarsh's longer than Miss

Bateman, would have none of it. Harry had always been vaguely surprised that his own able but timid secretary refused to be pushed around by The Paragon.

Marie Bateman was in her early forties. She was of medium height and thin, and from her fair hair to her long narrow feet she was perfectly groomed. Altogether she gave off a kind of restrained elegance, which deceived you into thinking she could at one time have been pretty.

Looking at her now, Harry understood why she intimidated most people. But no matter how off-putting her manner, she was a good business woman and secretary, or else his demanding father-in-law would never have kept her on.

'He's finished now.'

'Thanks.' He tapped on the communicating door and went in to Dave Rippon's office.

'Hello there. I expected you.'

Harry paused in the middle of the room and Dave Rippon added, 'I knew Esther wouldn't be able to keep that.'

'Keep what?'

'Keep what! The car, of course. I told her not to mention it until after the holidays, but that's women for you, same all over. Sit down, sit down. Well what do you think? Do you want it?'

'This is the first I've heard of it. You mean your car?'

'Oh, so she didn't tell you then.' Dave Rippon leant back in his high-backed, black swivel chair and laughed. It was a small sound coming from so large a man. Then he passed his hand over his forehead and on to his thick greying hair before he said, 'Well, I'm ready for a change, it's over two years. Esther said you liked it.'

'Yes . . . yes I like it.' His tone held no enthusiasm. 'But you always put your old one in for exchange, don't you?'

'Usually. But that one of yours must be dropping to bits.'

'It's a good car, it's only five years old.'

'Only five!' The voice was scornful. 'It might as well be fifty. Anyway there it is, it's up to you. As you know, it cost me nearly two thousand. They'll give me fourteen hundred for it or more but I'll let you have it for twelve fifty. It's up to you.'

Harry looked at his father-in-law, at his round fleshy face, at his round pale blue eyes, which you could have called a sailor's eyes, far-seeing; and the description was certainly true in his father-in-law's case for Dave Rippon was far-seeing where Dave Rippon was concerned. People said he was a handsome man, a fine figure of a man, a man you would never put fifty-five years to, fifty yes, even forty-five on some days. His body was big, thick and hard. He had been an athlete in his time and the effect was still with him in spite of his sly drinking, although that was showing now in a thickening above his belt.

He had never liked his father-in-law, perhaps because he knew that everything Dave Rippon did for him was really for his daughter. He was where he was, he knew, because he had married Esther. This knowledge hadn't irked him during the first years of marriage, but latterly it had got under his skin, more so as he took his father-in-law's real measure. He knew for instance that his father-in-law couldn't make a straight deal if his life depended on it. Even about the car he had to be crooked. He wouldn't get fourteen hundred for it; it had only cost him eighteen hundred in the first place not two thousand. If he got twelve hundred he'd be lucky, and that's what he wanted him to pay. Moreover the car wasn't two years old; by his reckoning it was three, nearer four.

'I'm a fool for letting it go in any case.' Harry blinked as his father-in-law leaned across the desk towards him. 'I'm just going to get the same type, same colour in fact I think, but you know after a couple of years things start going. Oh' – he leaned back again and flapped his hand towards Harry – 'that's bad business, isn't it? I'll have to look out, I'm slipping. Well, you know how she's been taken care of, there's nothing wrong with her really.'

Harry just stopped himself from saying, 'No, you've only beaten the guts out of her.'

Dave Rippon waited for Harry to make some comment, and when none was forthcoming he blew his nose on a silk handkerchief before adopting his business attitude and saying, 'Well, if it wasn't about the car, what brought you up on this the slackest morning of the year, for I don't expect there'll be two penn'orth of work done in the whole building today?'

Harry swallowed, wetted his lips, then said, 'I've come up about the Halliday estimates.'

There was a long pause before Dave Rippon spoke, and then he said one word, 'Yes?'

'Whelan got the estimate out.'

'I'm aware of that.'

'It was for six thousand, five hundred.'

There was another pause before Dave Rippon said, 'I'm aware of that also, so what?'

He held his father-in-law's eye as he said, 'The estimate was sent out to them for seven thousand, two hundred and fifty.'

There was no reply from Dave Rippon now and Harry, wetting his lips again, said, 'And there was another estimate sent to Halliday, apparently from Lovell's for eight thousand.'

'Now look here, Harry.' Dave Rippon was sitting very straight in his chair, his two hands flat on the desk. 'This is not in your department and I'll thank you . . .'

'But I think it is, Dave. You see, the letter came to me from Halliday; I got Whelan to make the estimate and that came to me too.'

'And then it came into this office. From then on it isn't your business.'

Harry took a deep breath and dared to say, 'I don't like it. To me it's bad business.'

If he had thrust out his arm and punched his father-in-law right in the middle of his face Dave Rippon couldn't have been more taken aback, so much so that he could only stare at his daughter's husband and think, once again, she let herself in for something there. But his agile mind told him at this moment that he would have to tread carefully with his son-in-law, because it would never do for this to get around, at least off this floor. He made himself lean back, take a deep, deep breath, and smile; then his voice calm-sounding, he said, 'You know, Harry, right from the first I knew

336

you weren't cut out for business, you're not ruthless enough. Now this is just a simple business deal; you've been long enough with the firm surely to realise that there are rules within rules, wheels within wheels.'

'You sent an estimate supposedly from Lovell's for eight thousand for the same job.'

Dave Rippon took a folded handkerchief now from his breast pocket and wiped something from the corner of his eye, stretching his mouth wide the while; then he said, 'Well, that's easily explained. But it shouldn't need any explaining because you know yourself you send out an estimate and some of these beggars will beat you down to the last penny. They say A, B and C have put in theirs at hundreds less; you know this quite well, you're getting them every day. Well now, the job was six thousand five hundred, right?' He paused, waiting for a reply, but when Harry continued to stare at him he went on, 'We put on another seven hundred and fifty. Why? Again because Halliday is a new customer and if we can drop a few hundreds, say, down to six five, the original estimate, we've got him for good and all . . . see?'

'Yes, yes, I can see that.' But even as he said it he knew that Halliday's estimate would never be dropped to six five not while his father-in-law was dealing with it.

'Now about the Lovell's estimate; nobody outside those immediately concerned knows we've taken over Lovell's yet. Lovell's was a small private building company; their work was very high class and you've got to pay for high class work; so, therefore, when Halliday sent to Lovell's for an estimate I gave an estimate according to the work that Lovell's would likely have put in . . .'

'But that's the point. You'll give this job to Bradley or Kershaw or one of the others; they're not of Lovell's standard.'

Dave Rippon closed his eyes and leaned against the back of his chair, and then he said, 'If you were getting an estimate in from one firm for seven thousand two hundred and fifty and for the same kind of work you got an estimate for eight thousand from another firm which would you take? Go on, tell me which one you would take? You know damn well which one you would take.' Again he was leaning forward, his forearms stretched across the desk now, his hands flat as before. 'We sent Lovell's out just as a matter of business. It's BUSINESS. We're not thieves or gangsters, we're business men. This is a business house. Oh lord!' He now rose to his feet, thrusting his chair back against the wall. 'At this stage of your career I shouldn't be giving you a lecture on business ethics.'

'Perhaps you should.'

'What!' Dave Rippon turned and looked down on Harry.

'What if Halliday, being a finicky kind of man, I don't know if he is, but just say he is, what if he plumps for Lovell's estimate?'

'Then he deserves to pay eight thousand, that's all I can say.' Dave Rippon was bending down to Harry now, his face on a level with his head, and below his breath he said, 'Why these scruples all of a sudden?'

Harry looked away from his father-in-law's face before saying quietly, 'I don't think they are sudden.'

338

Then he dared to add, 'A decent profit, that's business, but . . . but this is jiggery-pokery. And have you thought what this man's going to say when he discovers that Peamarsh and Lovell are one and the same firm.'

'I don't care what he thinks.' Dave Rippon was standing straight now and his voice sounded calm and cold. 'The point stands that Lovell's was a high class firm and had highly skilled workmen, we've taken them over; nothing has changed.'

Oh my God! Harry groaned to himself. What could you say, how could you come back at this kind of twisted thinking? Half of Lovell's men were scattered among Bradley and Kershaw's. Whatever good work Lovell's men had done as a combined force was finished, but could you convince a man like Dave Rippon that this was so.

'Look.' Dave Rippon's voice came in sharp and high. 'What you want is a holiday, or' – he poked his face forward again – 'a change of job.'

'Perhaps you're right.'

Harry got to his feet, and Dave Rippon, sensing the battle of words he'd have with his daughter should her husband for any reason leave his protection, swallowed deeply and his tone, conciliatory now, said, 'Come on, come on. Look, leave this to me. I'll straighten it out to fit your conscience. It's Christmas; come on, forget about it.' He put his hand on Harry's shoulder and walked him towards the door, and as he opened it he remarked casually, 'I'm off to York this afternoon; I suppose Esther told you.'

'Yes, she did say something about it.'

'It's a blooming nuisance. This fellow – he was my

Colonel, I hadn't seen for years until we met at a reunion a little while ago – he's in a bad way, dicky heart, lives on his own . . . well he's got a housekeeper, sort of. Anyway, he phoned me yesterday begging me to come up. And what can you do at Christmas, somebody lonely, eh?' They were passing Miss Bateman's desk and he turned his head towards her now and asked, 'Oh, by the way, did you get me the reservation?' And when she answered, 'Yes, it's here,' he turned to Harry again and said, 'There'll be thousands travelling today, and if this keeps on I can see us being stranded in some siding over the holiday.' He laughed his other laugh, a deep belly laugh, then added, 'But I must look in on the jollification for a little while, so see you again at three then.'

'It's beginning at two-thirty today.' They both looked at Miss Bateman, and she added, 'I'm having word sent round, so that everyone can get away earlier.'

'Half-past two it is then.' Dave Rippon nodded at Harry and Harry returned the nod, then went out and down the passage and to the lift and when he was inside he leant his head against the wooden partition. He had never felt so small and inconsequential in his life before. From the beginning to the end of the interview his father-in-law had treated him like a cross between a young clerk and a man depending on his livelihood from the perks of his wife's father.

When he opened his office door a girl was standing at the corner of his desk. He said, 'Oh, hello,' and she said, 'I'm Betty Ray. Miss Bateman sent me in.'

'Oh yes. Sit down, Miss Ray.'

Seated behind the desk, he picked up some letters

from the in-tray, saying, 'There's only about half-a-dozen, they won't take long.' He smiled at her now and said, 'Nobody wants to work this morning.' And she smiled back at him and replied, 'Oh, I don't mind. I'd rather work, it passes the time away.'

'Yes,' he inclined his head towards her, 'there's something in that. Now then, this is to Farrow, Barrett and Soames.'

As he dictated the letter he looked at her and thought, She's the one that sits farthest away from the window. The girls in the pool were mostly faces to him; they came in before he did in the morning and they went before he left at night. Sometimes he passed them on the stairs at lunch time but he had never managed to put a face to a body until now. Miss Ray looked a vivacious girl, medium height, black hair with a fine pair of eyes. Brown or black? He waited until she looked up again. Brown.

When she had finished typing the letters and she was about to go, he said, 'If it wasn't for the party you could go home now I suppose,' and she answered pertly, 'But what would I do there . . . Well I mean, I've got nothing to do at home; I'd rather stay for the party and risk being snowed in.'

'You would?'

She nodded at him, 'Yes,' and they both laughed, he freely.

'How long have you been here?' he asked.

'Just over two months.'

'Do you like it?'

She shrugged her shoulders. 'It's a job.'

Yes, they were all jobs, just jobs. He looked at her

341

now as a whole. She was what they would call petite. She sounded lively, different from poor old Ada. But Ada was twice her age. He guessed this girl to be twenty. When he said, 'Thanks, Miss Ray,' she said, in a manner which would surely have caused Miss Bateman's back hair to stand on end, 'Any time, any time, Mr Blenheim,' and went out.

He found himself still smiling as he straightened the papers on his desk. For the moment he had forgotten about Halliday, Lovell's and his father-in-law.

Three

The basement storeroom was crowded with staff, ranging from the second director to the tea boy. A transistor was blaring forth dance music, but no-one would have thought of dancing; they didn't dance at the office party, they just drank, talked and laughed.

Harry, carrying a tray of filled sherry glasses, stopped in front of a group of men and one of them said, 'Well, there's no need for the old seasonable advice today, Mr Blenheim, eh?'

'What's that, Barney?'

'Well, if you drive don't drink, and if you drink don't drive.'

'Oh yes, yes, that's true. Well, we're going to get something out of the snow after all, you could say.'

An elderly-looking man said, 'I've seen some snow in me time but never anything like this. I've never seen it so thick that you couldn't get your cars out of the yard.'

'They say the buses are only running on the flat; they can't tackle Brampton Hill or the cemetery road.'

'Well the weather's not going to worry me,' said

343

another man. 'I mean to get bottled and stay corked for the entire four days.'

Harry moved on amid laughter and went to a corner, where two girls were sitting on upturned boxes. As he neared them one got to her feet, saying, 'I'll go and bring Ada,' and Harry, offering the tray to the remaining girl, said, 'Well, Miss Ray, how are you doing?'

'Quite well, Mr Blenheim, quite well; I've still got some.' She raised her half-filled glass; then putting her hand out she added, 'But I'll take another, just to keep the kettle boiling.'

'To keep the kettle boiling!' Harry laughed down on the girl. 'It's a long time since I heard that one. Which part are you from?'

The pert face pushed up towards his and the voice, hushed a little, said, 'I'd better whisper it, Bog's End.'

'No! Well, the same here.'

'You, Mr Blenheim!' The brown eyes were stretched wide, the mouth agape.

'Yes, I was born there.'

'Well, I never. Small world. Some go up, some go down, and some just stay put. The last's me. Although we don't live actually in Bog's End, but not a kick in the backs . . . Oh lord!' She put her hand over her mouth and spluttered, 'Aw well, it's Christmas, I might as well say it.'

Harry was laughing freely again. She was a card, this one. He wondered how she ever became a shorthand typist; her kind always ended up in a store or a factory. There was nothing of gentility, faked or otherwise, that he had come to expect from the typists in Peamarsh's.

344

And she was a looker too, full of personality.

When her companion and another girl came scurrying back and sat one on each side of her he offered them glasses of sherry, and they giggled as they said, 'Oh, thanks, Mr Blenheim.'

He smiled widely at them, saying, 'It's my pleasure, ladies.' Then, again amid laughter, he moved on.

When he went to the trestled table to replenish his tray his father-in-law was standing talking to Graham Hall. Hall was senior to Dave Rippon, but by how much was anybody's guess. He suffered from a stomach complaint, and it was rumoured he was going to retire long before his time. Harry knew that his father-in-law could hardly wait for Hall's shoes, or for that matter Mr Walters, whom everybody said should have retired years ago.

Dave Rippon, showing his consideration for the staff, called in a voice that he aimed to raise above the din, 'You're seeing to everybody, Harry? How about Miss Bateman?' He pointed to where Miss Bateman was standing condescending to talk to Jim Whelan, it being the one day in the year when position and seniority were supposedly forgotten.

Harry looked towards Miss Bateman, but she was looking at her boss, and her boss was smiling at her and waving his hand. The atmosphere was very genial, very.

Mrs Streatham, who saw to the tea each day, was now busily filling glasses. As she piled half-a-dozen on to Harry's tray she said, 'What about yourself, Mr Blenheim? I haven't seen you take a drink yet.'

'You must have had your eyes closed then' – he poked his head towards her – 'I've downed three so far,

345

and there's still time to double it. They're saying back there we've no need to worry about drinking and driving today.'

'That's true, Mr Blenheim; we're going to get something out of it anyway.'

'That's exactly what I said.' They laughed together as if at a hilarious joke.

When he handed a glass of sherry to Miss Bateman she smiled thinly at him and said, 'Thank you, Mr Blenheim,' and he thought, 'That's your fourth to my knowledge and not even a sparkle in your eye.' She could certainly carry it.

As he was threading his way through the groups sitting and standing about the storeroom he bumped into Tom Vosey. He, too, had a tray in his hand and he bowed to Harry, saying, 'Can I press you to a drink, Sir?'

Vosey was the youngest of the directors. He had risen to where he was because he was related to Graham Hall. Nevertheless, to Harry, Tom was all right. They were buddies. And now, with a number of sherries down him, Tom was being skittish and playful; and Harry answered him in like vein. Assuming a pompous air, he said, 'Thank you, my boy, thank you. Well, just one to keep out the chill, or let's say because there won't be any bill. Hah! hah! hah! Doesn't sherry make you witty? Drink it, my boy, drink it.'

Tom Vosey put out his hand and pushed Harry in the shoulder, almost upsetting him and the tray. He was spluttering as he said, 'You know, that's old Walters to the tee; I could even smell the board room.' Then he added, 'I say, how are we going to get home? . . . We'll have to shank it, won't we?'

'I'm afraid so.'

'God, I've got a mile to go. But you've got two, or more. Harry, I say.' He was whispering now confidentially. 'Do these affairs bore you? Honest now, honest.'

Harry considered a moment, then said thoughtfully, 'Yes and no. At one time I used to look forward to them, but now . . . well.'

'Me too. I know what you mean. We enjoyed them when we were young, boy, when we were young.' Again he pushed Harry in the shoulder; then went on his way laughing.

At a given signal someone called for order and Mr Hall said his usual few words, apologising for the absence of their esteemed head director and thanking the staff, one and all, for their faithful service to the firm of Peamarsh.

Immediately this ritual was over, Dave Rippon came up to Harry and spoke as if the altercation in the office hadn't happened. 'Well, I'm off, Harry,' he said. 'Give my love to them all at home. It's a damn nuisance having to go to York on a day like this, but there it is. We let ourselves in for these things and have to stand the consequences. Well, have a good time.' He slapped Harry between the shoulders. 'And by the way, if it thaws, come down and take the car to the garage, will you?' He hiccuped slightly, then laughed as he added, 'It's going to be yours anyway, so you'd better look after it . . . Happy Christmas.' He slapped him again between the shoulders, then cried loudly to those about him, 'Happy Christmas, everybody. Happy Christmas.'

'Happy Christmas, Sir. Happy Christmas, Sir.'

When he came opposite to Miss Bateman he actually took her hand and shook it, saying, 'A happy Christmas,' and she, looking into his face, replied, 'A happy Christmas, Mr Rippon.' Then waving his hand about him he went out.

'That should have given her a thrill,' said Jim Whelan nonchalantly as he passed Harry, 'having your hand shaken by God. By the way, did you see him about that business?' and Harry replied, 'Yes, I'll go into it after the holidays, Jim.'

'Good. Well now, I'm off an' all. Happy Christmas, Harry.'

'Happy Christmas, Jim.'

Ten minutes later he was back in his office. His head was buzzing. He did not know how many sherries he had got down him, at least half-a-dozen. He had never taken on that many before. He'd better get a cup of tea somewhere before he arrived home; it wouldn't do to greet Esther starry-eyed. He gave a little laugh to himself, then sat down at his desk and rested his head on his hand. He felt he could just drop nicely off to sleep; but he'd better not do that, he had a trek before him.

He rose and got slowly into his outer things, looked around the office, switched out the light, and went down the stairs to the main hall.

The hall was quite empty and he stood listening for a moment. There was no sound in the whole building. Funny, fifteen minutes ago the laughter and chatter had been rising to the top floor. He went out through the glass door and into the porch, and was met by a flurry of snow. It was still falling in thick, steady flakes, and although it was only a quarter to four it was almost dark.

As he stood pulling his collar tightly up around his neck a small figure darted up the three steps in front of him, and as she brushed past him, she said, 'Oh hello. Hello again. I've forgotten my bag. Fancy doing a daft thing like that. And it's got me pay in it!' She pushed out her lips and blew the snow away from her face, then laughed before disappearing through the glass door. He went slowly down the steps into the street, and he had just reached the corner when she caught up with him again.

'Dreadful, isn't it? It's getting worse.'

'Yes. Have you far to go?'

'Pullman Street.' As she finished she slipped and one leg disappeared into what had been a gutter but was now an eighteen inch drift. As he steadied her he said, 'I know Pullman Street. I can go part of the way with you; we could cut across the Market, they've likely cleared that a bit.'

They had cleared the Market earlier in the day but the constant falling had beaten them for the Square was knee high in places. He said to her now, 'They're going to find it difficult putting their stalls up tomorrow, and they generally do a roaring trade on Christmas Eve.'

She turned her face towards him as she laughed and said, 'We always wait until the last minute and get our turkey at a throw-out price. My mother can remember getting one one Christmas Eve for half-a-crown. But they hadn't the big freezers then. But who needs a freezer in this?'

When they had to step over a drift to get on to the pavement he took her arm and said, 'Come on, jump it. One, two, three!'

She squealed as she landed on the other side, then cried, 'I've lost me shoe!'

When he dug out the high-heeled shoe he said, 'Why didn't you put on something sensible when you knew it was like this?'

'Oh, who wants to be sensible? Here, can I hang on to you while I put it on.'

He supported her with his arm around her shoulders and she held on to him as she bent her leg back and put on her shoe. And she squealed again, saying, 'Coo! it's freezing. Me other one is wet and warm but this is like ice now.'

The further they got away from the centre of the town the deeper the snow. In the side roads nobody had bothered to clear it away as yet and when they came to Taunton Square, from where his road lay in the opposite direction from hers, he said, 'You're never going to make this on your own, I'd better see you to your door.'

'Thanks.' She peered up at him through the falling snow. 'It's only about another five minutes' walk. At least it used to be; I don't know how long it will take us now.'

'Come on, let's see then.' And he laughed as he took her arm.

After they had gone a little way she pulled him to a stop and said, 'Listen! Isn't everything quiet, hushed like?'

He listened, then answered, 'Yes, nice and quiet,

hushed like.' He was smiling down at her.

'Do you like things quiet?' They were trudging on again now.

'Yes, moderately so.'

'Oh, I don't, I like bustle, plenty of people, talk, noise, laughter . . . life. That's what I like, life.'

Although he couldn't see her face he said, 'Yes, I can see you do.'

Her comment to this was cut off when they both slipped together and overbalanced in the snow. When they righted themselves they had their arms around each other, but only for a second, for, taking her arm again, he made the incident casual by saying, 'It's treacherous; you could break your neck.'

'We're nearly there; two more streets and up the cutting.'

In the cutting they had to walk in single file, lifting their feet high to make progress, and when they came to the end of it she pointed to the first house at the end of a short street and said, 'Well, we're here.'

He raised his hat now and said formally, 'Well, I'm glad you've made it. I think I'll make my way back into the Market and keep to the main roads; they must have made some attempt to keep them open.'

'But you're not going straightaway' – she was peering up at him again as she searched in her bag for her key – 'You're wringing and frozen as much as me. Come in and have a cup of something hot.'

'It's very kind of you but . . .'

'Kind, me foot! Come on in.'

He smiled to himself as he followed her into the house. She certainly was an uninhibited little miss,

351

and she certainly had no respect for rank or class distinction.

'Take your coat and things off, I'll switch the fire on. The house is warm, the boiler's always on, but we'll need something more than the boiler to thaw us out.' She had flung her coat and head scarf aside and now, balancing on one leg, she undid her stockings from her suspenders and dragged them from her wet legs.

'Here, give me your coat, I'll put it on the boiler.'

'Oh no, no. It's perfectly all right, it's waterproof.'

'Waterproof or not, it's soaking wet across the bottom. Here give it to me.' She almost dragged it from him. 'There now, sit down an' make yourself comfortable.'

As she went to go through a door she paused and, looking over her shoulder, laughed back at him, saying, 'Make yourself at home; it's Christmas . . . remember.'

He found himself sitting on a very comfortable couch before an electric fire which flickered over artificial logs and smiling widely to himself. Make yourself at home. Make yourself at home, because it's Christmas. She was a little star turn.

'Tea?' Her voice was calling from the other room, the kitchen presumably.

'Yes, please.' He listened to a kettle being filled and the plop of the gas being lit, and when she came back into the room she said, 'It won't be a tick.'

He looked at her standing in her bare feet, her dress coming just above her knees – Miss Bateman wouldn't allow mini skirts – she looked like a child, no older than Gail. For something to say he said, 'It's a very comfortable room this.' He spread out his hand.

'Yes, I like it.' She came and sat on the sofa, not in the corner but not close to him. 'My mother did it up; she's a dab hand with paper and paint.'

'Your mother does the decorations, not your father?'

'I haven't got a father.'

'I'm sorry.'

'Oh, don't be. I don't remember him; he died when I was young.'

'Have you any brothers or sisters?'

'No, just me and me mother, two lone women.' She laughed, and he laughed and said, 'Woman indeed!'

'What do you mean? Woman indeed! What do you take me for? A girl?'

'Well, yes, I would. I'd take you for a girl, a young girl.'

'Coo! that's nice.'

The kettle began to whistle and she jumped up and went into the kitchen, and from there she called, 'How old do you think I am?'

He thought for a moment and said 'Nineteen.'

'Thanks very much; I'm twenty-four.'

'You're not!'

'I am.' She came in with the tray and, putting it down on a pouffe to the side of the fireplace, she said, 'I'm shivering, I want something to lace this. How about you?'

'Oh, not for me, thank you.'

'Oh go on.' She went to a sideboard behind them and brought out a bottle of whisky. 'It's Christmas. Have you forgotten? It's Christmas, and we've just trekked through the Yukon, and you've saved me life and we've

353

come to the log cabin and we're going to be marooned here for three weeks.'

He was laughing loudly now; he couldn't help but laugh at her.

'There, get that down you.'

He'd never had whisky in tea before and he clicked his tongue against the roof of his mouth and said, 'Hmm! very nice.'

'I'll say it's nice; it's me life saver.'

'Yes?'

'Yes.' She drew in a deep breath and lifted her legs and put the soles of her feet towards the fire. Then leaning back, she said, 'Everything's nice at Christmas; everybody's nice to everybody at Christmas. Have you noticed it? For a couple of days everybody's nice to everybody, and for the rest of the year they're bitchy.'

'Is that how you've found life?'

'Mm! Well no.' She shook her head. 'There are nice people. You're nice.'

'Thank you.'

'But you are, seriously.' She now sat straight up on the couch and turned her body towards him until her knees were within an inch of his. 'That's what they said the first day I came to Peamarsh's. You'll like Mr Blenheim, they said; he's nice.'

'They didn't. You're teasing me.'

'Honest, they did, all the girls in the pool. They said there were one or two not bad, Mr Vosey and Mr Whelan, and one or two on the bottom floor, but for the rest they were stinkers. Oh, you should hear what they say. And they know some things about a lot of them an' all, all the darling goodie-goodies. Make your hair stand up on end, it would. But never about you.' She took another long drink from her cup, her eyes fixed on him all the while. 'A nice bloke, that's what they said you were, a quiet, nice bloke. And you know what else they say?'

His mouth was tightly closed, he was trying to stop himself from laughing. He shook his head. 'That you're above board.'

He stared at her, his face bright. He felt warm inside, the whisky was seeing to that. Yet it wasn't the whisky alone, it was a good feeling to know that people thought you a nice fellow, a nice bloke. Gail had said that too. It was worth being above board after all.

'They think Rippon, your father-in-law's, a stinker.'

'Oh, do they now?'

'Yes. He's rotten rich, isn't he? They say he's got more than Mr Walters, or Mr Hall or any of the others put together. They say he's loaded down with shares in everything from oil to ointment.'

He drooped his head on to his chest and bit on his lip. He should stop her talking but he couldn't; nor did he want to. It was all so good to hear that they thought Mr Dave Rippon a stinker. It was good to know that some people could see through his church façade.

'Have another sup?'

'Oh, no, thanks.'

'Come on.' She pulled the cup from him. 'You can only get really drunk once.'

He was leaning against the back of the couch laughing loudly. He had never laughed like this in years. Suddenly he put his hand over his mouth and said, 'Dear! dear! Have you got near neighbours?'

355

'Only Ma Tarrant next door and she's stone deaf. We're lucky . . .'

Half-an-hour later he had got through three cups of tea and almost the equivalent of three double whiskies; he had his shoes off and they were set at a safe distance from the electric fire drying. Betty was now in a knee-length, padded dressing gown because she had found that her dress was damp. She sat on the couch with her legs curled under her, her head and hands moving as she talked; and he lay back in bemused contentment and laughed at her. He had never met anyone like her. She was gay, happy, full of the joy of living and, strangely, she didn't make him feel old. He felt younger now than he could remember feeling in his twenties.

'Loosen your collar and tie.'

'No, no. What do I want to loosen my collar and tie for?'

'Go on, make yourself comfortable, there's nobody'll come in. Me mother won't be back until nearly eight. Here.' She had her hands at his neck, and they were struggling now; then she was lying across his knee looking up into his face, her hands still at his neck but quiet for a moment under his grip. He looked down at her in silence, and then he said thickly, 'You know, you're a naughty girl.'

'My! you've been quick finding that out. You're sharp.' Her tone, the deriding manner in which she said it, her candidness, set him off laughing again. And now she had her head snuggled under his chin and his tie was off and the buttons of his shirt were open.

'Have you any hairs on your chest?'

'What!'

356

'Let's see if you have any hairs on your chest.'

They were struggling again.

'Here, here! you little devil. Give over.'

She gave over and lay back on his arm, her head on the end of the couch looking up at him. Then, her hand coming out, she traced her red-nailed finger gently around his mouth, saying softly, 'You're nice, nicer than nice, sort of innocent nice.'

'What!' He tried to pull himself up in mock indignation and she emphasised now, 'But you are. Do you know what? If you weren't, you'd have had me clothes off afore now.'

'Oh, Betty. Really!'

'Oh, Betty, really!' She mimicked his voice, then tweaked his nose.

As she lay gazing up at him, her big brown eyes mere slits now, his sanity, rising on a strong wave, told him to get out of here and quick, and he muttered thickly, 'I'll have to be making my way; it's getting on and it's going to take me some time to . . . to get back.'

'Why go when you don't want to?'

'What do you mean, I don't want to?'

'You know what I mean. You don't want to go.'

They were staring at each other again, and he said softly, 'You seem to know everything, don't you?'

'Pretty near everything.' She was her skittish self again, her chin bobbing and her hand waving in the air. 'Anyway, I know enough that you don't want to go.'

'What if I prove you wrong?'

Her body became still for a moment. Then raising her head from the couch, she brought her face close to his. Her eyes, wide now, stared into his, and of a

357

sudden she was kissing him, holding him and kissing him with such a ferocity that it was like an attack. And it was seconds before he responded to her.

When she pulled him up from the couch and led him across the room and into a bedroom he made no resistance. When she switched on the light, one thing his bemused mind did notice was that the curtains were already drawn; it was as if she had prepared for it.

He sat on the edge of the bed, as much from weakness at the knees as pressure from her hands, and when, slowly unbuttoning the dressing gown, she slid it from her and stood before him stark naked, he closed his eyes against the sight of her. He hadn't seen Esther naked more than half-a-dozen times in his life, and then only when he had barged into the bathroom, when she had been quick to cover herself up. Yet here was this girl standing before him without a stitch on. It was unbelievable. For a moment he thought that he must be dreaming, until her hands came on him again and she pulled off his jacket.

All his life afterwards he was to remember the next half-hour. Even when he hated the thought of it, every incident and happening in it was to remain clear before his eyes. At night when they turned the key on him and he was alone within those four cold, soul-crushing walls, he was to remember. Later, through ostracism and shame, the memory was still clear. Even when his life flowed through a channel that brought him a peace he had never known before, the memory remained vivid. Bringing him out of sleep, pushing the sweat from his pores, bringing groans and remembered moans of ecstasy from him.

He had been married for eighteen years and he knew now that compared with her he was as inexperienced as a virgin boy. He felt ravished, raped. She was wild, savage, almost demented at times. Such intensity and passion coming from such a small frame was unbelievable; and more unbelievable still when he thought of her as a young girl. But once it was over he never thought of her as a young girl again.

He lay still on the top of the bed, nothing moving but his bare chest. He wasn't at peace as was the case after he had been with Esther; every nerve end in his body seemed frayed, yet he had a strange sense of exhilaration and achievement. But he had achieved nothing; the achieving was hers. He wasn't aware how long he lay unmoving, but when he turned his head and looked at her he expected to find, like Esther, she would have her eyes closed as she dropped into relaxed sleep. But instead, her eyes were wide, laughing, waiting. She said softly to him, 'Do you believe me now?' He did not answer but made a questioning movement with his head, and she replied, 'That I know everything.' He still did not answer her, but as he looked at her he thought, Yes, she certainly does. And where had she learned it? She looked nineteen, she said she was twenty-four, and she had the knowledge of an old whore mistress. The last thought brought him up on his elbow to stare down at her, and it was as if he was reading the words written on her naked body: She was a tart. A little prostitute, that's what she was.

He got off the bed and dressed with his back to her, pulling on his clothes with jerky movements. When he made for the door she said to him, 'Some people are never satisfied.' He turned and looked at her but could find nothing to say. As he went to close the door behind him she said, 'I'll be seeing you.' It sounded like a threat.

He pulled on his shoes, got into his coat, wound his scarf around his neck, took up his hat and let himself out into the street. It was still snowing heavily, and he stood for a moment bemused. He must have been stark, staring mad.

He entered the long cut, lifting his feet high with each step, and when he reached the end of it where the wind had drifted the snow to the side and left a small clear space he stood for a minute leaning his back against the wall. What had he let himself in for? This is what happened when men went abroad. Peter Thompson had told him why Arthur Rice went off on his lone tour at least once a year. It could happen abroad and no consequences. But this had happened in Fellburn, in the town where he was known by practically everyone, where he was known as a churchman, for the simple reason that he sang in the choir, and, as it happened, with a young girl in his firm, a girl he'd see every day in the week, even if it was only her head through the glass partition of the pool. God! What had he done? He must have been raving, barmy. He hadn't been all that drunk, he had known what he was doing. Or had he? He'd never had so much whisky at one go before. And on top of all that sherry. He rubbed his hand over his snow-covered face. It was no use making excuses for himself, it was done, and he, Harry Blenheim, had done it . . . Or had he? He was feeling again her bouncing, struggling bare body. But it didn't tie up

360

with the everyday picture of her, small, neat and soft. Yet he'd heard of women like her; he had heard body-hungry men easing themselves with stories of loving amazons. But she hadn't been just one amazon, she had been half-a-dozen. How long was he there altogether? He pushed his coat sleeve up to peer at his watch, then realised with deep dismay that he had left it in the bedroom. The strap had caught at her skin and he had dragged it off his wrist and thrown it on the side table. It was a gold watch with a gold link strap and had been Esther's present to him on their seven-teenth wedding anniversary and had an inscription inside to that effect. God! What was he going to do now? He'd have to go back. He turned, but didn't go immediately down the cut; he had to will his body to move.

He had just reached the end of the cut when he saw a woman standing by the door he was making for. She was banging on it as she kicked the snow from her feet. When the door opened he caught a blurred glimpse of the girl. Within a second the door was closed.

That settled that. He wasn't going in there and have to face the mother; no, not if he never got the watch.

When he again reached the end of the cut he stopped once more, his thoughts racing now. How was he going to face them at home, Esther and Gail? Gail? It would be harder to face Gail.

'You all right, mister?' The man coming out of the cut was looking into his face, and he pulled himself from the wall and said, 'Yes, thank you. Just a little exhausted. It's heavy going.'

'You're telling me . . . Far to go?'

'Holt Avenue.' They were plodding along side by side now.

'Oh, that's yon side, isn't it?'

'Yes, it's some way. But I'll cut across the Market and keep to the main road. That should ease things.'

'That's going out of your way,' said the man. 'Why don't you cut up Barrack Road. Look, we're coming to it. You cut up there; that'll take off the Market and bring you out in Champlion Place.'

'Oh, as near as that?'

'Yes,' said the man; 'it'll cut a good third off.'

'That's very helpful.' Harry nodded at him. 'Thanks, I'll try it.'

They parted at the corner of the next street, and the going here wasn't so bad as the people had attempted to clear the snow from the pathways. But when he came out into Champlion Place it was almost knee high again. As he crossed the Square his knees almost buckled under him. From the Square he cut up side street after side street; then of a sudden he realised he was walking down Baker Street. This was where Janet lived. In the ordinary way he would have approached his home from the other direction. So deep was the snow here that he had to support himself with one hand against the wall, and when he found his hand flat against a door he made out the number seventeen. Janet lived at twenty-three, three doors away. He would knock and go in and rest for a while. It would appear quite natural. He could say he had taken a short cut that had turned out to be the long way round. He was frozen right to the bone. When he had left the other house he felt that he would never be cold again, but now he was shivering, and he knew that it wasn't only with the cold but with the thought of entering his own home. He was aware that he was still slightly drunk and if he went in like this Esther would be sure to smell it from him; there were no secret Rippon breath formulae for him.

Within a few seconds of his knocking on the door of number twenty-three it was opened, and Robbie stood there, silent for a moment, until recognising the figure. Then he exclaimed loudly, 'Good lord! Mr Blenheim. Come in, come in.' He put out his hand and almost dragged him over the threshold, exclaiming loudly, 'Lor! you are in a state . . . Mam! Mam!' he called over his shoulder then went on, 'Let me get your coat off; it's sodden. You're all sodden.'

Some whimsical part of Harry endorsed this. Yes, he was sodden both inside and out.

'Why, Harry!' Janet Dunn was standing at the end of the passage. The name Harry sounded natural on her lips, yet she never used it in his house. She came forward holding out her hands, saying, 'How did you come down this way? Is anything wrong?'

'Let him thaw out and then he'll tell you,' said Robbie bluntly. 'Let's get him near the fire.' He spoke as if Harry was unconscious, and he could have been for he felt powerless to open his mouth. They went into the living-room, one each side of him, and lowered him into a chair before the open fire.

Harry now looked up at Janet. He wanted to explain to her but still found it impossible. But when she put her hand on his brow and said, 'You are hot, but you're shivering. You've got a chill. Bring a drop of whisky,

Robbie,' he made an effort and protested in a croaking voice, 'No, no! A cup of tea please. That's all, a cup of tea, or . . . or if you have c . . . coffee.'

'Yes, yes, certainly. You'll have it in a second.' When she left the room Robbie, dropping on his hunkers before Harry, asked quietly, 'You been out in this long?'

'An hour I think. No, longer. What time is it?'

'A quarter to seven.'

'No!' He sat up in the chair. 'As late as that? I . . . I should be home, they'll be worrying.'

'You haven't been home?'

'No. No. There was a party at the office.' He leant back in the chair again. 'Some of the staff had a job getting back, I . . . I helped them.' And how, he thought.

Straightening himself up, Robbie said, 'Well, another half-hour isn't going to make much difference; you're not fit to go out again yet.' He stood looking down at him. An office party. That's why he stank of whisky. He had been under the impression that he didn't drink. Perhaps that was only when in the house, Madam Blenheim being a strict teetotaller. 'What you want,' he said now, 'is something to eat; it'll steady you.'

'Oh no, no!' Harry shook his head, but Robbie insisted, saying, 'Never mind no, no; it's packing you want inside you I'd say. We were just about to have something, anyway.'

As his mother came through the doorway with a cup of coffee in her hand he said, 'It's something to eat he wants, what do you say?'

364

'Yes, indeed,' said Janet. 'That's the thing. So drink this, then sit up; it's all ready.'

Harry took a long drink of the scalding liquid, then muttered, 'No, Janet; I'm not going to trouble you any further.'

'Trouble!' Her voice was high. 'We're only too pleased to have company. And what better day than on the queen of the sabbath.'

He looked up at her enquiringly for a moment. Then lowering his head he said softly, 'Oh dear me, I forgot it was Friday, Janet.'

'All the better,' she said. 'We couldn't have wished for better company, so come on, drink that coffee up and we'll get started.'

She returned to the kitchen and brought in a large covered dish, which she placed in the middle of the table set to the side of the room. The table was covered with a white cloth and at each end was a candle in a tall holder.

He watched her lighting the candles and heard her mutter something as she did so. Then she turned to him, smiling, and said, 'They should have been lit at sunset but that would have been at half past three. Do you remember looking through the window when you were a lad and Dad going to the door to bring you in and you flying down the backyard as if the devil was after you?'

He shook his head and she laughed, 'Well, you did.' Then she motioned him to the table, and he rose slowly and took his seat.

Robbie was already standing at one end of the table. He had a bottle of wine in his hand and began to pour some in a glass while unselfconsciously saying, 'Blessed art thou O Lord, our God King of the Universe, who created the fruit of the wine.' Then he sipped it and poured out another two glasses. Next he lifted the white napkin that was covering a large object to reveal a loaf of plaited bread. Again he repeated the words he had said before, but adding now, 'Who bringeth forth bread from the earth.' Then nodding impishly at Harry, he added, 'All in English for your benefit. Geordie English. Funny that, but me yiddish isn't in Geordie, at least I don't think it is.' Janet and he now laughed together. Then he broke the bread, dipped it into wine and handed it to Harry, saying, 'It's very good chollah.'

'Thank you.' Harry put the bread on his plate, then looked at the wine glass in his hand. From the smell of the contents it was port and just the thought of it intensified the sickness that was already in his stomach.

When Janet lifted the lid from the dish in the centre of the table to disclose what looked like a stew and which gave off a strong aroma of herbs, she said, 'You do like fish, Harry, don't you? So you should like this, it's what we call cholent.'

'It's got everything in but the pan scrub,' said Robbie, laughing, 'and it's guaranteed to stick to your ribs.'

Harry smiled but said nothing; he was doing his utmost to quell the rising swell of sickness, but when Janet placed the plate of steaming chopped fish and vegetables before him it was more than he could stand. His head down, his hand to his mouth, he stumbled to his feet, muttering, 'Sorry, sorry, bathroom.'

'This way.' Robbie had him by the arm, and when

366

they got into the small kitchen, Harry, still pressing on his mouth, groaned, 'Lavatory.'

'That's outside, man,' said Robbie brusquely. 'Get it up in the sink here. Come on.'

Harry was now past protest and, leaning over the sink, he vomited. A strong smell of whisky and dead sherry and the stodgy meat pudding he'd had for his lunch in a restaurant in town erupted.

A few minutes later, when Robbie handed him a towel he wiped his mouth; then putting his forearms on the draining board he rested his head on them.

'Here.' Robbie pushed a plain kitchen chair towards him and said quietly, 'Sit down.'

He sat down; then looking up at the young man he stared at him for a moment in silence before saying, 'I'm so sorry, Robbie.'

'What's to be sorry for? You've been sick, and no wonder, the way you came in. I'll tell you something.' He put his head down to Harry and whispered. 'Gin does the same for me. Two glasses and I'm flat. She doesn't know.' He nodded towards the kitchen. 'She always thinks it's something she's cooked.' He was grinning now, but Harry couldn't grin back. Getting to his feet, he said, 'If you don't mind, Robbie, I'll make my way home.'

'Yes, yes, of course. And I'll come along of you.'

'No, no, you won't.'

'Well, you might as well stop talking because I'm comin'. I won't go in, don't worry, but I'm going to see you there. I don't want them to find you lying in the gutter stiff the morrow mornin'.'

At this moment Harry thought he wouldn't mind

being found in the gutter stiff tomorrow morning.

Janet helped him into his coat, and she pushed his fumbling fingers aside and tucked his scarf over his chest, then buttoned the coat. He said to her too, 'I'm sorry, Janet.' And her voice brusque now, she replied sharply, 'Don't be silly Harry. What have you got to apologise to me for? I'll remind you that I've had to hold your head before the day when you were sick. Do you remember the night we went to the fair and you went on the shoggies?'

He had a faint recollection of the event and he smiled at her weakly. And she went on, 'And that wasn't the only time. There were school treats when you stuffed yourself and got it up in the bus coming back.'

He could remember one such occasion. 'I must have a weak stomach,' he said.

'There.' She handed him his hat. 'Now when you get in go straight to bed and have a rest over the holidays. It isn't only today that has caused this stomach upset, it's doing that Father Christmas stunt. That Market Place is a death trap any day in the winter, even without snow. I don't know how Robbie escaped.'

As he looked down at her part of his mind registered the fact that Janet Dunn in twenty-three Baker Street was a different creature from Janet Dunn when she came to help out in Hollytree House, Holt Avenue. This was the Janet he remembered from years back, and he had never seen her for a long time because their meetings were always in his own home, with Esther in either the foreground or the background. He said, 'Perhaps you'll invite me to dinner some other time, Janet?' and she answered, 'Any time. You know you're welcome in this house any time, Harry. And you don't need an invitation. Dear, dear! you should know that.'

He looked at her face. It was plain, homely and good. Her hair was black and straight; her eyes were round and dark; her skin had an olive tint; her nose was not large but it was the nose of a Jewess. Yet somehow he had the impression she had just missed being a beautiful woman. She had a good figure, and as his grannie had said, she had a presence, a sort of dignity. She was a good woman altogether was Janet. He took her hand and nodded at her but said nothing, then they went into the passage where Robbie was waiting. She opened the door and let them out, saying, 'Go careful, the both of you mind. Go careful.' She spoke as if they were of one family.

As he went down the street with Robbie supporting him by the arm he thought, It's been the strangest day of my life.

Robbie left him at the bottom of the steps, saying, 'Now you do what Mam said and go straight to bed. And if I were you I'd stay there over the holidays; you're right down low if I'm any judge.'

'I'll see to it, Robbie.' He tried to smile. 'And thanks for your help, for everything.'

'You're welcome. There's nobody I'd rather give me shoes to, you know that.'

They peered at each other through the snow, then Robbie turned away and he went into the house.

When he reached the hall they all gathered round him, all talking at once, until Esther, her voice raised unusually high cried, 'Stop it! Be quiet, I can't hear myself think. Now' – she looked at Harry – 'you might

369

tell me where on earth you've been. They said you left the office before four, your car's still there. We couldn't find out anything from anyone with Father gone to York.'

Before he could answer Gail said, 'Let me get your coat off, Father. Oh! it's wet. And your shoes and trousers, look.'

'Well, don't stand there,' said Esther; 'the carpet will be filthy. Go in to the cloakroom and take them off. Get your father's slippers, Terry. And stop dancing about, Gail. John, put the kettle on.'

As she gave her orders she pushed Harry towards the cloakroom, and there he sat down and pulled his shoes and socks off and turned the bottom of his trousers up. When she bent down and felt them she said, 'They're absolutely wringing,' and at this he was forced to retort sharply, 'Well, perhaps you haven't noticed, Esther, it's snowing outside.'

She answered this with a stiff silence for a moment; then she asked in her usual controlled tone, 'Where have you been?'

He bowed his head and rubbed his brow with his hand as he said, 'After the party some of the staff couldn't get home, I . . . I helped one or two on their way, then I got sort of lost and found myself round by Janet's, and I was so exhausted I went in . . .'

'You mean to say you've been at Janet's all this time!' Her voice was indignant now.

'Not all the time; I don't know how long.' He couldn't say not more than twenty minutes. 'But I just had to call in, I was dead beat. You've got no idea what it's like outside.'

370

'She could have sent Robbie to say you were there. That's the least she could have done.'

'I wouldn't let her,' he lied. 'She wanted to but I wouldn't let her. Now if you don't mind, Esther, I want to get near the fire.' He got to his feet and pushed past her in the narrow space and went out into the hall, there to see John standing with his slippers in his hand. He took them from him, saying, 'Thanks'; then still in his bare feet he went into the sitting-room, and as he dropped on to the couch Gail took the slippers from him and slipped them on to his feet, then said, 'You should go upstairs, Dad, and change your trousers, they're very wet.'

'I will in a minute, dear.' He nodded at her.

'Do you want anything, a hot drink or anything?' Esther was standing before the couch, and without looking at her he shook his head and said, 'All I want is to get to bed.'

'I'll go and put your electric blanket on.' Gail ran out of the room and he pulled himself to his feet again, saying, 'I'll be all right tomorrow, I just want to sleep.' He had not looked Esther straight in the face yet.

When he entered the room Gail was turning down his bed, and when she came at him and flung her arms round his waist, saying, 'Oh, Dad, I was worried; I thought you had dropped into a drift or something,' he felt his whole body stiffen. She was the same size, the same height as Betty Ray. Her body felt like Betty Ray's. When she put her hands up on to his lapels to help him off with his coat he thrust her from him, and his voice rough, almost a growl, he said, 'Don't. Don't do that.'

371

It was the first time in his life he had repulsed her. Always he had opened his arms wide to her; always he had hugged her close. She stepped back from him, her hand up to her cheek, her eyes wide and slowly filling with tears, and then she was running from the room.

He followed her swiftly towards the door but when he reached it he stopped abruptly and closed it and leant his back against it. This was only the beginning.

Four

It was three weeks before Harry returned to the office, and if he was grateful for anything during that time it was for the respite.

When, on Christmas Eve, his temperature having risen with alarming rapidity, Esther sent for the doctor – who pronounced a severe dose of influenza – the one clear thought in Harry's mind was, Thank God I won't have to go in on Wednesday.

Looking back he didn't remember much about Christmas Day or Boxing Day, only that he had made his peace with Gail. She had come into the room several times and stood at the foot of the bed and asked politely, 'How do you feel now, Dad?' until he had made the effort to put out his clammy hands to her and croak, 'Come here.' And when she had stood at the bedside he had said, 'I'm sorry, pet. I'm sorry,' and she had answered without her usual gusto, 'It's all right, Dad.' He had moved his throbbing head slowly and said, 'No, I was rough with you but . . . but I felt ill, more so than I do now; I'd . . . I'd had a trying day, and the snow.'

'It's all right, Dad,' she had answered, and again he

had moved his head. Then pulling her down to the side of the bed he had whispered, 'Listen, pet. If ever again I'm bad-tempered and beastly take no notice, just tell yourself that I love you better than anyone else in the whole wide world, will you?'

On this she returned to the daughter he knew and she threw herself on his neck, crying, 'Oh, Dad! Dad!'

'There now. There now. Look, you'll catch this cold. But remember what I said.'

She had lifted her head and looked at him and dropped it to one side, saying, 'You never could be bad-tempered or beastly, not you.'

'I was last night.'

'It wasn't you, it was the flu.'

'Get up out of that, child! Do you want it too?' Esther's command had brought Gail to her feet, but she had smiled lovingly at him before leaving the room.

After this little incident he let himself dissolve into the sweating depths created by a hundred and four temperature.

But now the time of the respite was over and Esther was at the door to see him off, driving in her father's cast-off Jaguar. Under other circumstances he would have got a thrill out of driving the Jaguar. Who wouldn't? But passed over as it had been, almost in the nature of a gift, the joy of possession was tainted somewhat. He knew that his father-in-law wouldn't have let him have a smell of the car if it hadn't been that he wanted to please Esther. That was the only good point in his father-in-law's favour; his constant aim to please his daughter.

But the business of the car was not really bothering

him at the moment. What was tensing the muscles of his stomach and bringing his jaw rigid was the uncertainty of what attitude Miss Betty Ray would take towards him. Remembering her brashness he shivered with apprehension.

But he needn't have worried. After Mr Hogg had greeted him warmly there came the chorus of, 'Good morning. Nice to see you back, Mr Blenheim. You feeling better?' To all of which he had said, 'Yes, yes, thank you very much.' And then he was passing the window of the typing pool, and the girls inside, having heard the chatter in the hallway, all had their faces turned towards him, and they smiled at him. And among the smiling faces was Betty Ray's. He did not let his eyes linger on her but nodded through the glass to them as a whole. Then he was in his office and Ada Cole was taking his coat and saying, 'Oh, I am glad to see you back, Mr Blenheim.'

'Thanks, Ada.'

'Sure you're feeling fit now?'

'Fit as a fiddle, Ada. Well' – he paused – 'not quite. Let us say, I don't feel like dying any longer.'

Her round face smiling, she looked at him kindly, saying, 'It's an awful thing, flu. It gets you down. It's left its mark on you; you've lost weight, and your tan's gone.'

'Tan? I never knew I had a tan, Ada.'

'Oh, well, you know what I mean, you were a bit browny.'

'Well I suppose the snow bleached me.'

'Eeh! it did that. Wasn't it dreadful? A number of old people in the town died, and no wonder. We've never had anything like it for years; and we don't want it again, do we?'

'No, Ada.' He took his seat behind the desk, drew in a deep breath, then asked, 'Anything new?'

'One or two small jobs have been completed. Bradley's doing the alterations in Temple Street and Kershaw has finished the Council job. There have been some enquiries in, estimations . . . And Halliday, you remember, he accepted the quotation.'

'Halliday?' He lifted his chin upwards. 'Oh yes; I was dealing with that just before we broke up, at least I went to see Mr Rippon about it. There was a muddle about prices.'

'Well, they accepted the stated price.'

'And what was that?'

'Oh.' She screwed up her face. 'I can't think off-hand. I'll get it.' On her way to the filing cabinet she turned round and said, 'I've just remembered, we haven't got it. I had orders to pass on all that corre-spondence to the upper office.' She jerked her head towards the ceiling.

'Was it six thousand, five hundred?'

'Oh no, more than than, I'm sure. Now I remember. That was the estimate Mr Whelan put in but Miss Bateman told me they'd worked it out upstairs and that wouldn't cover it. It was over seven thousand. Yes, it was over seven thousand.' She was nodding her head now.

He looked down at his desk for a moment, then bit on his lip and asked, 'Who's to do the work?'

'Bradley's as far as I can make out. They're starting this week. Their estimate is likely in. It's bound to be, but I haven't seen it. Everything's been mixed up lately, hasn't it, Mr Blenheim? I mean not just lately, for months now. You don't know where you are, do you?'

'No,' he said slowly; 'you don't know where you are.'

She looked at him for a moment longer. He was vexed. She could always tell when Mr Blenheim was vexed. She turned and gathered up some papers from a side desk and went into her cubby hole.

Harry sat staring at the phone. He had a desire to pick it up and say what was on his mind, but he knew that he daren't; not if he wanted to remain in Peamarsh's. But it was damnable, damnable. Bradley's estimate would be in the region of five thousand five hundred, give or take a pound or two. When Jim Whelan had put the job down at six thousand five hundred he was giving Peamarsh's a good percentage for the small amount of negotiating work they were doing, but that didn't suit Mr Rippon. He had to put it up another seven hundred and fifty. And who would get a cut of that? Would it be ploughed back? Not if Dave Rippon had anything to do with it, it wouldn't; it would be fiddled into the directors' pockets . . . But how? Yes, how? There was Miss Bateman to get over. She must know a lot, Miss Bateman.

As bad as old Walters was, this kind of robbery hadn't been so blatant when he was active. Their percentage had never been moderate but they had usually stuck to Jim Whelan's figures.

What would happen when his father-in-law became head of the firm, which was very much on the cards? Would he be able to work directly under him? When Dave Rippon moved into Peter Walters' office, Frank

Nolan, Arthur McMullen and Tom Vosey would all move up a step and there would be a vacancy on the directors' board, and that vacancy would come to him; not because his father-in-law would want it like that but because Esther would want it like that. But what did he himself want? Well, it didn't matter what he wanted, did it? He was fast stuck under Dave Rippon's thumb. Everything that came his way would come via Rippon, that is, as long as he remained in this firm. And being Esther's husband, he couldn't see himself leaving it ever. He took his handkerchief from his pocket and wiped his face, he was sweating.

It was as he returned from lunch that he came face to face with Betty Ray. She stopped on the bend of the stairs. Standing above him and her eyes wide and bright, she looked into his face and said, 'I'm so glad you're better, Mr Blenheim.'

His answer to this should have been, 'Thank you,' but all he could do was to swallow and stare at her.

'It was the snow; it was dreadful, wasn't it?' Her eyes were swelling over with laughter; he could almost hear her gurgling inside. He couldn't believe that she was the same girl who had acted like that. His mind interpreted, in a flashing picture, the words 'like that', and he saw her naked, savage and writhing, totally uninhibited.

'Did you get my card?'

He heard himself repeating dully, 'Card?' at the same time seeing Esther holding out a card to him, saying, 'This one's got no name on. Gaudy-looking thing; it must be from one of the choir boys. Very nice though to think of you. That makes thirty-one altogether. You're doing well.'

'Yes, I sent you a get-well card. I didn't sign it.' Her voice was a mere whisper now. 'I thought I'd better not . . . By the way, I have your watch . . .' She stopped abruptly. She was looking over her shoulder at someone coming up the stairs and she finished in a clear voice, 'I'm so glad you're better, Mr Blenheim.'

As Miss Bateman came abreast of them he said, 'Thank you, thank you,' then followed the stiff trim figure up to the landing. When they reached the hallway Miss Bateman turned to him and, smiling quite genially for her, said, 'I endorse that, Mr Blenheim, it's very nice to see you back again.'

'Thank you, Miss Bateman. It's good to be back; you get very bored at home.'

Then they went their separate ways.

Standing at the window of his room he looked down on the street and breathed deeply. The pattern was set; she wasn't going to blab. She had taken the incident like a night out at the theatre say. He looked unseeing now across the street and wondered how many men she had practised on to become so proficient at her hobby, for likely that was what it was with her. During the days around Christmas when he was at his lowest he had thought the whole thing was a nightmare and had been relieved at the idea, but his temperature, returning to normal, had brought with it the unpleasant fact that it was no nightmare. Well, it was over, and there'd be no repetition, not if he knew it. Although it was a pretty uncomfortable feeling to have the awareness of this thing between them he imagined that he wasn't the only man that shared such a secret with her. He supposed he really should be getting a kick out of the incident. Many men would, but it held no kick for him, only revulsion; and this was mainly created by the thought that one so young could be so damnably knowledgeable, and, moreover, had used him and made him feel like a schoolboy fumbling at his first affair.

She had mentioned his watch. He was relieved about that. Now he was back she'd likely send it to him here at the office. Esther, fortunately, hadn't missed it. That was something.

But Betty Ray didn't return his watch; instead, she sent him a letter. Ada usually left his mail, the envelopes slit open in a pile to the right of his blotting pad. But the next morning on top of the pile, lay an envelope with the words 'Private and Personal' printed in bold letters above the address. As he picked it up he looked at Ada Cole standing in front of the desk, then said aloud, 'Private and Personal, huh!' He was smiling as he slit the envelope open. There was a single piece of paper inside and on it he read simply, 'I have something belonging to you, don't you want it?' He had no power to stop the blood rushing to his face. He folded the letter in four again, crumpled up the envelope and dropped it into the waste paper basket; then looking up at Ada Cole he remarked with as much casualness as he could muster, 'Something silly; I'll deal with this.'

'Yes, Mr Blenheim.' And on this she turned and went into her room and, being a woman, she thought, Now what could be in that letter that would make him look like that, absolutely startled, and red to the ears?

Harry did a lot of thinking during the day. Should he ignore the letter and wait until he met her, perhaps by chance on the stairs again, and ask her point blank if she would kindly return the watch. But remembering her volatile personality he could see her marching into his office, a wide grin on her face, and slapping it down on his desk . . . and in front of Ada Cole, or anyone else who might be there. One thing he decided he wasn't going to do, and that was write to her and ask her to return it by post, for if she was nettled in any way she was just as likely to send it to his home address. And then how would he explain it away? Finally, he knew that the only thing to do was what the letter suggested and go to the house for it.

Having made up his mind on what course to take he knew he mustn't put it off; that would just be piling up the agony; he must settle this business tonight. So he phoned Esther and told her not to hold up the meal as he had some outdoor business to attend to and would be a little late.

The staff left the office at five o'clock but he didn't leave until a quarter to six, gauging that this would give her ample time to get home. One other thing he was careful not to do, and that was to drive up to her door. He left the car at the bottom end of Carey Street, then went through the Cut, no longer knee deep in snow but brittle underfoot now with ash.

When, following his knock, he heard one female voice call out and another answer he hesitated whether to turn and run into the darkness. But too late; the door opened and a woman said, 'Yes?'

381

He was standing in the shadow and she in the light. He took her to be about forty, and she was as fair as her daughter was dark, and instantly he summed her up.

'Mrs Ray?'

'Yes.' Her tone was intended to appear refined but resulted in being mincing.

'I would like to have a word with your daughter if I may.'

'Oh. Oh, come in. Come in. You're Mr . . .?'

'Blenheim.'

'Oh yes, yes. Betty's told me about you, lots. Come in, Mr Blenheim. Oh, come in. Betty! Betty dear, here's Mr Blenheim.'

After closing the door she went before him along the passage, her arm extended, ushering him into the room like a stage servant before a personage.

Betty was standing at the bedroom door. She had a comb in her hand and after looking at him for a moment she began combing her hair, then said casually, 'Be with you in a tick. Sit down.'

'I . . . I can't stay.'

As he spoke the bedroom door closed and Mrs Ray, smiling with every feature of her over-made-up face, said, 'Oh, do sit down for a minute, Mr Blenheim. She always likes to tidy up after she's been in the office. You get sticky, don't you? So do sit down; you might as well get off your feet.' She was wagging her head at him. 'You're quite better now? Betty told me you had been ill. It was the day in the snow. You had a time of it, hadn't you? It was very good of you to bring her home. She told me all about it.'

Did she? he thought. I wonder. And yet he wouldn't

put it past her. He could see them sitting on this couch here roaring their heads off. He stared at the woman. He knew the label Esther would put on her after just one glance. Common. And if Elsie saw her she would go further. 'Common as muck, Mr Blenheim,' she would say. 'Common as muck. An old tart.' Like mother, like daughter. They were a couple of tarts. Yet Betty had a better camouflage . . . as yet. Anyway, she had deceived him. But perhaps in a way he was easily deceived.

Mrs Ray was now adjusting an ear-ring the size of a walnut; she was looking into the mirror above the mantelpiece and talking to him through it. 'We don't see much of each other, Betty and me; it's lonely for her. I'm so happy when she gets a nice friend.' She paused here and let her eyes rest on his before going on, 'You see, I'm on a twelve till seven one week and six thirty till midnight, or sometimes later, another. I'm at the Three Dolls, you know, on the main road. It's a restaurant like, and does a night show. Very popular. Very popular with motorists. I don't mind the twelve o'clock shift but I always feel a bit worried about the late shift, leaving Betty you know. But when she has a friend, I don't worry. It's a comfort.'

There was a solo he sang with the phrase repeated throughout 'Holy, holy, holy, Lord God of Hosts', now he found himself saying just that 'Holy, holy, holy, Lord God of Hosts . . .' It was strange. Although he went to church every Sunday he had never prayed very much, and of latter years not at all. When the prayers were being said he was thinking of the next hymn and hoping yet once again that Robbins would not drag the end out; or he was going over his solo, singing it in his mind. But now he was praying, actually praying; 'Holy, holy, holy, Lord God of Hosts, get me out of this.'

'Oh there you are, dear. Oh, that's nice. I always say you suit red.'

Out of habit Harry had risen to his feet when Betty entered the room, and now he stared at her in the tight fitting red woollen dress and red mules as she came towards him. She didn't speak as she sat herself on the couch, but her mother said, 'Well, I'll have to be away; time's flying, as the man said as he threw the clock at his wife.' This quip was followed by a high kick of a laugh; then hurrying across the room, she added, 'It'll never do if I miss that bus.' She was going into the bedroom when she swung round. 'Wait till we get that car, eh Betty? And we will, won't we, girl?'

'We will, Mam.' Betty jerked her head towards her mother and smiled; then she turned and stared at Harry. She stared at him for a full minute during which he could find nothing to say. Her scrutiny unnerved him; and when at last she spoke, she said softly, 'It's nice seeing you again,' he was more unnerved still.

Mrs Ray came hurrying back into the room. She was wearing a short green coat with a fuzzy fur collar turned up high and over her bouffant hair was lightly dragged a chiffon scarf. 'Well, I'm off, so I must say good-bye, Mr Blenheim. It's been very nice meeting you.'

He was on his feet once more, watching her pulling on a pair of fur-lined gloves, and when she smiled widely at him and said, 'Now, don't you be a stranger, just pop in when you feel like it. I know our house must appear homely and not what you're used to, but you're very welcome to what we have,' he groaned to himself. And following on 'Glory, Glory, Glory,' he added 'Oh Christ!' and the exclamation now had no connection with prayer.

'Bye-bye, ducks.'

'Bye-bye, Mam . . . Be good.'

'Well, you know your mam.' Mrs Ray went out laughing. And when the front door closed Betty looked up to where Harry was standing some distance away on the hearth rug, and her face unsmiling and tight now, she said, 'You didn't think much of her, did you?'

'. . . What do you mean?'

'Just what I say. You almost turned your nose up at her.'

'You've got a vivid imagination. How do you know what I think?'

'I happen to know men, that's how I know. And you dubbed her straightaway as a cheap piece, didn't you?'

'I did nothing of the sort,' he lied firmly.

'Well, you could have fooled me.' She uncrossed her legs, then re-crossed them, then said almost vehemently, 'She's been good to me, has Mam. She's worked for me all me life until I could do it for meself. She could have let me go into a factory as soon as I left school and that would have made things easier for her, but no, she wanted something different for me, so she sent me to the typing college and I passed out top. Do y'know that? Top! And if it wasn't for all the old frozen-faced nits in this town, especially in Peamarsh's, holding down the good jobs I'd have an office of me own instead of being in the blasted pool. But once the

Miss Coles and Batemans get in they're there for life; old maids' last hope.'

He didn't see what all this had to do with his visit, but one thing was evident, she was bitter about her position. He said, 'You could always move; there are always vacancies of the kind you're after in Newcastle.'

'Yes, I know I could, but I don't want to leave me mam; this is her home, she's made it.'

'It's very commendable of you.'

'Oh, come off it.' She swung round, turning her head fully away from him and looking across the room, leaving him feeling bewildered. She was talking from such a personal plane that one would have imagined that they had known each other for years. She turned her face towards him again, and now she was smiling, and her whole attitude underwent a lightning change as she said softly, 'Come and sit down, I'm being naggy.'

'I . . . I can't stay.'

'You can for ten minutes.' She patted the couch. 'Just ten minutes. Come on, sit down.'

It was impossible to refuse her request, and when he took a seat once again on the couch she curled her legs up under her as she had done on the first occasion they had sat together, but she didn't snuggle up to him or tease him; her tactics were different tonight. She kept her distance as she said, still softly, 'It's nice seeing you again.'

'Now, Betty.' Her name had a strange sound on his lips, and as he paused she put in, 'Now, now, don't get panicky, relax. I'm not going to eat you, you know.' She gave a little giggle. 'You're scared stiff of me, and it's funny.'

386

'I'm not scared stiff of you.' He jerked his head to the side. 'Only there's no point in going on with this.'

'Why?' The question was quiet.

'Because' – he brought his head round to her again – 'I'm a married man with three children, the eldest one not much younger than you.'

'Are you happily married?'

'Yes, I'm happily married.'

'I don't believe you. You've got a son seventeen, so you've been married eighteen years or more. It doesn't last that long, not eighteen months in some cases. You prove to me one middle-aged man in this town who's happily married and I'll enter a convent. And look, I'm tellin' you I'm not talkin' from hearsay, I'm talking from knowsay. I know a lot of men in this town, and I could spill some beans if I liked. But there's one thing about me, I'm not spiteful, I never have been. I don't want to cause trouble for anybody, but what I do want' – she paused, and, her hands gripping her forearms across her chest, she repeated, 'But what I do want, Har . . . ry' she drew out his name, paused again, then ended, 'is a bit of happiness. That's all I'm asking, just a bit of happiness.'

What could he say to this? For a moment he felt sorry for her, in sympathy with her, and he wished, he wished deeply that it was in him to make her happy, but he knew that if he was going to have an affair it wouldn't be with someone like her.

She was compelling him to look into her eyes as she went on talking. 'I liked you from the first time I clapped eyes on you, but mind, mind, I never planned anything, I just thought it was heaven sent that snow

387

and you bringing me back, like an answer to a prayer that you didn't know you had prayed. You know . . . sort of. After you had gone that night I knew I'd frightened you. You had never been with a woman had you, except, well, your wife? You knew nothing about it. To all intents and purposes you could have come straight out of a monastery. I know I'm a bit wild when I get going but that's me. I'm warm inside, hot, boiling in fact, like them volcanoes, just like them, burstin' out every now and again.' She shrugged her shoulders now and grinned slyly at him. 'But I don't need to tell you, do I? Anyway, there it is.' She leaned back from him and now stated flatly, 'I like you; I want to be friends with you.'

He turned from her and, leaning his elbow on his knee, cupped his forehead; and from this position he muttered, 'It's impossible, quite impossible.'

'Are you afraid your wife might get to know?'

When he didn't answer she went on, 'Nobody would ever see you come here; we're very fortunately placed in this house. You just need nip through the Cut and you're in. There's only six houses in the row and from when they come in at half-past five until they start to go out to the clubs or some place at half-past six the street's empty. And in front there's only a warehouse. It's a hundred to one chance you'd ever be seen, so what are you frightened of? And look, look, don't think me mam would say anything; me mam's the soul of discretion as they say.'

He almost sprang to his feet now and, looking down at her, said, 'It's impossible. You must take this for final. Apart from being a married man, we work in the same office. Then besides being a member of the church I'm in different societies in the town. What you're offering is most generous, I realise that, but I just cannot accept, I cannot be a hypocrite. You know for a fact that if I hadn't drunk so much on Christmas Eve the . . . the incident would never have happened. Now' – he undid the top button of his waistcoat, then did it up again, before adding, 'If you'll be good enough to return my watch I'll be grateful, and . . . and we can . . .'

'And we can forget it ever happened.' She was on her feet confronting him now, her eyes almost black, her mouth tight. 'You know what you are, you're a weak-bellied, pious bastard. That's what you are. Now you listen to me, Mr Blenheim. What if I have a baby?'

He had heard about people blanching, but now he was experiencing it. He felt the blood draining from his face down through his stomach. Even his words seemed white as he whispered, 'You're not . . .?'

'I don't know yet. It could happen quite easily; I wasn't prepared. I'm over me time, so I don't know.'

Holy, holy, holy, Lord God of Hosts . . .

'As things stand I think I'll just hang on to your watch, sort of mind it for a little while longer.'

'I want my watch, and I want it now.'

'Oh, Mr Blenheim, stop shouting; somebody might hear you next door. I know she's deaf but she has friends come in.'

He was no longer feeling blanched; the blood was pounding in his head. This was the kind of situation that other men got themselves into. From his own experience he had known of a number in his time; one had been a close friend, a churchgoing man and a

389

visitor to the house. Esther had liked him; she always thought Bill Caldwell such a genuine man. That was until he had got himself mixed up with a young married woman and the affair had ended in divorce. After that his name had never been mentioned again. Esther didn't hold with divorce; what God had joined together was a holy law with her. He had the wild idea of thrusting this blackmailing little tart aside and dashing into the bedroom and searching for his watch, and he might have done just that except that he knew that to prevent him she would come to grips with him, physically, and he wanted no more of that.

He picked up his hat and, without looking at her again, made for the door; and when he reached it she called, 'I'll write to you when I want to see you again.'

As once before he had stood at the end of the Cut and wiped the sweat from his face, so now he stopped at the same spot again and stood gasping as if he had sprinted from the house. What was he to do? He should get advice, tell someone . . . and make himself out to be as she said, a weak-bellied pious bastard. And what if she should be . . .? He couldn't even think the word pregnant. He saw his whole ordered world in fragments about him. He saw the chaos after exposure. He saw the reactions of the individual members of his family. First Esther; the ground cut from beneath her, her ideals and lofty thinking sullied by the sordid affair. But the reaction he knew he dreaded most was that of his father-in-law. What would it be? Wrath, yes, indignation, and of course the demand that the whole affair be hushed up for his daughter's sake; and for the remainder of his life he'd be under his thumb. And all this because he took a girl home in the snow. It didn't seem possible. If someone had put the situation to him as a hypothetical case he would have said the whole thing was highly improbable.

He got into his car and drove home . . .

The house was quiet when he entered the hall and after he had hung up his things in the cloakroom he went into the sitting-room, where Esther was sitting reading. She laid down her book and stared into his face, saying, 'You're looking peaky again. Why did you work so late when you're not feeling too fit?'

'Oh, I'm all right.' He went to the fire and held out his hands to the flames and asked, 'Where's everybody?'

'Terry's gone to his piano lesson, John's doing his homework, and Gail's having tea with Anna Birkett. By the way, are you going to choir practice?'

'Yes, yes, I suppose so. I'd forgotten about it for the moment.'

'I told Gail you might pick her up and bring her home before you went, but then I didn't know you were going to be so late.'

'I'll go straight off after I've had a bite and fetch her,' he said flatly.

'Good, I hate her to be out alone in the dark. I'll get your meal now, I've kept it hot.'

As she brought his meal into the dining-room, she said, 'Father rang a short while ago. Colonel Callow's housekeeper had just been on the phone to him. The Colonel wants him to go through again for the weekend, so he won't be coming into the office tomorrow and will likely stay in York until Monday night. He said he thinks the old fellow's lonely.'

'Hasn't he any relations of his own?' Harry asked, and she answered, 'No; I understand not. He's lived with the old housekeeper and a man-servant for years.'

'Is he wealthy?' Harry asked this question thinking it might give the reason for his father-in-law putting himself out for an old man.

'I don't really know. But he must have some money although he doesn't appear to spend more than is absolutely necessary. He's a bit of an eccentric I think, won't have the phone in, no television. The house-keeper's got to use a call box. Father said this was the third time she had phoned in the last three weeks, so he felt he was obliged to go. He's silly like that, about wartime loyalties. He seems to forget that the war's been over more than twenty years.'

When you enjoyed the war, as much as Dave Rippon did on his own saying, you didn't forget it easily. He could hear his father-in-law leading forth, his back to the fire, swaying on his toes as he regaled him with his wartime activities. 'Best years of my life, grand days, great days. Such comradeship'll never come again. Oh boy! did we have fun.' And all this from a training camp in a corner of the country where the nearest bomb had been dropped twenty miles away.

'What's on your mind?'

'What?'

'I said, what's on your mind? You've been staring at your plate for the last five minutes.'

'Oh. Oh, I was just thinking.'

'Can't you scrap the choir practice tonight?'

'No, Gregory's got the idea that the TV might do a

service from the church. As far as I know he's written away asking someone to come down and hear us.'

'I . . . I knew nothing about this.' She looked slightly affronted, and he said, 'Well, it's the choir business.'

'Well, the choir business is also the church committee business and nothing was said at the last meeting.'

'Oh, I think what he's done he's done since then.'

'I should hope so.'

She certainly was affronted. As he watched her taking some empty dishes out of the room, her back very straight and expressive, he thought, I wish to God that was all I had on my mind at the moment, whether or not Gregory had taken too much upon himself.

Fifteen minutes later when he was on the point of leaving her to pick up Gail, she said to him, apropos of nothing that had been mentioned since she showed her displeasure of the choirmaster's initiative, 'Does Father know of this?'

He had almost forgotten the matter and he turned a blank face to her and asked, 'Know what?'

'What's the matter with you tonight, Harry, you're miles away? What were we talking about just a short while ago. Gregory writing off to the BBC on his own?'

He stared her full in the face, then said loudly, 'I don't know, Esther, if your father knows about it or not, but if someone has omitted to inform him is that going be looked upon as a crime?'

'Harry!' She spoke his name in a tone that was weighed with censure; then she waited. But on this occasion he didn't as was usual when he had raised his voice to her, apologise immediately by saying, 'Oh, I'm sorry, dear' and so preserve the tranquil atmosphere of the home. On this occasion he just walked out.

Ten minutes later, when he reached the Birketts' house, he got the impression that Gail, for once, wasn't overjoyed to see him, and the reason was presented to him when Paul Birkett came out of the garage, where he had obviously been tinkering with a motorbike, and joined his sister Anna who was seeing her friend off at the gate.

When he started the car up and the waving had stopped Gail said to him, 'That was Paul, Dad.'

'Yes.' He raised his eyebrows and nodded at the windscreen. 'Yes, I think I saw him.'

When she took her elbow and dug him in the side he cried, 'Careful, careful! That's a police car just passed us; they'll have me up for drunken driving.'

'Do you like him, Dad?'

'Do I like Paul? Well, I hardly know him. I don't come across him much, him not being in the choir.'

'Well, he sits in the third pew on the left . . . no, on your right, and in the end seat; you can't help but see him.'

He was forced to chuckle. So this was it. He was glad. She was nearly sixteen and she hadn't had a boy friend yet. Some of them at the church were going strong at fourteen. He wondered if young Paul, like himself, could detect the butterfly emerging from the chrysalis. He doubted it. He said teasingly now, 'Oh yes, I remember seeing him. He's lanky, isn't he?'

'Oh, Dad, he's not; not lanky, tall.'

'Oh, perhaps I haven't got the right one. Has he got red hair?'

He could hear her swallowing. 'It isn't red, it's auburn, and it's lovely hair.'

They stopped at the traffic lights and he cast a glance at her as he asked softly, 'You like Paul?'

She dropped her head just the slightest as she answered, 'Uh-huh!'

'Does he like you?'

'Yes, Dad.' She was looking at him squarely now, but he kept his eyes on the road as they moved over the crossing; then he asked casually, 'He's told you so?'

'Well . . . well, not exactly. He wrote me a letter.'

'Oh, he did, did he?'

'He . . . he didn't give it to me himself, he gave it to Anna to give to me. He wondered if I would go out with him.'

'And what did you say?'

'Well, I haven't said anything yet. I'll write the answer tonight and give it to Anna tomorrow.'

He bit on his lip. For all the talk of being with it, of being groovy, of LSD and free love, for some youngsters love still started like this. He could understand young Birkett writing, he was a shy lad in spite of his red hair, or perhaps just because of it. The Birketts were a nice family. A bit starchy he thought, at least the parents were, but nevertheless nice.

Out of curiosity now he said, 'Have you just got to know him, I mean well? Doesn't he go to the Youth Club?'

'Not very often, and then he plays chess most of the time.'

They were about three minutes' ride from home when after a thoughtful silence, she suddenly asked, 'What's it like, Dad . . . I mean marriage?'

He actually grazed the kerb, and when he straightened out again he didn't know whether to laugh outright at her question or to treat it seriously. It was natural, he supposed, she should be thinking of marriage, even at fifteen, well near sixteen, but this was jumping the gun a bit. And what a question to tackle, and coming from her. Had it come from either of the boys he would have dealt with it in a straightforward manner; but even with them he knew he would have evaded the truth, because the young should not be disillusioned. If that was to come it should come only after they had tasted wonder. Had he ever tasted wonder? The answer was a little while in coming, and then it was, No. Happiness, a kind of happiness, but never wonder, because he thought that when you tasted wonder it would leave a mark on you. He had only once seen the result of wonder and he had been very young then. He had seen it on the faces of Mr and Mrs Fielding. They would sit in the front row of the church and often he would find himself singing his solo to them alone. They walked in the street hand in hand, and some of the choir boys said they were potty. They were of no account, the Fieldings. He had worked in an ironmonger's shop all his life, never even rising to manager, and she had done daily work until she fell and broke her leg. She died at seventy-three, and the following day he put his head in the gas oven.

'Dad! Did you hear what I said?'

'Yes, I heard you, dear; I was just thinking. But . . .

but I think it's a question you should ask your mother; she'd be able to tell you better than me.'

'Why?'

'Why? Well, because she's a woman; she'd see it from her side.'

'If I asked Mother I know exactly what she'd say.'

'You do?'

'Yes. "Don't probe; you'll know in God's good time."'

He gulped in his throat. Again he didn't know whether to laugh or to treat this seriously. That his young daughter could have got the measure of her mother utterly nonplussed him. That Gail, who was always obedient and loving towards her mother, should yet see her through a mirror of cool reasoning amazed him, for in that simple sentence was embodied Esther's character and, stemming from that, her way of life.

Thinking it advisable to ignore her statement, he said hesitantly, 'Well, marriage is a very wonderful thing if two people love each other . . . really love each other.'

'But how will I know, I mean really know. You see, I feel I really love Paul, I've been gone on him for ages. I've dreamed about us being married and all that, but I want to know if I'll still feel like this . . . well, I mean when I'm married and have a family.'

'Oh my dear! you mustn't trouble your head about such things yet. Look.' He swung the car round into the avenue. 'You'll have other boys, dozens of other boys. Well, if not dozens you'll know and like a lot of boys before you marry. What you want to do now is to enjoy yourself. Go to parties and dances. The summer will soon be here, you'll be playing tennis and you'll meet other boys and . . .'

'I don't want to meet other boys, Dad. I've just told you.' Her voice was earnest now. 'I like Paul, I always have.'

'Well then, go on liking him, there's nobody stopping you. And there's one good thing about it, your mother likes the Birketts.' He felt he shouldn't have said that.

'Do you love Mother, Dad?'

He was startled again by this question and he wanted to evade it by saying, 'What's got into you tonight?' but he knew what had got into his daughter. She was awakening to life; the puppy fat was slipping from her mind as well as from her body. She wanted to talk about this thing that was persistently with her and which took on the shape at present of Paul Birkett.

As he turned into the drive he said, 'Of course I love your mother.' When he stopped the car he found she was looking at him, and he wouldn't have been at all surprised if she had come out with, 'Then why do you have single beds? Because if you love somebody I would have thought you would always want to be close to them.' Or she could have said, 'Well, why have you stopped kissing mother when you go out in the morning and when you come in at night? You used to do it when I was small.' But what she said was, 'It's funny, Dad, but I can talk to you better than anybody else, even Anna, and we talk about some things I can tell you.'

He laughed gently and touched her cheek with his hand as he said, 'I bet you do. But I'm glad you can talk to me, I hope you always will.'

She said now, 'Aren't you coming in?' and he answered, 'No, I haven't time; I'm late for the squawking session as it is. It's an absolute nuisance having to pick up modern misses from parties.'

She put her arm through the window, her fist doubled, and aimed a punch at him; then said, in what she imagined to be a haughty grown-up voice, 'Will you look me up, Mr Blenheim, on your return?' And he answered in the same vein, 'It'll be a pleasure, Ma'am. A pleasure.'

As he drove the car round the circular flower bed and out of the drive again he thought: She could be married in two or three years' time. And the boys, too, for that matter. When they were gone there'd be only he and Esther. What would it be like, just he and Esther alone? But the thought brought no mental picture to the screen of his mind.

Five

It was a fortnight later when he saw the second letter marked 'Private and Personal' lying on top of his mail. Ada was in her office, her door open, but before he had finished reading the letter she was standing at the other side of the desk, and once again she saw his face giving him away.

The letter said simply: 'You can have your watch. I'll be in about the same time.'

He had given up all hope of getting his watch back and had decided to go into Newcastle, buy a similar one and have it engraved. In fact he would rather have done this than visit her house again. But then there was the damning inscription. With a thing like that she had a hold over him.

Ada was still looking at him as he folded up the letter and casually opened a side drawer and thrust it in. When she laid an order sheet on the desk and turned away without speaking, went into her room and closed the door, he quietly opened the drawer again, took out the letter and put it in his pocket.

Behind her closed door Ada Cole stood looking into space. It was a woman. He had got himself mixed up

400

with a woman. That was the only reason he would look like that. She bent down and opened the bottom drawer of her desk and from beneath some papers she took out a crumpled envelope and studied it yet again. There was something vaguely familiar about the writing. She had a good memory for people's handwriting. Well, so she should, she told herself; she had dealt with handwriting all her working life, and whoever had written the address on this envelope had got her claws into Mr Blenheim. Yet she couldn't imagine him going off the rails, him happily married and such a nice family. And besides which, he was such a nice fellow. But he'd had that scared look on his face again when he had read that letter . . . Now where had she seen that writing before? Something about the P. 'Private and Personal'. If she had seen it recently then, she deduced, it must be somebody in the office. Mentally she now went over all the female staff from the ground floor up. She went through the directors' secretaries, but the improbability of it being one of them was too high, two of them being over fifty and the others, Miss Bateman excluded, were of an appearance, she decided, that wouldn't attract any man, not a man like Mr Blenheim anyway. That left only the pool. Now who was there in the pool? Rose Weybridge, Betty Ray, Olive Standford and Mary Cheeseman. Mary Cheeseman was getting married next week. That left three, and she could count Olive Standford out; a man would be hard put to take on a girl like Olive, poor soul. There were plain girls and plain girls, but Olive was in a category of her own. That only left Rose Weybridge and Betty Ray. Now she wouldn't put it past Rose Weybridge to try it on with any man. She was a young madam was Rose Weybridge. And what about the other one? She was a cheeky piece, Betty Ray, always with an answer ready and brazen sort of eyes. But when would either of them have come in contact with Mr Blenheim? Christmas! The word hit her like a blow. When she returned after the holidays she found a note signed by Betty Ray stating briefly what work she had done and adding that she had filed the copies of the letters she had typed. Ada Cole remembered that she had commented to herself at the time about the handwriting, thinking, They get worse. She hadn't the note now, but she could easily get a sample of that girl's handwriting, and she would do so without further delay.

On their third meeting she said to him, 'You know I could love you or hate your guts,' and he replied, 'I'd rather you didn't do either.'

'What're you frightened of, anyway? Oh, I know.' She flapped her hand at him. 'There's your wife, and the church and the Choral Society and the Rotarians, and the Save the Children Fund Committee, and oh, God knows what. I know everything you're in, I've done my homework, but when all that's said I say, What are you frightened of? I'm not a blabber, I've told you. Have I let on in any way over these past weeks that I know you other than as one of the bosses?'

'No, I can't say you have. But you've written to me twice and your letters, to say the least, stand out. Private and Personal. You know yourself that when a letter like that comes into an office it means just that,

402

"Private and Personal". But there's very little of private business that one can keep from one's secretary.'

'Oh, if that's all you're worrying about. Old Ada wouldn't smell a dead pig if it was hung under her nose.'

'You'd be surprised.'

'Yes, I'd say I would be if I found out different. But anyway' – she turned her head to one side – 'you don't want anything to do with me, do you? I'm not your type. That's it, isn't it?'

'No.' He had to be kind. 'It isn't a case of you not being my type, it's a case of not wanting to be involved in anything underhand or—'He almost said unseemly, but that would have made her laugh. 'Oh!' He moved impatiently on the couch. 'We've been through all this before. You said you'd return my watch and that's why I'm here.'

She stared at him. She wasn't sitting on the couch tonight but on a chair to the side of the fireplace, and after a moment she said, 'If I give it you back, will you do something for me?'

He groaned inwardly. Another catch, another hitch. Not the bedroom again. 'It all depends what it is,' he said, 'and if I'm in a position to grant it.'

'Oh, you're in a position all right. I want to go up.'

'Up?' He bent his head towards her, not under-standing.

'Yes, up on to the top floor. Mr Noland's secretary is going to America; I'd like her job.'

He took his eyes from hers and looked into the fire. He was thinking rapidly. If he told her the truth that he had no power to help her here, it was just a possibility she might hang on to the watch. He listened to her saying, 'Mary Cheeseman's getting married and Rosie Weybridge hasn't got the sense she was born with. That only leaves Olive Standford and me. Now Olive has been there for over a year and her work isn't bad, but if you've seen her you'll know that she isn't what every man wants about the office.' Her mouth curved upwards now; then her face broke into a smile as she ended, 'So that only leaves me. A little word from the right direction, a little push, and I'll be upstairs. The last word, I know, is with Miss Bateman, but you could tell her that I've done work for you and it was all right. It was all right, wasn't it?'

'Yes. Oh yes.'

'Well then, will you? You could say sort of offhand like to her when you're going through the office to see his nibs, "I hear Mr Noland is losing his secretary. Who were you thinking of putting in her place?" And if she doesn't say me you could say, "Well there's that Miss Ray. She did some very good work for me."'

He was staring at her again. She really believed that this was how things could be done. She didn't think that Miss Bateman would be asking herself why he should want Miss Ray promoted, why his interest. He couldn't understand how she, being what she was, could be so naïve. He said, 'I'll do what I can.'

'You will?' She was laughing now. 'Good. You won't regret it. I'm a good secretary, I know me own worth, and if I've got somebody to take an interest in, and an office of me own . . . well, I'll go ahead like wildfire. I know I will.'

Not in Peamarsh's, he thought, not if I can help it.

404

He would, he knew now, never know a moment's peace as long as she was in the building.

He watched her get up and go into the bedroom, and when she came back his watch was dangling from her finger. She came and stood in front of him and swung it before his face like a pendulum. Her own face had an impish look as she said, 'The evidence.'

He put out his hand and took hold of the end of the strap, but she still held on to it and as she looked down at him she said, 'I hate to let it go; it was me only hold over you.'

Thank God for that, he thought, remembering the threatened pregnancy. He wanted to pull it from her hand, but restrained himself in case this should be a prelude to a tussle. He felt she was just waiting for that. He took a slow deep breath as the watch dropped on to his hand, and putting it in his pocket he said, 'Thank you.'

As he got to his feet she said, 'You won't forget about what I asked you, will you?'

'No, I won't forget.' He picked up his hat and walked out of the room and into the passage, and there, slipping before him, she put her hand on the sneck of the door and turned her face up to him as she said, 'Well, I suppose this is the last tête-à-tête.'

He made no answer to this and she said softly, 'You're a fool, you know; you could have had fun. I'm not a gold-digger. There's something I put much more value on than money, and I'll give you three guesses at it.' She put her head back now against the door and laughed a high cracking laugh, saying, 'You blush easily. I've never known a man blush like you; you're

405

like a lad in some ways that's never been tried out. All right, all right.' The slow movement of her hand before his face indicated he keep calm.

When the door was pulled open he stepped into the dark street and moved swiftly away towards the Cut, and he was some way along it before he heard the door bang. It didn't close, it banged.

For the third time he stood at the end of the Cut and got his breath. It was over. Thank God, it was over. It had been a lesson, a nerve-racking lesson. But he was out of it, clear. Never again would he let himself in for anything like that, NEVER, NEVER.

The third letter marked 'Private and Personal' arrived the day after Olive Standford was told to take over in Mr Noland's office. The letter said briefly: 'You're a dirty stinker! You didn't even mention my name to Miss Bateman. I asked her. Well, the last laugh might be on me.'

As the morning wore on the sick feeling in his stomach increased. She had said she wasn't a blabber, but that was when she imagined she had something to gain. Thwarted, God knew what she would do, or say! He even dreaded going out to lunch in case he would run into her on the stairs. The only thing to do was to get out early and return early. And he got the opportunity to do this when, at about ten to twelve, Jim Whelan phoned to say he would like a word with him and would he join him for lunch at 'The Oak'? Yes, Harry said, he'd be very pleased to. Was it something connected with the business? No, Jim replied, nothing connected with the business, but nevertheless it was of some importance. But more over lunch. How soon could he make it? Right now, Harry said.

Jim Whelan was waiting for him in one of the wooden-framed cubicles which distinguished 'The Oak', and after asking him if he would like anything to drink and Harry saying no, thanks all the same, they got down to ordering lunch. This over, Harry sat back and looked across at Jim and said, 'Well now, what's this you've got to tell me?'

'Ah, yes.' Jim tapped his finger tips gently together then asked, 'Am I right in thinking that you don't actually love your father-in-law?'

It was a moment before Harry answered very quietly, 'You're right; but why do you ask?'

'Well, for the simple reason I wanted to make sure, although I was pretty certain how you felt.'

'What you've got to say concerns him?'

'Yes.'

'Regarding the business?'

'Oh no. No, nothing to do with the business . . . By the way, do you know if he goes to York very often?'

'York? Yes. At least he's been a few week-ends this year.'

'Do you know why he goes?'

'To see this old colonel I understand. He's still war crazy. Good old days, and all that.'

'His old colonel? Oh, that's a good one! Now let me start at the beginning and put you in the picture from my side. It's like this, Harry. My in-laws live in York and they were celebrating their golden wedding at the week-end, and the wife and I went through on Friday night and for a treat we had arranged to take them to the new hotel that's been opened recently. The Splendide. In the ordinary way we would never go to a place like that but this was once in a lifetime. Well, it was when we were in the foyer, they were waiting for me, Marge and her mam and dad, and I was just coming out of the gents when I see a man and a very smartly dressed young woman being led to the dining-room by the head waiter. And the man was . . . guess who?'

'No!'

'Yes, Rippon. And the woman was Alice Howell.'

'Alice Howell and him, in . . . in York!'

'Alice Howell and your father-in-law in York, yes. You remember Alice Howell, don't you? She was in the storeroom. She married, and her husband had a nervous breakdown, two in fact. He's in the asylum now.'

'Yes, yes, I know.' There was an utterly bewildered note in Harry's voice. 'She was a member of the church. They were both members. She moved to York to stay with a cousin or someone last back end, in November some time.'

'Does that coincide with the colonel?'

Harry sat back and tried to digest this news. It was unbelievable. He said as much. 'It's unbelievable, Jim. Now are you sure?'

'Look, Harry; I know the old man, I knew him even before you did – I started in the business when it was a pup – and I also know Alice Howell.'

'He couldn't have just met her.'

'Just met her be damned!' Jim tossed his head. 'The head waiter was taking them in like old friends and head waiters are not given to charity; the only thing that causes them to stoop their backs is the thought of picking up crinkly paper.'

The stinking hypocrite; the psalm-singing stinking hypocrite! And all that business about his old Colonel. God! he could be sick.

'Well now, has that given you an appetite for your dinner?'

'Appetite? It's taken it away, I'm floored, Jim.'

'I'm not; I wasn't surprised in the least. I've had my own opinion about Mr Dave Rippon for many years; an' I've got a suspicion this isn't the first little offshoot he's indulged in. In fact, I've more than a suspicion. Dave Rippon never does anything for nothing, and if I've ever heard of him doing a good turn for somebody, a woman in particular, I've always wondered what she'd had to give him in return.' He paused and looked hard at Harry and asked, 'Aren't you tickled about it?'

'No, Jim, I'm not, I'm anything but. At this moment I'm flaming-well boiling, I'm bloody-well boiling.'

And that was putting the state of his feelings mildly, for he was hearing Esther down the years extolling her father's virtues.

'I'm sorry I told you, Harry.'

'Oh no, don't you be sorry, Jim. Thank you very much, and I mean that. You see I've had that sanctimonious old roué pushed down my throat for years; that was, when he wasn't being held up before me as a paragon.'

'Oh, I guessed that much, Harry. That was why I thought I'd like telling you. What you going to do about it?'

'I don't know, Jim, not yet. I just don't know, I'll see

how things work out. But there's one thing I do know. I feel in a stronger position than I've ever felt in my life before.'

'Good. Good. Then my spilling the beans has done something.'

'By the way,' said Harry now, 'did he see you?'

'No. As it happened he didn't, and that was because he was escorted to the Rose Room . . . It's a smaller dining-room, kept for select patrons or small parties I understand. But would his face have been red if we had bumped into each other! Yet being Dave Rippon, I bet he'd have talked himself out of it.'

Yes, thought Harry, being Dave Rippon he'd have talked himself out of it all right.

Harry ran up the office stairs, marched across the first floor, thrust open his office door, pulled off his hat and coat, and sat down behind his desk. He was still angry, but now his anger was being attacked by a form of reasoning that seemed to be defending his father-in-law. It said: He's a widower; if he wants to have a woman on the side that's up to him, isn't it? Yes, he came back, that was up to him. He could have had as many women on the side as he liked if he wasn't such a preaching prig, and if his moral code wasn't held up as a yardstick to himself . . . And what would Esther make of her dear papa when she heard of this? But there was the rub; he wouldn't be able to tell Esther, for the knowledge would break her. And there was another point. Would he be able even to tell his father-in-law he was aware of his double life? . . . He didn't know. Yet there was one thing certain, he wouldn't be capable of listening to him doing the Colonel Callow and the honour of the regiment monologue without retaliating in some way.

He sat now with both hands on the desk rolling a pencil back and forward between his fingers. Then, the action stopping abruptly, he put his hand into his inner pocket and brought out Betty Ray's letter again. When he re-read it, it didn't appear so obviously threatening now. The knowledge he had acquired over the last two hours had in an odd way rid him of some of his fears, not all, but some. His thinking pointed out that even if she did open her mouth he wouldn't have his father-in-law wagging his finger at him. Then his reasoning, turning on him, again, said, You're not in such a good position that you can wag your finger yourself. They would say you're worse than he is; a married man with three children! It wouldn't be much use protesting it just happened that once for who'd believe you? Certainly not Esther.

When the phone rang he lifted it abruptly and said, 'Yes.'

'Harry!' The name was rapped out, it was the great man himself.

'Yes?'

'Where've you been? I tried to get you at twelve o'clock.'

'I've been to lunch.'

'Going early, aren't you? Anyway, listen. I want you up here at four-thirty prompt. I'll likely be out of the board room then but if I'm not, wait.'

He held the mouthpiece away from him and looked at it. The man on the other end of the line could have been a schoolmaster chastising an errant pupil. He was about to speak when he heard the phone click down.

Well! Talking about having the wind taken out of your sails. That demand augured no pleasant interview. There was something amiss and he himself was involved, that was evident.

It was about ten minutes later when the phone rang again and he heard the voice of Miss Bateman on the other end. 'Mr Blenheim?'

'Yes.' He was bristling now.

'Miss Bateman here.'

'Yes, Miss Bateman?'

'Would it be possible for you to come up to the office now?'

He screwed up his eyes as he replied, 'But Mr Rippon's just been on the phone and told me he wants to see me at half-past four.'

'I know, Mr Blenheim; but I would like to see you now, if it's convenient to you.'

Where his father-in-law's tone had been, to say the least, demanding, Miss Bateman's was persuasive, and this he knew wasn't like Miss Bateman.

'Are you still there, Mr Blenheim?'

'Yes, I'm still here, Miss Bateman.'

'Can you come up now?'

'Yes, I can.' His voice remained stiff.

'Thank you.'

When he put the phone down he stared at it; then rising and passing Ada Cole's door, he called, 'If anyone should ring I'll be up in Mr Rippon's office, Ada.'

She opened the door and nodded at him, saying,

'Very well, Mr Blenheim.' Her expression caught his attention, and stepping back he looked at her and said, 'Are you all right, Ada?'

'Yes yes, Mr Blenheim.' For a moment he thought she looked frightened, but that he supposed was a ridiculous idea; she was just tired. 'Not another cold brewing up I hope?' he said.

'No, Mr Blenheim.'

He nodded at her now and went out across the hall and into the lift and up to the second floor. When he entered his father-in-law's outer office Miss Bateman was seated behind her desk apparently waiting for him. He judged this because her hands were on top of the blotter, joined together as if she had been sitting thinking. This, too, was an unusual pose in which to find Miss Bateman.

'Sit down, Mr Blenheim.'

He sat down and looked across the desk and noted that her expression, too, was different; she didn't look cool any longer, she looked sort of furious, yet in an odd way controlled. For something to say he said, 'Can I help you, Miss Bateman?'

Before answering she made a small motion of her head slightly to the side and her arched eyebrows moved upwards. Then, her voice even, she said, 'No, I don't think you can, Mr Blenheim; but I can help you.'

He found himself pursing his lips and bobbing his head and saying politely, 'That's very nice of you, Miss Bateman.'

'We won't waste time on being polite to each other, Mr Blenheim. I have twenty minutes' – she glanced at her watch – 'before I am due in the Board Room.' She sat up stiffly in her chair now, her hands still joined together on the blotter, then went on, 'Mr Rippon wishes to see you at half-past four. You will have gauged from his tone that he didn't sound pleased. You might be wondering what he wants to see you about. Well, I'm going to tell you so you'll be prepared. It's about Betty Ray.'

His stomach muscles jerked as if a bullet had hit them. The saliva left his mouth and his tongue seemed to swell making it impossible for him to comment in any way.

'The knowledge of your association with Miss Ray came to me through' – she paused – 'Miss Cole, but believe me, Ada . . . Miss Cole told me of this only because she was worried about you. She felt you were being blackmailed by this girl because of the letters you were receiving. She told me in confidence about it. Perhaps that was foolish of her, but she wanted advice. You must believe that she sincerely wanted to help you. Well, Mr Blenheim, I am secretary to Mr Rippon; I've worked for the firm a year longer than you and my loyalties have always been with it, especially to Mr Rippon and so I informed Mr Rippon of what Miss Cole had told me.'

The hell you did! Loyalty to the firm. He felt hot anger rising in him again, but it was checked when she said, as if she meant it, 'I'm sorry now that I did so, very sorry. I want you to believe that, Mr Blenheim.'

That was some comfort. He opened his mouth to speak but found himself still unable to do so. Instead he drooped his head and swung it slowly from side to side; but he brought it up sharply as she said, 'But you needn't be concerned as to what he will do to you because you've got a come-back on him, haven't you?'

'Come-back?' The word seemed to struggle over the thickness of his tongue.

'Yes, his visits to York.'

His eyes widened, his mouth dropped into a slight gape. 'You know about them?'

'I didn't until about an hour ago. I happened to be sitting in the cubicle in "The Oak" and heard you and Mr Whelan talking. I'm afraid I became interested and made a point of listening. It's odd that I should have gone into "The Oak" today, fate, you might say. I haven't eaten there more than half-a-dozen times before. Perhaps because it's a favourite with the men. Anyway, there I was alone in my cubicle and I had nothing to do but lean back against the partition and listen to two known voices talking.'

'You know it all then, Miss Bateman, don't you?' he said now with a slight touch of sarcasm, and she nodded at him and said, 'Yes. Yes, Mr Blenheim, I know it all. I also know that your father-in-law was looking forward to the ribbing he would be able to give you because of your relationship with Miss Ray, although he didn't know exactly what it was. Nor do I or Miss Cole for that matter. But being, as he terms himself a man of the world, he put two and two together.'

'He would.'

'Yes, he would, Mr Blenheim. I can also tell you that he had decided that he wasn't going to inform your wife, he didn't want her to be upset, but' – she paused – 'to use his own words he was going to take it out of your hide. Subtly of course. The means he was going to use was the business concerning the outside building contracts. He was going to give you carte blanche except' – again she paused – 'for the final word on estimates. He would make these himself, but they'd all be done through your office and you personally, and whatever trouble ensued he would see that you bore full responsibility. You have known your father-in-law a long time but even so it might seem impossible to you, even at this stage, that he could, under those circumstances, make trouble for you, but I can assure you, Mr Blenheim, that he could. His methods are legal and quite within the law, but dirty.'

Miss Bateman sneered as she said the word, dirty, and there was such bitterness in her tone that for the moment he forgot his own predicament and wondered what had happened to turn her against the man she'd worked for for so long. Surely not just because she'd heard of his affair in York. Yet women were strange creatures. Didn't he know! He asked her quietly now, 'Why are you telling me all this, Miss Bateman?'

She didn't answer for a moment, but, bringing her hands from the desk where she had kept them during all this time, she joined them tightly together and pressed them against her thin neck as she said, 'Because I'm leaving next week and I thought it might be a good idea that when you were called into the sanctum you should have in your possession some bullets to fire, not only for yourself but on my behalf, so to speak.' She began now to gather some papers up quickly from her desk, and when she rose he rose also and said, 'I don't quite follow you, Miss Bateman. I can't see how letting him know I'm aware of the real reason for his visits to York can affect you in any way.'

'That alone couldn't, Mr Blenheim, but when you tell him that you are aware that I have been his mistress for fifteen years, and that I have a child by him – adopted, she is now thirteen years old – and that I expected him to marry me when his wife died, you'll understand that you are firing for me. Also, that right up to this very week he has visited me as usual. My home is very discreetly placed on the outskirts of the town; he arranged it so.' She moved towards the door and his stunned gaze followed her, and there she turned and looked at him, her face, he thought, on the point of crumpling into tears. But her voice held a slight cracked sound like laughter as she said, 'I believed in Colonel Callow. Mr Rippon kindly phoned me from a call box during his visits. The Colonel, I understand, didn't like the phone. What is more, he actually made me feel sorry for the poor, lonely Colonel. I was a fool, wasn't I, to be taken in? But I . . . I really can't blame myself for my stupidity because Mr Rippon is a very clever man.'

'Oh, Miss Bateman, I'm very sorry.'

She turned her face towards the door for a moment but she didn't go out, and he spoke softly to her back, 'I won't say anything about this, Miss Bateman; you wouldn't really want me . . .'

'Oh yes, yes please.' She was looking at him now. Her eyes were full of tears but they weren't spilling over. 'I ask you to do this for me. I want you to do it. I want him to know that you know. It may not give you any power over him because you're not the kind of man who would use that kind of power, but it will prevent him from using you as a battering ram because of his dislike of you. And he dislikes you heartily, he cannot stand you. All crooks hate honest men.'

As they stared at each other in silence he had the strong urge to take her in his arms and comfort her. Then she said, 'I'm acting in strict accordance with the saying, there's no fury like that of a woman scorned, don't you think, Mr Blenheim? But I've kept my fury quiet because I'm averse to brawls, but it will nevertheless have results.' She blinked a number of times, then, straightening her shoulders and wetting her lips, she went out of the room. She didn't even deem it necessary to go to the cloakroom but marched straight to the Board Room, knocked once, then opened the door and went in.

He stood where he was staring into the empty hallway. Amazing, unbelievable, fantastic. The words were of the superlative degree, of which his mind was capable at the moment. The whole affair was past description, at least that part of it in which Miss Bateman was concerned. Poor Miss Bateman. He felt utterly, utterly sorry for her. All these years he had judged her to be an unfeeling, prim, less-than-human being, a sort of highly-powered machine. How wrong one could be. Yet, no-one could be blamed for thinking her otherwise for her attitude had created that impression. But he had just glimpsed the real Miss Bateman, an exceptional woman.

He forgot to close the door after him before he walked across the landing, and he was still in a state of bewilderment when he entered his office again, there to see Ada Cole standing in her doorway, her hand to her cheek. She went to say something as he passed her, but instead she broke down, and he turned quickly to her as if he had just recollected she was there and said, 'Why, Ada, don't. Don't distress yourself like that.'

'Oh! Mr Blenheim, I don't know what to say; I don't, I don't really.'

'Then say nothing.'

'But it was me.'

'Well, you did what you thought best.'

'I did, I did, Mr Blenheim. I was so worried. That girl's no good, I know she's not. I've found out things about her. I . . . I didn't know what to do. Miss Bateman was the only one, but . . . but believe me –' She now blew her nose loudly, then went on, 'Oh believe me, Mr Blenheim, I never thought for a moment she'd pass it on to Mr Rippon, I didn't. I would have died rather than open my mouth if I'd thought. And this morning when she phoned and told me, well, I nearly ran out of the place. Honest I did.'

'Sit down. Sit down.' He pressed her into a chair. Then sitting down himself, for he felt he needed support, he said, 'Now you mightn't believe me when I say that what you did was the best thing that could have happened.'

'Oh, Mr Blenheim!' Her head moved in wide unbelieving sweeps.

'It's true. It's true, Ada. You've done me a great service.'

419

'Oh, Mr Blenheim, if only I could believe you, but I can't; it's just because you're kind.'

'Kindness nothing, Ada. Look, I'm telling you.' He reached out and took her hand. 'You won't understand this, but I want you to believe me. Because of your concern and what you did you've given me a kind of strength, power you could say.' He didn't use the word his mind suggested, 'handle'. 'Yes, that's the right word, "power", that I didn't have yesterday.' And this was true, for if Miss Bateman hadn't heard of his connection with Betty Ray it was more than unlikely he'd ever have heard of her connection with Rippon.

She dried one eye after the other, then stared at him, her whole face showing perplexity now.

'I can't explain anything more to you, Ada, but I just want you to believe that you've done me a service. That's what you wanted to do in the first place, wasn't it?'

'Oh, yes, Mr Blenheim. And as I've said, I was so worried about you because I could see by your face when you got those letters that you were upset, and when I found out who they were from . . .'

'How did you find out, Ada?'

'Well' – her head drooped – 'by the writing on the envelope, comparing it.'

'You're very astute, Ada.'

'No, not really, Mr Blenheim, but . . . but when you're worried about someone' . . . Her voice trailed away then she blew her nose and went on, 'I knew enough about you to know that you would never get mixed up with a person like her, not off your own bat; there must have been something.'

'There was, Ada, but, but it's difficult to explain.'

'Oh, Mr Blenheim' – her lids were blinking rapidly – 'you've no need to explain. But she's no good, Mr Blenheim. But perhaps you know that already.'

'Well, I know very little about her really; I've only seen her three times.' He pursed his lips. 'The last twice following the "Private and Personal" letters.'

'Oh,' she seemed surprised. 'Then you won't know that her mother's done time for soliciting . . . and shop-lifting?'

His face stretched a little as he said, 'No, I didn't, Ada.'

'How that one ever became a typist at all passes my comprehension; commonness is sticking out all over her. Oh!' She put her hand to her cheek again. 'I shouldn't say all this but I feel I can, knowing your feelings are not concerned. They're not, are they, Mr Blenheim?'

She was agitated and on the point of tears again and he took her hand and patted it, saying, 'No, of course not, Ada. There now, no more tears, let's forget about it. But before the subject is closed, I'll say again that I'm grateful for your concern.'

'Thank you, Mr Blenheim. But there's just one more thing I'd like to know. Will . . . will there be any repercussions for you because of your father-in-law knowing?'

'I shouldn't think so, Ada.' His voice was firm as he got to his feet. 'In fact, I'm sure there won't be. Now' – he bent over her – 'do you think you could get us a strong cup of tea on the side?'

She fluttered to her feet, saying, 'Oh yes, Mr Blenheim. Yes, I'll see to it at once.'

'For both of us,' he added and she hurried away still sniffing but apparently reassured and he thought: Poor Ada, she was a small cog in the wheel of his life but her concern for him had gummed up the works.

Six

He was standing in Dave Rippon's outer office at twenty-eight minutes past four. There was no one there. At twenty minutes to five, as he was pacing up and down before Miss Bateman's desk, the door opened and she came in, alone. Going straight to her desk she put down a pad and some papers, and without looking up she said, 'He'll keep you waiting another twenty minutes or so. I'm leaving at five, a very unusual procedure for me following a Board meeting. It's what you might call working to rule.' She glanced up at him, her eyes cold and hard now.

He asked her quietly, 'What will you do?'

'Do?' Her chin came up high. 'I'll become secretary in another firm. That'll be no problem. I don't know whether you've realised it or not, Mr Blenheim, but I've practically run this business over the past ten years.' Her voice was steely.

'I have realised it, Miss Bateman.'

He noticed now that in spite of her tone her whole body was quivering, her hands, her shoulders, her head, it was like an ague. Her hands began fumbling at the papers on the desk; she opened and closed drawers;

423

she rose from her seat three times in succession and went to the filing cabinet, flicked over folios but did not take anything out. He felt he couldn't bear to watch her any longer. Her calmness had entirely deserted her and she looked possessed of a growing fury. He went to the window and stood looking out.

About three minutes to five she bounced up from the chair and, going to a cupboard, took out her hat and coat and handbag. She pulled on her hat without looking in a mirror and the result was slightly askew. As she got into her coat she said, 'If he wants to know where you got your information, and he's sure to, tell . . . tell him, I told you, just that.' She emphasised the last few words with accompanying dips of her head.

He stared pityingly at her as she fumbled with her bag. There wasn't a shred of her usual composure left. He said softly, 'What can I say, Miss Bateman?' and she turned to him and said, 'What? What do you mean?'

'I'm . . . I'm so sorry.'

Her lips worked soundlessly before she said, 'You shouldn't be sorry for me, Mr Blenheim, you shouldn't waste your pity on fools. But then you've been a bit of one yourself, haven't you?' When she made an effort to smile, even grimly, it was as if her skin had become stiff and was cracking in the process. As she went towards the door it was suddenly opened and Dave Rippon marched into the room; at least he took three steps inside then stopped and stared at Miss Bateman and said on a surprised note, 'You . . . you off?'

'Y-Yes, Mr Rippon, I'm off.'

He glanced quickly at Harry, then looked back at his secretary, questioning now. 'You not feeling well . . . Miss Bateman?'

'I never felt better, Mr Rippon, and never more sane.'

Again he glanced at Harry, furtively now, but his gaze was jerked back to her when she said, 'I'm leaving early because I'm going away for the week-end. It's a long time since I went away for a week-end, Mr Rippon, but now I feel I need a change. Good night, Mr Rippon.' Her voice and manner were touched with hysteria now. She moved towards the door; then, her head jerking round, she said, 'Good night, Mr Blenheim.'

Harry did not answer, he merely acknowledged her words with a small movement of his head; then he watched his father-in-law stare at the closed door that she had almost scraped past his face.

But now Dave Rippon was recovering himself. Definitely his mistress's attitude had astounded him, but he was covering it up well. He passed Harry without looking at him and, going into his own office, he called over his shoulder, 'Well come on; let's get this over.'

In the inner office Harry didn't wait to be asked to sit down. Pulling forward a straight-backed leather chair he placed it dead opposite his father-in-law and sat down.

'Now –' Dave Rippon rubbed the palms of his hands together as if about to relish a meal; then he moved from one buttock to another before he said, 'What I've got to say to you isn't going to be pleasant hearing.' He

425

waited, staring across the desk into his son-in-law's straight face. 'You've been up to something, haven't you?'

Harry made no movement. He did not even blink his eyes. He kept them fixed on the pale blue ones glaring into his.

'Well! what's the matter with you, man. You've heard what I said. You've been up to something. Keeping your tongue glued down isn't going to help. I'm going to start by telling you, you should be damned-well ashamed of yourself.'

'Oh, Esther wouldn't like to hear you using that kind of language, Father.'

Harry had no intention of being facetious but he just couldn't let the opportunity slip past. He felt for a moment like laughing, he felt drunk with power. He had it in him to break this man, this pompous, big-headed, conniving, sly, lecherous man. He knew also in this moment that the feeling he'd had for his father-in-law, had always had for him, had been hate. Not a Christian feeling; that being so, he hadn't put a name to it before.

'Are you drunk?'

'I could be.'

Dave Rippon brought himself forward in his chair, and leaning across the table peered at his son-in-law. He didn't look drunk, he didn't sound drunk, but there was something different about him. After a moment of dead silence he leant against the back of his chair again, and, nodding his head slowly, he said, 'You're going to brazen it out, eh?'

'Brazen what out?'

'Now look here. You know as well as I do what we're talking about. You've been having an affair haven't you, with the girl, Ray, in the pool?'

'Having an affair? Me? What on earth gave you that idea?'

Dave Rippon again sat in silence; there was no indignation in his son-in-law's voice. His denial was smooth, calm. He tried again: 'You've been getting letters from her, she's got something on you. She's been blackmailing you, hasn't she?'

'Blackmailing me?' Harry now dug his finger into his chest.

'Now look here, I don't know what your game is, but don't play it with me. Now stop acting the goat. I know you've been receiving letters from that girl, and a girl like that doesn't keep writing letters to no purpose. Now you either come clean or I'm going to go further into it. Take your choice.'

'What do you mean, go further into it?'

'What do I mean?' Dave Rippon's bushy eyebrows were moving up to his receding hair line. 'I mean just that, I'm going to get to the bottom of it. You happen to be my daughter's husband. You have a standard to keep up and I won't stand for any jiggery-pokery towards . . .'

'Shut up!' The spittle spurted from Harry's lips on the words, and if there had been bullets aimed straight at him Dave Rippon couldn't have been more startled. His face, in fact his whole attitude when he rose to his feet, looked comical. When at last he brought out, 'What did I hear you say?' Harry said in the same tone, 'Do you want me to repeat it? And I wouldn't bother standing up if I were you, it's going to be a longish session.'

'Have you gone mad?'

'Yes, slightly, because hearing you putting on a sanctimonious act is enough to drive anyone mad. And I'm going to tell you something. I've listened to it for the last time . . . Sit down!' He now stabbed his index finger towards the chair, but Dave Rippon didn't sit down, not immediately anyway; he didn't resume his seat until Harry said, 'I've told you, it's going to be a long session. Where would you like me to start? With Alice Howell, alias Colonel Callow, or nearer home . . . with Miss Bateman?'

He thought for a moment that his father-in-law was going to have a seizure. He watched his heavy face flush slightly, then turn a ghastly grey, a pasty doughy grey. He watched the blue eyes darken and swell out of their sockets; he watched the prominent Adam's apple jerk between the collar and the thickening chin. He saw one white hand, with its well-tended fingernails, paw at the end of the desk, and for a moment he thought the man was actually going to collapse; then he was sitting in front of him again, staring at him as if he was watching horns growing out of his head. He let him get his breath before he said, 'Well now, take your choice.'

Dave Rippon didn't speak but continued to stare at Harry. He was recovering himself, but not sufficiently to make any retort when Harry said, 'Of all the two-faced, mealy-mouthed, dirty old swines on God's earth, you beat them all.'

'Don't you dare speak to me like that.' Dave

428

Rippon's voice seemed to be dragged up from some great depths.

'I'll speak to you how I like. You've lauded it over everybody for years, held yourself up as a moral example – my home's been built on . . . Father's standards.' He gave an impression of Esther's voice. 'God, it's unbelievable. And all the time you've not only had one woman on the side but two.'

Dave Rippon made no rejoinder to this; he just continued to stare at the new edition of his son-in-law, and Harry went on, 'You'd like to know how I found out about your little games, wouldn't you? Well, I'll tell you this much because she asked me to tell you, Miss Bateman; she told me she's been your mistress for fifteen years and that she's had a child by you and that you've visited her twice a week, never failing. She must have felt pretty grim to tell me that, don't you think, a decorous, self-contained woman like Miss Bateman? She must have gone through something and been pretty cut up to give you away in one foul swoop like that. You'll have to ask her on Monday why she did it, for as she said, she'll be away for the week-end. I'd like to be here when you explain about Mrs Howell and the Colonel. And you'd better be careful what you say, you'd better not make a bigger liar out of yourself than you already are, because she knows a great deal does Miss Bateman.'

'Get out!' The words were thin, hardly moving the lips at all.

Harry didn't move. He knew he had said enough, more than enough. Whichever way things went this would likely be the end of him in Peamarsh's, but at

429

this moment he didn't give a damn, except perhaps that it would all come as a shock to Esther. In a way he was sorry for her because she was so damned fond of her father, too fond. That kind of feeling should be cut out, or at least filed down, when a woman took a husband. Looking back now he could see that Esther had never looked upon him as master in his own house; mentally she was still living under her father's roof. Well, there were lots of people going to get lots of jolts before this affair was over, but there was one thing he'd make plain to Esther from now on: he was running his own life, and hers, and the children's as long as the latter needed him. He thought quizzically that he might even have to do it on the dole, but however he had to do it he would do it.

Now, in his own time, he rose to his feet. But he had to drag his eyes from those of his father-in-law before he turned about and went out of the room.

The clock in the outer office said twenty-past five. In his own office he found Ada still there, her face full of apprehension. He said calmly, 'Everything's all right; there's nothing to worry about. Get yourself off home.'

There'd be plenty of time for her to worry when the lid blew right off, at present it was only eased up slightly. How quick and how high the lid went depended on his father-in-law's reactions and these in turn depended on the outcome of his meeting with Miss Bateman. He saw how things would work. His father-in-law would go straight along to her place now and try and patch things up. But with his new knowledge of Miss Bateman he couldn't see her allowing the rift to close; she had cut too deeply. Yet at the same time he couldn't visualise her opening her mouth wide; if she wanted to get another responsible post she wouldn't get it by blackening her last employer.

The week-end he saw as a time of waiting. Should he, he asked himself, use it to put his own case before Esther? Tell her everything that had happened since the office party? Then tell her why he was coming clean? He didn't know; he'd have to see how things turned out because bringing low in her estimation, at one go, the two men in her life would be too much altogether. It was strange but if he had the choice of whom to expose, he would have chosen to tell his own story because he knew it would have hurt her less. The knowledge wasn't pleasant to face up to but it was nevertheless true . . .

When he reached home Gail greeted him in her usual boisterous way and as she tugged off his coat, he said, 'Hold on, hold on, leave me my shirt. What's all the rush, anyway?'

In answer she said, 'I thought you'd never come.' Then taking him by the arm she led him towards the sitting-room and inside she pointed and said, 'There! Isn't that nice?'

He looked at the low table set before the fire and when he stood over it and saw only two cups and saucers and two plates arranged, he said, 'Where's everybody?'

'Mother was at the Young Wives' group meeting. She phoned to say she'd be held up, a committee or something, she'll be back about half-past six. And John is staying on for a lecture. Terry is down at Tony Barnham's and Elsie had to go to the dentist's, and so

431

I thought, tea for two before the fire. Isn't it lovely? And look' – she pointed – 'I've done a plate of toast, all dripping with butter, soggy.' She wrinkled up her nose. 'Sit down. There's your slippers. I'll just make the tea.'

As she dashed out of the room he looked after her and shook his head slowly; then he sat down on the couch and put on his slippers. From the hate-filled meeting of an hour ago to this. And would he ever have this again, tea before the fire, just him and Gail? As he turned towards the door and watched her coming in, her face bright, the teapot held out like a sacrifice, he thought, Oh my God! What'll it do to her when she knows? and of a sudden it became imperative that she shouldn't know, that all this messy business concerning himself and his father-in-law should be hushed up; no price should be too high to pay for his daughter to continue seeing him in the light of 'a nice bloke'. Esther didn't matter, not really, she could take care of her emotions, they were already set. Her reactions would be decided between her and God and she would receive comfort from righteousness. But not so his daughter; God would hold no comfort for Gail. If her father ceased to be 'a nice bloke', it would affect her whole life. For one wild moment he thought of getting on the phone to his father-in-law and asking him if he could talk the matter over again. When he gave an audible 'Huh!' Gail said, 'What did you say?' and in reply he smiled at her and answered, 'I've got the kindest, and most beautiful daughter in the world.'

When she fell across his knees he actually groaned – she was lying in the same position as Betty Ray had lain, and it brought back the incident as plainly as if it had happened yesterday. But, contrary to when Gail had put her arms around him that night up in the bedroom and he had repulsed her violently, he now took her hand gently in his and said softly, 'Don't ever stop loving me, Gail, will you?' and she, after a moment of surprise that brought her eyes wide and her mouth agape, said, 'As if ever I could, Dad. Fancy even thinking a thing like that.'

They were at their evening meal when Dave Rippon came into the room. Harry had his back to the door, and he did not turn round when Esther, from the far end of the table, said, 'Oh hello, Father. This is a surprise; I thought you were going away for the weekend.'

'I've changed my mind, I'm getting too old for jaunts. Have you a bite for a hungry man?'

Harry had been about to carry some food to his mouth, but when Esther had spoken the fork had become stationary in mid-air; now he returned the food to his plate and waited for Dave Rippon to come into view. He knew that Esther's attitude would have told her father immediately that as yet she knew nothing.

'Move up and let your grandfather sit down.' Esther was speaking to Terry when Gail said, 'Come and sit beside me, Grandfather.'

'Thank you. Thank you, my dear.'

Now Dave Rippon turned to his daughter and asked, 'Sure I won't be robbing anybody?'

'Don't be silly, Father.' Esther closed her eyes at such a question.

'Where's Mrs O'Toole?' He always gave his son-in-law's grandmother her full title.

'She's got a slight chill,' said Esther; 'I'm keeping her in bed.'

'Good idea, good idea.' Dave Rippon nodded in agreement.

That he had not addressed himself in any way to Harry was not really unusual; they worked in the office and this made formal greetings unnecessary.

As Esther helped her father to food, she said, 'I thought you were going to York to see the Colonel.' This was followed by a moment of complete silence; then Dave Rippon, looking down at his plate, said, 'Oh, I think the old boy was having me on. I'm not going to rush off at his beck and call. I'm getting a bit tired these days, feeling my age I suppose.'

'Nonsense,' said Esther soothingly. 'But anyway, I've always told you, you work too hard.'

'It's a modern complaint, my dear, and it's not going to get any better. And these two will find it out shortly.' He nodded from John to Terry, then asked, 'How's work going with you, John?'

'Oh, not too bad, Grandfather.'

'You really have got your mind set on this engineering?'

'Well, yes, I suppose so.' John smiled across the table, and the smile altered his face completely and made him appear strikingly good-looking.

'What about you, Terry? Still going to be an architect, eh?'

'No, Grandfather.' Terry shook his head solemnly.

434

'I've decided that my mission in life is to lead a pop group.'

John spluttered part of the food from his mouth; Gail let out a loud crack of a laugh; Esther, too, laughed; her father smiled; only Harry's face remained straight.

'You know what?' Dave Rippon wagged his fork, first at one boy, then at the other, as he said, 'You could both do worse than come into Peamarsh's. The firm's going places, getting bigger and bigger every year. You should think about it. And think about it very seriously from now on, with your father to be a director soon, and not exactly junior either.'

Harry lowered his knife and fork to his plate but held on to the handles. So this was it. In some way or other he had silenced Miss Bateman; now he was making sure of him. For a moment a gust of fierce hot anger rose in him and he thought, be damned if he will! Then Gail's hand came across the end of the table and touched his arm, and Esther was saying, 'Oh, Father! When did this happen?'

'Oh, it's been on the books for some time, but . . . but I like to be sure of things, know my ground so to speak.'

'Who's leaving?' said Esther now, excitedly.

'Well, we knew today for certain that Walters is resigning – it's his age with him – but Graham Hall is also giving up. Poor chap, he's in a bad way. So I thought of my son-in-law.' Slowly he lifted his head and looked at Harry. His blue eyes looked cold, almost opaque, and he said directly to him now, 'Of course it all depends whether your husband will

435

take one of the vacant chairs on the first floor.'

'Don't be silly. Don't be silly.' Esther was laughing, her voice high, her attitude almost girlish.

'Well, it's up to him.' Dave Rippon's glance was boring into Harry, and as Harry looked back at his father-in-law the expression on his face brought a sudden quietness to the table. They were all staring at him now. What he might have said if Gail hadn't at that moment got up and, coming to his side, exclaimed excitedly, 'Haven't you anything to say, Mr Director?'

He turned and looked at her for a matter of seconds, then muttered thickly, 'It's come as a sort of surprise, I wasn't expecting it.'

'He who expecteth nothing.' Terry's voice was mimicking their minister. Then speaking as his perky self once again, he added, 'But I'll tell you what I expect, Pop. I expect a car the minute I'm seventeen, but I'll settle for a scooter to be going on with.'

Amid laughter, in which she joined, Esther said, 'You'll have nothing of the sort to be going on with! And don't call your father Pop. I've told you about that before.'

'All right, Ma.'

Whether Terry realised it or not he was creating a diversion for which Harry was grateful; but shortly there came a lull in their laughter and chatter and they were all looking at him again, all, that is, except Dave Rippon. He was eating his meal with apparent enjoyment, and into the waiting silence he said, 'This is an excellent casserole; I can never get Mrs Hunter to do steak like this.'

'Excuse me.' His voice mumbling, Harry got to his feet.

436

'What's the matter?' Esther looked concerned for a moment, and he patted his stomach and said, 'Over-eating I suppose, but carry on.'

When he reached his room he dropped heavily into a chair. So this was how it was going to be; promotion, as a gob stopper. Working on the same floor and hating each other's guts. Miss Bateman had said that his father-in-law disliked him. Now that feeling had turned to black hate; it had poured out of his eyes as he had stared at him back there at the table. And on his part, the feeling was returned in full. And so how could they work together? He couldn't do it. He just couldn't do it . . . but the alternative was to bring everything into the open . . .

It must have been twenty minutes later when Esther came into the room. She stood looking at him for a full minute before she said, 'What's the matter with you, Harry?'

'Me? Nothing, just tummy.' He punched his middle.

'Aren't you coming down?'

'No; if you don't mind I'll turn in.'

'You're going to BED!' Her voice was high in disbelief. 'And after Father bringing you this news.'

He could only stare at her until she said, 'Talk about gratitude; you didn't even say thank you. What's come over you lately?'

He got to his feet and went to the dressing table and took off his collar and tie, and he said to her through the mirror, 'What have I got to thank him for? If he hadn't done it off his own bat, you would have seen he did it off yours; so it was cut and dried anyway, wasn't it?'

'Aha!' She moved her head from one side to the other on the exclamation. 'Now I have it. Well, let me tell you, Harry, you should be thankful and glad that there are people who have your welfare at heart, because, left to yourself . . .'

He swung round, saying sharply, 'Don't say it, Esther, don't say it. I've heard it for years and once more would be just too much.' He watched the colour flush her pale face. Then she swung round and went out. But she didn't bang the door behind her; that wasn't Esther's way.

He returned to the mirror and looked at his reflection. She had explained his reactions to her own satisfaction; he would leave it like that and let things ride. For how long? He didn't know.

It was a nine-days' wonder in the office, Miss Bateman was leaving. Why, nobody seemed to know; there were various rumours. She was going to be married to a man abroad with whom she had been corresponding for years; and this could have been so because nobody knew Miss Bateman's business. She'd had money left her; perhaps she'd won the pools, with an X for secrecy, who was to know? Some more astute guessers said, perhaps she'd had a row with old man Rippon for he had been acting like a white-skinned devil during the last few days.

But Ada Cole thought that she was the sole reason for Miss Bateman leaving and she said so to Harry. 'It all stems from Friday, Mr Blenheim, and what I told her. And then you going up there.'

He assured her again and again that his own affair had nothing whatever to do with Miss Bateman

438

leaving, until he finally convinced her, and then she said, 'What will they do without her?'

'Everybody can be done without, Ada.'

'But she's got everything at her fingertips, she's a wonderful organiser, you know she is, Mr Blenheim.'

'Yes, I know Ada. But someone else will take her place and will soon get into the way.'

'They'll never suit Mr Rippon, he's very particular.'

'Yes.' He endorsed her statement. 'He's very particular.'

'They have had nine replies to the advertisement in the evening paper,' she said.

'Well, that's hopeful.' He nodded at her. 'Now let's forget about the business of the upper floor and get on with this one.'

Ada Cole looked slightly hurt. Never before had Mr Blenheim told her in so many words to get on with her work . . .

By Thursday it was all over the office that Mr Rippon had picked his new secretary. She was a woman in her forties with good references and she was to start on Monday.

Miss Bateman left on the Friday evening without any fuss, not going round, as some of the other staff would have done, to say good-bye to her colleagues. And there was no presentation made to her. She had asked Ada Cole to see definitely that there was no collection taken on her behalf.

On the Monday morning Olive Standford told the other girls in the pool that she had seen Miss Bateman waiting for a bus on the Friday night and she was sure she was crying, and on this she was howled down. Mary

Cheeseman said, 'That would have been quite impossible, as the paragon hadn't any tear ducts.'

On the Monday afternoon when Harry came back
from lunch, Ada informed him that Mr Rippon said she
had to take over the management of the pool until the
new secretary got into her stride.

The new secretary gave her notice in at the end of
the week; but this was no nine days' wonder, everybody
expected it.

The next secretary stayed a month. It was when the
news went round the office that she had given her
notice in, too, that Betty Ray spoke to Ada Cole. She
waylaid her in the main hall.

'Miss Cole, can I have a word with you?' Her tone
was deferential, but the look Ada bestowed on her was
cold and her tone prim, as she said, 'Yes, Miss Ray.
What is it?'

'Well, I'll come to the point. It's no use beating about
the bush. Mr Rippon . . . above' – she jerked her head
– 'nobody's staying with him; I want the chance to try.'

'You!'

'Yes, me. Why not?' The deference had gone out of
the tone. 'I've been here nearly six months; I've got the
hang of the work. Me shorthand's better than anybody
else's. It's a hundred and twenty a minute and me
typing's sixty. And what's more I can pick things up
quick. I want a chance to try.'

'Well, you're not getting it, Miss Ray. And take that
as final.'

Ada was utterly indignant. That girl daring to ask to
be sent upstairs. She felt like telling her all she knew
about her. If she had her way she'd dismiss her on

440

the spot; cheap little blackmailing guttersnipe!

There was only one answer to a further advertisement for a secretary in the evening paper, and this applicant's inexperience disqualified her immediately. There was nothing for it but Ada should send someone up from the pool. But it certainly wouldn't be that Ray piece; on that she would remain firm if Mr Rippon never got a secretary. So she sent up Rose Weybridge; and on the second day Rose came downstairs crying, and stuttered, 'He to-ld me to ge-t out.'

When Ada went to the pool with the intention of sending the newest recruit upstairs, she found the typewriters quiet and the girls waiting for her. They all wanted to be the first to tell her that Betty Ray had taken her pad and things and gone upstairs to Mr Rippon's office. They thought that Miss Cole was about to choke and they waited for her to grab the phone. Instead, they watched her march out and across the hall to the lift.

Ada Cole was incensed. That's how she would have termed her feelings; but flaming mad would have been a more accurate description. When she reached Dave Rippon's office the outer room was empty. Knocking on the private door and being told to enter, she saw Betty Ray seated at one side of the desk and looking as if she had been there for ever. For a moment she was unable to speak; then almost spluttering she said, 'Mr Rippon . . . Mr Rippon, I didn't send this girl up here. She came on her own accord. She's . . .'

'Yes, she's just told me. Well, she can't be any worse than I've had lately. If she is she'll go. In the meantime, you can leave things as they are, Miss Cole.'

She stared at Mr Rippon; then she looked down on the girl, and she had the most disturbing desire. She wanted to slap her face, not just once, but twice, three times, go on slapping it. She hurried from the room, and in the lift she said to herself, 'And he knows about her and Mr Blenheim. There's going to be trouble. Oh dear, there's going to be trouble. And what will poor Mr Blenheim say?'

Seven

'Do you like it?'

'I think it's smashing.'

'Truly?'

He looked at her proudly. In the last three months she had put on inches; her puppy fat had almost disappeared, her legs were long and beautiful, she carried herself well, holding her head up as if, like the song, she was attempting to walk tall. Yet she had no need to try; two months past her sixteenth birthday she was already five foot five. Her face looked warm and kind and beautiful and so, so young.

She said, 'It isn't mini-mini, it's only three inches above.'

He smiled as he looked at the cream wool lacy thing she was wearing. Not mini-mini, as she said, but showing a surprising length of leg. He dropped his chin down and pushed his eyebrows up as he asked, 'Has your mother seen it?'

'Yes.' She pulled a long face.

'She said definitely no, until she saw Anna's. Coo! Hers is mini-mini-minus. But she said it was as well she wasn't with me when I went to buy it.' She hunched

443

her shoulders. 'It was lucky I hung on to my birthday money, wasn't it?'

'I'll say it was.'

She came slowly across the room and sat on the edge of the bed and looked at him as he stooped to tie his shoe laces. Then, her head on one side, she asked, 'Could I have come with you to the dance if I hadn't been going to Paul's party?'

'Yes. Why not?'

'You would have taken me?'

'Of course . . . Why do you ask?'

'Well, Mother says I couldn't have gone in any case, it being a staff do; but you're taking John, so I said I didn't see why I shouldn't have gone, that is if I hadn't been going to Paul's. And she got ratty with me.'

'But you are going to Paul's, so why bother arguing?'

'Oh!' She wagged her head. 'It's just a matter of getting things straight . . . Sort of standing up for me rights, as Elsie says.'

As he got into his dinner jacket he said, 'But you'd rather go to Paul's party, wouldn't you?'

'Huh! Yes, I think so . . . Dad!'

'Yes?'

'Do you really think I'm pretty?'

He came slowly to the side of the bed and put his finger under her chin and looked down at her. 'No, I don't think you're pretty.' He moved his head from side to side. 'Pretty is such a weak word. I think you're beautiful.'

'Oh Dad!' Impulsively she leant her head against his waist and put her arms around his hips. 'Do you know,

444

you're the only one who's ever said I'm beautiful; Paul says I'm not.'

'What!' He jerked her head up. 'You mean to say he's told you you're not . . .'

'Yes. We were talking one night and he said I wasn't beautiful I wasn't even pretty, I had the wrong features. But he said I had something. And when I asked him what it was he couldn't tell me, he just said I had something that . . .' She stopped and chuckled, and he prompted, 'That what?' and she blinked her eyes and bit on her lip before she ended, 'That got him.'

He laughed deep in his throat and walked to the wardrobe, saying, 'Well, I'm glad you've got that something an' all, but he's wrong.'

'I don't think so, Dad.' It was her quiet tone that made him look over his shoulder at her. Her face was straight, almost solemn as she said, 'You're the only one who sees me as beautiful. There's not another soul in the world thinks I'm even pretty . . . If Paul doesn't . . . well!'

He turned his head away, opened the wardrobe door and took out his overcoat, and he didn't speak until he was ready to leave the room. Then, standing in front of her, he said, 'People will come to my way of thinking before long, you'll see.'

She stood up and put her hands on the lapels of his coat and drew them together and buttoning the top button, she stared at it as she said, 'I'm worried, Dad.'

'What about?'

'You. You haven't been well for weeks.'

'Nonsense. It's just the pressure of work. Fitting into a new job. Responsibilities and all that. But I'm all right.'

She still played with the button as she said, 'Mother's worried about you; we all are.'

When he didn't answer she raised her head and looked at him, and then he said softly, 'Well, you can stop worrying for there's nothing to worry about. Now you go out and enjoy yourself.'

She smiled at him, then said, 'It won't be much fun for you without Mother. Of all the luck, to go and sprain her ankle the day before the one night in the year she looks forward to.'

'Did she say that?'

'Yes. She said she loves the staff dance. Didn't you know?' Her voice was high with surprise.

'Not really; I always thought she looked upon it as a bit of a bore, a sort of duty.'

She seemed surprised by his answer as if it appeared odd that her father didn't actually know what her mother thought. She picked her coat up from a chair and they went out together, down the stairs and into the sitting-room, where John was waiting.

John at eighteen was an attractive boy, being above average height and startlingly blond. When he was happy he looked handsome, and he looked happy tonight.

From her position on the couch Esther surveyed her son with pride. She loved her first-born with a deep secret love that even outdid the feeling she had for her father. The affection she felt for her husband had never, even before she gave birth to her son, been given entry into the private chamber of her being. It could be truthfully said that only she and God were aware of such a place and the secrets it held.

446

She looked from one to the other now and said, 'Well, that's it; you're all ready then.' She didn't comment on her daughter's appearance but addressed her with, 'Don't keep your father waiting when he comes to pick you up . . . And mind what I told you.'

'Yes, Mother.'

'Well then, don't stand about, get yourselves away.'

This remark could have had a dampening effect, but Terry, sitting on the head of the couch, said, 'I don't see why I couldn't go to the dance. I've kicked more ankles than most at the Club; I can do everything from the Charleston upwards, so why?'

'Because you're still in short trousers!' John pushed Terry's head with his hand, and Terry, jumping off the couch and taking up a battling stance, said, 'Watch it! watch it! said Mary O'Toole.'

At this moment Mary O'Toole came into the room and she exclaimed loudly, 'Who's taking me name in vain?' Then she paused before adding, 'Oh now! don't you look grand, each and every one of you. My! it's a family to be proud of.' She bent and kissed Gail, and Gail hugged her; then she said, 'Let me have a look at your new dress.'

When Gail opened her coat Mrs O'Toole covered her eyes and exclaimed, 'What's the world coming to? It'll be nappies you'll be getting back to next.'

'Gran!' After the note of censure, Esther exclaimed, 'Let them get away, they'll be late.' And Mrs O'Toole said tartly, 'Well, there's nobody stopping them.'

With an exchange of bye-byes Harry, John and Gail left the room somewhat self-consciously, but when they reached the front door Gran O'Toole was behind them, and she patted their backs one after the other as if they were all small children, Harry included, and said, 'Have a good time. Have the time of your lives. Forget about everything and enjoy yourselves.' She gave Harry an extra pat and he turned and smiled at her; then bending he put his mouth to her ear and whispered, 'I'm going to get blind drunk,' and she cried in a smothered laugh, 'Now that's the best idea you've voiced in years. Just do that. Do that, me lad.' And she pushed him out of the door.

The staff dance was always held at the old 'Coach and Horses'. The word old was a misnomer, because although the hotel was half-timbered and could date its beginnings back to the eighteenth century, its interior was modern, yet complementing the old beams rather than at variance with them. The cuisine was of the highest standard; and what was more, the hotel was situated on the outskirts of the town in a setting of woodland and pasture land; and lastly it provided parking facilities for over a hundred cars.

The staff at Peamarsh's numbered fifty-two. Add to these wives or sweethearts and a couple of friends per head of staff – the inviting of friends was always encouraged – and you had a company of two hundred or over. This number always provided for the dance floor to be well covered even while the bar and cocktail lounge were crowded. Everyone's enjoyment was provided for at Peamarsh's staff dance.

Harry was standing at the bar in company with Tom Vosey, Ossie Ferndale, who owned the timber yard, Jack Lucas, a dentist, and Peter Jones, an accountant.

The two latter were there as guests. Their wives were at present dancing and in the respite the men were drinking hard. The company were all well known to Harry, all his friends you might say, being members of the Round Table.

This time last year, even this time six months ago, Harry would have been laughing at their risky jokes, telling himself he must try and remember this one, and that one; he never did as he couldn't tell jokes, but that didn't stop him from enjoying them. But tonight he didn't laugh, he only drank. He had started on sherry; then, as on another memorable night, he went on to whisky, not doubles this time, just singles, but they came regularly, and as their number increased so did the anger inside him. Every now and again his thoughts would be punctuated by the term 'the dirty old swine!' Once he thought, and her playing up to him openly, brazenly. Well, she'd get all she was asking for. But this trite term, he knew, didn't really apply to the situation because Betty Ray would be very disappointed if she didn't get what she was asking for. Four times, to his knowledge, the old sot had danced with her; that would never have happened if Esther had been here, oh no. Like the good impartial employer he was his dances would have been doled out if his daughter had been present. And what was more, if Esther had been here her father would never have come near the bar. As it was he'd been in and out all evening throwing them back.

A few minutes ago he had stood in the doorway watching the dancers, trying to keep his eyes on John wriggling in front of his young partner, trying not to let

449

his fuddled gaze rest on his father-in-law whirling the dirty little piece round the floor. He seemed to have lost all sense of propriety, and didn't care a damn what anybody thought, yet he must know that tomorrow all the staff would be talking.

Harry didn't have to be told that there was a reason behind his father-in-law's flouting, he was doing it because he imagined it would upset him. Doubtless the little bitch had put him well in the picture. And now Mr Dave Rippon was thinking that he had him on a hook; he was showing him that he was in a position to enjoy something denied to himself. If it had been possible to explain the truth to him he would still have remained unconvinced. In his own eyes he was a dashing fellow, swiping his son-in-law's mistress from under his nose. God! It was all so sickening.

And Betty Ray? She too, in her own way, was showing him. He could almost hear her saying, 'All I wanted was to be secretary to somebody on the top floor, anybody, but you put a spoke in me wheel, and see what happened. In one jump I'm at the top. Now what do you think of that, Mr Blenheim?'

'What's up with you tonight, Harry? You look about as happy as a whore at a rectory tea.' Ossie Ferndale pushed his big red face close to Harry's. 'Come on, what is it? Worrying about your missus not being here? Look, boy, count your blessings; go and have a dance. I've never seen you on the floor the night. You used to trip a pretty measure. Didn't he, Peter?'

Peter Jones, a thin dapper man, nodded and giggled. 'A pretty measure. That's funny. Makes you sound like a ballet boy. A pretty measure.' He giggled again into his glass; then almost aggressively he said, 'You know somethin'? Those ballet boys on telly, they make me sick. How a fellow can push himself into those tights. I tell you, they work me up.'

This brought a splutter from the group, and Tom Vosey, his arm round Harry's shoulder, his mouth wide with laughter, said, 'Listen, it reminds me. Talking of ballet, there was this fellow. He was doing a film and he had to do the splits . . .' At this point Tom Vosey lowered his head and his body shook with the outcome of his story, and just as he was about to go on the band stopped and Ossie Ferndale put in, 'Come on, Tom man, get on with it. They'll be here in a minute.'

'Oh, they'll enjoy this one.' Tom Vosey flapped his hand. 'I'll wait for them.' He took his arm from Harry's shoulder and turned towards the door where some of the dancers were now entering; then he turned back again and asked, 'What you say, Pete?' And Peter Jones muttered quickly, 'Not before mine, Tom; she's funny that way.'

'Break her in, break her in . . . And where you goin', Harry?' Tom Vosey reached out and grabbed Harry's arm; and Harry said thickly, 'I've just remembered, it's time I picked up Gail.'

'There's another hour to go yet, man, and they've got an extension to the end.' He nodded towards the bar.

'Sorry.' Harry's face muscles were working as he mumbled, 'The child'll be waiting.'

'Child! Go on with you.' Tom Vosey pushed him roughly in the chest. 'Sixteen. Gail's no child. They don't thank you for butting in, not at sixteen they don't these days. She'll be glad of a little necking time.' He

451

now left the crowd and walked unsteadily with Harry across the room, saying, 'What's up with you these days, anyway, Harry? You're not yourself. You want to take a pattern from your old man. Now he's had a real randy night. Never been off the floor, and at his age. As for knocking 'em back . . . whew!'

Harry's teeth ground together. But he forced himself to speak calmly as he said, 'I've left Esther at home; she'll be worrying. Oh, not about me.' For a moment he adopted Tom Vosey's manner. 'But she doesn't like them being out late.'

'You know something?' Tom Vosey leant towards him now, swaying slightly. 'There's something I've wanted to say to you for a long time as a close friend . . . privileged friend, an' it's just this. You never brought her up right, Esther. You should have put your foot down from the start. She's still daddy's girl. You should assert yourself, man . . . Here, Harry, just a minute, just a minute. Don't go off like that, man.'

But Harry was away, hurrying erratically across the hall to the cloakroom.

When, a few minutes later, he returned from the cloakroom he saw John standing talking with two girls, and he beckoned him over, and even in his fuddled state he noticed that his son looked different tonight because his expression held no trace of surliness. He tried to space his words as he said to him, 'I'm going to pick Gail up; I'll be about half-an-hour; I don't want to have to wait for you when I come back mind.'

John stared at his father closely before he answered briefly, 'OK,' then turned and walked back to the girls . . . And Harry thought, There'll be no need for you to tell your mother that your father's been drinking; it'll be self-evident tonight. But will you tell her about your grandfather? Ah! that was a point. John wasn't blind, nor was he stupid; he knew what his mother thought of her father; he was also aware of the handsome presents in the form of cash she received from him and which rubbed off on to himself. No! John would doubtless consider the matter carefully for he was cunning was John. Oh yes, he had to own that, among other things, his son was cunning . . .

The party was still going strong at the Birketts when he collected Gail. But her reluctance to leave was compensated by the fact that Paul came out to the car with her.

Harry had just started the car up when she leaned towards him and said in a confidential whisper, 'Dad! you've been drinking.'

He gave a short laugh and said, 'How per-spic-acious of you, Miss Blenheim.' When he stammered on the word she burst out laughing. 'And I was forbidden even to take sherry!'

'What! Who forbade you?'

'Mother, of course. That's what she said before I left, you remember? No, you don't. Well, she said, "And mind what I told you." She had warned me upstairs that I hadn't to touch drink of any kind. And here's you bottled!'

He put his head back and laughed a great rollicking laugh, and the car swerved as he cried, 'You sound like Gran, and that's good, that's good.' Then he asked, 'Did you have a good time?'

'Smashing! Oh really smashing. I jived till all my

bones rattled. Mrs Birkett had cleared one room right out. I danced with Paul nearly half the night. Roma Allsopp was mad, she's after Paul, you know.'

'Is she indeed!'

'Yes, but Paul couldn't care less. He told me so.'

'That was very chi . . . chivalrous of him I must say.'

'Did you have a good time, Dad?'

'Well, you've just said I'm drunk so I'm bound to have had a good time, eh.'

She leant her head against him as she said softly, 'I didn't mean it nasty . . . Did you dance much?'

'I didn't dance at all.'

'Not once!' She straightened herself up away from him, her voice high.

'Not once; there were no beautiful girls about. Now if you had been there my shoes would have been worn out.'

'Oh, Dad, you're sweet.' When she dragged on his arm and snuggled up to him, he said, 'Here, here; be careful. Look, I'm having my work cut out to drive this thing as it is, I'm seeing double.'

She laughed and sat back in her seat and, sighing deeply, said, 'Oh! am I tired. And it's school tomorrow. Oh lor! Oh lor!'

'Well, get in the back and lie down. John will want to sit in front in any case.'

'That's an idea. I'll climb over.' As she made to clamber over the seat he said, 'Wait, hold on, we're nearly there.'

When he drew up in front of the hotel and got out of the car an attendant came up to him and said, 'Would you mind going to that side, Sir?'

454

'But I won't be a minute, I'm just going to collect my son.'

'Well, you see, Sir, if anyone wants to come out' – he pointed to the left of the building – 'they're going to have a tight squeeze getting past you with the other cars parked alongside. You see, you've stopped at the narrowest point, Sir.'

'Oh, all right.' He got into the car again; then putting his head out of the window, he asked, 'Where do you want me to go?'

'Just along here, Sir. Look, there's a space just round the corner.' He walked by the side of the car. 'There, Sir, I'm sorry to trouble you, Sir, but we've had a job tonight. We've moved those we could from the drive – the careless ones who leave their doors open.' He grinned, then walked ahead and beckoned Harry on.

There were a number of cars parked around the side of the building and the attendant, coming up to Harry again, said, 'We don't usually stack here, but there was an overflow from the main park, very unusual. Most times it can cope, but the whole town seems to have come out the night. Will you be long, Sir?'

'Not more than five minutes,' said Harry. Then taking off his overcoat, he leaned into the back of the car, where Gail was now curled up on the seat, and put it over her before asking, 'Will I put the light on?'

'No. No thanks; I'll be clean off in two minutes flat. And don't wake me when we get home, just carry me in. Do you hear?'

'I hear, Ma'am. Certainly, Ma'am.' He sounded jocular, and when he closed the door and turned about the attendant said, 'You could come in the side door here, Sir; it leads straight to the lounge.'

'Thanks,' said Harry 'but my son'll likely be waiting in the hall for me and I don't want to be waylaid at the bar, if you see what I mean.' And they both laughed.

The hall of the hotel was a large room with an open fireplace fronting the door and lounge chairs dotted about on the thick pile carpet. The reception desk was at the far corner on the right hand side, and on the left hand side were two passages, one leading to the gents cloakroom, the other leading to the ladies. The door leading to the ballroom gave off from this side of the hall, and as Harry made his way towards it there emerged from the second passage the blue mini-dressed figure of Betty Ray.

'Well, well! Hello!'

Harry had paused for a moment, long enough to give her a cold wavering stare, but when he made to move on she stepped quickly in front of him, saying, 'I've never had a chance to have a word with you tonight, or any other time for that matter. You're very elusive, aren't you?'

He didn't answer her, he just continued to stare at her. For weeks now he had ignored her; even when her voice came over the phone saying politely, 'Mr Blenheim, Mr Rippon would like a word with you,' and adding, 'at your convenience,' he never gave her an answer. And when he passed through Rippon's outer office he kept his eyes averted from her, although highly conscious all the time that she had hers fixed tightly on him and that they were laughing at him, as they were doing now.

'Have you enjoyed yourself the night?'

456

When he still didn't answer she gave a little hick of a laugh and, her voice low, she said, 'You're in a misery, aren't you? All the time you're in a misery. You're frightened of your own shadow, frightened to enjoy yourself . . . Look, hang on a minute, don't dash off' – she put her fingertips lightly on his sleeve – 'or I might raise me voice, I've had a few drinks; an' I'm never dependable when I've had a few drinks, not to be counted on, you know what I mean?'

He knew what she meant. They were staring at each other now and her eyes were no longer laughter-filled as she said, 'You wanted me out of Peamarsh's, didn't you? You were terrified of me; you wouldn't believe that I would play square. All I asked was to get on to the other floor and make something of meself, but instead of giving me a helpin' hand what did you do? You kept mum; and if you could you would have got me the push, wouldn't you? But I got on the top floor, didn't I, right into the sanctuary. And now I'm in a position to have anything I want. Did you hear that, Mr Blenheim? Any-thing-I-want?'

'How nice for you.' His words were flat, lead-weighted.

'Yes, isn't it. He's barmy about me. At first he just did it to get one over on you. Oh, he knows all about it; I told him. Apparently he knew afore; old Cole had done some snooping and she told Dame Bateman. Oh, I know all about her an' all, Bateman; he's come quite clean with me, he's not a damned hypocrite like you. And he knows how to enjoy himself. And let me tell you something else, he's quite willing to pay for it. Do you know something?'

'I'm in a hurry, Miss Ray; will you excuse me?'

Her fingers came on to his sleeve again, tightly now. 'No, I won't excuse you, Mr Blenheim; you're going to listen. This is the only opportunity I've had.' She glanced about her, then said, with mock primness, 'It wouldn't be right in the office, to talk like this. I mean . . . As I was saying, do you know where I'm going on me holidays and for a full month, eh? Do you? Well, I'm going on a cruise, on a first-class liner. He's taking me. All very discreet of course; we meet up on board . . . It's a free world. As long as you have the money you can go anywhere, get anything. Me mam's gettin' her car an' all. Isn't that nice, Mr Blenheim?'

He had the terrible desire to choke her and he closed his eyes as she said, 'Dear, dear! Does it shock you? But perhaps if I was a relation it would be all right. How would you like me for a mother-in-law?'

'Huh!' He now allowed a twisted smile to spread over his face, and his voice a deep sneer as he replied, 'If an attractive and first-class business woman like Miss Bateman couldn't bring it off then I hold very little hope for you, Miss Ray.'

His tone brought her dark brows together and her lips into a tight straight line and she wagged her head for a moment before hissing back at him, 'You'd be surprised! I have me methods. He's waitin' in the car for me.'

As they glared at each other the ballroom door opened and John came through with a girl. He stopped abruptly and looked hard at them, then said, 'You're back early.'

Harry turned to him. 'Get your things, I'll be waiting

outside.' His voice was thick and shaking. He didn't look at her again but went outside and stood on the top step gulping in great draughts of air in an effort to cool the heat of his anger. Mother-in-law! My God! She could do it, too. Yes, he believed her, she could do it.

It was as the door opened behind him and she came out that he heard the scream. It came from the direction of the cars parked to the side of the hotel. When it came again he lifted his head like an animal, scenting danger. The scream in a way was recognisable although he had never heard it before. It wasn't a giggly scream, or the scream of lovers, it was a terrified scream, and now he was running, leaping over the ground.

As he rounded the corner he saw through the dimness the shape of a man backing out of his car; he was straightening himself up as Harry reached him, and he spluttered. 'Sorry, sorry. Thought it was mine. Left it . . .'

Gail, crouched in the corner of the seat, her hands cupping her face, was making strangled sounds and Harry's mad, fury-filled gaze jerked from her to his father-in-law taking in his disarrayed clothes. Then with a deep oath he had him by the throat.

He was never clear in his mind about what happened in the first few moments but he did remember banging the big body against the wall, and when it fell to the ground he remembered using both his fists and his feet on it, and all the while the screaming went on, not Gail's now, but Betty Ray's as she tried to pull him off. Then other hands came on him and forced him to the ground. But even as they held him his limbs still reacted to the desire to flay.

When they allowed him to get up someone sat him on a box and he leant against the side of a car, but they still held on to him. The place was crowded with people now; their voices were torturing his ears. Dimly through the red haze that seemed all about him he saw John talking to a policeman, and he heard Betty Ray's voice, high, hysterical, yelling, spluttering, jabbering.

When they led him to a car, which was not his car, he thought clearly again and said, 'Gail. My daughter,' and John said, 'She's all right.' John did not look at him as he spoke, but kept his head down. He became vitally aware of this, and remained aware of it for a long time afterwards.

When he reached the police station he passed out, and while they were awaiting the doctor's arrival they brought him round by douching him with cold water. It was the sergeant's pet treatment for brawling drunks.

Eight

'Keep away! Don't come near me.' Esther was standing near the head of her bed and Harry at the foot of it.

'You've got to believe me,' he said.

'I'll never believe you. That girl, your . . . mistress' – she hissed the last word – 'got round him, like she got round you.'

'She only got round him because he wanted her to get round him. And for the tenth time she's not my mistress, and never was my mistress. I've told you, I've explained. It was only that once. It was snow-madness you could say, but I can't expect you to believe that if you won't open your eyes to the fact of what's been going on for years.'

'My father's a good man.' Her voice was low and trembling. 'He always has been; you or no-one else will be able to convince me otherwise.'

'He's not a good man, Esther; he never has been. The fact that he's been good to you because you were his only child doesn't make him a good man. Nothing will ever make him a good man, in business or anything else.'

'Shut up!' Her lips were covered with spittle and she

dragged her handkerchief first one way then the other across them. Then she said, 'Even if he wasn't a good man was that sufficient reason for you to try to kill him? And you would have killed him if they hadn't torn you off; they all said that.'

'It's a pity they succeeded,' he said grimly. 'But I've told you why I went for him, I've told you. He must have frightened her to death when he tried to . . .'

'Shut up! Shut up, will you?'

'I won't shut up.' His voice rose high now, almost to a shout. 'He . . .' When she put her hands tightly across her ears he bowed his head. Then after a moment he turned about and walked to the window, and from there he said, 'The fact that he thought it was the Ray girl makes no difference. And you don't believe he was sodden drunk, even though it might act as an excuse for what happened, but you believe I was drunk.' He turned his head now slightly towards his shoulder and said slowly, 'And in a way you're to blame for the final incident, because if you hadn't persuaded him to let me have his car there wouldn't have been two of a kind, and he wouldn't have mistaken it for his own.'

When he heard her moan he turned about to see her sitting on the edge of the bed, her head deep on her chest. He made no attempt to go near her, but from where he stood he said, 'I'm sorry, Esther.'

Now her head jerked up and, her face cold and tight, she cried at him, 'And you'll be sorrier still before you're finished. I don't know where you've been these past three days so it might be news to you to know that Father's seeing this thing through to the end, and if he's so full of guilt as you infer he is, do you think he would dare do that?'

'Your father is capable of doing anything; he's an expert at chicanery and everything underhand. He was clever enough to keep Miss Bateman hidden for fifteen years.'

'I don't believe it, not a word of it.'

'Then you'd better go and ask her, hadn't you? And she might introduce you to your half-sister.'

He was sorry he said that for her face now looked utterly bloodless.

After a moment of bitter silence she said through clenched teeth, 'It isn't my father's misdeeds that've brought us low, it's yours.' She gripped her forearms and rocked herself backwards and forwards now, saying, 'We'll not be able to lift our heads in the town again. And what about Gail? And you were supposed to worship Gail, weren't you; she was the apple of your eye. Now who's going to look at her after an incident like that, her name splashed across the papers?'

His neck jerked violently up out of his collar as he said, 'There's no need for her to be mentioned.' He held out the paper he had been holding the while. 'She's not mentioned here, not a word about her. The whole gist of this article is from Betty Ray's point of view, that I was jealous of her leaving me and therefore beat up my rival, that's how it reads. There's no need for Gail to be brought into this at all, although if she was I might be able in future to lift my head up in the town, as you term it, because what I did was in defence of my daughter, not through jealousy. God no! Yet' – he paused – 'I know that what I did to him was what I've wanted to do for years, and all because of you. You were at the bottom of it.'

'What! Me? You're blaming me now. You're mad.'

'I'm not mad, and you know it. And you also know you've never really been a wife to me. You've given me children, yes, but first and foremost you've remained your father's daughter. You should never have married; you'd have been perfectly happy being Daddy's little girl and after your mother died keeping other women from him . . . Yet you'd have had a hard job doing that; he would have beaten you at that. And you know something else? He was jealous of me having you. At first it wasn't apparent, he was being the kind father-in-law; then I knew deep down in me he was out to humble me in your eyes, belittle me; any rise in the world I got must come through him. Even in this house I've had no say, I've never been the master in this house; you've been the master under the direction of your father.'

Slowly she rose to her feet, and her eyes looked remarkably like her father's as she stared at him, and her voice held a semblance of her old control as she said, 'In that case you won't mind leaving the house. I've thought it over, and it's quite impossible that we remain under one roof.'

Vaguely he had imagined that this might come about but as yet he hadn't faced up to it. He had in a way visualised some form of reconciliation; he had imagined that at least she would see her father for what he really was; but now he knew that had been a vain hope. He said, 'What if I don't choose to go, this is my home, my children are here?'

He watched her draw a deep breath into her flat chest

before she answered, 'This is my house, it is in my name; all the furniture in it was bought with my money. All your salary has done over the years is maintain it. Everything here is legally mine, including the children.'

'Oh no. No!' He lifted his hand up like a traffic warden. 'Hold on, Esther, hold on. Talking of legality. You can have the things and the house, but when it comes to the children I've got a say there, and the law isn't so rigid that it's going to say that I haven't. Gail is mine.'

'Oh yes,' she put in quickly; 'Gail is yours, it doesn't matter about the other two. Well, we'll see who Gail belongs to. I'm seeing my solicitors tomorrow with regard to a separation.'

'Good, good,' he said now; 'that suits me. But don't think you're going to separate me from the children because you're not.'

'You propose to take them to prison with you? Because if my father's injuries prove to be as extensive as they suspect, you're not going to get off lightly!'

The look on her face, her voice, her manner, all told him that she prayed he wouldn't get off lightly. He felt shaken and suddenly frightened. He looked at her for a moment longer, then went out of the room, along the corridor and, knocking on Gail's door, he waited. When there was no answer he opened it, but the room was empty. Very tidy, unlived in, it looked as if it had never known Gail.

Within seconds he was back in the bedroom. 'Where's Gail?'

Esther had her back to him as she replied, 'She's staying with friends.'

'Which friends?' He was bawling now.

She was standing in front of the mirror putting her hat on as she said, 'I'm not going to tell you.' Then swinging round and arching her body towards him, she ground from between her teeth, 'And if it's left to me you'll never see her again.'

She now whipped up her coat from a chair and made for the door, and when she was abreast of him she said in a thin, bitter whisper, 'You've taken everything I value from me; don't try to take Gail. I'm warning you.'

He watched her walking firmly across the landing and down the stairs; then he leant against the stanchion of the door and closed his eyes. He was like that when a hand came on his arm and Gran O'Toole turned him about and led him into her room; and there she pressed him down into a chair as she said brokenly, 'Where've you been? I've nearly been out of me mind.'

He screwed up his eyes and placed his fingertips on them. Then after a moment he looked up into her face and asked, 'Of my many friends who do you think came forward to support me?'

She shook her head, then said, 'Tom Vosey? Mr Nolan?'

When he still continued to stare at her she went on, 'Mr Ferndale of the timber yard?' She paused, waiting, then said with slight impatience, 'Then who?'

'Nobody.'

'Nobody?'

'I had to get in touch with Peter Thompson, the solicitor, you know, and he bailed me out, but he didn't ask me home. But you can't blame him for that, I suppose,

466

for he'd be under the impression I'd come straight back here.'

'Well, where did you go?'

'To Janet's.'

'Janet's?' She sat down slowly and joined her hands in her lap and repeated, 'Janet's? She was here yesterday and never said a word and knew we were worrying . . .'

'You might have been worrying, Gran.'

'No matter, no matter, she should have told us.'

'I asked her not to.'

'But why Janet's?'

'I felt I couldn't face Esther right away and I had to go somewhere to calm down. If I'd gone into one of the hotels it would have felt like sitting on a hilltop, I'd have been exposed to everybody. No, it suddenly came to me that the only place I could go and be safe would be Janet's.'

Some seconds elapsed before she said, 'And what are you going to do now?'

'Wait; that's all I can do.'

She now started to nip at one finger after the other as she said, 'I was on the landing, I heard what you said about not letting Gail be involved, but don't you realise that's your only hope of getting off lightly. If you tell them what he was up to, they won't touch you, not for trying to defend your daughter, they won't, but if you let things go along the line that the papers are indicating then I'm afraid you'll be in for it.'

'I can't help that, Gran; I don't want Gail dragged through the Court. As it is this is going to have a bad enough effect on her, but if she has to stand up there and say what happened, she'll never get over it. She's in the Galahad state of life and a sponge for impressions, and in that Court she'll soak up all the dirt they'll bring up, real and imagined, because no one's going to believe that I was only with Betty Ray that once.' He leant forward now and gripped his grandmother's hands. 'You believe me, Gran, when I say this, don't you? I was only with her that once on the day of the office party. I was tight and mad if you like. Once it was over I knew I'd been mad; I also knew that I wouldn't repeat the madness. I swear to you that it was only that once.' He waited, looking into her worried wrinkled face, and when she didn't speak he asked, 'How could all this have come out of one mistake in a man's life?' When still she said nothing, he muttered thickly, 'I'm bitter, Gran, bitter, because I'm having to pay for that old bastard's misdeeds; and Gail's having to pay, and Esther's having to pay, the lot of us are having to pay . . .'

'Be quiet! Be quiet!' Her voice came at him low and sharp. 'It's no use throwing blame right and left now, you've got to face up to something, Harry. As you say, it was only once, but once was enough. Now look here, lad. You're the only thing in life I've got to live for; I've never said this to you afore but everybody could drown as long as you could swim. But I'm going to tell you this to your face. It wasn't what the old fellow's done that's caused this, it was just that once you had with that girl, that's what caused it. He's an old swine and you couldn't hate him more than I do, but it was you and that girl that brought this present situation about, and you've got to face that fact.'

468

'Aw, Gran, hold your hand. Don't you go to the other side; I couldn't bear it.'

She was on her feet now holding him by the shoulders, glaring down into his distressed face. 'I'm not going to the other side, I'm with you whether you're in the right or wrong, but I want you to see this thing clearly. Don't apportion blame, but at the same time don't carry the whole can yourself. When you're brought up you tell them exactly why you lathered into him, and my God' – her voice dropped and she shook her head – 'you did that. I went with her yesterday to see him. Lad, you all but murdered him. I doubt if he'll ever be his self again. Looking at him I couldn't believe that yours was the hand that had inflicted such punishment on him. It wasn't like you; you must have gone clean mad.'

He moved away from her hands and went to the dressing table, and he leant his body over it as he said, 'Yes, I must have gone mad, but it was coming. I'd reached the end of my tether. From the night he came in and stopped my mouth with that directorship I've never known a minute's peace or self respect. He's played me like a puppet for weeks now; every time he's looked at me that hate has oozed out of him, and it got that way I couldn't bear to face him in case I lashed out. It had to come, it was bound to come; the only thing I'm sorry for is that Gail was involved.' He turned to her. 'Do you know where she is, Gran?'

'No lad; Esther wouldn't tell me. And she's right there, because she knew I'd pass it on to you.'

He went to her again and took her hands and said, 'Will you try to explain the whole thing to her when she

469

comes back? You're the only one that can put it over; she'd listen to you.'

'I don't suppose I'll be here when she comes back, lad.'

His face stretched. 'Where you going?'

'I'm not sure yet, but there's one thing certain, when you're gone there'll be no place here for me.'

'Now don't be silly, Esther's not like that; this is your home.'

'As long as it was your home it was mine. And I'm quite sure Esther would be willing for me to stay, but I wouldn't want to stay.'

'Gran!' He pressed her hands tightly. 'Stay, please. I want Gail to have someone to rely on, someone sensible. Well, what I mean is not biased, somebody who can see the two sides. Gail thinks the world of you, she'll listen to you. Stay, please, at least for a while.'

She bobbed her head slowly. 'Well, don't concern yourself about that. Just leave it, I'll see how things go. That is, until I know what is going to happen to you.' Her face now dropped into trembling creases and she asked almost in a whimper, 'They wouldn't send you to prison, would they?' and he replied, even heartily, 'Don't be silly. No, of course not. A fine likely, heavy. But prison? Of course not!'

II

ROBBIE DUNN

One

'There, Mam, do you like it?'

'Yes, it's a nice chest.'

'Lor! Mam. It's not just a chest, it's a Georgian piece.'

'I'll take your word for it.' Janet Dunn smiled fondly at her son.

'Look at the frieze.' Robbie ran his finger around the ornamentation below the top of the drawers; then swiftly pressing a button at the top of the lower section of the tallboy, he said excitedly, 'And a shelf. Look, a sliding shelf.'

'Yes, that's nobby,' said Janet; 'very unusual.'

'I'll say it's unusual. I'll bet you a shilling I've got a find here. Just look at those handles. Original, or I'm a Dutchman. And I'm not, am I?' He poked his face towards her and grinned, and she laughed and pushed him none too gently in the chest. Then she said, 'Fancy people parting with things like that. Why do they do it?'

'Because they're daft. But mind, in a way I was sorry when I took these. There was the old girl staring at me and her daughter talking away at her. "You can't take that old thing into a new house, Mother, it just won't

473

fit in. Anyway, there isn't room for it." And you know what? She had the nerve to put her hand out for the money, but I turned a blind eye an' handed the fifteen quid to the old girl. I would have made it sixteen, aye and more, believe me, Mam.' He lowered his voice to almost a whisper. 'I would have made it twenty-five to get that piece, but whatever I'd made it that madam would have had her hands on it within a minute. God, an' they call us mean.' He stared at Janet, and Janet stared back at him, and then they both laughed together.

She turned now from the back room and walked towards the door that led into the shop and, standing there, she said, 'The window looks lovely but why don't you put more in it.'

'Put more in it?' He raised his black eyebrows at her. 'Can't you get it into your head that this is a classy shop, little and good. It's not the market, Mam; I'm not having this place chock-a-block with rubbish.'

'No, I didn't mean that, but you've only got that sofa table and that other one. What do you call it?'

'Pembroke.'

'Well, that one, and that little couch . . .'

'. . . Hepplewhite period settee, Mrs Dunn.'

'Hepplewhite period settee.' She bowed her head towards him. 'Well, that doesn't seem much to get anyone inside.'

'You'd be surprised. There's tricks in every trade as you know, and in this one there's dozens, and that's one of them.' He patted her shoulder. 'I know what I'm up to, Mrs Dunn; the last two years or so've been as good as a University education to me.'

Janet looked at him, pride in her dark eyes, and shaking her head slowly, she said, 'I can't understand how you remember all the names and periods.'

'Oh, any fool can do that, it's buying the pieces that's the thing, knowing what to buy, where to look. For instance, who would have thought I would have come across that gem' – he thumbed over his shoulder towards the workroom – 'at Bog's End. And it in such good condition.' His voice dropping, he said, 'That old girl loved that chest. She mightn't have known its value but she loved it. And you know, Mrs Dunn,' he grinned at her now, 'I love folks what loves furniture.'

'How much are you going to ask for it?' asked Janet practically.

'Fifty.'

'No, Robbie!'

'Why not?' His chin poked forward. 'Put that in a shop in Newcastle and you wouldn't get it under seventy-five. And run it up to London and then the sky could be the limit. I'm getting fifty for that.' He wagged his finger at her. 'I'll mark it up fifty-five an' I'll get fifty.'

'Do you think anyone round here will want it?' She sounded sceptical, and he answered roughly, 'No, Mam, nobody around here'll want it, but they come down from Brampton Hill, don't they, an' from Newcastle. And I bet you what you like if I stuck it in the window the morrow I'd have a few hawks after it. It's genuine, it's old, it's got the stamp on it, an' those fellows know what they're after. And boy, so do I.'

'All right, all right,' she said calmly. She looked fully

at him now and her voice dropped to a soft note as she added, 'You're a good boy, Robbie.'

He blinked rapidly at what was high praise from her, then with an upward thrust of his chin that tossed his lank hair back from his brow he said, 'I'm only startin',' to which she nodded endorsement.

He had turned from her, but quickly looking at her again, he said, 'It's close on six, I'll be shutting up. Let's take a run over and look at the house.'

'What, again? But we were there yesterday.'

'Well, we can go the day an' all, can't we? I'll tell Sid I'm locking up; he can go out the back.'

As they drove through the town they were both silent. Five minutes later they were on the main road running into the country with the fells rolling away on both sides of them, until, turning into a lane, they came upon a slag heap that looked like a huge carbuncle blotting the landscape, and beyond it reared a disused mineshaft and workings. For another five minutes the road wound slowly uphill terminating in a narrow lane. They crossed a wooden bridge, under which a burn gurgled, then went through a wide aperture in a tangled hedge. And there it was, the wreck of a house.

But when Robbie alighted from the car he stood gazing up at it as if at a mansion; then turning to Janet, he said, 'I was thinking in the night, we'll strip the ceiling in the hall and expose all those beams and soak them with boiled oil.'

'But they're all worm-eaten.'

'Well' – he nudged her – 'don't people pay for worm holes?'

She laughed and looking upwards as they walked

towards the door, flanked on each side by glassless windows, she said, 'Before you start thinking of boiled oil it would pay you better to concentrate on slates, with only three of the rooms dry.'

'All in good time, all in good time.' He pushed her gently up two worn wooden steps and into a hallway, where, in spite of the ventilation coming through the windows, the smell of dry rot met them. The hall, about thirty feet long, had once been half-panelled but all that remained of the original wood were odd pieces which were pegged to the crossbars and had resisted being wrenched off by marauders. A wide flight of stairs, as worn as the outside steps, mounted from the end of the room upwards, and the daylight from a gap in the roof showed the broken balustrade that had once graced the narrow gallery.

It was with something of secret despair that Janet looked about her. She still thought her son stark, staring mad to saddle himself with a two thousand pound mortgage for this wreck of a place standing on a piece of barren land. No doubt, once it had been a beautiful house, but it had been empty when she was a child thirty years ago. She remembered her mother and father walking her out here one Sunday and they picnicked on the hill behind the house, and she in her turn had brought Robbie here. And that was a mistake, for the first ride he took on his second-hand bicycle had been to Scarfield Mill. She didn't know why the house was called a mill for there was no sign of a mill within miles. The only prominent feature on the landscape, and that could only been seen from the hill behind the house, was the pithead. It was a desolate enough place

477

in summer, God knew what it would be like in winter. Up to now everything her lad had touched had turned to money, but she could only see this place eating money, it would take thousands and thousands to put it into shape. When she had put this to him, all he said was, 'I've got plans,' and she hadn't pressed to know what they were because, whereas he could be as open as the fells he could also be as close as a clam.

She walked across the hall and through a door into what had once been the kitchen. Now it hadn't even the usual iron stove to which it could lay claim; that had been ripped out, as had most of the piping. She saw the task ahead as so formidable that she turned a distressed face to Robbie. 'I can't help it,' she said, 'but the more I look at it the more hopeless it seems. Why, as I said in the first place, you could have got a nice bungalow for just a bit more if you wanted to get away from Baker Street so badly . . .' The look on his face checked her voice now and when he stared at her blankly she ended, 'I can't help feeling like this about it. Where are you going to get the money to make this habitable, eh? Where?'

He still continued to stare at her, then with a swift jerky movement characteristic of him he grabbed her hand and pulled her forward through the back door, across a paved yard thick with weed and grass, over a mouldering gate lying where it had once hung, across a narrow field, and up a steep incline, and having arrived at the brow of the hill, he commanded sharply, 'Sit down.'

She was gasping and half laughing as she obeyed him. Then dropping on to his hunkers by her side, he pointed down to the house, saying slowly and thickly, 'From the first time I saw that house I've hated Baker Street.' As he watched her face stretch in genuine surprise he said, 'Aye, that's news to you,' then went on, 'I must have been about twelve when I vowed that one day I'd have a place like this, some place worthy of the mezuzah on the door, but as I grew older I knew that even with things going well I'd have to wait ten, fifteen years or more before that dream could come true, unless I joined the fiddles, an' I could have an' all.' He inclined his head towards her. 'I've been tapped more than once, but you know me, I never liked little rooms.'

She ignored his grin and his jest and said, 'But it's going to take you a lifetime to get this place to rights; and how can you do the buying, see to the shop, and do this an' all, all on your own? It's impossible.'

He looked away from her and down on to the broken roofs of the house that was now his, and he said slowly, 'I don't intend to do it on me own.'

'What!'

He slanted his eyes at her. 'You heard what I said, I don't intend to do it on me own.'

'You've got somebody to help you?'

'Yes, just that. In two months' time I'll have some-body to help me.'

'NO, Robbie! No!' She was on her feet staring down at him, her lips pressed together, her face tight, and he looked up at her and asked harshly, 'Where's he going to go then when he comes out? Have you asked your-self that? He wouldn't come back to Baker Street; he knew he was putting us out for the few nights he was

479

there. It'll be a room in some grubby back street until he gets started, and God knows when that'll be in this town. The only chance for him is to move away . . . and you don't want that, do you?' His last words were slow and emphatic, and Janet stared back into his eyes but made no answer. When her face began to work he got to his feet and said, 'Look. I know how things are with you; I've always known.'

'Be quiet, Robbie.'

'I'll not be quiet. I'm not a kid, I'm not even a young fella, I've never been a young fella, I somehow skipped that stage, I'm a man. I've always had to think as a man because I've had to think for you, so I know how things 've been, an' not only the day or yesterday, but for years back.'

When she turned from him and stared away over the sloping land he said, 'There's nothing to be ashamed of, woman. And it's funny but I've never been jealous of him, just the opposite. Somehow I've always looked on him as a sort of father. I think it's because he started me up with that ten quid. An' what's more I knew years ago why you went to the house to help, not for the money but just because he was . . .'

'Robbie!' Her voice was deep and pain-filled, and he drooped his head for a moment against the sound of it. Then his chin was up again and he said, 'I've got it all worked out if you'll only listen. He could come an' live here and he could occupy himself with the wood-work. He took up carpentry in there because he wanted to use his hands; well, he can go on using his hands . . .'

She turned her body slowly towards him and her

480

voice held an unusual disdainful note as she said, 'You're just using him as cheap labour.'

His fists were clenched and his arms were extended to the fullest length as he flung himself first one way and then the other, crying, 'God in Heaven! Christ alive!'

'Don't use that term, Robbie!' She was snapping now. 'It might mean nothing to us, but I don't like to hear it.'

'Well, Mam.' He shut his eyes tightly and his head swung as he ground out, 'You'd make a Rabbi curse. Using him? Of course, I'm using him.' He was glaring at her now. 'And, aye, for me own benefit, but at the same time it's for his benefit. But besides anything me or him'll get out of it I'm doing it for your benefit, an' you're a fool not to see it.'

'Robbie, stop it. Be quiet for a moment and listen to me.' She paused until he was looking at her again. 'The truth is that Harry Blenheim doesn't know I'm alive except as good old Janet; Janet who lived upstairs above him for years; Janet who first took him to school, because I was six and he was five; Janet who would go into their house and mind him when his mother was out. Then it was Janet who would go and help his wife out.' She paused again and wetted her lips before saying quietly, 'Never, even as a young girl did I imagine anything could come of it. Harry Blenheim was not only Church of England, he was in the choir, and his voice brought him quickly to the fore, to people's notice, and there was us, practising Jews. Had my father ever thought that I had any private thoughts about Harry Blenheim he would have had me transported to some far-off place; he was quite capable of it. He picked your father for me; and your father was a good man, yet I might have protested if there had been the slightest hope for me in Harry's direction. But as I've said, he didn't even know I was alive in that way. And he doesn't to this day, so you can save your plans and your schemes, Robbie . . . And one small point you seem to have overlooked is, he's still married and has a family.'

'Huh! Married and his family? If that's marriage then I'll find me a woman to live with.'

'Don't say things like that, Robbie.'

'I will say things like that, Mam, and I mean them. He stepped off the white line once and that was enough for her. And his family. God! his family. An' not one of them's been to see him during all this time.'

'You forget Terry; he came and asked after him.'

'I'd have thought a damn sight more of him if he had made the journey to Durham.'

'He's only a boy.'

'Boy, me granny's aunt! Anyway, apart from that what do you think is going to happen when he comes out? Are his friends going to rally round? They were pretty scarce before he went up. As I see it he's only got us and that Mr Whelan. But he's in Doncaster now, so where's he going to go . . . prisoners' aid?'

Janet bowed her head and covered her eyes with her hand. 'You make it sound so awful.'

'It is awful, Mam.'

'Couldn't you offer him a job in the shop? You said you wanted somebody presentable, different from Sid, and he could get lodgings in the town.'

'I could, but I know damn well he'd refuse; he won't be able to face the town. He'll want time and a place to recover in, and this is it.' He pointed down the hill. 'Mind.' He raised his hand, palm upwards, towards her. 'I'm not saying I took the house because of him. Oh no. But the whole thing fell into place, his need an' mine.'

'I still think it's making a convenience of him, using him.'

'But it's a job for him, Mam, be sensible. And I'll pay him. It won't be builder's rates but I'll pay him, he'll feel independent.'

'But he'll be here with me all day and I couldn't bear that.'

Her voice was low now and it stopped him from yelling 'Aw, for crying out loud!' Instead, he gripped hold of her arms and shook her slightly, saying, 'Well, that's something you'll have to get used to, because if I have anything to do with it he's coming here; and he can stay until he gets on his feet and then it's up to him.'

She looked at him for a long, long moment. Her eyes travelled from his black hair to his equally black eyes, over his big nose and thin mouth, then down his stocky body, and she said slowly as if drawing on familiar thoughts, 'You'll marry one day . . .' But she got no further before his chin jerked up and out, and his words came rapidly on brittle laughter as he said, 'Don't make plans for me in that direction, Mam; you forget you're talking to Robbie Dunn, who, if he knows nothing else, knows what his assets are in the marrying market. Whoever says "I will" to me is going to want a fine dowry along of me, such as a big house' – he again nodded down the hill – 'furnished with antiques, and a nice fat bank roll. She'll want the prestige money can buy, and as it's goin' to be some little time afore I can offer me beloved that, we'll forget about it, eh? . . .'

'But, Robbie . . .'

'Look, Mam, I said forget about it. I know what chances I have in that direction.' His voice had moved from sarcasm to bitterness now. 'Girls I have an eye for look upon me as a Jew boy, fast talking, slick and common. Aye, common. Even those of me own kind don't want to know me. I don't spend enough for some, and the others, like Olive Stein, who you'd think'd be glad to jump at anybody, are waiting to see what I make of things . . . Aw, Mam, don't, don't cry; for heaven's sake don't cry.'

'Oh, Robbie. Oh, my dear.' When she leant her head against his shoulder he put his arms around her and stared down the hill to the substitute for loving he had saddled himself with, and there came a swelling in his throat that threatened to choke him, and he beat it off with, 'Christ alive! Don't you start.'

Two

The sale, in a private house just outside of Prudhoe, was almost at an end. Robbie was pleased with himself. He had not only got what he came for, an Adam-style wine cooler, but had picked up a couple of good quality plated cover dishes for almost a song. The last lot of the sale was an outsize clothes basket, full of books and oddments. The oddments were a dented copper kettle and stand, and an old tea caddy, the lid and sides heavily rococoed. The lead had been stripped from the inside and the box-lids were missing, yet he thought he might have a find here.

When the lot was knocked down to him for fifteen shillings he knew he was all right, for the books alone should bring ten bob. He didn't intend to take them back to the shop if he could help it, he didn't go in for books. There was a second-hand bookshop on the main road to Newcastle just beyond Jesmond; he decided to stop there and try to flog them.

At twenty minutes past five he pulled the van up to the kerb opposite the shop and saw he was just in time, as a girl was clearing a table of books that stood outside the doorway.

The bookshop had a single window, but this was deceptive he saw as he entered the shop, because before him was quite a large room with racks down the centre and the walls lined with book-filled shelves, and overall the permeating musty smell that is peculiar to second-hand bookshops seemed stronger than usual. It was a depressing place.

The girl was bending down stacking the books on the floor to the side of a rack, and seeing the feet standing a yard or so from her she turned her head and said, 'I'm sorry, we're closing.' Her voice trailed away on the last word and she straightened up and stared at Robbie, and he at her. Then he said, 'Why, hello. Fancy seeing you here.'

He watched the colour flood up over her pale face; it was as if she had been caught in some misdemeanour. 'You work here?' he now asked. It was obvious that she did, but he could find nothing else to say at the moment.

'Yes,' she said flatly. 'And I'm about to close.' The colour was receding now.

'Oh, that's awkward.' He grinned at her. 'I had some books on the van; I wondered if you'd be interested. It says outside you buy them.'

'Yes. Yes, we do, but Miss Frazer is out at the moment, she does the buying.'

'I'll call back then.' He nodded at her.

'Yes, you . . . you could do that.'

He stared at her. You couldn't say she was breaking her neck with enthusiasm at the sight of him. She had changed. Well, she would, wouldn't she? It must have changed the entire Blenheim family that do. It was

486

over two years since he had seen her last. She hadn't
grown as tall as he imagined she would. She wasn't
much bigger than him, well perhaps an inch or so. He
had imagined, at one time, she would turn into a
looker, but she hadn't. She still had all the bits and
pieces necessary, yet there was something about her
face that stopped short at the word beautiful or pretty,
or even attractive. Likely it was due to her expression,
it was surly.

She turned away from his stare, saying, 'Miss Frazer
won't be in until eleven tomorrow.'

'Good. I'll call in then. Tara!'

He was making for the door when she said, 'How is
Janet?'

He looked back at her now with interest. Her
question took some of the uppishness out of her
manner and he replied, 'Oh she's fine, grand. How's
your people?' The short space before she replied
conveyed to him that his question wasn't entirely
tactful.

'They're very well, thank you.'

'Good.' He nodded at her. 'Be seeing you then.' He
had turned from her again and reached the door when
her voice, hesitant yet hurried, asked, 'How . . . how is
your business going?'

Slowly now he faced her. His eyes narrowed as he
looked at her across the gloomy room and he knew
instinctively that she didn't care a damn how his business was going; the question she was asking was,
'How is my father?' Her expression had changed, the
dead look had lifted, and he saw she was agitated
because her hands were clasped tightly together on the

487

counter as if to prevent her from spurting something out. He looked from her face to her hands and back to her face again before he said, 'It's going like a house on fire.'

'I'm glad.'

'Thanks.' He thought a moment while she dropped her gaze from his, unclasped her hands and started tidying the counter, then he said, 'You going straight back home?'

'Yes.'

'By bus?' One of them might come to pick her up, you never knew.

'Yes.'

'Well, I've got the van outside. I'm going that way, I could drop you.'

'Oh no. No thanks.' Now she was agitated again. Her fumbling hands upset a stack of paperbacks and as she reassembled them she repeated, 'Thank you,' then added, 'I wouldn't want to trouble you, I might be some time.'

'The evening's me own, I can wait.'

'Thank you all the same.'

As he continued to stare at her, fumbling with one thing after another, the old animosity welled up in him, until he was not seeing her any more but was looking at John Blenheim. Had his real education been garnered from school, he would, because of the pride that was inherent in him, have smothered his feelings, taken no for an answer and left, seeing he had no personal interest in her. But his education had come mostly from the market and from men without inhibitions who said what they thought, more often than not without thinking. Daily contact with such types had also ousted in part the inborn reticence that was his, and so he said now, 'Are you frightened of being seen with me?'

She jerked her head up and for a moment she looked like the Gail he remembered before the affair, and she sounded like her too, impetuous, kind, as she said, 'Of course not, Robbie. Why do you say such a thing?'

'Well then, what's stopping you riding back with me in the van?'

Her gaze dropped again and she said, 'It's . . . it's only that . . .'

He finished the sentence for her. 'Some of your family might see you, your John for instance.'

She was looking him full in the face now and she answered him truthfully, 'Yes, it could be that.'

'Huh!' He laughed, then said, 'Well, what if I drop you this end of town? You could pick up a bus there and you won't have half-an-hour to stand in the queue, like down here.'

He watched her wet her lips, fumble with the books again, droop her head and think, before saying, 'Very well, I'll . . . I'll be out in a few minutes.'

'Good enough.' He turned without further words, went out and got into the van, and as he sat waiting he thought, 'It'll give her the opportunity to ask; but she's got to ask, I'm not tellin' her else . . .'

But she didn't ask, she hardly opened her mouth during the whole of the journey except to say yes or no, until they reached the outskirts of Fellburn, and then she said, 'Would you mind dropping me here, please.'

'OK.' He pulled in abruptly to the kerb, then leant across her to open the door and pushed it wide, and when she stepped on to the pavement he said, 'See you the morrow then.' As he watched her eyes widen for a moment he put in, 'I'll be bringing the books.'

'Oh yes. And thank you for the lift, Robbie.'

'Any time.' He nodded his head at her, pulling the door closed, then started the van off with the same abrupt movement as he had stopped it. As he drove along the road he watched her in the driving mirror until he turned the corner, and then he muttered aloud, asking himself, 'Did you see her face when I said I'll see you the morrow? She had forgotten about the books, but the look on her face. Well! She needn't worry.' He swung round another corner and spitting out one word now he said, 'John!' Then he added, 'To blazes with John, and all his breed.'

As soon as he entered the house, and before Janet could ask her usual question, 'Well, how did you get on?' he said flatly, 'Who do you think I saw the day?'

'Someone you're not used to seeing, evidently,' she answered him, smiling and waiting.

'Gail.'

'Gail! Where?'

In a few brief words he told her where, and as he ended he was unable to keep the bitterness out of his voice. 'She was scared to death to be seen with me.'

'Don't be silly.'

'I'm not silly, Mam. Most people can see through curtains but I can see through brick walls; it's been me trainin'.'

'Oh, Robbie.'

'Anyway, she said she was.'

'Gail said that! No, she would never say that. I wouldn't believe it.'

'Well, I'm telling you she did, and on account of Master John.'

'Oh . . . well now, that's possible and understandable.'s

'Is it?' His voice was aggressive.

'Well, you know you couldn't stand the sight of each other before all this happened, and he's bound to know you've been to see his father.'

'How's he bound to know? Not one of them've been within a mile of Durham in case they would get the smit.'

'That may be true, but news travels and by very odd pathways . . . Did she ask after him?'

'No, she didn't.' He pushed his eyebrows almost up to his hairline. 'That's the point, she didn't, and the only reason she came in the van with me was to find out something about him.'

'Well, why didn't you tell her?'

'What! Not on your life. Look, Mam; she's not dear little Gail any more, she's a girl of eighteen, and if she had any spunk she would have gone and seen him. You haven't to be told that he thought the sun shone out of her, and she was supposed to be clean mad about him. It wouldn't really have mattered so much about the lads. Master John; well, he'll never live the stigma down, one couldn't expect him to go visiting at a prison. And Terry after all, as you pointed out, he did come and ask how his father was faring. And the old grannie would have been there like a shot if she hadn't had that fall. But our Miss Gail was the one he cared about. I know this much, he wouldn't have cared a damn about the others as long as she had gone, if only once.'

'She had a very bad experience, you must remember that,' said Janet calmly. 'It was bound to leave an impression on her mind.'

Robbie turned away from her and went into the scullery, and as he took off his coat he called, 'It hasn't only left it on her mind it's left it on her face. She gave you the idea years ago she was going to look something.'

'Well, doesn't she?' Janet came to the scullery door and he said, 'No. It was a kind of shock when I saw her; it was her and yet it wasn't her, she's plain.'

'Gail plain?' Janet gave a laugh. 'You don't lose beauty overnight.'

'It's been a long night, nearly two years, and I tell you any looks she promised have given her the slip. Her face is dead, blank looking, no life in it.'

Janet stood looking at him as he washed himself and she said quietly, 'Well, if you're right that's one of the worst things that could have happened, for she did promise to be beautiful, and he was so proud of her. But perhaps she'll still look beautiful to him when he sees her.'

He blew into the towel, dried his face hurriedly, then said, 'If he sees her.'

'Well, if she won't come to him he could go to her now you know where she works.'

'That remains to be seen because he's altered an' all. You know he has. He was never a boisterous fellow but he's so quiet now he could be dumb.'

'It's the place,' she said; 'it doesn't induce conversation.'

'No? Well the others talk and seem glad to talk.'

Later, as they sat down at the table, she said, 'It's only six weeks and I'm dreading it in a way. Oh, not for me.' She shook her head. 'For him.'

'Yes.' He paused before picking up his knife and fork. 'You know you could be right; I think he's dreading it an' all. Last time, when I said to him, it won't be long now, he just looked at me. And it was as much that look as anything, I might as well tell you, that settled the question of the house, me taking it.'

She was holding his glance, and now she reached her hand across the table and touched his, saying, 'You're a good boy, Robbie, a good boy.'

He attacked his meal and after bolting a mouthful of food he said roughly, 'Don't give me credit for being . . . altruistic.' He jerked his head at her now and laughed out loud. 'That's a good 'un, isn't it? I read it somewhere, but I'd like to bet I haven't pronounced it properly. Anyroad, you know what I mean, 'cos what I do, Mam, first, middle and last is to look after number one because if I don't nobody else will.'

She nodded at him solemnly now, saying, 'Yes, I know you're full of vices, but being your mother I'm blind to them, so to me you're a good boy.' When he spluttered on his food and burst out laughing again she laughed with him.

Three

The following afternoon Robbie took the books along to the shop and was met by Miss Frazer. Miss Frazer was a woman in her fifties. She was tall, lean, and sparing of words. She quickly looked through the assortment of books, then said, 'There's only two I'd buy but I'll give you seven-and-six for the lot.'

His natural response to this would have been, 'You won't. Twelve-and-six or nothing,' then following a little bargaining he would have walked out with ten shillings, but Gail was standing at a bookcase with her back to him and he knew she was listening, and although he thought, It's going to cost me that much for petrol, he said, 'All right; I just want to get rid of them, I don't deal in them.'

'You're a dealer?' Miss Frazer raised her eyebrows just the slightest, but even so they expressed disbelief, and he stared hard at her as he said stiffly, 'Aye. Yes, I'm a dealer.'

'In what?'

'Antiques.' His voice was much louder than the answer in the ordinary way would have necessitated, but this old dame didn't believe him. For a moment he almost turned to Gail and said, 'Tell her what I deal in,' but Miss Frazer was handing him the seven-and-sixpence and although his maxim had always been pennies make shillings and shillings make pounds, he almost said grandiosely, 'Keep it; you need it more than me.'

During the time he was in the shop Gail did not acknowledge him in any way, she did not even turn and look at him, and when he was in the car once more he found himself swelling with anger and, as usual, talking to himself. 'God! some people. Who the hell do they imagine they are! Royalty? The Aga Khan's lot? Or what?' But it wasn't quite evident whether he was referring to Gail or to Miss Frazer, or to both.

It was three weeks later when he met Gail again, and in an unusual place, the Roxley Eventide Home.

It happened that he received a letter from a Mrs Bailey saying that her friend, Mrs Scott, had sold him some pieces of furniture and had recommended him to her. She herself had a few articles at her son-in-law's but he was moving away and didn't want the things, so would Mr Dunn care to look at them, then come and see her?

So, after he had found among Mrs Bailey's old-fashioned furniture a beautiful eighteenth-century grandfather clock, and an envelope card table, he gladly went to talk terms with her at the Eventide Home.

It was as he was crossing the main hall that he saw Gail; she was going out of the front door. He stopped in his stride for a moment, then hurried after her, and when he came up to her he said airily, 'You retiring?'

For a moment she looked startled, then she said stiffly, 'Well, hardly.' When she walked on, her gaze directed ahead, he felt, as he put it later to Janet, a bit daft her taking it like that.

Before he reached the main gates he had decided to let her get on with it. If she wanted to play the madam and remain aloof it was OK by him, but then she took the wind out of his sails for when they reached the street she stood in front of him and with her head slightly lowered, she said, 'I'm sorry.'

'Oh, that's all right; I was only meaning to be funny.'

'Yes, I know, Robbie.' She was looking straight into his face now. 'And you must think me awful. And the other day when you came into the shop. And I know what you meant just a minute ago, but, but with one thing and another I get upset.'

'Don't we all?' He grinned at her.

'Yes, I suppose so.' She looked away from him. 'You get it into your head that you're the only one who's got troubles, but to see Gran in there upsets me . . .'

'Your gran in there?' His voice was loud, his arm extended back towards the gate. 'Mrs O'Toole you mean?'

'Yes.'

'Good God, no!'

Immediately her manner was on the defensive again. 'It isn't our fault, you can't blame us, she insisted on going. My mother tried to stop her. She did . . .'

He didn't say, 'I'll take your word for it,' but something in his expression must have said it for him for she insisted harshly, 'I'm telling you she did, she tried everything to stop her going in.'

'How long has she been there?' The question was quiet, and she gulped in her throat before she answered, 'Eighteen . . . nineteen months or so. She arranged it all herself after she fell and hurt her hip. We didn't know anything about it until it was done.'

He now said, 'Your father's had letters from her but he doesn't know about this. He's going to go mad.' Without thinking he had given her an opening. He watched her now as she turned her head right round to her shoulder, and his brows beetling he said, 'Turnin' your head away won't rid you of the fact that he's still your father. And I'll tell you this. No matter what you or anybody else says, he's a decent bloke; just unfortunate that's all, and them with sense see it that way.'

When she put her hand up to her mouth and pressed it tightly he thought, She's going to cry; but she didn't, and after a moment he asked, 'Would you like a cup of tea, I'm parched meself? There's a nice café along there by the river . . . pleasant.'

Her ready acceptance surprised him, so much so that when she said 'Thanks' and stepped off the pavement on to the road in the direction of the green, he walked by her side until they reached the café without again opening his mouth.

When he ordered a pot of tea for two and a plate of cakes, she did not go and take a seat at one of the tables outside but stood waiting until he was served; then carrying the plate of cakes, she followed him as he made his way to the far end of the garden. 'There,' he said, as they sat down. 'Isn't this nice?'

'Yes.' She looked about her. 'It's lovely. I never knew this café was here.'

'Well, I didn't meself until last year. I go to the Home sometimes because the old ladies want to sell bits and pieces. I've got the name for givin' them a fair crack of the whip; they trust me not to diddle 'em. Barmy, aren't they?'

When she made no answer to this but continued to stare at him, he said, 'Well, aren't you going to pour out?'

'Yes, of course.' She seemed flustered.

This was new too, because the girl he had met in the bookshop wouldn't, he had imagined, know how to be flustered. Agitated yes, but not flustered. He watched her from under lowered lids as she poured out the tea. He couldn't get over the fact that she seemed to have lost her looks. He wondered what her father would think when he saw her. Get a bit of a gliff he supposed, and blame himself for the change in her. He had been determined he wasn't going to mention her father to her but he had, and now he found himself saying, 'Your father'll be free in a fortnight's time. Do you know that?'

'A fortnight?' Her lips moved with the words but made no sound.

'Have you thought what's going to happen to him when he's out?'

'Yes, yes, I have. All the time.'

He took no heed of the terseness of the words or the pain in her voice, but leaning across the little round table towards her said harshly, 'Well, why didn't you go and see him and try and find out?'

Gail stared at him. His face was not more than six inches from hers. His eyes were coal black, and his short lashes so dark and thick one could imagine they had been touched up. In the twice they had met, not counting the day he had sold the books to Miss Frazer, he had been kind to her. She could, in a way, understand him sympathising with people's problems, as he did with the old ladies in the Home, but she couldn't imagine him understanding if she said, 'I was afraid to,' for he would come back smartly, asking, 'Afraid of being seen visiting him in prison?' And the truth was just that, she would have been afraid of being seen visiting the prison. Nevertheless, she would have gone if it hadn't have been for her mother.

At one time it could have been said that she adored her father and loved her mother, it could have been said up to the night in the car park; since then she had ceased to question her feelings towards her father, but her feelings towards her mother she knew were no longer of love but of deep resentment, even of fear, and, at times lately, kindled an emotion she dared not face up to. Although she no longer attended church she still considered it a terrible thing to hate one's parent.

At times she thought it was unfair to blame her mother for her attitude because she hadn't started all this; yet when her thoughts touched on the person who had been the instigator of all the trouble that had come upon them she directed them hastily away, for she couldn't blame him, not really, except when awaking from dreams in which she imagined herself screaming at a girl who kept talking and talking and talking. In the dark she could always see Betty Ray as she had that night, and hear her yelling at her father as she struck out at him, 'You didn't want the cake, but you didn't want anybody else to have it.' She hadn't understood about the cake then but she had the next day when her mother made it plain to her. It was odd the things that stuck in your mind. For days afterwards she could only think that the girl was the same size as she was. She had kept her mind dwelling on the girl at that period, not letting it touch on her father . . . or her grandfather; no, certainly not on her grandfather. The thought of her grandfather made her physically sick, even now, and at that time she hadn't cared whether he died or not. It was only when she realised the consequences to her father should this happen that she began to pray that her grandfather might live.

She had never seen her grandfather since that night. Her mother had said to her, 'You mustn't blame your grandfather; he wasn't a married man with a family, he was a free agent.' At first Gail couldn't understand her mother's differing attitude towards the two men. She had put her husband out of her life altogether, yet every day for two months she went to the nursing home and visited her father, and after he returned home, hardly a day passed when she didn't go and see him; this was when he wasn't taking one of his long holidays. Gail wondered for a long time whether her grandfather went on these holidays alone, and as recently as two weeks ago, when having another verbal battle with her mother she had dared to hint of such a thing, she thought for a moment that Esther was going to strike her. But instead she had stood with her back to the door and told her for the countless time in that cold monotonous penetrating way what a changed man her grandfather was. How he was still quite incapable of carrying on his business, and never again would he be able to work as he had once done, and it was only thanks to his past industry that he could exist now.

She had dared her mother's wrath again by saying, cynically, that his past industry must have been very lucrative because his way of living went on as before; added to which, he now kept them . . . At least he kept her mother and the boys, together with the house and car; he did not keep her.

Nothing would induce her to go back to school after she had returned from the protracted holiday her mother had forced on her. She had been lucky to get the job with Miss Frazer almost right away. The other thing she had wanted to do at this time was to leave home, but that had been a hopeless desire. Even now, at eighteen, it was still hopeless. Whereas the boys were free to go where they liked, her mother almost timed her movements. And this was while her father was in prison; what it would be like when he came out she dare not think. She'd likely send John with the car to pick her up. But it couldn't go on for ever. No, it couldn't go on for ever.

'Did you hear what I said?'

'Yes. You asked me why I didn't go and see him and find out what he's going to do?'

'Well, why didn't you?'

'Because I couldn't.' Her head was drooped now, and he looked at the crown of it for some time before he said, 'Your mother wouldn't let you, is that it?'

When she didn't answer he sat back, picked up his cup and saucer, sipped at the tea, then said, 'This's got cold, is there a drop more hot in there?'

After she had poured him out another cup he pushed the plate of cakes towards her, saying, 'Aren't you going to have one?'

When she took a cake from the plate he helped himself also and they both ate in silence for a few minutes, until he asked quietly, 'Will you come and see him when he comes out?'

She looked up at him now. 'I don't think I'll be able to. I mean . . .'

He was leaning towards her again. 'Well, if you could, I mean if there was nobody stoppin' you, would you then?'

She stared at him, then said softly, 'But where would I see him?'

'Our place.'

'He's going to stay with you at your house?' Her mouth remained slightly agape.

'Yes, but not at Baker Street. We're movin' on Monday.'

'Oh.'

'Do you know Scarfield Mill? It's about three miles out beyond the old Beular mine.' When she shook her head he went on, 'It's a big house, not much to look at now, with only three rooms habitable, all the rest let in water, but wait till I get it finished. My! It'll be a grand place. I've had me eye on it since I was a lad.' His voice was laden with pride.

'Really! . . . And you've bought it?' She was smiling. It was the first time he had seen her smile, and for a

503

brief instance he saw the young Gail again. Her eyes looked warm, her face alive. She said now, 'That's wonderful for you, a great achievement. Janet must be pleased.'

He pulled a wry face at her. 'Not as much as me. There's about ten years work ahead of us, and she's not really taken with that.'

The smile faded as she said, 'And my father's going to live with you?'

'Well, that's the idea, sort of. At least' – he wagged his head – 'until he gets on his feet. He'll need time to find himself. You know what I mean.'

'Yes.' Her voice was a mere whisper. She hung her head again and remained silent, then surprised him somewhat by almost jumping to her feet, saying, 'I'll have to be getting back.' She glanced at her watch. 'A bus goes in five minutes.'

'Why not save the fare?' He was grinning up at her. 'All right, all right, I know. But like afore I could drop you off outside the town.'

'It's very kind of you.'

'Kind, nothing.' He jerked his chin up. 'Same amount of petrol, won't cost me any more.' When he saw the smile creep into her face again he urged it outwards by saying, 'I never do anything that's goin' to cost me money. Now it's a different story if I'm going to make a bit. Oh, I'd even tackle climbing up a gum tree if I thought there was sixpence at the top.'

'Oh, Robbie.'

He had succeeded and the smile was on her face again, and when she said, 'Thank you for the tea and everything,' he put in brusquely, 'Well, come on; we'd better take these things back else they'll charge us for being waited on.'

When they put the tray of dirty crocks on the counter the woman behind the tea urn said brightly, 'Oh, that's kind of you; thanks.' And after he had said, 'You're welcome,' he muttered under his breath as they made their way outside, 'Now if I'd known that you weren't expected to bring the empties back I wouldn't have wasted me strength on them.'

She cast a sidelong glance at him. Her eyes were still laughing but her voice was touched with sadness as she said, 'You're the one person who hasn't changed in all these years, Robbie.'

He put on a long face. 'Well, that's bucked me up. Here's me reached the state of manhood, owner of the best antique shop in town, not forgetting the stately mansion, draughty as yet but nevertheless stately, and you tell me I haven't changed.'

When she laughed outright he felt a sense of real achievement and he said eagerly, 'How would you like to run out and see the place, it'll only take about twenty minutes?'

'Thank you, Robbie, but I can't today, I'll . . . I'll have to be getting back. I . . .' When she hesitated he put in quickly, 'Fair enough, fair enough. Well, here we are.' When he stopped in front of the Cortina she seemed surprised and said, 'I . . . I thought it would be the van.'

'The van?' His tone was haughty. 'The van on a Saturday afternoon! No, Ma'am, no van on a Saturday afternoon. Nor for weddings an' funerals.'

She was still smiling as she took her seat and asked

him, 'Is this the one you first bought?'

'Good Lord no. You mean that Christmas?'

'Yes.'

'I've had three since. No, no, this is the fourth, all second-hand, and all bargains. And they were still bargains when I sold them again an' all.'

Gail sat back in the seat. She couldn't tell how long ago it was since she felt so relaxed. Her body felt free; it was as if it had been encased for years in something tight and she had at last unloosened it, or Robbie had. He was nice, kind and nice. But it was true what she had said, he hadn't changed at all. He still acted like a smart Alec, that was John's term for him, among others less complimentary. She knew a moment's stiffening of her body again. If John were to see her with him there would be trouble. He had nearly gone mad when he knew that her dad had stayed with them after he had left the house. She understood it was only for a few days but that was enough to make John go almost berserk. The fact that their father had gone to the Dunns seemed to concern him more than the reason for him having to go to the Dunns. Her mother had not sent for Janet from that time, and neither of the Dunns had been mentioned since, not in her hearing anyway.

What would happen at home when John found out that his father was going to live with the Dunns again? Her mother's reactions, she felt, would be that her father was dropping to his original level and she'd likely leave it at that, but John's reaction would likely take an active form. She had known for a long time now that John was vicious; if he didn't see eye to eye with you he'd take it out of you in one way or another.

Perhaps it was merely passing you day after day in the house without speaking until you were forced to make a move towards reconciliation. Or his retaliation might take the form of light table chat around the doings of Paul Birkett who was now at the Technical College.

The Birketts, like most of their friends, had faded away when the scandal hit the town. Not continuing at school, she lost touch with Anna, and Paul, the recipient of her adolescent painful love, slid from her horizon like a ship to an unknown destination. Only at times when she had incurred John's displeasure would she hear with whom Paul was now voyaging. First it was Tracy Meekan, an art student; next it was Gwen Stapeley; then one evening at supper he told his mother of Paul's engagement to a Miss Linda Ratcliffe, whose uncle was a lord. This was the night that Terry had bounced up from the table, exclaiming, 'You make me sick!' Terry didn't like rows and it meant a lot that he had stood up to John, and on her behalf, on this occasion.

'Do you go and see your grannie every Saturday?'

'No, one week I'm on duty in the shop until six; that week I go and see her on a Sunday.'

'Well then, I'll work that out,' he said, 'and pop over and let you know how things are. What about that?'

'Thank you.'

'What's your usual time for coming?'

'Around two-thirty.'

'OK then. When he's settled in I'll come and let you know. That's if we don't run into each other afore then.' He cast a swift glance at her, but she was looking ahead. Her face was straight and he thought, 'Aw, we're back to square one.'

When he dropped her on the outskirts of the town she stood on the pavement looking down at him as he sat with his hands on the wheel, and again he had the glimpse of the young Gail, for she smiled widely now and said, 'Thanks, Robbie. I've . . . I've enjoyed this afternoon.'

'Me, too.' He grinned up at her. 'Well; be seeing you.'

'Yes, Robbie. Good-bye.'

'Bye.'

He set the car off with a zoom. My, my! Would you believe that? Wonders would never cease; she was quite human. Wait till he told his mam he'd had Miss Gail Blenheim out to tea, and she had promised to come and see Harry. What would she say to that? She'd say her son was a clever lad, that's what she'd say, and he felt a clever lad. In this moment he felt powerful, capable of achieving anything he set his mind to, anything.

Four

Robbie was waiting when Harry stepped through the prison gate. He did not immediately speak to him because for once he felt embarrassed. It was Harry who said quietly, 'This is good of you, Robbie.'

'Me mam's waiting along the road.' He jerked his head towards the car and they both turned and walked towards it.

Janet was sitting in the back of the car. She looked up as Harry looked through the window; then when Robbie opened the door for him he bent down and when he was half in he twisted round as if he was going to speak to her, but he turned away again and settled in his seat, and no-one spoke until they were well out of town. Then Robbie came out with the only thing his mind gave to him. 'It's a grand day,' he said.

There was a moment's pause; then Harry repeated his words, 'Yes, it's a grand day, Robbie.'

As if Janet had been released by a spring she now bent forward and touching Harry's shoulder, said eagerly, 'Oh, it's good to see you . . . Harry.' She had just prevented herself from adding, 'Out.'

He put up his hand and placed it over hers and

turned his face towards her. 'It's good to see you, Janet.' He looked into her face, then turned his eyes to Robbie, and said huskily, 'What would I have done without you both?'

'God provides,' said Janet.

'Huh!' Harry's laugh was quiet, even gentle, but mirthless, and he swung his head for a moment, then stopped suddenly and, bringing his eyes back to her, he said, 'Well, there may be something in it after all, He provided the both of you.'

Robbie now broke in, his voice holding an excited note. 'I've got a surprise for you, Harry.'

'Yes?'

'I've bought a mansion.'

'Oh, our Robbie!' Janet clicked her tongue. 'Don't exaggerate so.'

'Who's exaggeratin'?' When he turned round as he spoke to her she cried, 'Look where you're going, you'll have us in the ditch.'

'Well, that will learn you not to contradict me. As I said, I've bought a mansion, Harry.'

'Dropping to bits with woodworm and dry rot,' said Janet under her breath.

'Do you know Scarfield Mill, Harry?'

'Yes, Robbie. Yes, I know Scarfield Mill.'

'Well, that's the place I've bought, and isn't that a mansion?'

'You've bought . . . Scarfield Mill? But wasn't it derelict? Is that the same place?'

'That's the same place,' put in Janet. 'He's mad, but I couldn't talk him into sanity.'

'You don't live in Baker Street any longer?'

'We don't live in Baker Street any more, Harry.'

There was a pause before Harry said, 'It sounds interesting, Robbie.'

'It is. Just you wait until you see it, Harry. The prospects are endless.'

'You've said something there,' muttered Janet.

'I wish you'd shut up woman; if I have any more of your old buck I'll put you in lodgings.'

'Any time, any time,' said Janet, laughing now. 'It would suit me. Life would be much easier, I'll tell you that.'

And so they talked, trying to lighten Harry's first hour of freedom. And it was almost an hour to the minute when they passed the pithead, turned down the road and up the narrow high-banked lane towards the house.

'There! What do you think?' Robbie swept his hands from one corner of the house to the other, and as he did so Janet went in through the front door, saying over his shoulder, 'Don't tell him all at once, Harry; it might be too much for him.'

Harry looked at the paneless windows, the gaping roofs, the damp mildewed walls, and what he thought was, He's joking. Then he looked at Robbie's face and he knew it was no joke. He knew that young Robbie Dunn had taken it on and was proud of it. He nodded at him now, saying, 'As you say, I think it has prospects, although it will require a lot of work.'

'Oh, that will get done with the years. But isn't it in a lovely setting? There's three acres of land with it and open country all around, and you can't see the pithead unless you go up the hill beyond there; and then even that looks good. But come on in, I'll show you your room.'

'You've got it furnished?' Harry sounded surprised as he walked slowly towards the front door, and Robbie said over his shoulder, 'Just the stuff from Baker Street. But that won't have house room once I really get going. I mean to have the place lined with antiques. Mam laughs, but I'm serious.'

In the hall Harry looked about him and said, 'It must have been a beautiful place at one time.'

'Aye, an' it will again. Come on through this way.' Robbie led him down a passage and into a room that was cluttered with furniture and full of sunshine, and there Janet, busying herself at a calor gas stove, said, 'We're in an awful mess, Harry, but I'll get straightened up within the next few days. Sit down, sit down and have a cup of tea and a bite.'

Harry sat down and forced himself to eat the beef and tongue and salad that Janet heaped on his plate. It was odd, but he missed the clatter of the tin plates and the distinctive smell of men, imprisoned men. During the whole course of the meal he hardly spoke, leaving the talking to Robbie and Janet, who both, in their own particular ways, were trying to make things easy for him. He knew that he should say something off his own bat, but he couldn't. That was one of the things he'd have to get used to again, talking, starting a conversation. Yet there were words gnawing at his mind, forming a simple question: 'Have you seen anything of Gail?' But they were impossible to get out. Then Robbie gave him the answer without the question having to be asked. Leaning towards him, he said, 'I've got some good news for you.'

His face moved into what should have been a smile as he waited.

'I've seen Gail a couple of times lately . . . an' she's going to come an' see you.'

Harry put his cup slowly down on to his saucer and stared at it; then he rubbed one lip over the other several times before he asked simply, 'When?'

'Well, it could be next Saturday or Sunday, Sunday likely. Yes, it'll be Sunday.'

'But where will I meet her?'

'I told you, she's coming to see you here.'

'Oh.' Harry straightened his shoulders and, his voice slow, he said, 'That's almost a week ahead; I couldn't put you out like that.'

'What you talkin' about?' Robbie's voice was high now. 'You're going to stay along of us.'

'Oh no. No!' Harry looked at Janet who was sitting quietly at the end of the table crumbling some bread on her plate, and he added, 'It's more than good of you, but . . . but I just couldn't.'

'Well, where do you intend to go?' Robbie's voice was rough and Harry turned towards him, saying, 'Well, I'll, I'll get a room, and a job of sorts.'

'You've said it, Harry. And it'll be a job of sorts.'

'Robbie!'

'You be quiet, Mam.' He wagged his finger at her. 'Harry knows what I'm talkin' about. He's got no more chance in this town than snow in hell and he knows it. Now look.' He was bending towards Harry. 'I've got all this planned out. I've got a job for you, an' it'll keep you going for years.'

513

Harry was looking at him now as he asked, 'What sort of a job?' There was no interest in his face; the only name you could put to his expression was blankness.

Robbie glanced at his mother and the glance said again, 'Now you be quiet.' Then looking back at Harry he said slowly, 'Rebuilding this house.'

'What!'

'You heard. Rebuilding this house. Now look at it this way, Harry. I've got to pay a man to help me, I can't do this all by meself; in any case, it's going to take years, and if I employed a bloke regularly, let's face it, it would be union wages. Now I'm not going to offer you union wages, all I can offer you is board and lodgings and six quid a week to start. As I make a go of it in the shop, I'll put it up. I promise you that.'

Harry was shaking his head in small movements. 'It's very kind of you, Robbie, but . . .'

'It's not very kind of me,' put in Robbie swiftly. 'As usual I'm thinkin' of number one. I'm asking you to do me a good turn, an' I look at it as this way. Take it on just for a few months until you feel your feet, until you get yourself sort of acclimatised again, an' then if you find you don't want to stick, well and good, there'll be no harm done. I'll be thankful for what you've done by then.'

'But Robbie, I know nothing whatever about building. I did a bit of carpentry . . . in, in there, and that's all.'

'That's all you need to know, man. It's carpentry that's needed here; window frames, door frames, panelling, roof rafters, the lot. When it comes to the brick-laying and plastering we'll both learn as we

514

go, but it's the woodwork that's important.'

Harry looked from Robbie to Janet, but Janet had her eyes lowered. Her hands were still now on her lap. It was as if she was saying, I'm having nothing to do with this.

'Janet.'

She looked up as he spoke. 'What do you think about all this? I've got the impression that it's all being done for my benefit and I don't want that, I don't want to be carried, not by anyone.'

'Oh, it isn't like that,' Janet put in quickly now, and her voice was earnest because in this she knew she was speaking the truth. 'You'll be helping Robbie, doing him a good turn, doing us both a good turn. But one thing' – her voice dropped. 'If you want to go, you do that, Harry. Don't let either of us stop you.'

Again he looked from one to the other, then said helplessly, 'But where would I go at the present moment? I . . . I feel lost, all at sea so to speak. The funny thing is' – he looked down at the table and, taking up his knife, he began to move it around the plate like a man doodling with a pencil – 'I've been thinking for some time that the best thing to do would be to get as far away from the town as possible, yet I knew I wouldn't be able to. As long as Gail's here I knew I'd hang around, take anything just to see her and try to explain, if that's possible. She might understand now she's older, that is unless her mind's been completely turned against me.' He slanted his tired gaze towards Robbie. His eyes looked like those of a man who had gone a long time with little sleep, and Robbie looking into them, said quietly, 'I don't think you'll find that.'

'No.' Harry looked thoughtful now. 'Whatever brainwashing was done, Gran would counteract it. That's the only thing that's given me comfort all this time.'

Gran. Robbie looked swiftly at Janet, and she made a small motion with her head and he thought, Aye, best leave that for a time; he's got enough to get on with at present.

But everything else was going according to plan. He felt he could congratulate himself. He had done Harry a good turn and he had no doubts about that, but at the same time he had done himself one outsize good turn, for give Harry a year or two on the house and with what he could do himself and perhaps a bit of help on a Sunday from Sid, and the place would be ready enough for him to put his big idea into practice. Boy! Yes, that would be something, his big idea.

He had forgotten for a moment why his mother wanted Harry to stay.

It was twenty-past three on Sunday afternoon and Robbie said they would be back around half-past. Harry was standing in front of the house near a ladder that was leaning against the rough scaffolding. He was on edge, apprehensive. He thought that if it was Esther who had been coming, he wouldn't have felt worked up like this, for now he had no feelings for or against Esther; where she was concerned there was a neutrality in his life. There was only one thing he blamed Esther for, and that was keeping Gail away from him during those weeks before the trial.

The past week had been surprisingly pleasant. He

had worked ten hours a day and would have been willing to go on, only Janet had put her foot down. Janet, he found, was a surprising woman; apart from his knowledge of her as a child, and a young girl, when he remembered her being full of chit-chat, and merry, and then during her visits to help in the house when she had appeared slightly reserved, he had really known nothing about her. Yet this week he had found out a lot about her. She was sympathetic and kind. But he had always known that much, that had been made clear in the black days two years ago. But during the past week he had come to recognise her as an intelligent woman. Her conversation was bracing; she even made the future appear bright. And that was something, for his future was a dark patch, of which he was afraid.

As he stared towards the road he thought, If everything goes right this afternoon I'll be as happy as ever I'll be.

When he heard the car turn into the lane he went hastily indoors, across the hall and into the kitchen, where Janet had a substantial tea all ready spread out, and he said to her, 'I heard the car, Janet. Do you mind if I see her in my room?'

'Of course not. You go on and I'll send her in.' He nodded and, turning hastily about, went down a passage and into a small room that held, along one side of it, a single bed, a chair and a chest of drawers. On the bare floor at the other side were two tin baths and a large earthenware dish, the last hole in the rafters of that section of the roof explaining their presence.

He sat down on the edge of the bed, and put his

joined hands between his knees. He could hear Robbie's voice now and Janet's muted tones, but he heard no sound of a third voice. His teeth were gritting against each other when the tap came on the door.

He only had to rise and take one step to open it and there she stood, his daughter, and he hardly recognised her. She was thinner, as he knew she would be, and her features were the same as he remembered them, but when he remembered them they had promised beauty, exceptional beauty, yet the girl before him was almost plain. Her fair hair that had flowed like sunlit water down on to her shoulders was pulled tightly back over her head. She was eighteen, yet she could have passed for an age up to twenty-five.

'My dear.' The words were thick. He extended his hands tentatively towards her, but she didn't take them and she didn't speak. He gulped in his throat before he stepped back to let her enter the room; then he placed a chair for her and she sat down, and he sat on the bed again facing her.

His hands gripped on his knees now, he said softly, 'Oh, Gail; it's good to see you.' He waited for her to speak, and when she didn't he said formally, 'How are you?'

She was staring at him, her eyes wide, her whole face tense. He watched her lips part as if she were about to speak; then there came a sound from her throat as if a balloon had burst inside. The eruption was painful, for she gripped her neck, closed her eyes tightly and swallowed. His hands were moving out to her again when, as if the past two years had never been, she flung herself forward and into his arms and, sobbing loudly, she cried, 'Oh Dad! Dad!' And he held her as he used to do and rocked her silently, his own eyes tightly screwed up now against the pain and happiness that was filling him. He hadn't lost her, she was still his.

Five

'Why are you doing your hair like that?'

Gail looked through the mirror at her mother, then said, 'Because I want a change.'

'It suited you better drawn straight back.'

'It didn't.'

'Don't answer me in that fashion, Gail; I've told you before.'

'Well, it didn't. And you know it didn't.'

Esther looked at her daughter, her eyes narrowed. The change in her was more startling today. Could it be she had a boy? No, that was impossible. She had rejected the idea before. But she was different. Something had happened . . . Could it be that she had seen him? No, that was impossible too; John picked her up from work most evenings, and when she went to the pictures she herself accompanied her. The only place she went to alone was the Old People's Home. Well, she would find out today if there was anything going on there.

As Gail pushed past her to go out of the room she said, 'Terry's going with you to see Gran.'

'What!' Gail stopped dead. 'Terry? Why? Not one of you's bothered to go and see Gran before, so why is Terry starting now? . . . Oh, don't tell me.' She thrust her head forward. 'I know.'

'What are you talking about?'

'You know what I'm talking about.' She marched out of the room, across the landing and down the stairs, to see Terry standing in the hall looking somewhat shamefaced.

She paused on the bottom step and stared at him, and he lifted his gaze quickly from hers and looked upwards to his mother standing on the stair head. Then turning abruptly, he went to the front door, jerked it open and hurried out.

Gail followed more slowly, and she resisted coming abreast of him until they reached the street, but as soon as she came to his side he muttered under his breath, 'Don't blame me, I didn't want this. It isn't my idea of a Saturday afternoon out.'

'Then why didn't you tell her?' she snapped at him, but kept her gaze directly ahead. And he came back, his tone equalling hers, 'Well, it was either me or John, and I thought I was the lesser of two evils for you.'

'John would never give up his rugger.'

'That's all you know. He was quite prepared to do it if I hadn't said I would come with you.'

They were looking at each other now and she said, as if the knowledge was new to her, 'He hates Dad more than she does.'

Terry made no answer to this but he looked ahead again as he asked softly, 'Have you seen him?'

'Yes.'

'Is that why you've been late this last couple of times?'

'Yes.'

'Where is he?'

'He's staying with Janet.'

'Janet Dunn?'

Again they were looking at each other. 'Yes, Janet Dunn. Why do you sound shocked, he's got to stay somewhere?'

'. . . But that place in Baker Street.'

'They don't live in Baker Street any more.'

'Where then?'

'Robbie's taken a big old house out beyond the Beular Mine, it's called Scarfield Mill. Dad's helping to rebuild it.'

'Dad helping to rebuild a house?' His voice trailed away.

'Yes.' Her head was thrust out towards him now, her voice cold again. 'He learned to do it in prison.'

'All right, all right, you needn't shout.' He looked about him. 'There's enough people know already.'

They were waiting for the bus when Gail, looking pleadingly at him, asked, 'What are you going to do? I mean, are you going to tell her?'

'What do you take me for?'

She smiled faintly at him, then said, 'Thanks, Terry.'

He hung his head until she asked, 'Would you like to come along with me and see him?'

His head still remained bowed as he muttered, 'There'd be the devil to pay if she found out, or worse still if John found out, and especially as it's Robbie

Dunn he's with. You know what he thinks of him. There'd be murder.'

'They need know nothing if we're back in time.'

He raised his head. 'You think it'll be all right?'

'Yes.'

'OK. I'd . . . I'd like to see him. How is he?'

'He's, he's fine, but sort of quiet. It'll make him happy to see you.'

He drooped his head again and they remained silent; but when the bus came she said, 'Let's go on top.' For a moment she was a young girl again, eager for excitement, even if it was only riding on top of a bus. Life wasn't so awful. She had her dad again and Terry was on their side.

Six

The days drifted into weeks and the weeks into months, during which life seemed to stand still for Harry. He felt he was marking time; as a prelude to what he didn't know. There was enough work on the house to keep him busy for another two years, but was that what he wanted? He just didn't know. What he did know was that if he had wanted to leave tomorrow he wouldn't have done so, because his gratitude to Robbie and Janet would have compelled him to stay as long as they required him.

When thinking of gratitude he put Robbie first, for he knew it was he who had made this quiet retreat possible. And living here was like a retreat. Except for the picnickers who came on to the hill behind the house on a sunny day, and Gail who came every Saturday or Sunday, accompanied by Terry, he saw no-one other than Janet and Robbie; that is except on a Sunday or a Wednesday when Robbie would drive him out to see his grandmother. And if it would have been possible to get out of these visits he would have done so, for the sight of that high-spirited old woman sitting among thirty other old women was one of the worst things he had been called upon to bear, equal in its way to his early estrangement from Gail.

There had been suggestions from both Gail and Robbie to alter the situation. Robbie suggested bringing her out as soon as he got a room ready. Well, he had got a room ready but she wouldn't come. And then there was Gail's suggestion that they should find a little place and the three of them live together. He hadn't given his grandmother the opportunity to refuse this suggestion because he had never put it to her. He knew that his lack of enthusiasm for her proposal had upset Gail. She couldn't understand why he wasn't for it and he couldn't tell her. How explain that he didn't feel capable of taking on responsibility of a home ever again? How to explain that he felt so unsure of himself that at times he wished he was back in that small room where he had no control over his own life, where his every action was set to a timetable?

When he allowed himself to think he likened his present existence to the life in an open prison; he knew what work he had to do, his meals were put before him, and in the evening he could read, or look at television, and for privileges there was the occasional jaunt in the car. It was all he wanted.

And then came the morning that Robbie said, 'I've got an idea, Harry. Like to hear it?'

'Fire away.' Harry smiled, picked up a piece of toast, put some marmalade on it, bit into it, then looked across the table at Robbie, who was leaning back in his chair with a cup of tea in his hand.

'Well, before I start,' said Robbie, now looking at Janet, 'I want you to be quiet, Mam, because before I open me mouth I can hear you say, "Oh, no, you don't"; so will you oblige me, Mrs Dunn, by keeping yours closed?'

'That all depends.' Janet nodded at him. 'If it's anything hare-brained . . .'

'Hare-brained, tatty haired, long haired, it doesn't matter, it's something I've been chewing on for months. I thought I'd have a chew on it for another year or so, but because Harry there has done such a good job I could get going anytime.'

'Something about the house?' asked Harry now.

'Something about the house, Harry . . . The roof's all done, all the windows in the front are done, the whole front's presentable, and the front's what I want. The long room's done . . .'

'Look! I don't know what you've got in mind but you said that was going to be our sitting . . .'

'It will be, it will be. Didn't I tell you to keep it shut.' He leaned towards Janet. Then looking at Harry again, he went on, 'As I said, the long room's done and you've done more than half the panelling on the hall. Now how long will it take you to finish the woodwork there?'

'Oh' – Harry paused, thinking – 'another month I should say. Perhaps a bit longer.'

'Four weeks, five weeks, six weeks, that'll be fine. Now this is what I propose.' He put his cup on the table and laid a hand palm downwards at each side of it. 'I aim to furnish the hall, an' the long room as show-rooms, period rooms, and that'll only be a start . . .' He now lifted one hand sharply in Janet's direction, saying, 'What did I tell you? Now keep it quiet for a minute until I'm finished.' He drew in a deep breath; then

526

addressed Harry again. 'It could be asked who's going to come out here from Fellburn to buy antiques, they're not an antique-minded lot except those on Brampton Hill and they're thinning out fast? Well, I'm not going to look for my market in Fellburn. I have four good customers in Newcastle and I'm sending stuff the morrow to a house in Doncaster. Now what I propose when these Newcastle lot come into the shop is to bring them out here. They're moneyed people, two in shipping, one in oil, and one running a chain of shops, so many now he can't count them. Nor can he speak English; and his wife's even worse. I could give them some pointers, that'll tell you how bad they are.' He nodded and grinned at Harry. 'But they've got this thing about furnishing the house with antiques and he, being a business man, got the idea that if he can pick up bargains locally why go further afield. Now from people like them it's only a step to the American market, and that's where I'm going, and not through half-a-dozen middlemen either. Well, what do you think, Harry?'

Harry stared at Robbie; then he looked at Janet, and he said, 'Well, it isn't what I think surely, it's your mother, isn't it?'

'Look, I can manage her, I always have.' His grin in Janet's direction was wide now. Then again he said, 'Well, tell me what you think?'

'I think it's a very astute business idea and I can see you making it work.'

'I can't on me own.'

'No?'

'No. I can't be in two places, or three places for that

527

matter at once, at the sales, at the shop and here. Sid is not bad in the shop, but then again he's not good. I've got to put up with Sid and pray to God he won't give the things away while I'm out. But here I want not only a salesman, but . . . well. Well, to put it bluntly someone with a bit of class like yourself.'

'Aw, Robbie.' Harry shook his head heavily.

'Now don't aw Robbie me in that way, I mean it. What I'm offering you is a partnership.'

Harry's head came up with a jerk. 'A partnership? But you know how I stand, I've got . . .'

'You've got everything I want. You've got the ability to build this place, which you're practically doing on your own an', as I've said, you've got a presence, you'll be able to talk to people . . .'

'Oh no, no.' Harry's tone was definite now. 'I don't want to talk to people, Robbie.'

'But you've got to talk to people sometimes, Harry. Look, I've been wanting to have this out with you. You've got to talk to people, you've got to get out and mix. You've done a marvellous job here and you'll go on doing a marvellous job, but you're not in a monastery, man. And that's how you've been living except for the one female here.' He nodded towards his mother.

'He's right, Harry.' Janet's voice was soft, and Harry turned and looked at her, and she said again, 'He's right in all he says. He nearly always is. He knows what he wants, but he can't do it on his own. If you turn it down, it won't mean that he'll give up the idea, he'll only have to get somebody else, and they won't be one quarter as good as you.'

Harry's chin was now deep on his chest and his voice was a thick mutter as he said, 'It's all so one-sided.'

'One-sided, be damned!' Robbie rose to his feet. 'I never do anything unless I think there's a good profit in it for me.' He stabbed his finger across the table. 'Make no mistake about that. Anyway, man, your own sense should tell you I've been making a profit out of you for weeks; where would I get anybody to do the work you've done for six quid a week? You've put thousands on this place. Wait till that little squirt, Pearson, comes to value it the next time; he won't see it being two thousand down the drain, bet your life he won't, he'll be falling over himself to put up the premium. Well now, what do you say?'

'What can I say, Robbie?'

'It's settled then. Everything you sell here we split the profit.'

'But I know nothing about period furniture, Robbie.'

'I've thought of that, and I bet when you get through the two dozen Apollo's I've got in the back shop you'll know twice as much as I do; then you can come to one or two sales with me just to get the feeling. Look; what about coming down to the shop this mornin'? I got a load of stuff in on Friday. It's been knocked about a bit, but I'd like you to see it as it is afore it's done up. What d'you say?'

'There's the hall; if you want it finished I should be getting on with it.'

'Look, the hall can wait for one morning.' Then, his voice dropping, he added, 'You've got to come into town sometime, Harry, and this morning's as good as any.'

Harry looked from Robbie to Janet, and she said quietly, 'He's right, Harry.'

An hour later when Harry, standing in the back shop, looked down on a jumble of chests of drawers, Victorian chairs with the stuffing sticking out, old fashioned couches and battered card tables he thought, I wouldn't give them house room.

Pointing to a couch, Robbie said, 'You won't recognise that piece when you see it again, it'll be done in Regency stripe and be known as a chaise-longue. Thirty pounds, madam, very reasonable.'

'Never!' said Harry on a small laugh.

'It's a fact. I'm tellin' you.'

Harry shook his head.

'And wait until you see it against the dark panelling of that hall. That's the setting for it. An' you needn't believe me, only time will tell, but in some cases that setting will double the price.'

Again Harry shook his head. It was all he could do.

It was just after twelve when they left the shop and crossed the market, and it wasn't until they turned the corner by the bank that Harry realised that he must pass Peamarsh's and the thought checked his step. It wasn't that he hadn't been aware of how close he was to the office; all the way to town he had thought of the possibility of running into one of them; but listening to Robbie in the shop and sharing, in a way, his enthusiasm for the new venture had for the moment pushed Peamarsh's to the back of his mind. But now, there it was across the road, big letters heading a stone façade, and down the steps into the street almost opposite to him were walking three men, Arthur McMullan, Tom Vosey and a man who was a stranger to him.

Arthur McMullan stopped for a perceivable second, looked at him, then walked on; Tom Vosey paused a little longer, then he joined the other two.

Robbie looked at Harry. He was standing as if glued to the pavement. If he had been facing the other way he could have pretended he was looking into the windows of Howard's the jeweller's, but he was standing half-facing the steps across the road. 'Come on, man.' Robbie touched his arm, and Harry allowed himself to be led away like a blind man.

They had gone but a short distance when there came hurried steps behind them and a voice said, 'Just a minute.'

They both stopped and Robbie turned, but Harry stood looking straight ahead.

'How are you, Harry?' Tom Vosey stood to Harry's side and Harry, moving his neck slowly round, looked at him and said, 'Oh, I'm all right, Tom. How's yourself?'

'Fine, Harry, fine.' Tom Vosey now glanced at Robbie, then back to Harry and his voice was tentative as he said, 'Would . . . would you care to come for a drink?'

'No, thanks, Tom. I'm . . . I'm on a piece of business.'

'Oh!' Tom nodded, again glancing at Robbie. Then he said, 'Everything all right with you, Harry?'

'Splendid, Tom.'

'That's good. I'll be seeing you around some time, then?'

'Yes, Tom, be seeing you some time. Goodbye.'

'Goodbye, Harry.'

Tom Vosey went one way, Harry, accompanied by Robbie, the other, and when they reached the end of the street and Harry hadn't opened his mouth Robbie said, 'What about having a bite to eat in town?'

It was some seconds before Harry replied, 'If it's all the same to you, Robbie, I'd rather get home.'

'It's OK with me; I always like me mam's cooking better than anything they give you in a restaurant.' He made the remark sound light but it fell flat.

In the car Robbie began to talk. He talked rapidly, asking himself questions and giving himself the answers, and all the while Harry sat silent, until they came to within half-a-mile of where they turned off the main road into the lane. This stretch of the road was on an incline and had a sharp bend in it. It was when they were approaching the bend that Robbie cut off what he was saying to exclaim loudly, 'Look at this madman tearing up here; he's passing two cars behind me and we're almost on the bend. God! will they never learn? You could wish somethin' would happen to teach him a lesson. An' look!' His voice was even higher now, drawing Harry's attention to the passing car. 'It's full of kids.'

As the car passed him within yards of the bend Robbie blasted his horn once. He was about to do it a second time when his hand became still and he almost closed his eyes as he saw the car swerve quickly in front of him to avoid the oncoming bus. If he put on his brakes he knew the cars behind would pile up into him. He held his breath, kept his pace steady, and they were around the corner, the car full of children speeding away in front.

Harry was sitting on the edge of the seat now and he asked quietly, 'You all right, Robbie?'

'Aye. Yes, just.' There was a slight quiver in his voice. 'But only just I'm tellin' you. That bloody, mad swine. God! if only I could get me hands on him. And the car full of kids. You saw them, there must have been six.'

As they turned into the lane he drew in another long breath; then relaxing in his seat, he said, 'You know what? I can tell you what's going to happen to that lot. Very shortly those kids are going to say, "Why are we wearing haloes, Daddy?" and Daddy'll say, "Because I was a clever bugger."'

Why are we wearing haloes, Daddy? Because I was a clever bugger. That was funny. And the way Robbie had said it. Oh, that was funny. Why are we wearing haloes, Daddy? Because I was a clever bugger. Slowly Harry's shoulders began to shake, his head drooped and he put his fingers to his brow. The chuckle came into this throat and when it passed through his lips it had turned into a laugh; and then it grew louder and louder.

When Robbie had seen that Harry was amused he had laughed too, but now his laughter had faded away because Harry's laughter wasn't merriment. He wanted to say to him, 'Give over, man.' The sound was embarrasing, it was sort of hysterical. When Harry's hand groped out towards him and touched the wheel he stopped the car. And now, to his concern, he saw that Harry was no longer laughing, he was crying; the tears were spurting from his eyes and running over his spread

533

fingers. His shoulders were hunched and his body was curved downwards. Robbie said quietly, 'Aw, man, don't take on like that. Nothing's worth feeling that much over.' He ended harshly, 'You'll see your day with the lot of them yet, you mark my words.'

When Harry groped at the handle of the door and, pushing it open, got out, he leant across the seat and said, 'Where you going?' And Harry, unable to speak, pointed to the hill behind the house, and at this Robbie nodded at him, then watched him go round behind the car, jump the ditch into the field, then cross it.

When he drove up to the house Janet came to the door and, seeing him alone, asked anxiously, 'Where's Harry?'

He pointed upwards over the house, saying briefly, 'He's gone up the hill.'

'Up the hill?' Janet followed him closely indoors. 'Why's he gone up the hill?'

'He ran into some of his old pals near the market and they cut him, except one. He came back, but he made it as awkward as hell. I think it was the last straw. He broke down just along the road; I'd leave him until he gets over it.'

Janet walked slowly across the hall, down the passage and into her own room, and there, sitting on the foot of her bed, she gripped the rail and laid her head against the wooden post. Would this make him leave? Go away somewhere by himself, or perhaps with Gail and Mrs O'Toole? Either way it would be like death to her. She had never been so happy in her life as she had been during the last five months, but at this moment she was sick deep down in her soul, sick with fear that this wonderful existence – and to her it was a wonderful existence – was about to end.

She didn't know if Harry had any idea of her true feelings for him; she doubted whether he had because some men, good men like him, couldn't see what was under their noses. She lifted her head and stared at the wall and, like a moving picture, she saw her life in it; all her young days subject to her parents' religious bias, her married life without joy, except when her son was born. He had been the only comfort she had had but it had never been enough, there was always a gap in her, and only one person could fill it.

She rose to her feet, opened the window and stepped over the low sill into the courtyard – she didn't want to run into Robbie at this moment. She walked across the yard, through a gate in the rough fence, across the field and mounted the hill.

He was lying on the grass in the shelter of an outcrop of rock when she saw him, and she knelt by his side and touched his shoulder. It was a moment before he raised his head, and she was surprised by the look on his face. She had expected anguish, bitterness, anything but the calmness she saw there, and his voice too was calm when he said, 'It's all right, Janet, it's over.'

'They're nothing but a lot of nowts,' she said.

'Aw, it wasn't only that. It had to come. It's as well it did. I feel better.' He brought himself into a sitting position by her side and he stared across the valley for a moment before he said, 'It's as if I've been swimming under water for years and at last broke surface. I feel free, freer than I ever remember being before. Yet nothing has changed. It's funny, but I know this is

535

another starting point and I won't go back. As Robbie said, I'll see me day with most of them. Not that I want that but . . . but I want to get moving, do something.' He looked at her and she asked in a voice scarcely above a whisper, 'Does that mean you're going?'

'No, no.' His reply came quickly. 'Robbie's given me a chance; I'm going to take it up, but in an entirely different way from what I expected to do this morning.' He put out his hand and covered hers now, saying, 'I don't know what I would have done without you both. It frightens me remembering the state I was in a few months back and where I might have drifted if you hadn't been there that morning . . . you've been a good friend, Janet.'

They were looking straight into each other's eyes as she said, 'I'll always be ready to be whatever you want me to be, Harry.'

There was no mistaking the implication of her words. His eyes widened slightly. Janet and him. He'd never thought . . . Well, yes; years ago, his mam and dad used to chip him about Janet because he could never go out back or front without he ran into her, but he only took that as the result of the proximity of Janet living upstairs and they down and of sharing the same backyard. Anyway, she had married before him, and to an orthodox Jew. As he looked at her he saw her as she was when a young girl. There was the same look in her eyes. Poor Janet. And all these years coming back and forward to the house helping; he had never guessed. Well, now that he had what about it? He was still married, wasn't he? But say he wasn't, then what about it? He received no answer to this, only another question. How would he like living without Janet now? And to this the answer came promptly, he wouldn't. No, no, he wouldn't. Janet brought him a sort of peace, security; yes, that was the word, security, for although in the last half-hour he had come to know where he was going, he also knew he was a man who would always need security, the security of a home and a woman.

Apart from Gail it was almost three years since he had touched a woman and when Janet fell against him he held her stiffly until she began to tremble and to mutter his name over and over again. Then his arms tightened about her and he buried his face in her black shining hair, and there returned to him a feeling he hadn't known since the early days of his marriage. But the feeling was immediately punctured by the thought of Esther, and her moral point of view rose before him like a battlement through which a divorce would never penetrate.

Seven

For the second time within four days Esther Blenheim was experiencing a feeling that really terrified her, for she was being consumed by a rage that urged her to get something into her hands and smash it. All her life she had assumed a calm exterior. Daily small tribulations had never ruffled her; the greater issues occasioned by family life might have disturbed her inwardly but on the surface she appeared in control. Her mother had once said to her that emotions not only tear you to shreds inside but they aged you, and you could say that on this advice Esther had based her life, because deep down she was a vain woman, and this had been proved, if only to herself, within the past few days.

When she had received the letter from the solicitor stating that her husband was seeking a divorce, the façade of years had cracked. She had read the letter at breakfast and she didn't remember leaving the table and getting upstairs into her room, but she did remember picking up the first thing she saw, which was a petticoat, and rending it from top to bottom.

The coaching of years had quickly cried a halt to the fury of her hands, but not to her mind. She had sat pulling one finger after another listening to the knuckles cracking like castanets while startling vituperations frothed from her lips. Six months out of prison and he had found another woman! And in Fellburn – he had gone back to that girl, that dirty slut. She had imagined he hadn't come back to the town after he had come out of prison or he would in some way have tried to get in touch with Gail. But the solicitor's letter was from Fellburn, so from that she gathered he was still here. And this fact alone disturbed her, for she couldn't imagine him being in the town all this time and not trying to contact Gail.

It wasn't until this morning she had answered the letter, and to the effect that her husband knew her views on divorce and she wished to receive no further communication on the subject.

She had mentioned the matter to no-one, not even her father, for she told herself there was no need, as nothing was going to come of it, and since the letter was posted her calm demeanour had taken control again, at least on the surface.

But now, here was John telling her something that was engendering rage even more fierce than the previous bout. She wouldn't believe it. When she could speak she said just that to him, stuttering on the words. 'I . . . I don't believe it. You've . . . you've made a mistake. No. I can't believe it, I won't, I won't.'

'Mother! Sit down.' He took her by the shoulders and pressed her into a chair; then bending over her and staring into her face, he said, 'It's true, I've told you. For weeks now I've suspected our Terry was up to something because he's gone with her on Saturday afternoons without a murmur; and you said yourself she'd changed.'

The perspiration was hanging in beads on her brow and around her lips, even her neck was running sweat, yet her flesh felt cold. She gulped as she said, 'Robbie Dunn?'

'Robbie Dunn.' John gritted his teeth on the name. 'There he was, waiting outside the home, and out they came and got into his car and drove away.'

'But . . . but your father? You're sure?'

'Of course I'm sure. Didn't I follow them? When they turned up Cooper's Lane I knew it led to a dead end to that old derelict house . . . It used to be derelict, you should see it now.'

'And you're sure it was Janet?'

He bared his teeth and the word sounded like a hiss. 'Yes. Yes, I've told you. She was standing with him watching the others sliding down the hill, the three of them were laughing and acting like lunatics.'

She closed her eyes and began to pray, beseeching God to take this terrible anger away from her. Her fingers were plucking at each other, desirous again of rending something. With her eyes still closed she said, her voice beseeching now, 'But, but about the other. You're not just making it up about Gail and him . . . be . . . because you don't like him?'

'That's stupid reasoning.' He straightened himself, pushed his shoulders back and drew his chin in. 'I told you, when they were going back to the house they kept way behind the others. I lost sight of them for a bit because I had to move along the hedge but when I next saw them they had their arms around each other.'

Again he was talking through his teeth. 'If ever there was a two-faced little brat it's her. She goes around here looking like someone in a closed order, but if you could have seen her today, snuggling up to that filthy little Jew. Ugh! I wanted to vomit. It was all I could do to stop myself from dashing out and knocking him silly.'

'What . . . what time is it?' She had her head down.

'Ten-to-five.'

'They should be here any minute; leave it to me.' She raised her head now. 'Do you hear? Leave it to me.' As she finished speaking there came to them the sound of the front door opening and she rose from the chair and walked round the couch towards the fire and, turning, she stood with her back to it. She could always manage situations better standing on her feet.

Gail and Terry had learned to alter their expressions as soon as they entered the drive. They always came into the house soberly, Terry assuming an air of slight resentment, while Gail's expression suggested acceptance, if begrudgingly. They hadn't planned their attitudes but they knew they were a necessary extension of the whole deception.

Today they found it harder than usual to put on their masks. Gail couldn't remember enjoying herself so much for years. That slide, and them all laughing, and the wonderful tea after, and Terry being amused and her father looking happy. Yes, he had looked happy. She must remember that, he was happy.

When he had first told her he wanted to marry Janet she had been amazed and frankly a little shocked. Janet who had worked for them, Janet who was a Jewess,

Janet who was the mother of Robbie, and Robbie was . . . Well, what was Robbie? A typical Jew, a market Jew, as John called him, brash, go-getting, common – but behind it all, kind, thoughtful, a good friend, as he had proved to be to her father. If her dad married Janet it would make him Robbie's step-father and Robbie and her step-brother and sister. Neither of these facts appealed to her. That was until her dad had taken her up the hill and had talked to her about things that she had never heard mention before, his early life where he had lived almost in the same house as Janet, and her own devotion to him, which he had been too blind to notice.

'Are you going to ask Mother for a divorce?' she had said, and he answered, 'Yes.'

'Do you think she will?'

'I don't know; I doubt it.'

'Then . . . then what'll you do?'

When he had said bluntly, 'I'll live with Janet,' she hadn't been shocked.

She knew that her mother must have received her father's application for the divorce earlier in the week but she had made no reference to it, she wouldn't. It was another shame-tinged secret to add to her martyrdom.

They had hung their things in the cloakroom and together they entered the sitting-room and together they stopped just within the door and looked to where Esther was standing on the hearth rug, and John at the head of the couch, both apparently waiting for them.

'Well, what are you standing there for? Are you afraid to come in?'

Terry blinked and glanced quickly at Gail, but Gail was staring across the room at her mother.

'Where've you been?' The question was addressed directly to Gail and before she answered it she felt Terry moving away from her side. If there was any lying to do he was going to let her do it; Terry hated upsets. 'You know where I've been, to see Gran,' she said.

'And after?'

Gail slowly turned her gaze from her mother to John. So that was it, they knew. John had been snooping. Looking back at her mother, she said boldly, 'You know all about it, so why ask.'

'I want to hear you tell me where you went after visiting the home.'

Gail lifted her shoulders high up around her neck; it was an attitude, she knew, that always angered her mother, but that was a small issue now. And she walked towards the other end of the couch from John before saying, 'Well, I don't suppose I can enlarge on what my dear brother has told you but I've been to see Dad.' As she looked into her mother's face she saw the bitterness swamp it like a tidal wave.

'You lying, cheating, little . . .!' As Esther clenched her hands together her flow of words trailed away and Gail put in harshly, 'Who made me lie and cheat? You did, you! Anyway, I've a right to see him, he's my father.'

'You have no rights, as you say, you're under my care and protection . . .'

'Don't be silly.' The tone was scornful. 'You're talking as if we were early Victorians.'

'Don't dare speak to me like that, do you hear?'

543

Esther moved to the front of the couch, her body arched. 'I will not be spoken to in that manner.'

'Well, don't talk nonsense. You can't tie me up, although you've had a jolly good try.'

'Don't you make any mistake, my girl, I can tie you up; there's ways and means of tying silly girls like you up to protect them from men like him.'

'Men like him! What do you mean? Men like him.' Gail's eyes slowly widened. 'You talk as if he was a mad beast or something. It's as if you had never known him. Anyway, I know now that if he had told the truth about why he hit Grandfather he would never have been given the outrageous sentence. He let them put the wrong construction on it to save me any more worry and embarrassment. Yes, and to save your face from getting red. And it would have been red, wouldn't it, if the truth had come out about your dear father?'

Esther was beyond words; she could only stare at this daughter, who dared to recall the shocking incident that had wrecked their lives. Even when Gail went on harshly, 'But I know what's getting you now, it's the divorce, isn't it? You don't want him yourself and you don't want anyone else to have him, least of all Janet.'

Esther couldn't speak, that was until John, looking at her, repeated, 'Divorce?' Then she stepped back from the couch, put her hand to her cheek and muttered, 'What did you say? Janet?'

It was evident to Gail that the matter of the divorce had come as a surprise to John, but the association of Janet's name with her father was acting as an even greater shock to her mother. When Esther exclaimed again in a low voice, 'Janet! Janet Dunn?' Gail felt a

544

momentary feeling of pity for her because she was remembering how she felt when her father had broken the news to her.

'Is this true? He's asked for a divorce?' John's hand was out touching his mother's arm, trying to draw her attention towards him; but she didn't look at him as she said dully, 'Yes, yes, it's true.' And now her face moved into a mirthless smile, her upper lip showing all her even teeth, and she nodded at Gail as she said, 'And so he wants to marry Janet Dunn. Your father wants to marry Janet Dunn. Well, he's sunk to the right level, but he'll never marry Janet Dunn, not while I'm alive.'

Gail was staring at her mother as if hypnotised. The room was utterly quiet now until, her voice breaking the silence like a high whistle, she almost screamed, 'Then he'll live with her. You can't stop him doing that.'

The silence fell on them again, and during it Esther drew herself to her full height; she moistened her lips while the muscles of her face twitched and those in her neck stood out like cords. She was letting the silence say that the matter was closed. She had for the moment forgotten Robbie Dunn, but John hadn't, for now moving towards Gail he demanded, 'And what about you and that Robbie Dunn, eh?'

Gail stared at him. She was in no way intimidated by his attitude. 'And what about me and Robbie Dunn?' she asked, her eyes widening.

'You must be hard up for a fellow cheapening yourself with a dirty little Jew like him.'

'Don't you dare call him a dirty little Jew.' She even advanced a step towards him. 'He's got more in his little finger than you've got in your whole body. It's jealousy that's always hit you with regards to Robbie, you're jealous of him.'

'Oh my God!'

Esther didn't chastise her son for blasphemy at this stage, and John went on laughing scornfully now, 'You must be joking, jealous of that! The point is, I won't stand for a sister of mine necking in public with a little runt like . . .'

'You're lying! I've never . . .' She had to force herself to say the word, 'necked in public with him or anyone else.'

'Look.' He was yelling now. 'Face the fact that I saw you. I saw you with my own eyes today. My dear brother there' – he cast a swift threatening glance to where Terry was standing at the far side of the window – 'my father and' – he paused – 'his mistress were trotting on in front, but you two stayed behind, remember? And don't tell me you weren't necking.'

Gail's mouth was hanging wide, her eyes stretched. She was remembering that she had stepped on to a frozen puddle in the field and had slipped, and Robbie had put his arm out and caught her and they had stood laughing together for a moment. She had felt odd, sort of excited at the close contact with him; it was the first time he had touched her, he had never even helped her in or out of the car; and then, all of a sudden she had been close to him, pressed to his chest, her cheek near his chin, his breath, like white smoke, fannning her face. When he had released her she had been unable to speak, and he hadn't said anything either. But, necking! She defended herself harshly now, 'I slipped; he

546

stopped me from falling, that was all. Do you hear. THAT WAS ALL!'

'Oh, Lord, with the experience you've had lately I would have thought you'd have come up with a better one than that.' His tone was derisive, his eyes blazing. 'Who do you think you're talking to?'

'I know who I'm talking to, a low down sneak, that's who I'm talking to. You've always been a sneak, you always will, you couldn't be straight if you tried, even since you were small . . .'

'That's enough! That's enough!' Esther was holding up her hand; and once more she addressed herself solely to Gail. 'Listen to me,' she said, her voice sounding strangely calm. 'I forbid you to see that boy. Do you hear? You are not to associate with him in any way. If you do I'll take steps . . . legal steps to put a stop to it. I suppose you've heard of being made a ward of court?'

'Ward of court!' Gail's voice was full of scorn. 'Don't be so ridiculous. You know what you are? You're ludicrous. Now listen, 'cos I'm going to tell you something.' She was bending over the end of the couch, her body strained forward as if she was aiming to bring her face in contact with her mother's. 'And listen carefully, because I mean it . . . I'm going to marry Robbie Dunn, so what do you think of that, eh? Whether you divorce Dad or not I'm going to marry Robbie Dunn.' She swung her angry gaze from her mother to John and, bouncing her head at him, she cried, 'And you can do what you damn well like about that.' The silence fell heavily on the room again and no-one broke it as she turned and rushed out.

547

She almost fell into her bedroom, such was the speed with which she ran across the landing and flung herself at the door. Once inside she didn't put on the light but groped her way to the window and, extending her arms, gripped each side of the framework. Her whole body was shaking with a mixture of amazement, fear and cold. What on earth? what in the name of heavens! what . . . WHAT? had possessed her to say such a thing! Marry Robbie Dunn when he had never even looked at her in that way, never even as much as touched her hand until this afternoon? She must have gone stark staring mad. What if John went to him? What if her mother wrote? Her head sank deep on to her chest. She would die of shame. She didn't love him, he didn't love her, then why? why had she said that? Oh God! She turned about and threw herself face downwards on the bed and she bit tightly on the corner of the pillow, but she didn't cry. She mustn't cry, she told herself bitterly; what she must do was to think, and think clearly of what she was going to say to Robbie when he asked her for an explanation . . .

It was about seven o'clock on the Monday evening when Esther, without announcing herself in any way, went into Gail's room and, closing the door behind her, looked at her daughter and said quietly, 'I want to talk to you.'

Gail was sitting at the dressing table and after one quick glance in her mother's direction she lowered her head and started to sort among some oddments on the tray in front of her.

While Esther Blenheim stood looking at the back of

her daughter's head, she told herself that she must keep calm. She couldn't believe that only two days had elapsed since Saturday, for she had crowded so much painful thinking into them that they appeared like months. The outcome of this cathartic process was that she was about to waive her moral principles in order to save her daughter years of unhappiness, she was choosing the lesser of two very real evils. At least that's how it appeared to her.

'Look at me, Gail.'

Gail slowly raised her eyes from the tray, and looked at her mother's reflection through the mirror. She didn't know what she was up to now but undoubtedly it would be something twisted, but she didn't really care what it was as long as she didn't hear her say 'I've written to Robbie Dunn'. Her mother hadn't spoken to her during the past two days and she'd been afraid to break her silence.

Esther, looking at the young tight drawn face, said, 'I want to make a bargain with you.' She paused, then went on slowly, 'I don't believe in divorce. Your father has always known that; I've . . . I've already refused his request but' – she swallowed twice and nodded her head a number of times before ending, 'I'd be willing to give him want he wants if you'll give up all idea of marrying that boy.'

Gail was facing her now, having swung swiftly round on the stool, and Esther, taking this as a prelude to a verbal onslaught and a refusal, held up her hand and cried, 'Now listen, listen. In the first place, and I mean this, it's you I'm thinking of. That boy . . . that boy's not in your class, you know he's not. You wouldn't be married to him five minutes before you were ashamed of him. I know what I'm talking about. He's . . . I'm going to say it, he's a Jew, he looks a Jew of Jews; he thinks like a Jew, he acts like a Jew. You would be more likely to be at ease with a Negro than you would with him after a while . . . you have nothing in common.' She paused again while she stared down into her daughter's face, and her voice dropping to a whisper, she said, 'There it is, it's in your hands. I'll give your father the divorce if you'll do this, break off . . . break off all connections with Robbie Dunn.'

Gail slowly lowered her gaze from her mother's face; then her head moved downwards. She had the desire to laugh. It was gurgling in her. She felt sick with relief. She kept her head bent as her mother went on talking, almost pleadingly now, saying, 'You think me cruel, but you'll thank me later on.'

Esther stopped and stood staring down at the centre of the bent head. The fair hair looked beautiful, alive and springing, and she remembered that at one time all of her daughter had promised to be beautiful. And she could be yet. But whether she changed or remained as she was, the thought of flesh of hers being associated with that low, common individual was unbearable. She said now, 'I'll give you time to think it over.'

She was turning away when Gail muttered from under her breath, 'If . . . if I do it, will you let me do it my own way; you . . . you won't approach Robbie, or let John?'

There was a pause before Esther said 'Very well.'

'When will you see to it? I mean about Dad.' Her head was still bowed.

'As soon as possible.'

'I won't stop seeing Robbie until they've got it in writing.'

'Gail! I've given you my word.' Esther was bristling.

Gail's head was up now and she was staring at her mother. 'That's how it must be. When the solicitor says it's all right, then I'll tell Robbie, not until. Take it or leave it.'

Esther let out a long drawn breath, then went swiftly out of the room.

Staring at the closed door Gail cupped her face in her hands and pressed her cheeks so tightly that her lips pouted. Then, her hands dropping into her lap, she turned to the mirror again and watched her eyes cloud over and her face crumple as if she was about to burst into tears. A few minutes ago the whole situation had seemed marvellous, even funny. Her father was getting what he wanted because she was giving up something that she'd never had, Robbie Dunn's love, but now she had signed that something irrevocably away. Once the divorce proceedings started she wouldn't be able to see Robbie again.

Eight

Robbie lay, his hands behind his head, staring up at the ceiling. It was Sunday morning and Sunday morning as a rule meant a long sound sleep until Janet would shake him by the shoulder, saying, 'Come on, have this cup of tea. Do you know what time it is?' But this morning he had woken around four o'clock and couldn't get off again; it was all the talking last night before they had gone to bed. They were all worried . . . Well, for himself he couldn't say he was worried, not really worried. If that's the way she wanted it, well, there wasn't much he could do about it, was there? If her dad couldn't get her to come out here then he hadn't much chance, had he? But why had it happened all of a sudden like that? Was it because the social gap had just struck her? No! No! It wasn't that. Then what? Aw, why was he bothering his head? What did it matter? Now let him get this straight and not kid himself any more. In his own way he was as much concerned about her change of attitude as the other two, although he hadn't let on to them. And it wasn't that he had fallen for her, lor no! That would have been something, wouldn't it? The reception she would have given to any advance from him would have knocked his ego so far down that he would be getting his pension by the time he retrieved it. Oh no, he was too cute to let himself in for anything like that. It was just that they seemed to get on well together, pally like. And then she writes that letter to her father, saying that she wouldn't be able to come on a Saturday any more and perhaps she could see him in town sometime. Just like that, cool like as if she owed them nothing. But don't let her forget it, she did owe them something; she, in a way, owed them her father, for where would he be now if they hadn't stood by him? . . . Aye, that was a question he'd like to ask Miss Blenheim.

He moved restlessly in the bed now, turned on his side, brought his knees well up and his head down towards them, and he lay like this for some time before he muttered aloud, 'It's me. It's not Mam, it's me. Let's face it, it's me, because she accepted the fact that her father wanted to marry Mam all right, and when Harry put in for the divorce she was as anxious as any of us to know what her mother would say. It was from that Tuesday night when she came unexpected, she was changed then, acting like she did at first, quiet, offhand; yet on the Saturday she'd been gay like I'd never seen her afore. Then what happened in between? I did nothing . . . Aw no, it couldn't be that.' The thought brought him on to his back. 'Because I caught hold of her?'

He stared upwards again remembering now the feel of her as his arms went around her and her face laughing into his, and he remembered thinking she could still be beautiful at that if she was happy. Her body had felt warm and soft and it trembled a bit, but he had done nothing, not even tightened his hold, he had let her go. Her face had been close enough to his to kiss. Not that he would have dreamt of doing that, but it had been.

When the front door bell rang he jumped as if he had been shot and, resting on his elbow, he stared across the darkened room. When it rang a second time he scrambled out of bed and into his slippers and dressing gown and went out into the passage and across the hall. When he opened the door there stood a policeman, and one that was known to him. Constable Tallow had been on market patrol when he first set up his stall.

It was the constable who spoke first. 'Hello, Robbie,' he said. 'Sorry to get you up at this hour.'

'It's all right, it's all right, but . . . but what's the matter?'

The constable paused for a moment, then said, 'It's your shop. It's been tarred.'

'Tarred?' Robbie's cheeks moved up until they almost closed his eyes. 'Tarred?' he repeated. 'What do you mean, tarred?'

'Well, you know, there was a carnival on yesterday and that's a signal for some of them to go clean mad. They were at it in the town until two o'clock this morning. They get up to all kinds of things. They've stuck a Joey on St Stephen's steeple. Imagine that; one of them must have been a steeplejack . . .'

'But my shop, how tarred? What do you mean tarred?'

'I think you'd better come along.'

'Aye. Yes, I think I'd better,' he said loudly. 'But

come in. Come on in a minute until I get me things on.'
As he closed the door and indicated to the constable
to take a chair Harry came into the hall, asking, 'What
is it? What's the matter? I heard the bell.' Then
he stopped dead as he saw the policeman. 'Something,
something wrong?' His voice, his whole manner apprehensive, for policemen would always have an
intimidating effect on him now.

Robbie, going quickly past him, said, 'Shop's been
tarred. Believe that?'

'What!'

As Robbie disappeared along the passage Harry went
slowly forward and if the policeman was surprised to
see Mr Blenheim apparently living with the Dunns he
gave no sign of it, but he said courteously, 'Good
morning, Mr Blenheim.'

'Good morning,' said Harry. 'What is it, is it bad?'

'Well,' the policeman jerked his head and said very
softly, 'put a tar brush into the hands of somebody who
doesn't like a Jew and you know what to expect.
Though why anyone should have their knife into
him puzzles me; he's well liked, and respected in most
quarters if it's only for the guts he's got.'

'Yes, yes.' Harry nodded absently; then his tone
quickening, he said, 'I'll get dressed and come in
with him.' When he passed Robbie's room the door
was open and Janet was inside and she turned her
face towards him, asking, 'Who would do a thing like
that, Harry?' He didn't answer her but, looking
beyond her to Robbie, he said, 'I'm coming in with
you.'

Robbie made no reply. He was pulling on his coat

555

now, and he said to Janet, 'Don't worry; it mightn't be anything, just those mad hats letting off steam.'

'Mad hats?' she repeated. 'With a tar brush!'

Within ten minutes Robbie drew the car up opposite his shop. He didn't get out immediately but sat looking through the window at what the headlights revealed. The writing started at the beginning of the wall three feet to the side of the window; it crossed the window and finished up on the shop door. The letters were two feet high, and they said 'Dirty little Jew'. The tar had run down the glass in streaks, and it appeared as if the words were crying black tears.

Then he opened the car door and stood on the pavement. Dirty little Jew. It was the word little that focused his attention. This writing was no insult to a race, this was a personal insult to a man, a little Jew. Twice as a boy John Blenheim had called him just that to his face: Dirty little Jew, and every time he had looked at him since his look had said, 'Dirty little Jew.' Ever since he could remember he had hated John Blenheim and the feeling, he knew, was returned with equal force. At times he had wanted to lather into him but, knowing how his mother felt, had checked his fists. The fact that Blenheim had for years been head and shoulders taller than him made no difference. He knew that given the chance, he could knock him out, and by God he would knock him out for this. He turned and looked at Harry and for a moment he hated him as much as he did his son.

There were two policemen on the pavement now. One of them was saying, 'It must have been done between three and four because we had them cleared

556

from round here just after two, and at ten to three I drove past and all was quiet.'

'We can't do much until tomorrow morning when the school opens,' said Constable Tallow now. He paused, then ended, 'This stuff takes some getting off.'

Robbie had not spoken one word. He now moved towards the door, unlocked it and, stepping inside the shop, switched the lights on. He looked round him expecting to find the furniture all defaced but it was just as he had left it last night.

The second policeman, stepping in behind him, asked, 'Everything all right in here?'

When Robbie didn't speak but walked away down the shop the policeman turned to Harry, who was within the door now, and said, 'Enough to make a man mad when all's said and done. It's things like this that starts trouble off; this is how it started in London a few years ago. Some lunatic dabbed one place then others followed. Ten to one they're Nazis or' – his voice dropped – 'somebody's got a grudge against him in the market; you can get on too quickly for some folks.' He looked to where Robbie was standing at the end of the long room, his hand moving slowly back and forwards over the top of a small table. Then looking at Harry again, he said, 'I suppose you'll be around for some time, we'll be back later.'

When Harry joined Robbie he stood looking at his grim face for a moment before he said, 'Don't take this to heart; as the constable said you're highly respected in the town and . . .'

'Huh!' There was a slight pause after the exclamation; then again came the 'Huh!', louder this time, and now Robbie's eyes were hard on Harry as he asked, 'Have you any idea who could have done this? I mean a vestige of an idea, can you think of anybody?'

Harry had to force himself to keep his gaze on the face before him. Youth seemed to have left it; he had to look into the eyes in which he recognised a hate as deep as was in his own son, and it hurt him. He had never connected Robbie Dunn with hate. Hate and John, yes. He had recognised hate in his son at a very early age. Hate of everyone who opposed him. In the early days the hate had taken the form of sulks, but now it had matured and taken a tar brush in its hand. And the reason for this was twofold: he wasn't only tarring a Jew, he was tarring his father who was divorcing his mother to marry a Jewess. Gail's reaction to his connection with Janet was hurtful, and not quite understandable, but his son's attitude was frightening. Yet in a way he had been expecting it. The action had shocked him but not surprised him. What would have surprised him would have been John's acceptance of the situation.

'Well, do you?' Robbie asked again, his voice hard and the question pointed. And when Harry lowered his head and shook it, he once more emitted the telling syllable 'Huh!' and looked at the man who was shortly to become his step-father and whom up to a short while ago he had liked better than any other person in his life, except his mother. But now he wanted to yell at him, 'Well! I'll tell you who it was, it was your son.' But were he to do that, the relationship between the three of them would be severed for good. This was something he must accept, at least for the time being; but let him

558

meet up with Master John Blenheim on the quiet, then by God there would be a settlement.

Dragging his coat off, he said, 'Well, it's no use standing here. Petrol'll be the best thing; there's a can out in the back although I don't think that'll go very far . . .'

And it didn't. It took four cans of petrol and five hours work to clean off the three words. The hardest part was getting it off the brickwork, and during the whole process they hardly exchanged a word. It wasn't until they were cleaning themselves up in the back shop and the outer door opened and Sid came in, that the conversation took on a lively note.

'What's this I'm hearing?' said Sid. 'The shop's been tarred? I had just gone into The Stag when I heard. Bloody lot of mad bastards. What they want to go and do that to you for? You're well liked . . . Well, aren't you?'

Robbie looked at his assistant. Sid was a big individual, honest enough but without an overdose of intelligence, yet in a three-worded statement and a similar worded question he had pointed out the difference between their nationalities. They had both been born in this town, within a stone's throw of each other but it was as if he and his kind were, at best, tolerated: 'You're well liked.' The inference was, he was a tame wolf being singled out of a pack.

Around Bog's End there were Indians and Arabs, West Africans, Jamaicans, Chinese, and Greeks, but their businesses were not stamped with their nationality in tar, perhaps because, except for the Chinese and Greeks, none of the others had businesses. His was

559

not the first shop that had had Jew written across it, and for a different reason from that which motivated John Blenheim. Jealousy was at the bottom of a lot of it, jealousy, because most Jews had the knack of surviving in the business world. They could build on a shilling; some had started on even less. Sid worked for him but whether he was aware of it or not he envied him, and yes, gormless as he was, dared to despise him.

He made himself say evenly, 'It was the carnival spirit, I suppose, an' it's a pity you didn't hear of it two or three hours since, we could have done with a hand.'

A few minutes later, as Robbie was locking up, Sid said, 'What about the night? They might try it on again. Don't you think we should stay on watch, take our turns like?' And Robbie replied, ' I don't think it'll be necessary.' Then glancing over his shoulder at Harry, he asked, 'What do you say?'

For the moment Harry made no reply; the look and the question certainly meant more than they said. He gulped before he answered, 'The carnival's over, they'll have cooled down.'

It was about eleven o'clock on the Monday morning when the three young men entered the shop. One had longish hair, one wore a brown tweed jacket over a purple pullover, the third one was in blue jeans and a windcheater; they could have been three lads from Bog's End, but Robbie knew immediately that these were the Technical wallahs.

'Mr Dunn?' It was the one in the windcheater who spoke. He didn't say 'I want to see Mr Dunn'; he seemed to know whom he was addressing and Robbie said abruptly, 'That's me.'

'We're from the Technical College.'

'Aye.'

The young man hesitated then said, 'We represent the Carnival Committee and I understand that we . . . I mean some member of the College has been blamed for disfiguring your shop window.'

'That's right.'

Again the young man hesitated, then said, 'Well Sir, I want you to believe that all the fellows who were in the carnival have been up before the Principal and they have sworn they had no hand in what was done; in fact they are incensed that they are being blamed for it.'

Robbie stared at the young man. He was a good six inches taller than himself. He had called him Mr Dunn, and Sir. He could scarcely remember being called Mr Dunn before, and never, never, had he been addressed as Sir. He liked this fellow in the wind-cheater and he wanted to say to him, 'That's all right; I don't blame any of you,' but he did blame one of them and he'd like to bet Mr John Blenheim wasn't among the number who were indignant. What he said was, 'Well, there's one thing for sure, it didn't get there by itself.'

The young men stared at him, they were obviously embarrassed; even their spokesman didn't know what to say next until Robbie said, 'Well, anyway, I appreciate you comin' along,' then one of the boys who hadn't yet spoken said, 'Well, we felt obliged to as it was a stigma on us an' all.'

Stigma. They didn't like having a stigma put on

561

them. It was a stigma on us an' all. The word Jew was a stigma.

Perhaps it was the look on Robbie's face that told the spokesman that his companion had made an unfortunate remark for he said quickly, 'I'm . . . I'm glad you understand, Sir; I hope you won't have any more trouble.'

Robbie nodded to this and the three of them, speaking almost simultaneously, said, 'Good-bye, Sir.'

Again he nodded. Then he watched them go out of the shop. He watched them until they were out of sight across the road and he told himself not to let that remark turn the chip on his shoulder into a plank. The fellow hadn't meant it like that; they were decent blokes else they wouldn't have come along and apologised.

Yet this moderate attitude did nothing to lessen the overall feeling of rage that was seething in him. He felt burnt up inside. If he could have talked to his mother about the matter it might have helped but if she even thought it was Harry's son who had done this to him she would immediately lay the cause at her own door. But there remained one person he could talk to; he could go to Miss Blenheim and give her a message for her bloody brother, a warning message. Yes, that's what he would do, and now. He'd catch her coming out at lunch time; it wasn't likely that the family watchdogs would pick her up to take her to lunch . . .

It was just on twelve when he stopped the car some little distance from the shop and prepared himself to wait until one o'clock if need be; but it was only two minutes later when he saw Gail come out of the shop and walk rapidly down the street.

Abruptly he started the car and drove along the kerb, but lost sight of her when he had to round a parked car, and when she came in view again she was standing on the corner waiting to cross. In a second he had brought the car alongside the kerb and looking out of the window, he called, 'Gail! Hi there, Gail! Get in.'

She had been about to step into the road and when she heard his voice and turned and saw him she swayed a moment, then stepped back on to the pavement. Her head was shaking as she said, 'No, no.'

'Get in, I tell you. If you don't I'll follow you. I'm holding up the traffic, get in.'

'I can't . . . no.'

He was leaning sidewards, one hand on the handle of the part open door, and he let it swing wide as he said, 'Do as I tell you, get in.'

He watched her look swiftly along the street from where was coming the impatient tooting of horns. He was on the corner of a narrow road at an angle that would make it a danger for anyone to pass him. He bawled now, 'I'm stayin' until you get in.'

When with a flounce of her body she entered the car he started up almost before she had closed the door and, rounding the corner, he shot up the street, crossed an intersecting road, then made for the quiet outskirts of Jesmond.

It was she who spoke first. 'Stop the car, I want to get out,' she said.

'You'll get out when I say what I've come to say.' He kept his eyes on the road ahead while he spoke. 'What you frightened of? Catching something? Leprosy, say?'

'Robbie!' Her voice was pleading now. 'Don't go any

563

further, please. I've got to be back in half-an-hour, Miss Frazer's got an appointment.'

'Poor soul. Then I'm afraid she'll have to break it.'

'Robbie, please, please stop.'

'I'll stop when I'm good and ready and not afore. You can wave your hand out of the window; there's the polis ahead. He'd have the squad car after me in no time. Go on and try it.'

'Don't be silly.' Her voice was no longer pleading, but harsh.

With a screeching of brakes and an abruptness that brought her brow almost in contact with the windscreen, the car came to a halt.

Her head was still bobbing when she said angrily, 'What are you trying to do, kill us?'

'I shouldn't be a bit surprised.'

'You're mad.'

'Aye, I am.' His face was thrust towards her now. 'But not in the way you mean.'

She turned her head away from him and, drooping it slightly, she said, 'Look, I explained all I can explain.'

'Oh, that's another matter altogether.' His voice was airy now. 'We'll come to that later. I'm not mad about you deciding not to condescend to visit us any more; we should I suppose, have been grateful for your previous visits.'

She was staring at him now and he, ignoring her distressed look, went on, 'Your retaliation to the fact that your father was going to marry me mother took the form of cutting us off so to speak. But your brother's retaliation took a different form altogether. It's that I want to talk about.'

564

'What!' Her head was poked forward. 'What do you mean? Which . . . ?'

'Oh, you needn't say which one. Terry's no sneak in the night; Terry wouldn't hide behind a carnival to do his dirty work, then let other folk get the blame for it. No, you know which brother I'm referring to and it's ten to one you know what he was up to. You don't tar somebody's shop in a hurry without getting messed up, unless you wore overalls, and then you'd have to put them somewhere . . .'

'Robbie.' His name was just a whisper now and she repeated it again, slightly louder, trying to get him to stop talking. 'Robbie, what . . . what are you saying?'

'Haven't you been listening?'

'You're inferring that John tarred your shop?'

'I'm not inferring any such thing, I'm damn well tellin' you straight out. He left a message on it in tar, the letters two foot high, and they said "DIRTY LITTLE JEW".'

Her hand moved slowly up to her cheek and her fingers cupped her ears as if in pain.

It seemed a long time before she said weakly, 'No! He wouldn't.'

'Wouldn't he? Well he did.'

'But . . . but have you proof?'

'Yes, yes, I've proof.'

'How?'

He paused before he said 'The word "LITTLE". DIRTY LITTLE JEW. Some other bloke would have just put DIRTY JEW, but your dear brother had used that term on me afore.'

Her fingers were tapping nervously at her lips now

565

and she looked away from him and down the road as she said, 'I can't believe he would go to those lengths.'

'No?' His voice was high. 'But you do believe that he would be capable of doing somethin', don't you?'

She turned to him again and now she said quietly, 'Yes.'

'Oh, well, that's somethin'.'

They stared at each other in silence for a full minute and then Robbie, suddenly turning from her, said, 'Blasted bloody swine, that's what he is, a cowardly blasted swine; getting at me because he can't get at his father or me mother.' And rounding on her again he said, 'I want you to go back and tell him that I know it was him an' that if he makes just one more move in my direction in any way I'll have the polis on him so quickly he won't know what's happened till he's hanging on to his cell bars. You tell him that from me.'

Again they were staring at each other in silence; and then, straining his neck out of his collar, he said, 'Well now, I've had me say and you're free to go. I'll drive you back if you like or you can get off here, it's all the same to me.'

When he saw her lips tremble he thought, Oh, my God. Let me get out of this. 'Well, what's it to be?' His tone was thick and rasping, even ugly. 'You getting out or am I to have the pleasure of your company for another few minutes?'

'Robbie.' Her eyes were lowered, focusing on a point on the car floor between their knees. 'I . . . I just want to tell you that I'm not against Dad and Janet getting married, I'm glad. I said that in the first place and I meant it. I want them to be happy, but . . . but' – she swung her head and her lips opened and closed as if they were trying to find words. And then she ended rapidly, 'It's my mother; she's . . . she's very lonely. She's . . . she's cut herself off, she has no-one, she has no friends; if . . . if I were to continue visiting Dad at your house under the present circumstances it would upset her. She's . . . she's so alone . . . you understand?'

He was looking straight into her eyes now. Yes, he understood; he had known all along it was her mother.

'It isn't that I don't want to come, Robbie.'

He continued to stare at her. Then, his voice almost a whisper, now he said, 'It's all right, don't upset yourself. I'm . . . I'm glad you told me.'

But when she turned quickly from him and opened the door he said flatly, 'You're getting out then?'

'Yes.' She was speaking from the pavement now. 'I can get a bus.'

'Please yourself.' His voice, chin and whole manner were cocky again.

'I'm . . . I'm very sorry about the shop, Robbie, really I am.'

'Oh, don't let that trouble you. A mere detail that; just a mere detail.' His heavy sarcasm made her close her eyes; then straightening up, she said, 'Good-bye, Robbie.' Her voice was cool now.

'Good-bye to you, Miss Blenheim.' He inclined his head deeply towards her, then turned quickly to the wheel with the intention of starting up the car. But he didn't start it up; instead he watched her hurrying along the street towards a bus stop. He no longer felt anger concerning the defacing of his shop; what filled him now was a deep pain which was rising from its birthplace of resentment, bred in its turn from trials and purgatories of which he had no personal knowledge. Slowly he brought his face round to the car mirror and gazed at himself, and on a deep oath, he said, 'Blast her! With you one minute – "It isn't that I don't want to come, Robbie"' – he mimicked her voice – 'an' spitting on you the next. It isn't as if her mother or their John would see her around this quarter, an' at this time of the day. She doesn't want to be seen with me; it's as plain as that. She never did. The mother's a good excuse. Who does she think she is anyway? Workin' in a crummy bookshop and her dad done . . .' He pulled himself up. 'Aw, to hell!' He started the car and drove away, passing her at the bus stop without a flick of an eye towards her. This was the end of him worrying about her; she could rot for all he cared.

III

THE OUTCOME

One

The dawn was just breaking as Harry stepped quietly out of the back door and, crossing the courtyard, went slowly up the hill. When he reached the top he turned and looked back at the house. It was standing with its feet in mist giving it an ethereal appearance and for the first time he saw it, as Robbie had always seen it, as something beautiful. It was a year since he had first started on it. There was a lot still to be done but what he had accomplished he could be proud of; he had in a way served his time on the house. As he stood looking down on it he had a strong wish that it was his, that he owned it; but he would never own it, it was Robbie's house. Yet it was to be his home for the remainder of his life, his and Janet's. That was agreed. And today was his wedding day . . . and he was sad.

From the moment he had entered his room last night his mind had been filled with thoughts of one person, and that person wasn't Janet but Esther, and how she had looked on that first wedding day over twenty years ago. He had risen early on that morning, too; too early to find the church open, and it was the church he had wanted to go into then. But he had walked to the river and sat on the bank and thought how lucky he was, and how he would love Esther until the day he died.

Last night he had said to Janet, 'This is the last parting,' and as she had pressed her lips to his he had felt a deep sense of happiness at the thought that life ahead would revolve about her. But once alone, there had come over him a strange feeling; it was as if Esther was in the room telling him that it was wrong to take another wife when the first one was still alive. And he had paced up and down thinking, She's right, it is. And the feeling had persisted and grown. And now as he watched the first rays of the sun breaking up the mist, he said to himself, 'Don't be a blasted fool; if she had wanted you you would have run back; there's nobody to blame for the present situation but herself . . . at least' – he qualified this thought – 'for the continued separation and the divorce.' Doubtless she had suffered. Of this he had been left in no doubt when Gail had said, 'I'm not coming to the house, it's hurting Mother. And now the divorce is going through.' And then she added quickly, 'I'm not blaming you. Don't think that. I want you to marry Janet, but the fact remains that Mother's upset.'

Knowing his wife, he felt sure she was in some way putting a screw on Gail, and as time went on he had become more convinced of this, for he sensed his daughter's hidden unhappiness.

Janet, however, said that she could see Esther's point of view and if she was in the same boat and Robbie went visiting the other woman, she'd be torn in shreds.

He now walked to the other side of the hill and leaned against the rock. The mist on this side was covering the valley in great white waves; it was going to be another fine day; it had been beautiful for the last fortnight. Janet had said yesterday that she hoped it kept fine, yet she didn't mind if it poured. She had looked excited and young. It was odd but she seemed to have got younger over the past six months. She was happy as he had never seen her happy; it was good to know that he could do that for someone, make them happy. The thought came at this moment that there were other women he could have made happy. Betty Ray for instance. God! Betty Ray. He was back to the bedroom. He was where he was at this minute because of that half-hour madness – how did other fellows get by for years on the same racket. He didn't know. He only knew that he himself was the type that could never get away with anything. It happened with all men like him, fundamentally nice blokes. Three women had wanted him. Not much of a record perhaps, yet he had been branded a Casanova. It was laughable, if you could laugh at it.

Thinking of happiness, what about himself? Was he happy? No! But he could be. Yes, yes he knew he could be happy with Janet. And not just in placid acceptance, for she aroused in him a feeling that he thought had died for want of use. It was the transition from Janet Dunn to Mrs Blenheim that seemed to be frightening him at the moment. If only it was this time tomorrow, and it was over, then he'd feel different; Esther would be irrevocably in the past . . . and John? Ever since the tarring episode he had gone in fear of his son's further

573

reactions, and the nearer the day came the deeper his fear had grown.

He started visibly when he saw Janet come out of the mist. She didn't speak until she was close to him, and then she said, 'I knew you'd come up here this morning. I wonder you didn't come out in the middle of the night. You haven't been to sleep, have you?'

He didn't answer her but took her hand and made to draw her close to him, but she resisted. Yet still leaving her hand in his, she said, 'You're not the only one who's been thinking, Harry.'

'The time for thinking is past, Janet.' He moved his head slowly. 'It's deeds that are required now.'

'Not necessarily.' Her dark eyes were looking into his. 'Harry, listen to me, and I mean every word I say . . . You don't have to marry me; I'm not demanding the final sacrifice. No! NO!' She held up her free hand. 'Listen. Listen. I'll be quite content to live with you. I'll be proud to live with you. I said as much on this very spot some months ago but you didn't take me at my word. Well now, I repeat the offer, and I repeat it because I know you want me, whether it's as a wife or a mistress doesn't matter. In either case there's one thing I'm sure of: this is going to be our wedding day, Harry Blenheim.'

'Oh, Janet. Janet.' He was holding her tightly. This is what he wanted, what he needed, firm reassurance. When he kissed her it was hard and long and loving. Then with her face cupped in his hands he said softly, 'Roll on eleven o'clock.'

★   ★   ★

They had a table booked at the Crown Hotel and as the head waiter ushered them to it he guessed that it was a wedding party, and he hadn't to exert his powers of perception to gauge that it wasn't two of the three young people present who had been married, but the two older ones, for apart from the feeling that seemed to pervade the group was the fact that the girl was dressed very ordinarily, and one of the two young men looked as if he was rigged out for a tour on his bike.

And the waiter was exactly right in this, for Terry was dressed as he was most Saturday mornings since he had joined the motor-cycling club, and Gail was wearing the same clothes as those she had worn yesterday for the shop.

No mention had been made at home about her father remarrying, but she knew that the thought was in the forefront of her mother's mind all the time. Yet this past week it hadn't been her mother's attitude that had worried her, but John's. He had been in one of his sulks again. She called his mood sulking for want of a more correct definition of his withdrawal. Right up to this morning she felt that he might do something to prevent his father marrying Janet. She didn't ask herself how he knew it was the day; she only knew that both he and her mother were aware of it. Their knowledge emanated from them like a dark fog and filled the atmosphere of the house.

But now it was done. Her father had married Janet, and he looked happy; he looked as if he had been injected with new life, and all because of a dull and emotionless ceremony in a dusty office. Marriage was odd when you came to think of it. A few words read out of a book, a couple of questions, and the signing of a name and that tied you to a man for ever; or until such time as you wanted to get free, and then you sinned. Oh, she didn't want to think about it. Marrying, unmarrying, she hated it all.

She was grateful to Terry for having come, for he was making them laugh and that took some of the embarrassment away. Terry was a smoother of situations. He was telling them about his pal at the Art School in Newcastle. 'It's a fact,' he was saying, 'everything happens to Jackie's mother. He has me rolling. But this is honest, and it happened because she's stone deaf. You know the Marsden line down Shields way. Well, whether you do or you don't, it's a little railway, not passenger, just for goods, and the engine driver sees this woman crossing the line and he pulls his blower like mad. Honk! honk! honk! honk!' He demonstrated. 'But she didn't seem to hear him and he couldn't pull up in time, and so he hit her side on and she was dragged twenty yards and broke about ten bones. Yes, it's true, honest it is. Jackie was in the hospital sitting by her bedside when she came round and she ups and yells. She always yells with being deaf; you should hear him imitate her. Mind, he likes her, oh he likes her a lot, but he gets a lot of fun out of her. Anyway, there she was covered in bandages and she says, "That you, our Jackie?" and he says, "Aye, Mam, it's me." "Where am I?" she says. "In hospital, Mam," he says. "Eeh!" she yells, "I feel I've been kicked doon the street. Eeh lad, have I had a stroke?" "No, Mam," he says; "you were knocked down by a train." "Oh, was that it?" she yells. "Well, thank God I didn't have a stroke."'

They were trying in various ways to suppress their loud laughter. Janet had her hand held tightly across her mouth; Harry had his teeth clamped on to his bottom lip; Gail had her head down, and Robbie was bending over sideways hugging himself. It was as he straightened up that Gail raised her head, and as he looked into her face he thought, It's nearly six months since I saw her. She's changed. It's right after all, she's going to blossom out. She looks bonny the day, sort of sad, yet bonny.

And Gail, looking into the round black eyes, thought, It's a new suit he's got on. Grey suits him. He looks nice. But when his gaze remained hard on her she blinked and turned her eyes from him and on to Janet. Janet looked nice too, even pretty. No, Janet couldn't look pretty, she looked handsome. Her father was looking at her as if he were proud of her. Up to an hour ago her father had still been hers, solely hers because her mother had rejected him, but not any more for now he had Janet. The aloneness this thought engendered swamped her and she knew a moment of horror when she realised she was about to cry. But Terry was looking at her and saying, 'Remember, Gail? Remember the time when I told you about Jackie being gone on that girl and taking her home to Bog's End, remember?'

Gail blinked rapidly and smiled and said, 'Yes, yes. Tell them; that was funny too.'

Their attention was again focused on Terry, and he rose to the occasion and told them the tale of the

577

refined shy girl meeting up with Jackie's eleven brothers and sisters in a small sitting-room, the mother yelling her head off first at one and then the other, and Jackie's three married brothers scaring the daylights out of the girl by telling her what Jackie expected out of marriage, one small item being that he hoped to produce a larger family than his father.

There was more laughter at this, and altogether the wedding lunch could be said to have been a great success. And it was almost quarter to two when they left the hotel and went towards the car and the van parked on the driveway. But there, embarrassment seemed to envelop them, until Janet, offering her hand to Gail, said softly. 'Thanks, Gail; thank you for coming. I'll . . . I'll never forget it.'

For a moment Gail was about to make the polite reply, 'Oh, that's all right, Janet, I wanted to come,' but instead impulsively she put her arms around Janet and kissed her, and the gesture set a seal on the day. It took a weight from Janet's heart and a weight from Harry's mind. He held his daughter tightly for a moment before looking into her face and saying, 'Remember what I said years ago? Well, it still holds. My love for you is a thing apart. Janet understands this.'

The words were like warm oil on a sore. It was more difficult now to withhold the tears so she merely nodded, then turned away.

Janet and Robbie did not embrace, they just looked at each other, and he jerked his head at her, saying, 'Well, I suppose I'll be seeing you the morrow night. Why the devil you can't make it a week is past me. All right, all right' – he wagged his hand at her – 'I know.

We've been through it and I'm not capable of lookin' after meself yet. Have it your way. Get in.' He pushed her unceremoniously into the car, and there was more laughter.

But before Harry took his seat he stood in front of Terry, and he said simply, 'Thank you, son.' And Terry, no longer laughing and lost for words now, flushed red to his ears.

There was no verbal exchange between Robbie and Harry, but they looked at each other and their glance, full of understanding, cemented the partnership that was already between them.

When Harry took his seat behind the wheel, not one of them could have guessed his thoughts, for behind his smiling face he was feeling weak with relief. All during the short ceremony, even during the lunch, he had expected something to happen. What, he didn't really know, but something instigated by John. But now it was over. If he had intended doing anything he would have done it before this. He started up the car, then he and Janet called their final good-byes.

The three of them waved the car along the drive and out of sight; then Robbie, stretching his neck out of his collar and buttoning his coat, said briskly, 'Well, that's that.' Then looking directly at Terry, he added jocularly, 'The van's at your disposal, me Lord; I can drop you where you left your bike, right?'

'Right!' said Terry, laughing again. 'Fine.' Then he turned to Gail, and she said, 'I've got some shopping to do, I'll get the bus.'

At this Robbie almost groaned aloud. God Almighty! she was still going to keep it up. After a lunch like they'd

579

had, all jolly good pals together, she was going back into her shell. Well then, let her. He hadn't pined because he hadn't seen her for months. He had been about to make some crack about her being his step-sister. God, it was just as well he hadn't, she would have swooned. Yet she had been all right with his mother, putting her arms around her and kissing her. It all went to prove what he had known all along: it wasn't his mother marrying her dad that had brought on the ice age, it was him. She couldn't stand him. Well, to hell with her! The feeling was reciprocated. Aye, and with interest.

'OK, let's get going,' he jerked his head at Terry as he walked away adding, 'the party's over. I've got a business to attend to.'

Terry watched him go towards the van, then in an undertone to Gail, he muttered quickly, 'Why can't you come? He can drop you off before you can get anywhere near home.'

'And have our John see us?' Her tone was equally low and when after a moment he nodded at her, she said, 'Go on, don't keep him waiting.'

Terry now made his way to the van and took his seat beside Robbie and within seconds they were flashing down the drive, passing Gail as if she was a stranger.

It was half-past two when Robbie returned to the shop. He felt in a vile mood, ready to go for the first one that crossed him, but he had to warn himself not to go for Sid because Sid had done him a favour in working through his dinner-hour, and he was going to ask a further favour of him. He wanted him to stay on until six o'clock, or to such time when he returned from the house. There were a number of pieces he wanted to take out to finish off the long room, besides which he had an appointment to view some pieces at a private house around three-thirty.

He felt mad at himself for feeling mad. He shouldn't be feeling like this, he told himself, not with Monday before him. So much could happen on Monday; it could be the beginning of big things, real big things.

Some weeks ago an American had come to the shop and bought three pieces and paid well for them. They had got talking and the American seemed to take to him; anyway, he had put some business in his way. He said he was looking for an eighteenth-century lowboy and one or two Louis XVI pieces, a secretaire in particular, and a Louis XV commode. Did Mr Dunn think it possible he could come by them? Robbie didn't think it was possible not at short notice anyway, but he intended to have a damn good try.

He hadn't taken the man out to the house on that occasion, although he could have done because he had some attractive pieces there already, but his alert mind was, as usual, giving him the completed picture and he could see these French pieces lining the walls of the long room and the overall impression it would have on the American. Ten to one he wouldn't take the pieces he was after, but the lot.

He had, after much searching, managed to get hold of all the pieces except the commode, but he'd had to pay through the nose for them. Yet what he lost on the roundabouts he'd gain on the swings on this deal, he told himself, or his name wasn't Robbie Dunn.

The visit to the private house proved disappointing

and he came out thinking, They've got a nerve; I wouldn't put that stuff in the market. So his frame of mind hadn't lightened when he entered the lane and first smelt the smell of burning. He looked down towards the floor and sniffed. Perhaps it was his exhaust. He had reached the mine before he realised the smell of burning wasn't coming from inside the van but from outside. He put his head towards the open window and sniffed again. It was a strong smell now lying heavy on the air. He looked towards the old mine buildings at the back of the wheelhouse. Likely somebody was up to something in there. Kids, he'd bet. Yet there was no smoke to be seen.

He didn't see the smoke until he rounded the pithead. And there it was before him, spiralling up into the sky and spreading along the horizon, and filling the world, his world. He hadn't been conscious of bringing the car to a stop; he wasn't conscious of his hands gripping the wheel while his chest was pressed against it. One minute the car and he were still, the next minute they both seemed to be flying through the air.

When he tumbled out of the car in front of the house he became still again; not only his body now but his mind seemed incapable of movement. No thought penetrated the stupor as he gazed up at the flames licking out of the upper window; the floor of the house was a complete red glow that hissed and crackled. He didn't see the man in the tee-shirt and the two policemen come towards him. When the constable said, 'I'm sorry about this, Mr Dunn,' he turned a slow gaze towards him and his mind began to move again, but not around the enormity of

582

the situation. What he thought was, He's one of the fellows that was on patrol the night the shop was done; he's a Jonah.

'The Fire Brigade should be here any minute but I'm afraid it's a bit late. You see, we knew nothing about it until this' – he nodded to the man in the tee-shirt – 'this gentleman phoned in.'

'Well, it wasn't me that phoned, it was me son, Tony.' The man was gesticulating now. 'He must have run a mile and a half along the road to the phone. And to think I saw the bloke do it. But it didn't dawn on me at the time. You see, Mister.' He was bending his head down from his six-foot-four to Robbie's level. 'You see, Mister, I'm from Wallsend and it just happened I had the feeling that I wanted to show me lad where I used to fish when I was a nipper, in the burn yon side of the sugar lump.' He nodded towards the hill. 'This house used to be empty in those days. We used to run in and out of it, build fires in that room there. Not as big as this one though.' He stopped on an embarrassed 'Huh!' then went on, 'Well, as we was passin' on our way down the burn I stopped an' had a look. There seemed nobody about an' I was interested like, so we climbed on the wall round there just near the stables. I wasn't goin' to come over, just have a look, as I said. An' then, as I told the polis here, up comes this car. Not right up; it stops along the road there' – he pointed back – 'an' this fellow comes carrying a can, a petrol can. He passed us within two arms' length. Me and Tony saw him plain as I'm seein' you, but you see at that time I thought he was the boss, the owner like. When he disappeared round yon side of the house we scarpered

583

along by the wall, but as we was passin' the gate there, or the place where the gate was, I saw him opening the windows, so naturally I took him to be the owner. Well . . . we went on to the burn but there wasn't any fish, not like there used to be – the chemicals have poisoned the pool down there – an' so we came back, 'cos I had a fancy to sit on top of the hill, there and eat me bait like I did as a nipper, as I said. An' then when we rounded the old mine we saw the smoke, an' like lightning I put two and two together. That fellow was carryin' a petrol tin, I said to our Tony. God, did we run! But when we got here all the bottom was ablaze and even if I could have found the stopcock and a hose I couldn't have done anything, so I sent Tony flyin' for the polis. But, Mister, I'll pick that fellow from out of a million for you.'

Robbie still hadn't moved. He didn't move even when the fire engine came jangling into the yard. When someone shouted, 'Where's the stopcock?' he just pointed.

The man in the tee-shirt was speaking again, he said, 'I thought I'd be able to save some bits. I went round the back, but that was worse than the front, everything was burning like matchwood. He must have set half-a-dozen places goin' at once. He knew what he was doin' leaving the windows open.'

They all began to cough as a cloud of smoke enveloped them, and the policeman, taking Robbie by the arm, said, 'Come over here, Sir.'

It was the contact of the hand on his arm that seemed to break through the shock and return him to life, for he startled both the policeman and the man by racing

584

away from them and round to the back of the house, and there, dragging a coil of hose from a shed, he dashed with it to a tap on the side of the stable wall and, having attached the nozzle to it with hands that shook as if they had palsy, he ran with the end of the hose through the smoke towards his bedroom window.

Just that morning he had left three paintings stacked against the wall in there. He had learned a bit about paintings during the past three years, and about one of these paintings he had a feeling. He had picked them up from among the contents of an attic he had bought and the feeling told him he might have a find in the picture that showed the face of the Madonna and Child under the dirt and grime of years. On the back of the picture was a torn label with a few words discernible, indicating that it had at one time been hung in a gallery. Even when one of the firemen, coming up to him, shouted, 'I don't think you can do much there, Sir,' he still kept the hose directed through the window.

Coughing and choking and almost overcome by the smoke, he staggered back across the yard and leaned against the wall and there standing sightless for a moment, he cried from deep within him, 'Oh, God! Let me die. Let me die.'

'Come away, Sir; there's nothing you can do.' When the man went to help him he shrugged him off and picked his way over the tangle of pipes, through a patch of hissing steam and to the front of the house again, where the policeman met him, saying, 'This gentleman's given me a full description of the man. Do you know anyone like this?' He looked at his notebook. 'About six foot tall, fair. Very fair, you said?' He looked towards the man again, and the man nodded and said, 'Yes, unusually fair, sort of silvery like.'

'About twenty to twenty-three years old,' went on the policeman. 'His clothes I suppose wouldn't be of much help, but he was wearing a conventional suit and collar and tie. That's so, isn't it?'

'Aye,' said the man. 'He was dressed as if he was going into the town, Newcastle or some such place. That's why I thought he was the owner like.'

Tall, six-foot, fair, silvery like, twenty to twenty-three. He didn't need any description, he knew. He had known since he had smelt the smoke. Like a dam breaking, the rage swept through him, sundering the remaining stupor and the shock into fragments.

Once again he startled the policeman and the man by running but now towards the van. Once inside he threw the gear into reverse but his backward move towards the gate was immediately impeded by the rear end of the fire engine. The policeman was shouting to him. 'Where can we contact you, Sir?'

'What?'

'I said, where can we get in touch with you?'

'I'll be back shortly. Yes' – he nodded to him – 'I'll be back shortly.'

'Very good, Sir.' The policeman continued to look at him, then he beckoned him forward and indicating to him to turn his wheel hard down right. This done, the road clear, the car shot backwards and within seconds it was bounding over the road towards the mine, past it, then along the lane and on to the main road.

During the journey to Holt Avenue Robbie wasn't

conscious of forming any plan as to his actions once having arrived there, yet when he drove the car to a grinding halt outside the gate he didn't make for the front door, but ran along the road and entered by the gate marked 'Tradesmen'. The lonicera-hedged path led to the square of cement outside the kitchen door and it wasn't until he had his hand actually on the knob of the door that he paused. Lifting his hand gently off it again he sidled towards the window and looked into the kitchen. It was empty. They'd be at a meal. The dining-room window looked on to the side of the house to his right, but he didn't make for it. Instead, he went back to the kitchen door and, slowly opening it, he stepped inside and stood taut as he looked about him. Everything was neat, clean and prim – a portrait of Esther Blenheim. He wanted to see Esther Blenheim. Oh yes, he wanted to see Esther Blenheim. But after he had seen her son. And he wanted to see her son now when he was still feeling like this, mad, crazy, wanting to kill. This feeling, once it had subsided, would never return. Never, he knew, as long as he lived would anything happen to make him feel like this again, for every fibre of his being demanded that he should get his fingers into the flesh of John Blenheim and tear that flesh, rend it, scar it, leave it so that the six-foot silvery blond bastard would not be recognisable, even to his mother.

Swiftly and quietly he crossed the kitchen, and as he entered the hall the thought came to him for the first time, What if he isn't in? Well then, he would wait until he came in, and neither Esther Blenheim nor a hundred like her would stop him.

The dining-room door lay along the passage to the right of him and, still on tiptoe, he was making for it when the sitting-room door opened and he froze to the spot and looked across at Gail who was now standing staring at him as if at an apparition. Before she spoke his name she glanced apprehensively to the side of her and up the stairs, and then she whispered, 'Robbie!'

It was at this moment that a door banged overhead and now they both looked towards the stairs, to the head of it and to John Blenheim, who had come to a stop on the first step, one hand gripping the banister, the other flat against the wall. And there he stood for a space that seemed timeless.

'Well, aren't you coming down? I'm waiting for you.'

Before her brother could make any reply, Gail cried, 'What is it? What is it?'

Robbie didn't look at her but he answered her. 'I'll tell you what it is,' he said in a slow, deliberate, frightening tone. 'Your brother's burned me house down, right to the ground, and everything in it.'

'No! No!' The two words were like a thin scream, and now Gail was at the bottom of the stairs staring up at her brother, shouting, 'You didn't, John! You didn't!'

Again Robbie answered her. 'He did.'

'He's mad.' John Blenheim's voice was cold, incisive, the tone scornful. 'Always has been. He's potty.'

Gail now turned and looked at Robbie, and, her voice appealing, she said, 'He couldn't, Robbie, he couldn't. Not that, not your house.'

Robbie's eyes hadn't flinched a fraction from the tall

588

figure poised above him, nor were his lids blinking. His stare fixed and fanatical never left the face that was almost as pale as the hair above it.

When Gail stood in front of him, saying pleadingly, 'He didn't, you heard him, Robbie. He wouldn't. Not that,' he thrust her roughly away with his outstretched arm and she landed up against the wall to the side of the drawing-room door, and there she stood with both hands stretched across her mouth and watched her brother move slowly down the staircase.

When John Blenheim reached the last step he paused and from this added vantage point he looked down on to the dark, hate-filled countenance, and he spat at it, 'Get out of here!'

The answer came in a spring that brought him from the stair and whirling into the middle of the hall. For a matter of seconds they faced each other like two judo combatants. Then they were locked together, struggling, tearing, clawing.

As if throwing off a small clinging animal, John Blenheim now tossed Robbie against the main balustrade of the stairs, and there he lay in a huddled heap until like a cobra uncoiling, he slowly brought himself to his feet, and again he sprang. It wasn't the action of a man, it was more like some primitive beast, and it brought another high-pitched scream from Gail.

Robbie's hands this time made straight for John Blenheim's throat and by the sheer frenzy of his effort they found their target, and when he felt the flesh beneath his fingers he hung like a limpet to a rock, and although John Blenheim swayed and thrashed and grappled with the hands he couldn't dislodge them. The next moment they were both on the floor, rolling and tossing, Robbie on top one second, John Blenheim the next. Both their faces were now covered in blood, but whereas a few moments before John Blenheim had been using his rugby tactics, now with the pressure tightening on his gullet, they were becoming ineffectual.

'Robbie! Robbie! Oh Robbie, for God's sake leave go. Leave go of him!' Gail tried pulling him off by his collar, then by tearing at both his hands with hers, but when she couldn't unloosen his grasp she beat at him with her fists, yelling all the time, 'Robbie! Robbie! Do you hear me? Do you hear? Please! please!'

It was this scene that met Esther Blenheim as she came through the front door and heard her daughter scream at her, 'Help me. Help me get him off.'

Now it was as if another wild beast had joined the fray for Esther Blenheim tore not only at Robbie's hands but at his face, and when at last her son was free she fell on her knees beside him, crying, 'John! John!' When he didn't speak she took him by the shoulders and lifted his limp head upwards and shook him, all the time, crying, 'John! John!' as his chest swelled and he drew in a deep intake of breath she almost dropped him back on the floor with relief. Then, cradling him she looked across at the madman her daughter was supporting and she cried, 'You insane beast. Get out of here.' And when Robbie made no move but continued to lean against Gail's supporting shoulder, she screamed in a voice that rang through the house,

'You filthy, murdering little beast! Get out! Do you hear? Get out!'

It did not strike Esther Blenheim at the moment that her son was not only head and shoulders taller than his attacker but that he could also give him breadth all round. When she saw that Robbie Dunn neither moved nor made answer she yelled at Gail, 'Get away from him. Do you hear me, girl? Get away from him.'

Shivering from head to foot, Gail stared at her mother holding John in her arms. It was like the picture of Christ taken down from the Cross; but John wasn't Christ and her mother wasn't Mary. And so she yelled back at her, 'You know what he's done, our John? He's burned Robbie's house down. Do you hear me? He's burned Robbie's house down!'

Esther Blenheim now looked at her son, who was pulling himself from his knees to his feet, and her lips moved, but no sound came from them. And Gail was yelling at her again. 'You could have stopped him, you could, you could. You knew he was up to something. All week he hasn't spoken. You knew what that meant, you knew he was up to something.'

Esther Blenheim now rose from the floor and, following her son who was shambling towards the drawing-room, she touched his arm as she said, 'Did you? Did you do this?'

Looking straight back into her face he said, 'No, of course I didn't. He's mad, insane. I'll have him for this.'

'He's a liar, a dirty, stinking liar!' They both turned and watched Robbie stumble forward. They watched him wipe the blood from his mouth before saying, 'He was seen by two people, they've given the police his description, but I wanted to deal with him in me own fashion afore they got their hands on him.'

Now Esther Blenheim was cupping her face with both her hands, and her voice, without strength now, muttered, 'No, no! You're mistaken. You're mistaken.'

'I'm not mistaken. Six foot, the men said, blond, silver blond, an' going into the house, my house, carrying a can of petrol. The man said he's only waiting to recognise him. No, Mrs Blenheim, there's no mistake.'

John Blenheim was now in the drawing-room, and Esther, following him, cried, 'John! Look at me. Do you hear? Look at me.' And when he turned towards her she demanded, 'Did you do this, this thing?' And when he said slowly and bitterly, 'Yes, I did it, and I'd do it again,' she closed her eyes and bowed her head and held her hands over her ears as if to shut out his voice. After a moment she turned towards Robbie, who was still standing in the hall, and she said to him, 'What are you going to do?'

'What do you think, Mrs Blenheim, eh? What do you think? I'm going to leave it to the polis. I don't know what the sentence is for arson and tarring a shop but I should imagine it'll be more than his father got, an' if there's any justice it will be. An' without your permission, Mrs Blenheim, I'm goin' to use your phone.'

As he stepped towards the side-table Esther Blenheim came through the door. Her hands joined tightly against her breast, she pleaded, 'Robbie! Please,

please, wait. I've . . . I've lost everything and . . .'

'So have I, Mrs Blenheim, so have I. An' not only me home but the best part of me business. That ground floor was full of antiques, specially got for a client who was comin' on Monday. I've lost everything an' all, Mrs Blenheim.'

'But . . . but you will have it all covered with insurance.' She was gulping on each word and he smiled at her, a deadly smile, as he said, 'Practical to the last, Mrs Blenheim, aren't you? Now, aye, you would think a sharp-shooting Jew like me would have the sense to cover the lot. Two thousand cover, that's all they would give me on the building when I took it. Six months ago they gave me four, but last week I put in to raise it to ten. An' that's what it was going to be, ten thousand, but it wasn't signed, so there I stand with four thousand cover, and the furniture in there was worth more than that. An' that's not covered, only when it was in the shop. So there you have it, Mrs Blenheim. And to think, as Gail's just said, you could have stopped that maniac, but you didn't, because somehow you knew that the day your man was marrying me mother, an' you let your retaliation have rip through him. Well, everything's got to be paid for, Mrs Blenheim.'

'I . . . I understand that, nobody better, everything's got to be paid for.' Her voice was bitter, her manner haughty again, and now she said, 'Give me a little time, please, time to think.'

Robbie's hand was on the phone.

'I'll . . . I'll make up the difference, at least my father will. You won't be out of pocket, only please, I beg of you, don't take this any further.'

'What! You're jokin'. Let him get off with this? Leave him free to do me down again? Oh no.'

'Robbie!'

He turned and looked at Gail; she was standing against the hall wardrobe as if she was afraid to leave its support. Her hands were pressed flat against the wood and she muttered, 'Don't do it, please. She's . . . she's got to have something left, because I'm . . . I'm leaving.'

Robbie stared at her. Her reasoning was beyond him at the moment. Why should she think that her leaving home would affect his decision? But before he could find an answer his attention was drawn to Esther Blenheim, because her manner, no longer beseeching or persuasive, or even haughty, she was rounding on her daughter, crying, 'You won't! You can't. You promised.'

Now Gail brought her body stiffly from the wardrobe, and, nodding towards her mother, she said slowly, 'Yes, yes, I know what I promised, but I also know that if I stay here I'll likely go berserk and finish what Robbie attempted a minute ago.'

'You promised, girl, you promised . . . you swore. Remember?' Her mother was almost screaming at her now. 'I gave your father a divorce solely because you promised that you wouldn't marry him.' She thrust her arm back, her thumb out towards Robbie. 'You promised faithfully, you promised on your honour.'

Robbie's hand moved from the top of the phone to the table and he leaned heavily on it as he stared first at Gail then at Esther Blenheim, then back to Gail again. What had she said? She had promised she wouldn't marry him and that was how Harry had got his divorce? But he had never asked her. Marry her? They'd hardly been civil to each other; they had never necked or courted as it were. He had touched her that once when she had slipped on the ice. Marry her? His mouth was filling with blood from the slit in his lip and he swallowed and blinked as Gail cried at her mother, 'Promise or no promise, I'm leaving. And with him. And now. You can't do anything; Dad's married.'

'Oh . . . yes . . . I . . . can. Oh . . . yes . . . I . . . can.'

'Don't be silly Mother.' Gail's voice although trembling now, was scornful, deriding. 'Robbie has you in the hollow of his hand. You try to stop me leaving and he'll use that phone, won't you, Robbie?'

He stared at her. His mind was in a whirl, caught as it were in a strong current leading from the main stream of his hate. He looked at the hand now clutching his arm and when she said pleadingly, 'Come on, Robbie, let's go,' he moved a step with her before pulling himself to a halt and saying, 'Wait a minute. Hold on. Wait a minute.' His body too had shrugged off her suggestion and he had turned half from her, only to turn quickly to her again and grab the hand that had left his arm, and he gripped it tightly and stared at her for a second before speaking to her mother again, saying, 'That would be simple, wouldn't it, just to walk out, but it's not going to end like that, oh no.' He slowly swung his head the width of his shoulders and this action, more than further words said plainly that he wasn't finished, not by a long chalk.

595

When, still holding Gail by the hand, he stepped towards the sitting-room door, Esther cried at him, 'Don't go in there. Don't you dare go in there!' and he paused for a moment. Then ignoring both her and the restraining pressure that Gail was now putting on his hand, he stepped into the framework of the door. And once more he looked at John Blenheim, who was sitting now, his hands massaging his throat, and he said to him, 'The greatest pleasure I can think up is to see you goin' out of this house atween a couple of polismen, but besides your dear mother' – he laid emphasis on the dear – 'there'd be somebody else who'd feel guilty over you. And that's your father. But, prison aside, you're not going to get off with it. By God, no, you're not. I want it down in writing what you've done. Do you hear? IN WRITING. And signed.'

'No, no. Don't, John.' Esther was now standing near her son, and she looked down at him, saying, 'Don't you do any such thing.'

'He's got no choice, Mrs Blenheim, an' you know it. So listen to me, both of you. Even as things stand, even if I don't phone for the polis, there's still this man and his son, an' they'll be on the look-out for you.' His lips left his teeth as he paused and returned in full the baleful glare of John Blenheim before going on, 'So I'd advise you not to run. D'you hear?'

Slowly now he turned his attention to Esther, saying, 'Whatever's goin' to be done it'll be done legal. You have him at the solicitor's on Monday morning. No' – he shook his head – 'Monday afternoon, say three o'clock. These things've got to be arranged an' me

596

solicitor, by the way, is a Jew. You won't be able to miss him; his name's Steen, three doors down below my shop. STEEN. Do you hear that, Mr Blenheim?' He was bawling now. 'His name is Steen. And if you're not there on time then I'll do what I'm itching to do now, that is if you've not already been picked up, you dirty white-livered swob you!'

When John Blenheim, his face ashen, made to get up from his chair, Esther restrained him, and she glared at the pair standing hand in hand before her. Then her eyes focused on her daughter, boring into her until Gail, turning away, tugged once more at Robbie's hand, murmuring, 'Come on, come on.'

As Robbie looked at Gail he was seeing her clearly for the first time since he had entered the house. He couldn't quite take it in that she meant what she had said but she had said it. 'I'm leaving with him.' And now he said to her, more in the form of a command than a request, 'Go and get your things.'

'No, no.' She shook her head. 'I don't want any things.' She knew that if she went up the stairs she would be trapped, and either by force or persuasion she'd be made to stay. 'I'm going as I am. Come on.'

'Gail!' Esther Blenheim made one last attempt. 'Think, girl, think what you're letting yourself in for.'

Gail turned and looked at her mother and she repeated, 'Letting myself in for? Huh! That's really funny because whatever I was letting myself in for couldn't be any worse than the life I've been forced to lead over the last three years in this house. You've treated me like a prisoner.'

Esther Blenheim remained silent for a moment, and

her chin seemed to flatten itself out under the pressure of her jaw bones. Then she said, 'And where do you think you're going to stay if . . . if he no longer has a house? Give yourself time, girl and . . .'

'That'll be my business from now on.' Robbie's answer cut her off. 'And that should be the least of your worries, Mrs Blenheim. What I would advise is you concentrating on Monday an' getting your son to Mr Steen's, together with . . . an' let's not forget this, the difference in the money, and that should be around six thousand pounds. No, don't let's forget the money, Mrs Blenheim, the money's very important to me. Come on.' He went to turn away, then looked back and into the staring eyes of John Blenheim, and he said, 'As for you. You can remember for the rest of your days that you were nearly finished off by somebody half your size, a dirty little Jew.' He paused, then ended, with a threat in his tone now, 'Until Monday, you swob, or else.'

When they went through the front door Gail attempted to run, but he pulled her to a walking pace, saying, 'Steady on, what's your hurry?' And that was all he said until they were on the main road and nearing the lane leading to the mine. And then he glanced at her and asked softly, 'You all right?' And in reply she lowered her head but didn't speak.

When he entered the yard the house was still blazing. As he got out of the van the policeman came up to him, but didn't speak. Instead, his eyes ranged over him from the long deep nail scratch down his cheek to his split and swelling lower lip over his blood-stained shirt and torn coat, the pocket ripped away exposing the lining. An hour ago the little fellow had looked spruce. He'd heard he had just been to a wedding, his mother's wedding; now he looked as if he had come out of the wrong end of a wrestling match. He said to him pointedly, 'Did you find who you were looking for?' and Robbie, returning his look, was about to say, 'What do you think?' but aware of Gail standing by his side he said nothing. When he looked at her she was staring at the house and her face was awash with tears. They were silent tears, flowing from pain, and he took her by the arm and led her over the tangled hoses, around the side of the house, across the smoke-filled yard where the firemen were still fighting the flames, and into the stables that Harry had turned into a workshop; and guiding her to a wooden form near a long bench he pressed her gently downwards, then sat beside her, but looked at her dumbly as her crying became audible. At the height of her sobbing she gasped, 'Oh, Robbie, Robbie, I'm s . . . sorry.'

'It's all right, it's all right.' He made to take her hands but they were covering her face, so he pressed his own between his knees and bent his head deeply over them, his teeth gritting against each other to prevent himself now from crying with her.

After a while her sobbing eased and he looked up at her, to find her eyes on him. She was still gasping as she said, 'It's dreadful, Robbie, dreadful. I can't believe any . . . anybody could be so cruel, so vindictive.'

It was some time before he answered her; then to his own amazement he found his stiff lips moving into a smile, and he said, 'It . . . it doesn't seem so bad, nothing seems so bad now.' He was holding her gaze. 'Back there you said that . . . that you had promised not to marry me . . .'

'Oh, Robbie.' Her chin was on her chest now, and her voice was a mumble. 'She . . . she forbade me to see you. John had been spying on me coming here. I don't know what possessed me, it just came out. I . . . I said I would marry you. It was just something to say in defiance. It was then she made the bargain with me. If . . . if I stopped seeing you she would give Dad his divorce. It was fantastic. It seemed an easy way out at the time, I mean to get Dad his divorce, but . . . but as time went on it got harder, I mean not seeing you.' Slowly she lifted her eyes to his again and she saw in them a strange expression, for Robbie Dunn and humility didn't go together; but that was the expression on his face, a soft humility.

He now caught hold of her hands and his voice was gruff as he asked, 'Do you really mean it, Gail? You're not just sorry for me, or anything like that?'

'Sorry! Oh no, no. I admire you, Robbie.'

'You admire me?' The phrase was a question, a soft doubtful question, but she nodded quick confirmation. 'Yes, oh yes. I know now, I always have.'

'I'm a Jew, Gail. As your John so aptly put it, a little Jew, not dirty, no, I won't have that word attached to me, but still a little Jew. Some Jews don't look like Jews, except that their noses might give them away, but every bit of me looks a Jew. Mind' – his voice now became a tone higher – 'I'm not makin' excuses for meself, I'm not ashamed of being a Jew, but if a girl like you married me some people might say you must be hard up for a man.'

'Oh Robbie, don't. Don't.' She pulled his hands towards her breast.

'It's true, because you've only got to look in the mirror. I thought a while back that you'd gone off, gone sort of plain, but now you're just like you promised to be, you're bonny beautiful, an' you'll get more beautiful.'

'Robbie!' She gathered his hands so tightly to her that his face was only a few inches from hers, and her eyes moved over each prominent race-translated feature before she said, 'If I don't marry you I'll marry nobody. I thought after that business with Grandfather that I couldn't bear a boy . . . a man near me, ever, but from that day I saw you in the bookshop I knew I could you, but only you.'

When their mouths touched the pain from his cut lip stabbed through him, but it was as nothing because he was holding Gail Blenheim in his arms, he was kissing Gail Blenheim. Gail Blenheim had said that if she didn't have him she'd have nobody. She was beautiful, lovely, and she wanted him, him, Robbie Dunn. The aching secret that he had pressed deep down into himself over the past years, refusing to recognise it, even to acknowledge its existence, surged upwards and filled his body with power.

When at last he released his hold on her she still remained leaning against him, and he held her gently now and they were both silent. After a while he said, with a catch in his voice, 'It's getting on, we'll have to find some place for you to stay the night. There's a little hotel near . . .'

She raised her head from his shoulder and asked, 'Where are you going to sleep?'

He thought for a moment, then said, 'The back shop will do me; there's a studio bed in there. It only came in last week, it must have known. I'll kip there tonight, and we'll have to think up something before they come back the morrow. An' that's another thing, they're going to be shocked to the core, especially your dad, because he'll blame himself . . . still he'll have you near him now and that should make up for . . .'

'Robbie.'

'Yes, love.' Even using the ordinary endearment brought a slight flush up under his dark skin.

Her lips were trembling and her eyes half veiled as she said, 'I don't want to go to a hotel, I . . . I don't want to be separated from you, ever, ever. I'm . . . I'm frightened, Robbie. I'm frightened that if ever I lose sight of you something will come between us.'

For what seemed a long while he stared into her eyes, then gently took her face between his hands, and, his voice scarcely above a whisper, he said, 'This time next week we'll be married; we can do it by special licence; in the meantime, I'm not goin' to take anything from you that you'll regret later on. Understand? . . . All right? all right?' He shook her face gently. 'We'll be together, nothing or nobody will put more than a few yards atween us until we're married.'

The tears were in her eyes again and her voice

cracked as she whispered, 'I love you more every minute, Robbie.' Then after a moment, she added, 'Do you love me, really?'

He stroked her cheeks now and brought his hands down her neck, round her shoulders and up through her hair before he muttered thickly, 'What I feel for you, Gail, couldn't be said with just "I love you". Adore, worship, all kinds of words aren't big enough, they don't fit. I can only say this, that the feeling that's in me now has made that out there' – he jerked his head towards the door – 'of little importance, an' if you knew me like I know meself then you'd know that all me life I've been workin' towards building that house, owning that house. It was what you would call a kind of lode-star, the pinnacle of all my dreams, and, and now it doesn't seem to matter much . . . So that's what you mean to me, Gail. You understand?'

When she moved her head slowly he said, 'No, you can't, you can't, an' it'll take a lifetime to prove it to you. But I'll work at it, you'll see. An' I'll tell you another thing. By the time I'm finished you won't be seeing me as five foot five Robbie Dunn but as I see meself inside, big, capable of achieving anything I set me mind to . . . aye, an' capable of loving you like you never dreamed of being loved. An' by that time we'll have a family an' you'll be mistress of a fine house. Aye, I promise you that an' all, for it'll be re-built.' He again thumbed towards the door. 'But above all else . . .' His face now underwent a change. The natural arrogance went out of it and the bumptiousness out of his tone, and, his head dropping to her shoulder, he murmured,'Above all else, and although I may never mention it again, I want you to know now I'll always be grateful to you for having me.'

'Oh Robbie! Robbie Dunn!'

THE END

THE MALTESE ANGEL
by Catherine Cookson

Ward Gibson knew what was expected of him by the village folk, and especially by the Mason family, whose daughter Daisy he had known all his life. But then, in a single week, his whole world had been turned upside down by a dancer, Stephanie McQueen, who seemed to float across the stage of the Empire Music Hall where she was appearing as The Maltese Angel. To his amazement, the attraction was mutual, and after a whirlwind courtship she agreed to marry him.

But a scorpion had already begun to emerge from beneath the stone of the local community, who considered that Ward had betrayed their expectations, and had led on and cruelly deserted Daisy. There followed a series of reprisals on his family, one of them serious enough to cause him to exact a terrible revenge; and these events would twist and turn the course of many lives through Ward's own and succeeding generations.

0 552 13684 0

JUSTICE IS A WOMAN
by Catherine Cookson

The day Joe Remington brought his new bride to Fell Rise, he had already sensed she might not settle easily into the big house just outside the Tyneside town of Fellburn. For Joe this had always been his home, but for Elaine it was virtually another country whose manners and customs she was by no means eager to accept.

Making plain her disapproval of Joe's familiarity with the servants, demanding to see accounts Joe had always trusted to their care, questioning the donation of food to striking miners' families – all these objections and more soon rubbed Joe and the local people up the wrong way, a problem he could easily have done without, for this was 1926, the year of the General Strike, the effects of which would nowhere be felt more acutely than in this heartland of the North-East.

Then when Elaine became pregnant, she saw it as a disaster and only the willingness of her unmarried sister Betty to come and see her through her confinement made it bearable. But in the long run, would Betty's presence only serve to widen the rift between husband and wife, or would she help to bring about a reconciliation?

0 552 13622 0

THE GOLDEN STRAW
by Catherine Cookson

The Golden Straw, as it would be named, was a large, broad-brimmed hat presented to Emily Pearson by her long-time friend and employer Mabel Arkwright, milliner and modiste. And before long it was to her employer that Emily owed the gift of the business itself, for Mabel was in poor health and had come to rely more and more on Emily before her untimely death in 1880.

While on holiday in France, Emily and the Golden Straw attracted the eye of Paul Steerman, a guest at the hotel, and throughout his stay he paid her unceasing attention. But Paul Steerman was not all he seemed to be and he was to bring nothing but disgrace and tragedy to Emily, precipitating a series of events that would influence the destiny of not only her children but her grandchildren too.

The Golden Straw, conceived on a panoramic scale, brilliantly portrays the rich vein of English life from the heyday of the Victorian era to the stormy middle years of the present century. It represents a fresh triumph for this great storyteller whose work is deservedly loved and enjoyed throughout the world.

0 552 13685 9

A SELECTION OF OTHER CATHERINE COOKSON TITLES AVAILABLE FROM CORGI BOOKS

13576	3	THE BLACK CANDLE	£6.99
12473	7	THE BLACK VELVET GOWN	£5.99
14633	1	COLOUR BLIND	£5.99
12551	2	A DINNER OF HERBS	£6.99
14066	X	THE DWELLING PLACE	£5.99
14068	6	FEATHERS IN THE FIRE	£5.99
14089	9	THE FEN TIGER	£5.99
14069	4	FENWICK HOUSES	£5.99
14050	7	THE GAMBLING MAN	£4.99
13716	2	THE GARMENT	£5.99
13621	2	THE GILLYVORS	£5.99
14468	1	THE GIRL	£5.99
14328	6	THE GLASS VIRGIN	£5.99
13685	9	THE GOLDEN STRAW	£5.99
13300	0	THE HARROGATE SECRET	£5.99
14087	2	HERITAGE OF FOLLY	£5.99
13303	5	THE HOUSE OF WOMEN	£5.99
10780	8	THE IRON FAÇADE	£5.99
13622	0	JUSTICE IS A WOMAN	£5.99
14091	0	KATE HANNIGAN	£5.99
14092	9	KATIE MULHOLLAND	£5.99
14081	3	MAGGIE ROWAN	£5.99
13684	0	THE MALTESE ANGEL	£5.99
10321	7	MISS MARTHA MARY CRAWFORD	£5.99
12524	5	THE MOTH	£5.99
13302	7	MY BELOVED SON	£5.99
13088	5	THE PARSON'S DAUGHTER	£5.99
14073	2	PURE AS THE LILY	£5.99
13683	2	THE RAG NYMPH	£5.99
14602	X	THE ROUND TOWER	£5.99
13714	6	SLINKY JANE	£5.99
10541	4	THE SLOW AWAKENING	£5.99
10630	5	THE TIDE OF LIFE	£5.99
14038	4	THE TINKER'S GIRL	£5.99
12368	4	THE WHIP	£5.99
13577	1	THE WINGLESS BIRD	£5.99
13247	0	THE YEAR OF THE VIRGINS	£5.99